Against a Crimson Sky

Also by James Conroyd Martin

Push Not the River

Against a Crimson Sky

James Conroyd Martin

THOMAS DUNNE BOOKS
ST. MARTIN'S PRESS   ❧   NEW YORK

This is a work of fiction. All of the characters, organizations, and events portrayed in this novel are either products of the author's imagination or are used fictitiously.

THOMAS DUNNE BOOKS.
An imprint of St. Martin's Press

www.thomasdunnebooks.com
www.stmartins.com

Map design by Paul J. Pugliese

Library of Congress Cataloging-in-Publication Data

Martin, James Conroyd.
    Against a crimson sky : a novel / James Conroyd Martin.—1st ed.
        p. cm.
    ISBN-13: 978-0-312-32682-1
    ISBN-10: 0-312-32682-3
    1. Poland—History—1795–1830—Fiction. I. Title.

PS3613.A779A75 2006
813'.6—dc22

                                                                    2006042248

First Edition: August 2006

10   9   8   7   6   5   4   3   2   1

For Scott, Barbara, John, Rick, Faye, Bob, and Jeanie

Acknowledgments

This novel and its predecessor would not have been possible without the help and encouragement of my friend John A. Stelnicki, whose ancestor's diary provided the basis for *Push Not the River*. His translation proved a princess' ransom. I offer sincere thanks to Sally Kim, Thomas Dunne, and Sally Richardson of St. Martin's Press for their enthusiasm for the two projects. Guiding me through the novels with his justly celebrated expertise has been my agent Al Zuckerman.

For exceptional editing skills, I thank longtime friend Mary Rita Mitchell, as well as Pam Sourelis and Carolyn Chu. The late Frances Dwral's folk papercuts (*wycinaki*) add visual charm to the words. The rendering of the Polish eagle is the work of Ken Mitchell. For help on things Polish and otherwise, Donald and Edward Kaminski's support and suggestions have been invaluable. A host of people have aided me in my quest in ways too numerous to mention. Some of these are Piers Anthony, Francie Arenson, Marilyn Bricks, Ken and Penny Brown, Judi Free, Scott Hagensee, Dr. Peter Hicks, Gary Holtey, Patrick Keefe, Kevin Kelly, Jan Lorys, Sister Mary Paul McCaughey, O. P., Mike McCaughey, Kitty Mitchell, Michael O'Malley, John Rdzak, Sandra Riley, Mike Rusnak, Angela Turley, and members of the Green Door Studio, Chicago, 2003-04.

Glossary

czapka (chap-ka)—cap; a high, four-cornered hat with regimental insignia on the front, sometimes adorned with feathers or rosettes

czepek (che-pek)—cap; ceremonial cap of the bride on her wedding night

dog's blood—damn; damn it

kasza (kasha)—porridge

kolacz (kaw-watch)—bread made for the wedding celebration

kurtka (kurt-ka)—jacket; military jacket

Marzanna (Mah-jahn-nah)—the Polish Goddess Death, depicted in white and carrying a scythe; in spring an effigy of Marzanna made from sheaves of grain was "drowned" in a river or pond as a year-long protection against sickness and death

"Napoleoni Magno Caesari et Victori!"—"To Napoléon, the Great Caesar and Victor!"

opłatek (aw-pwah-tek)—an unconsecrated bread wafer usually shared among those participating in the wigilia meal; while sharing the wafer, each participant forgives past transgressions and wishes everyone health, luck, wealth, and—after death—a crown in heaven.

owczarek niziny (awv-char-rek nee-zhin-nee)—the lowland sheepdog

Shepherds' Watch—Midnight Mass on Christmas Eve

starosta—the local magistrate

ix

szlachta (shlach-ta)—the gentry; officially of equal status, in actuality their wealth and holdings often varied greatly

Szkoła Rycerska (Sh-koh-wa Ri-tser-skah)—The school of knighthood, a military school founded by King Stanisław

Third of May Constitution—Ratified in 1791, the first written constitution in Europe initiating democratic reform; overthrown in 1794 when certain disgruntled Polish magnates invited Catherine of Russia to protect their interests; Poland's final partition occurred in 1795 with Russia, Prussia, and Austria dividing the spoils

wigilia (vih-gee-lee-ah)—the Christmas Eve meal and celebration; it is valued more highly than Christmas Day.

Name Pronunciation Key

Halicz = Hah-leech

Jan = Yahn

Jósef = Yu-zef

Kościuszko = Kawsh-chew-shkaw

Kraków = Krah-koof

Michał = Mee-how

Paweł = Pah-vel

Radziwiłł = Rah-gee-view

Sochaczew = Saw-hah-chev

Stanisław = Stan-neess-wahv

Wilanów = Vee-lah-nooff

Europe 1812

- French Empire
- French Dependent States
- French Allies

North Sea

Atlantic Ocean

| 0 | 100 | 200 miles |
| 0 | | 200 kilometers |

NORWAY

DENMARK

OLDENBURG

UNITED KINGDOM

Dublin

London

Paris

CONFEDERATION OF THE RHINE

FRENCH EMPIRE

KINGDOM OF ITALY

Corsica

Rome

PORTUGAL

Lisbon

Madrid

SPAIN

Sardinia

Mediterranean Sea

MOROCCO

ALGIERS

TUNIS

Prologue

Whom the gods love
die young.

–POLISH PROVERB

Poland, 1794

2 November—All Souls' Day

Swollen with recent rains, the river heaved and churned, flowing rapidly away from Warsaw, its burden of bodies propelled carelessly along like so much flotsam.

A partially clad woman clung to something as the current took her. A log? A piece of planking from the broken bridge? Delirious from the fall, she was certain she was dying—or had died. Her faith—or the hazy filaments of a childhood belief that she conjured now—suggested she might expect to ascend into heaven as if on wings. Or plummet to a hell she had thought little about.

But she was being carried in an undulating line—like a weightless twig—through the drumming rush of water. The sparkling interplay of the afternoon sunshine on the water was deceiving, for the river was brutally cold.

The woman's mind inexplicably fastened on to the mythical river that was thought to usher one to the Greek underworld. Her cousin had told her about it—the River Acheron, was it? She dared not open her eyes.

What was she to expect in the underworld? There would be the fee for the ferry boat operator. Did she have any coins? She thought not, and without a coin he would not bring her across. Everyone knew that. Might she use her charms on him? Were charms of her kind taken as legal tender in the underworld? She had her doubts.

Her heart felt the icy fingers of the river upon it. How was she to account for her life? The things she had done?

The numbing water seemed to run faster now—like her fear—rushing her to her fate.

The ancient Poles had believed that those who died by drowning were doomed to become water spirits, forever residing in the waters where they had met death. She imagined Marzanna, Goddess Death, waiting for her at the river's end, dressed in white and carrying her scythe.

The woman pushed the Polish deity from her mind. At the age of twenty-one, she had run out of time. So? What of it? She had often proclaimed that the years of her youth were golden ducats to be spent. Wishing she had lived a better life was useless. Just as well, she thought—she had never been one for apologies. Or regrets.

She was cold, cold to the bone. She took in a mouthful of water and coughed. Despite the urge, she knew not to move a hand to her face. To do so would cause her to lose her grip, and the river would draw her to its bottom. Her arms and hands remained frozen in position, locked on to the object they were holding . . . holding.

And if God was the Christian God of her parents' beliefs, she wondered, would he forgive her?

With the numbing cold, she felt darkness descending—and the angry resignation that death was imminent, certain as the fall of night's curtain. . . . *Dog's blood!* How had she come to such an ignominious end?

The villagers who had hurried down to the river's edge stared in horror at the cargo the River Vistula was carrying past them. Those transfixed with wide eyes were mostly women, their men having gone off to fight with Kościuszko against the invading forces. An old man gawked much like the others—in silence—as the flotilla of human bodies moved steadily along. Sometimes a corpse became enmeshed in the weeds and water plants at the bank of the river, but the force of other bodies following a similar fateful journey goaded it once again on its way—or the deeper currents drew it down.

In disbelief, the old man turned toward Warsaw; the city was a great distance away, twenty miles upriver, but he could see an eerie, orange glow and above that, thick black smoke rising high into the air. Had the capital fallen to the Russians? *God help us all,* he prayed. Then aloud: "God and the Black Madonna!"

The man's grandson had braved the sight, going close to the shore.

The old man called him back. This was no sight for a sixteen-year-old, even one already wounded in the patriots' cause. The boy seemed not to hear.

"Jerzy, come back!" he called again.

His grandson turned, a queer look on his face, and waved him forward.

Without questioning, the old man obeyed.

When he came to the shore, his eyes widened at the sight that held Jerzy spellbound. A raven-haired woman clung to what looked like planking that had become caught in the thick reeds and tubers at the river's side. Her skirt was red as blood, and she was naked above the waist. She was both young and beautiful. . . . Something about her told him she must certainly be noble.

The old man saw now what Jerzy had seen. Little bubbles at her mouth. *Damn!* The woman was gasping for breath. She was alive!

The peasant understood what his grandson meant to do and moved closer to assist.

Jerzy immediately stepped into the water, reaching for the woman with one arm while the other linked him to his grandfather and to the river's bank.

Jerzy tugged at one of the woman's arms, trying to force her to let go of what held her afloat. Her skin was a grayish blue. "Let go! Let go!" he cried.

She remained insensible to his directions. The mouth seemed to twist and tighten. Her talonlike hands held fast.

The current spun her body now, pulling her, whipping her legs and lower body out toward the river's middle, as if the river had mighty hands that would not allow her to be rescued.

Jerzy held on, persisting in loosening her grip, pulling back one finger, then another. At last her hand came free and came to clasp his as he pulled her to him. Her other hand willingly released that which had held her afloat the long distance from Warsaw, and as the old man aided his grandson in pulling the woman to safety, he saw that she had set free the red uniformed body of a Russian soldier, its mustachioed face blue and bloated beneath the waters.

Part One

The doorstep of the
palace is slippery.

—POLISH PROVERB

1

Warsaw, 1794

The West Gate, 13 December

Her heart contracting in fear, Anna returned the ice blue gaze of the Russian soldier who stared up through the open doorway of the covered carriage—and she thought she could do murder.

Here was a man with power, the power to keep her from the home she had not seen in three years, from the child who had been sent to safety there five months before, and from the man who should have been her husband in '91 had it not been for fate and the interference of others. . . .

The soldier's beadlike, wolfish eyes moved over her, and Anna instantly felt a shiver travel up from the base of her spine—until she had to fend off a trembling at her shoulders. She would not be cowed. Her back stiffened as she steeled her nerves.

"What is your destination?" he demanded in broken Polish for the second time.

"Sochaczew." She kept her voice steady. "To my family home." Her reply came in Polish. She would not let him know she could speak his tongue.

"Papers!"

His brusqueness did not surprise Anna. Nothing since the fall of Warsaw into Russian hands surprised her anymore. "Here," she said, handing him the parchment Paweł had given her.

She tried not to watch as he officiously perused the documents. Her upper teeth tore at her lower lip as she silently cursed him—and a fate that had brought thousands of such interlopers into Poland, catapulting them into positions of power.

The open door allowed for the coach interior to go cold as a vault. But Anna had more serious concerns and a chill that ran deeper. What if she was denied egress from the city? What if he saw fit to take her into custody? What if—?

"Your purpose in Sochaczew?" he barked, failing to address her properly. The man was impudent. She knew that if he could read, he had to be aware of her title.

"My mother is near death."

His eyes narrowed as if to assess her veracity. "Too bad."

It was a lie, of course, but Anna felt confident that he could have no way of knowing both of her parents had died in '91. She neither flinched nor averted her gaze. The ruddiness of his face—that not hidden by a great black mustache—was enlivened by the red of his uniform.

"And when will you return to Warsaw?"

"I am not certain. Such things are hard to predict."

"Of course," he said without a trace of empathy. "And this?" He nodded toward the passenger opposite Anna, as if she were a parcel.

"Lutisha, my servant."

He looked from one to the other. "Any weapons to declare?"

"No."

"Certain?"

Were they to be searched? "I am quite certain, Captain." Anna smiled nicely. She knew well the soldier's uniform was that of a lieutenant. It couldn't hurt to inflate his stature a bit.

He did not correct her. "Very well." Without further questions, he handed the document back to Anna and slammed the door. "Move on!" he called to Anna's driver.

The carriage lurched and rumbled forward, passing through the city's western gate. The fingers of her right hand moved over the folds of her dress, lightly tracing the object stowed in a hidden pocket—her pistol.

Anna smiled at the wide-eyed Lutisha, hoping to reassure her, but her own heart continued to race. *The swine! The filthy swine!* She had won the little battle with the Russian soldier but cursed him nonetheless. He, with the assumed power he held over her, *had* put fear into her breast, and she was tired to death of being fearful.

As the carriage moved away from the city, Anna took herself to task, for it was fear that had made her draw closed the leather window curtains at the outset of their journey. In leaving Paweł's town house on Piwna Street, they had passed through the Outer Courtyard of the Royal Castle, and Anna could not bear to look at the palace, knowing as she did that Poland's monarchy was most likely at an end. Even less did she want to see across the River Vistula to the once-vibrant suburb of Praga, now in charred ruins, her aunt's pristine white town house on the bluff burnt to cinders. She smiled tightly at Lutisha's puzzlement and gave no explanation for shutting out the light.

The cobblestones now gave way to the hard earth of winter, and the carriage started to bounce and roll through the countryside at a moderate clip.

Anna's fear ebbed. The journey—barring the unforeseen—would take less than a day. They should arrive at her estate in time for supper. She would be home. She felt lucky, indeed, for her family estate remained intact while Jan had lost his estate at Uście Zielone and home in Kraków, and her cousin Zofia had lost both the family estate at Halicz and the town house in Praga, all to the invading Russians.

Anna and Lutisha sat in silence and semidarkness for half an hour.

"May I open my curtain, madame?" Lutisha asked at last.

"What? Oh, yes, of course." The briefest of knowing looks on Lutisha's face told Anna she had misjudged her, that the servant knew exactly why Anna had closed it.

Anna opened her own curtain now, too. The sun was shining brightly for a cold December day. She sat at the small window, her eyes on the passing flat expanses of whitened fields, patches of birch and evergreen forests, an occasional manor house—and myriad cottages and huts where people tended to their animals, living their lives as their ancestors had done. Each blink of the eye produced a new living portrait. She wondered at the sights, for they gave no clue to what Poland had endured, no clue to what had befallen her country. The sights touched a place in her heart, a joyless place, because she knew that this was merely the appearance of things, for the peasants' losses were as heartrending as those of any other patriot. A close examination of the passing scenes revealed many more women than men at their tasks. A multitude of their men had willingly taken up scythes at the call of Tadeusz Kościuszko. Many of them had been slain by the allied powers of Prussia and Russia. They would not be returning to their modest homes.

Lutisha sat across from Anna, her large round face a stoic mask, her fingers moving over the beads of a well-worn rosary. Still, the gray eyes of the old and corpulent servant could not veil their sadness, blinking at long intervals like the eyes of a falcon. *How loyal she is,* Anna thought, *loyal and brave and strong!* With the Russians descending on Warsaw, she had chosen to stay with

Anna and Zofia in the city rather than leave for the safety of the country with her daughter's family.

"You'll see Marta and her family in time for supper, Lutisha."

The woman's toothless smile lifted Anna's spirit. It struck her how alike was this peasant to Aunt Stella, the countess Lutisha had served all her life. One noble at birth, one peasant—and yet both born with Polish hearts and souls. Aunt Stella . . . Anna's own heart caught. Countess Stella Grońska had been fortunate in that she had not lived to see the destruction of her Praga town house, the fall of Warsaw, and the impending dissolution of her beloved homeland. Anna turned her gaze again to the passing landscape. She could not help but wonder whether her own son would grow up to call this land *Poland.*

The thought cut to the quick, and Anna tried to think of other things. It was good fortune that they had left a Russian-held Warsaw with so little fuss. How had Paweł made it possible for her to leave? In early November, after the Russians retook the capital, they threw about it a fine net of security, tightening it as if the city were the Golden Fleece. How had he produced the documents? Had he bribed someone? "Anna," he had cautioned her earlier that morning as he helped her into the coach and provided her with the traveling papers, "this document refers to you only as Countess Berezowska-Grawlińska. No mention is made of your having been recently named princess. I suggest that remain a secret."

What was this concern over her title? She guessed that being a member of the *szlachta,* the minor nobility of which there were many, made her less suspect than being of the higher nobility—or even the magnate class. But there had been no time to question Paweł in the matter.

King Stanisław August had meant the title as a reward for her patriotism, but because he ignored the warning she had dared to bring him detailing the untimely uprising against the Russians, it mattered little to her. And what gave an even more hollow ring to the appellation of princess was that for decades now, titles came to Polish citizens only through foreign powers; Stanisław had bestowed her title under the auspices of Catherine of Russia. Her body tensed at the thought.

Anna stared out at the blur of scenery. Thoughts and time fell away.

At last, her eyes found focus and she realized the landscape was becoming more and more familiar. She was returning home to Sochaczew. She thought how much her life had changed since she had left her family manor house more than three years before. Both she and her country had changed. There was much to regret, things best forgotten.

The carriage moved now through a forest, the daylight dimming as if dusk had fallen. With a start, Anna recognized an almost indiscernible path that led into a thick patch of evergreens. She took in a deep breath, then expelled it slowly. When she closed her eyes, the old memory washed over her, uninvited, like the cold, dark, and turbid waters of the pond she knew lay a few miles into the blackest heart of the forest. Her usual powers of repression failed.

For the moment, she was alone again in the dense and eerie woods on the shore of that pond. Night had fallen, a moonless, starless night. Everything about her was still and black, and she could not help but recall the superstition that the forest was home to the devil. With her sprained ankle, she had lain in the pungent fall leaves for hours, like a wounded bird, awaiting the rescue party while holding off the bone-chilling cold and fighting the ignition of real panic.

She could not imagine what was keeping Zofia, who had gone for help. And then came the sense—alarm—of someone, something, lurking nearby. Something dangerous. Watching her. A long moment passed with only the drumming sound of her own beating heart.

Suddenly a figure stumbled out of the shrubbery and moved toward her in a deliberate and menacing way. Despite the injury, she stood and began running—running—insensate to pain—fear propelling her on, her feet padding along the water-parched bank of the pond.

A tree trunk provided only a momentary hiding place, and when the beast found her, she managed to push him into the pond. But he held fast, pulling her with him into the cold, murky depths. Struggling to free herself, she worked her way to shore—knowing he was close behind.

Then came the clawlike hand upon her back—the stink of liquor on his breath—the earth rising up—and a white-hot explosion as her head hit the stony ground. His body on hers—crushing her—rending her—terror giving way to torn flesh and raw pain.

Then, oblivion.

Anna pushed the memory into the dark and empty place inside her where she held it prisoner. She did have to admit to herself that from that violent and terrible night in the forest had come Jan Michał, her beloved child. Who could explain that? He was at Sochaczew, where he had been taken for safety's sake before the Russian onslaught.

And Count Jan Stelnicki was there at Sochaczew, too, waiting for her. Anna felt hot tears beading in her eyes at the mere thought. Her fears seemed to vanish. In the letter she carried near to her heart, Jan had pledged his love and proposed marriage. He would adopt Jan Michał. Anna wondered whether he would be allowed to keep his title, for he had fought with Kościuszko against the allied forces. Perhaps even she would be denied her nobility. But what did it matter? They would be together. She would have him at last. Happiness was within reach. She suppressed the thought that years before it had seemed within reach, too.

Anna recalled, as she often did, that warm afternoon in September of '91, before *it* had happened, that night in the forest. They had met in a meadow at midday. Jan, with his blond hair, cobalt blue eyes, and dimpled chin, was the most handsome man she had ever seen. In but a few weeks she discovered that beneath his iconoclastic leanings, bold gaze, and glib forwardness lay a sturdy foundation of patriotism, passion, gentleness. Her love for him took root and endured—increased—in the intervening months and years, years in which they saw almost nothing of each other. It frightened her now to think she might at last live her life with this man, find contentment with him. Did she deserve happiness? Was it truly a possibility? she wondered, for caution had set up a barrier about her heart.

She recalled now the saying that the most important things in life happen only once. Such was the meeting with Jan Stelnicki. Before the tragedies . . .

And yet, somehow she had lived to see this day. A day of reunion. There was a God. There was! A mere six weeks earlier, she had miraculously survived the flight from the Russians across the burning Praga bridge—just before it collapsed into the River Vistula. Her cousin Zofia had not been so fortunate. Anna made the sign of the cross now. Her heart went out, guiltily, to her cousin, but she tried not to linger upon the loss, as she had all this while. . . . Today she would be reunited with her son and with Jan. It was not a time to dwell on the past and the dead . . . not today! The carriage trundled on.

In no time they came into Sochaczew. The Market Square seemed oddly deserted. Soon they would pass the cemetery. Anna felt her pulse quicken. "We're not far now! A few more miles out of town." Her family home, Topolostan—Poplar Estate—was named for the twin columns of trees that lined the long curving drive from the road to the house.

She remembered that Lutisha had never been to Sochaczew. "Oh, don't put your expectations too high, Lutisha. It's not as large as Aunt Stella's estate at Halicz, mind you, or as elegant as her Praga town house."

A flicker of hurt in Lutisha's eyes halted Anna's train of thought. She immediately regretted the mention of the two homes where Lutisha had spent the bulk of her years. Lutisha had taken lessons in the French ways of tending a home and had passed on the methods, as well as the etiquette, to her daughter and granddaughters. Barring outright ownership, she could have been no prouder of those residences. The town house was destroyed, as was nearly all of Praga, and the Groński manor house—"the great house," the servants called it—had been burned in the summer of '93 soon after the Russians invaded in support of the Confederacy of Targowica, the gathering of Polish magnates that had so foolishly invited Catherine into Poland to depose the Third of May Constitution.

While Anna was grasping for some comment that would assure Lutisha that her new home would be safe and welcoming, someone outside the coach shouted, and the vehicle ground to an abrupt halt. Her excitement at being in Sochaczew was immediately snuffed by a dark presentiment.

"What is it?" Anna called to the driver. She could hear his raised voice amidst several others. She called out again.

"It's the Russians, milady," the driver called back, urgency in his tone. "The town's been garrisoned. They want you to step out for interrogation."

Interrogation. Looking to Lutisha, whose eyes had waxed like twin moons, Anna attempted a smile that she hoped would calm the aging servant and belie the cold terror that had seized her own heart.

Haunted by memories of the frigid river, the woman lay in the dark, unable to fasten her mind to any sustained thought. Despite a heavy counterpane and a fur covering over that, she shook continuously against the cold. Her eyes remained closed. When she shifted, even slightly, pain ran through her like a hundred piercing knives. Beneath her was the consolatory scent of fresh straw. She knew that she had come close to the surface of consciousness many times before this, hovering only briefly in the presence of strange, whispering voices. Somewhere, too, were the sounds of animals. Her mind did not attempt to distinguish what kind. Then she would again descend into a welcoming darkness that benumbed every sense.

It was the silence, the terrible and empty silence, that now worked at her, keeping her from her descent. Her eyelids lifted slowly, grudgingly, like tiny weighted curtains. What she saw, she saw with stark objectivity, for her mind was unable to think. Gray light was beginning to filter in through the square, four-paned window on the wall to the foot of her bed. The play of the morning rays passed through the *wycinanki* that served as curtains, the delicate papercuts casting a striking design of flowers on the beaten earth that formed the floor. Her eyes moved to the opposite wall, where a little table held a shrine consisting of icons and candles. Framed religious pictures hung on the wall above it. To the right of the table was a doorway through which a bread stove glowed white in the dimness.

To the right of the door hung a voluminous red skirt she vaguely recognized. On the floor rested once-elegant black boots. These, too, seemed familiar. Her eyes took in all of this, but it was not until she heard a door open and close that her mind formed real thought. *Who is entering?* She could hear footfalls. And for the first time, an alarm went off somewhere within her, breathing life into her dormant nerves. *Where am I?*

These cramped and rustic surroundings were unknown to her—and less than pleasing, although she wasn't sure why. She closed her eyes. She could hear bits of conversation between a man and a woman in the other room. They spoke in a low Polish dialect, their tones hushed. Who were these people?

The whispering lessened as the sounds of preparation for a meal began. The little room she was in—more an alcove, really—took on warmth as the stove was fed. She pulled the cover up to her neck, lulled into drowsiness by the smells of chickory and baking bread. She slept.

Some time later, she came suddenly awake. Some instinct told her she was being observed, and she immediately opened her eyes. An hour or two had passed. Daylight brightened the room. Two figures stood just a pace away, looking down at her.

"I told you she moved, I did," the peasant woman said.

"You did," said the weathered old man at her side. He smiled now. "It is good to see life within you, milady." He had few teeth.

The woman wished they had not disturbed her, longed to fade back into the comfortable straw of her bed. But it wasn't her bed. Hers was made of—what? Something softer? Goose down? She struggled to remember. How had she gotten *here?* And even though she knew these people were in no way connected to her, she could not recall faces or names of people who *were* important to her. Like sudden storm waters, panic rose.

She stared at the two. Fragments of memory began to eddy, flash, and stir. She remembered their faces poring over her, talking to her, forcing her to drink and eat. How long had she been here?

The blond woman smiled at her as her large hand clenched the folds of her colorless sacklike dress, allowing her to drop into a clumsy curtsy. "Is milady hungry?"

"No." The word was scarcely a breath. When she lifted herself up onto her elbow, the pain cut through her, and she felt herself growing weak. She coughed, her chest tightening like a fist.

"You're pale—you must rest, milady," the man said, moving away. "You will eat later, when it's ready. Rabbit, a good fat one, too! I'll leave you to my daughter for now."

His daughter nodded. "You'll want to use the chamber pot, I expect."

The woman could not deny it. And she realized that the experience of having people there to see to her needs was a familiar one. These were peasants—and *she* was not one of them.

She was helped then—at considerable pain—to sit up and slide off the bed onto the cold chamber pot.

When the peasant woman came back to collect the crude and coverless container, she introduced herself as Danuta.

"Thank you, Danuta," the woman murmured, shivering. She sat on the side of the narrow bed, exhausted by her effort.

"And you . . . what are we to call you, milady?"

Strangely, it was only now that the woman's own identity came to her. She stared blankly at Danuta as the horror of what she had been through came back to her in galvanizing waves—Praga being put to the torch—the Russians on horseback descending—sabers raised, falling, and flashing red in the sun—the cries of women and children unheeded on the smoke-filled acrid air. She felt faint again.

Danuta stood before her, grasping the pot as if it were a tureen, waiting.

"How did I get here?"

"You were in the river. My son fished you out, he did."

"Your son?"

"Yes, milady. Jerzy." She nodded toward the other room. "My father helped, too."

"I see." She fought off the faintness. "How long?"

Danuta shrugged. "Some weeks, milady."

Weeks! Was it possible?

"Thank you," she heard herself say. She had not always treated her own servants with respect, but these people had saved her from certain death, and she knew that her life was still dependent on them. She would have to behave accordingly, and she attempted a smile now. "I'm cold, Danuta."

"I'll fix you a bowl of *kasza*. It'll warm your bones, Lady . . ." Danuta persisted in her need of a name.

"Grońska," the woman said, coughing and falling back into the straw mattress. "Lady Zofia Grońska."

Count Jan Stelnicki smoothed over the plaster and stepped back to look at his work. The fissure in the wall was the last of several that had been in need of repair in the large reception room of Anna's manor house. With the owner of the premises absent for three years, the estate had gone without the diligent care necessary to keep it up. He sighed, less than satisfied with the result of his labors. He was better at soldiering, it seemed, but he was glad to be doing something physical. It gave him less time to think, less time to worry. Paweł had sent the message about Anna's arrival only the day before, prompting Jan's concern about the dangers of such a trip in Russian-occupied territory. And he would deny it if someone were to ask him, but he was nervous about seeing Anna again.

The woman he had loved from afar for so long was just hours away. Never mind that his own family estate at Uście Zielone and town house at Kraków had been sequestered—booty to the allied powers. Never mind that it was at Anna's estate that he waited. He would put aside tradition and pride. In very little time, he would see Anna.

"Much improved, Lord Stelnicki," Jacob Szraber said, coming in from the rear of the house by way of the music room. He approached the mended wall.

"Think so?" If only there were more time before Anna arrived. So much still had to be done around the estate.

"Indeed. I've finished with the roof."

"I told you to leave that for a younger man."

Jacob shrugged. "None younger around. Walek is just as old, unless you count his young son Tomasz."

"Then *I* would—"

"Oh, no," Jacob interrupted, "that wouldn't be proper. A few new evergreen shingles and it was done."

"Well, you made it leakproof, I trust?"

"We'll know come spring." His laugh coaxed one from Jan. "And don't worry, I took care not to disturb the storks' nest. They'll find it this spring just as they left it."

"You've been a tremendous help, Jacob, but . . ." Jan's words trailed off.

"The estate's not the same place the Countess Anna left, you mean."

Jan nodded. "Nor is anything else in Poland."

"Well, in such times as these it is enough that the countess is coming home to her son and to . . ." Jacob paused, his eyes averted in embarrassment that he may have overstepped himself.

Jan smiled, taking his meaning. *To you, Jan,* he had meant. Jan thought of Anna's little boy. She was coming home to him, too. "Where is Jan Michał?" he asked.

"He's with the wife. Good for her to have someone to fuss over, after—" Jacob's voice caught with emotion, and he was unable to continue.

Jan nodded in understanding and compassion. He silently thanked God for Jacob and Emma Szraber. Without them the estate would be in even greater disrepair. At the start of the conflict, Jacob had fought as a Polish patriot, joining the contingent of Colonel Berek Joselewicz, the first Jewish regiment since biblical times. He had seen serious action, survived, and come home to resume his duties as estate manager, but Jan's heart went out to the middle-aged couple, for they had lost their daughter Judith and her newborn son. It had been confirmed only three days before: The two had been among the twelve thousand caught up in the chaos when the Russians took Praga.

The Warsaw uprising had so incensed Catherine that she sent a general notorious for his ferocity—Aleksandr Suvorov—to level Warsaw. His forces descended from the east like red locusts, destroying the suburb of Praga and putting thousands of its citizens—men, women, and children—to the sword. Only a burnt bridge and the River Vistula held the enemy at bay from the capital walls long enough for the bloodlust to cool, allowing for the city to capitulate peacefully.

So many of the large Jewish population had died violently that day, cut down at the bridge, on the streets, in their homes. Jan's blood iced over to think it might just as easily have been Anna who had not made it across the burning bridge to safety behind the Warsaw city walls. The Szrabers' daughter and grandson were not their only losses. Their well-loved son-in-law had died at the ramparts that same day, defending the city's suburb from the Russians. There would be no regeneration for this good and proud Jewish family.

Jan had been there, too, and had suffered two wounds and the indignity of capture. The signing of the peace treaty, however, had allowed for his release.

Marta entered to announce the afternoon meal, a worried smile flickering on her earnest face. Jan knew that she was concerned over her mother, Lutisha, who had stayed in Warsaw to take care of Anna's needs. They would both be in Sochaczew in a matter of hours now, he thought, and the whole household would breathe easier.

Jan and Jacob moved to the dining room where Emma and little Jan Michał were already seated. Jan watched as Marta's daughters Marcelina and Katarzyna began to serve the mushroom soup. Just before the Russian invasion, Walek, Marta's husband—a patriot himself—had managed to spirit his little family away from the doomed suburb of Praga. He had taken Jan Michał also, disguised as his own child. How Jan wished that he had taken Anna, too, but anyone of nobility would have been detained, placing everyone in jeopardy. As it was, no one much cared about a little retinue of peasants.

"Lady Anna," Emma said, "will be home for the evening meal, I should think."

Jan paused for a few moments, a spoonful halfway to his mouth. Had she been reading his mind, just as Jacob had done? The mere mention of Anna's name—the thought that he would see those amber-flecked green eyes before the day was through—made his heart pump faster and his mind wander.

He found himself staring at his spoon and suddenly felt a bit ridiculous. A man who had seen the kind of bloodletting that had come his way, a man who had had to kill, should not be so emotional, he thought. Holding back tears, he put the spoon to rest in the bowl. He looked to the tawny-haired, dark-eyed child he had offered to adopt. "How is that bread, Jan Michał?"

Chewing with relish on the fresh rye, the boy looked up with adoring eyes to Jan. "Good." He pronounced the single word with such enthusiasm that crumbs went flying.

Everyone laughed.

A few minutes of silence passed. It was Jacob who broke it. "It is all very well, Lord Stelnicki, your having us take our meal here to give you company, but when Lady Anna comes home, we will eat in our cottage."

"What? Nonsense, Jacob!"

"Oh, that's the way it must be, Lord Stelnicki," Emma said. "It's hardly proper for an estate manager and a governess to be taking meals in the Bere-zowski dining room. And you and Lady Anna will have such a lot to catch up on when she arrives. So many preparations . . ." The woman stopped midsen-tence, her face reddening.

Jan smiled at her and started again on his soup. He tried to fend off the blood he felt rising into his face. That he and Anna would marry seemed to be common knowledge.

Soon Katarzyna cleared away the bowls while Marcelina brought in a huge tureen of *bigos*. Little Jan Michał's eyes bulged, sparkling brown at the sight and fragrant scent of the stew. Jan studied Anna's child. In truth, he felt uncomfortable that the boy had taken to him so quickly. Why was that? It was, after all, in his nature to be protective. He could not explain his own feel-ings to himself. Was it a fear of taking on such a responsibility? Was it the memory of the child's father? He would not wish away the existence of the lit-tle innocent. But he could—and did—hold himself responsible for the circum-stances that had led to the boy's entrance into the world. That day at the pond was a day Jan would regret the rest of his life. Even now, years later, no day went by without his thinking, *If only* . . .

A long moment passed.

"Lord Stelnicki," Emma said, "you've hardly eaten a thing."

"I'm just taking my time, Emma," he said. "It's delicious." Jan was im-pressed by the little meal. War had left the country poor, the storehouses of even the manor houses and castles nearly empty, but Marta and her girls had somehow conjured up the most savory *bigos* he had tasted in years, and when Marta came out from the kitchen on some errand, he told her so.

By custom, compliments to the cook were seldom made in the dining room, and the attention caused a rise in the servant's color. In her embarrassment, Marta changed the subject. "Oh, Lord Stelnicki, it will be so good to have Lady Anna here, safe and sound."

"That it will, Marta," Emma concurred. "Not to mention having Lutisha, your mother, back!"

The thought put Jan's mind on a happier path. He could not bring himself to say anything for fear of tears. How he longed for Anna, had since they met in '91, and now they were to make a life together.

As Marta retreated to the kitchen, Jan sopped up the gravy of the stew with his rye bread and began to chew, savoring the familiar afresh.

"Lord Stelnicki," Emma ventured, as she helped Jan Michał with his meal, "Lady Anna—has she had no word about her cousin?"

"No, Emma." Jan kept his eyes upon his plate. "I'm afraid that Zofia was among the many lost in the waters of the River Vistula."

"May God rest her soul," Emma said.

Zofia, Jan thought. He certainly wished no one dead, but just the mention of her name brought on a tide of grim emotions.

Zofia came suddenly awake, flushed and perspiring. The Praga massacre—with all its horror—had unfolded in a hellish nightmare. She could taste in her throat the acrid smoke of the burning homes, hear the screams of women and children being mowed down in the streets like shafts of wheat, see the glint of scarlet-stained cutlass and saber blades rising and falling. Even after the bridge collapsed into the Vistula, the Russian legions—lancers in the lead—continued to bear down on the populace, propelling them off the bridge and to a watery grave.

The Russian soldier that had pulled her atop his Arabian had stolen from her what jewelry she had worn—all but one ring. So it was that—on horseback and in the midst of the killing—they struggled over the diamond ring Zofia was intent upon keeping. It had been her mother's. She had only just managed to place it in a hidden pocket in her skirts when the cries of the people around them rose to fever pitch.

It was then that both she and the Russian realized that they were inextricably caught up with the masses that were being forced toward the jagged precipice of the broken bridge that jutted out over the roiling waters. The Russian soldier's face went pale as a ship's canvas as he sought—futilely—to direct his horse to safety. Zofia held to him with a viselike grip as fear—so un-familiar to her—coursed through her. The press of the crowd tightened then, and the horse rose up in panic.

They teetered at the edge of the broken bridge for what seemed a long moment, the sight of the swiftly moving Vistula below. In the water, their heads bobbing and limbs flailing, a thousand souls that had escaped the blade and bullet would not escape the current.

Then came the crush of the crowd, and suddenly the horse was pushed from the precipice and they were falling—falling—falling.

Zofia shook her head now in an attempt to cleanse it of the memory. She pulled herself into a sitting position at the side of the bed, dizzy at her own emotions. It was night, and the cottage was quiet as a crypt. A low fire off in the main room of the cottage tossed a dim, flickering light into her little al-cove. Her eyes went to the ruined skirt hanging near the doorway. Summon-ing a hidden strength, she was suddenly off the bed and moving toward it, her bare feet cold on the earthen floor.

She took down the skirt and fumbled for the hidden pocket. Her fingers came upon the ring then, and a wave of relief washed over her. She might very well need something of value to pay for her restoration to Warsaw. She with-drew the diamond ring and held it up to the weak, glinting hearthlight. The facets of the perfect stone twinkled coldly, like a star.

2

Anna had been kept waiting in the frigid room for more than two hours. Outside, twilight had darkened into the pitch of night. When she had been shown into the office, a Russian soldier had asked her questions in his language, and she had responded in kind. She had come to be with her dying mother, she told him, showing him her papers. Had she signed with the Confederacy of Targowica? he asked. The question startled her, and she felt her face flushing hot. Yes, she told him, hurting anew to think of it.

"It is good that you have signed, Countess." He seemed satisfied.

Anna thought the little interview over. She stood to leave.

"Sit down, please, Countess Berezowska-Grawlińska," he said. "You are to wait here."

And so she waited. Another hour.

The details of the office in which she was confined—labels on a file, a flag, a man's sash hanging on a hook—indicated that its occupant was a Pole. He collected clocks and sundials, it seemed, for they were present in abundance—gathering dust on the desk in front of her, on tables, and on the walls. The steady ticking and signaling of the clocks began to work on her fragile nerves. This was time being stolen from her, minute by minute.

How had she come to find herself caught up in such a lie? Violating her dead mother's memory in order to provide a likely excuse for a return to Sochaczew—it made her feel small. Oh, it was true that her name had been affixed to the Confederacy of Targowica, but it was her cousin Zofia who—without consultation—had added their names to those of greedy and misled nobles, men who should have known better than to ask Russia's Catherine to intercede and overthrow the democratic Third of May Constitution. Aunt Stella had been astute in predicting that Catherine would want more than to help crush the seeds of democracy in Poland, that she would want Poland, as well.

But Anna had to admit to herself that lies might have their place in a truthful world, for the lie about her mother would admit her to her home and a new life with Jan Stelnicki—just as the traitorous placement of her name with the Confederacy had already served her well. Zofia had once told her that lies were more useful than truth. Had she been right? And were such means justified?

The door opened now, and the Russian soldier entered, followed by a man in the old-fashioned Polish garb of Eastern influence—a long coat over tight trousers, a colorful sash at a thickening waist, and a ruff at a fleshy neck. He seemed to have been taken away from a meal, for he was still chewing and wiping at his grizzled mustache. Anna thought him to be in his mid-fifties. He appeared vaguely familiar.

"This is Countess Berezowska-Grawlińska," the Russian pronounced, failing to introduce the Pole to her. "I am finished with her. You are to question the good countess and make a report. If she does not cooperate, she is to be detained."

"I understand," the Pole said.

"Good!" The Russian made his exit, his bootheels hitting hard upon the wooden floor. He left open the door that led to other offices.

"Now, Lady Berezowska-Grawlińska, we will have a nice little chat in our own tongue, yes?" The Pole went to the chair behind the desk and took up a quill.

He avoided calling her countess. Like most of the *szlachta,* the minor nobility, he did not use titles in direct address, for they thought it too imperious to do so. Anna was buoyed by the thought that they were Poles of the same class and dared to hope she would find an understanding ear and quickly be put on her way home. But there was something about his eyes and deep, gravel-like voice that gave her pause. What was it? And it was odd that a Pole should carry such weight in a town garrisoned by Russians.

"You have been away some time," he said.

"Yes, I have . . . and I am hoping to return to my estate as soon as possible."

"Topolostan—ah, yes. Of course, I understand. This should not take long."

"That's very good to hear." Anna's reply was all bluster. In reality, his familiarity with her estate's name unnerved her.

"When did you leave Sochaczew?"

"The summer of 1791."

"A long time."

"I've lived with my aunt in Halicz and more recently in Praga."

With each of her answers, the man scratched away at a bit of paper. "And what has prompted your return?"

Anna felt a pressure in her chest. This time the lie came with a great uneasiness—still, she could not change her story now. "I've . . . I've come to be with my mother. . . . She's in ill health."

One of his bushy eyebrows lifted now, and he held the quill suspended. "Dying, isn't that what you told the lieutenant?"

Anna swallowed hard. "Yes. . . . It is reason enough, I should think."

"Ah, yes. But these Russians are suspicious souls, are they not?" He gave a sly smile.

Anna felt awkward. She would not allow him to place potentially dangerous words into her mouth. She affected a non-smile, the type her mother had used as a mask for displeasure. What she longed for was the protection of her father, long dead.

The official grew tired of waiting for a verbal reply. "And we Poles are a resourceful lot."

"I don't wish to be held up any longer. My servant must be freezing in our carriage. She's elderly, and I'd like to get her home."

"It is hard to lose a parent. Myself, I have lost both."

"I'm sorry. Then you understand—"

"What I don't understand, Lady Berezowska-Grawlińska," he said, his small, milky blue eyes fixed on her, "is the reason for your deceit."

"Deceit?" Anna's pulse tripled in time.

"Come, come, my lady," he said, his voice taking on a gruffness. "You know as well as I that when you left here three years ago, you left your parents stone cold in the ground!"

Anna couldn't think; she could only stare dumbly at this smug creature who suddenly seemed quite capable of anything.

He was smiling, as if he had just brought down a deer.

"How do you know—?"

"How do I know? I am the *starosta* here in Sochaczew, have been for nearly twenty years."

"The *starosta?*"

"Ah, our Russian hosts do not always show good manners. The lieutenant didn't introduce me. I am Lord Grzegorz Doliński."

Anna's back went rigid, but she attempted to maintain her composure. While she had seen him only once, years before, the name now brought home to her his identity. He was indeed the croaky-voiced magistrate of Sochaczew. It was he who had investigated the murder of her father and taken into custody the peasant who had killed him. And it was he who had somehow allowed the murderer to escape. An old wound opened, loosing a bitter poison into Anna's bloodstream as she recalled how, on her deathbed, her mother had cursed the name of Doliński.

Anna could scarcely believe that she stood before him—and at his mercy.

Doliński laughed. "You're wondering what I'm doing here, Lady Anna! Here at my old desk with my sundials and clocks—and amidst a contingent of the red devils!"

When Anna merely stared, he smiled. "Captured your thoughts, have I?"

Anna suppressed the bile that rose up within her and said nothing.

"We Poles are resourceful, always able to survive, yes? Well, the Russians are clever ones, too, they are. When they take over a town or a country, they don't replace the old bureaucracy with their own. Oh no, they're smart enough to keep things and people in place whenever and wherever they can, so that life goes on—or *seems* to go on—much as it had before their frontier violation. Their invasion appears less invasive, if you take my meaning. People adapt and are less likely to rebel. And so here I am at the desk I came to years ago." His eyebrows pushed upward. "Of course, I must answer to them."

Words failed Anna. She had been caught in a stupid and useless lie. What had prompted her to risk all? It was a foolish gamble. And she had lost to a longtime family enemy. Her arrest was all but certain. Perhaps the best she could look forward to would be a return trip to the capital. And the worst . . . Well, she knew of nobles who had been deported to Siberia. Now, as if to ring out her sentence, the six-o'clock bells and chimes on the many clocks began to peal.

"Come here, Lady Anna." Doliński stood, driving back his chair, and moved across the room. "Come quickly and look at this one."

Reluctantly Anna obeyed.

"It's a beauty, isn't it?" Doliński was referring to a cuckoo clock of linden wood hanging upon the wall. The yellow painted bird was just now delivering its final call. "It's Austrian."

"It's 'cuckoo' in any language, Lord Doliński."

He looked at Anna, paused for a moment, and laughed. "Marvelous, Lady Anna! I shall remember that one."

Anna did not laugh.

"Oh, you needn't be afraid. You may miss the evening meal at your manor house, but there's no reason why you shouldn't be home tonight."

"Then you won't–?"

"Tell our new Russian landlords of your little lie?" He moved toward a window as he spoke. Was he looking out at her carriage? Anna wanted to curse the man but knew to say nothing. He returned to where she stood. "I must write my report, Lady Berezowska-Grawlińska. It may be dangerous for me to write something other than the truth."

Anna remained silent, already suspicious of his intent.

"We Poles survive, do we not, Anna? May I call you that? Oh, not all of us, of course, but the smart ones do. Come . . . come back to the desk." He took hold of Anna's arm to lead her.

Anna smiled and disengaged herself. Walking back to the desk, she felt the bile rising again and imagined herself running from the room. But where would that lead? Certain arrest? Confinement? She thought she would be ill. When they seated themselves again, she welcomed having the desk between them.

"Should I choose to clear you to leave, my dear, you would be in my debt."

Anna concluded that the man was suggesting a bribe. "I have but little money on my person, but I can request some from Warsaw."

He waved his hand in a dismissive gesture. "I hear the mint's been shut down, despite Stanisław's pleas to his old lover Catherine. Oh, I have more money than things to spend it on, my dear." Elbows on his desk, he placed the tips of his fingers of one hand against those of the other. "I appreciate your concern, but I'm not hinting for money, Anna Berezowska-Grawlińska."

Anna looked into his fleshy face. His eyes–like blue stones–confirmed her suspicion. Her heart swung out over an abyss. What was she to do?

He smiled. "Nonetheless, I am a man who likes to be appreciated."

Anna stiffened in her chair. "Your favor to me would be much appreciated, Lord Doliński. But if you are a true Pole and a man of conscience, such a favor might redeem you of a past failing."

Surprise spread over Doliński's face. "Failing, you say?"

Anna stood. "You were in charge of confining the man who killed my father. Feliks Paduch managed to get away under *your* watch. I should think you would be glad to have the opportunity of doing Samuel Berezowski's daughter a good turn."

"Oh my, you *are* your father's daughter!"

"I take that as a compliment!"

"Ah! I like a woman with a bit of fire inside." Then, in a harder voice: "Please sit down, Lady Berezowska-Grawlińska."

Anna pushed down the rage she feared would spill out in invective. She sat.

He leaned forward over the desk now. "Your eyes are magnificent, Anna. . . . You see, I can be appreciative, as well."

"Tell me, Lord Doliński, do you collect women as you do clocks?"

Doliński turned crimson and drew back, as if stung. Was he angry? Or did he still have enough of a sense of decorum to be shamed? Before the *starosta* could do or say anything to reveal himself, the Russian came clumsily into the room.

"Well?" the lieutenant asked. Doliński coughed and looked down at the paper on which he had scribbled, the nib on his pen long dried up.

Anna felt faint. This man with the stones for eyes had her life in his keeping. What would he say?

The Russian glared at Anna, then at Doliński. "Come, come," he prodded. "I don't have all day."

"I . . . I have yet to finish the interview, Lieutenant."

"Very well. She'll have to keep, then. I've another for you to question. This one looks more promising . . . but not nearly so pretty." The Russian winked at Anna.

When the door closed behind them, Anna heard the lock fall into place.

Zofia was unaware of how many days or weeks had passed in the pitifully tiny cottage. The fever held on tenaciously. She slept constantly, dreamt deeply, allowing herself to come to the surface of awareness when Danuta sponged her body, helped her to eat broth and bread, or aided in the use of the chamber pot. Occasionally Danuta's father forced foul-tasting herbal potions upon her. Her son—the boy who had rescued Zofia—was not in evidence.

For a long while, Zofia thought she would not live—and often prayed that the end would be quick and painless. Her days of parties, balls, and castle intrigue seemed a lifetime ago. But in time, the fever broke, strength seeped back into her bones and flesh, just as spring carries life to a cold and dead land. Although spring was still months away, it was with a start that Zofia realized she would survive.

As her physical condition improved, so did her spirit. She began to wonder about Anna. Had she made it safely across the bridge? Had she survived? And Jan? Had he survived the Russian deluge? Most of the time, however, she worried how she would be able to return to Warsaw . . . and what she would find there.

Wearing a cotton shift, she was sitting in a crude and cushionless chair one day when she heard someone enter the dwelling. Danuta and her father had left for the village not long before, so she was immediately put on guard.

"Mother?" came a gentle voice.

Zofia saw a face appear around the corner, then disappear. "Come in, come in," she called.

Slowly a figure came into the doorway.

"Your mother's gone out. You must be Jerzy."

He nodded uncertainly.

"You fetched me from the river," Zofia said, marveling at his resemblance to another.

He nodded again.

"Come in. A few days ago I would have scolded you for not letting the river do its work. But today I am able to thank you."

The boy dared to take two paces. He seemed confused.

"How old are you, Jerzy?"

He cleared his throat. "Sixteen, milady."

"I see. I think your mother has sent you out of the house, no?" Zofia nodded toward the bed. "Is this yours?" When he colored slightly, she asked where he had been sleeping and eating.

"In the barn, milady." The boy shifted from one foot to the other. "It's not so bad."

"With the chickens and that damn rooster I hear?"

"Yes, milady."

"And with the goats that go on braying the livelong day?"

"Bleating. It is donkeys that bray."

Zofia laughed. "You have those, too?"

"No, milady."

"Sheep?"

"A few." Jerzy shrugged. "They stay outside except in blizzards or hard rains."

"And then?"

The boy lifted his blue eyes to the ceiling. "There's an attic above."

"Above?—Above *me,* you mean?"

He nodded. "We have a ramp to the rear of the house."

"You do?" Zofia asked, imagining a little Noah's ark overhead. "Hardly a *petit palais,* to be certain," she said with a smile, confident he would not understand. She offered her hand. "Thank you, Jerzy."

The boy stepped forward, unsure what was expected of him. He looked at his own hands, filthy from the morning's work, then dropped them. It was an awkward moment, and Zofia tried to stifle the giggle that tickled upward in her throat—to no avail. Of course, he had never kissed a lady's hand. What was she thinking? He was blushing now.

She dropped her hand and attempted small talk while she studied Jerzy more closely. His clothes were those of a peasant farmer, scarcely more than filthy rags, the boots well-worn and caked with mud. But he was already tall and nicely built. The dusty blond hair framed a face more aristocratic than peasant. He was a striking boy, with his deep blue eyes, and he would be a handsome man. Here amidst stark poverty and ugliness was this golden child favored by the gods.

Zofia knew she was making him uneasy—as much with her talk as with her eyes. Oddly, the sight of him squirming in discomfort gave her pleasure.

"I must go now," Jerzy said at last, turning for the door.

"If you must, Jerzy . . . but come visit again, will you?"

The boy's blush deepened, and he disappeared.

Zofia laughed aloud when she was alone. It felt good to laugh. As if she had only just started to live again. It felt good, too, to enjoy handsome male company. Even one so young as Jerzy.

She returned to her bed with its straw mattress, scarcely believing how the short interchange had sapped her strength. She lay back against the lumpy pillow. The little burst of energy had come and gone. The weakness made her worry that it would still be some time before she could hope to leave this place. *How long?*

Zofia allowed herself now to reflect on the realization that had come upon her the moment the young boy walked in. A sweet nostalgia filled her as her mind slipped back a decade. She remembered the many trips from her parents' house at Halicz to the neighboring Stelnicki estate at Uście Zielone, where an aristocratic replica of Jerzy had welcomed her. *Dog's blood!* Jerzy was the very image of Jan Stelnicki!

Count Jan Stelnicki. The nostalgia drained away almost at once, memories quickly turning bitter. She had counted on—plotted—an alliance with Jan to avoid a marriage betrothal to another made by her parents when she was a mere baby. But that was before the arrival of Anna at Halicz. Little Anna Maria with her reddish-brown braid and wide green eyes! How had her cousin won his affection? How had *she* lost it? The mystery still irked her.

Well, she had had the satisfaction of foisting off on Anna the man to whom she had been engaged, Antoni Grawliński. She could not help but smile to herself. What a crafty piece of work that had been!

The smile disappeared. How could she have known the tragic end that marriage would come to? . . . *Well, better her than me,* Zofia thought. And yet a little truth that she had always held below the surface rose up now—before Anna came on the scene, Zofia had been interested in Jan mainly as a way of avoiding an arranged marriage, but after Anna seemed to win his affection, her own interest in Jan increased to a white heat. She *had* been jealous of Anna.

Still, she loved her cousin. A little mystery, that. Had she survived the Russians? Zofia had done what she could to get her safely across the bridge. She hoped—and somehow instinctively felt—that Anna had indeed survived. Zofia had told her to go to Paweł's Warsaw town house. Is that where she was? The Russians would not harm her, for Zofia had affixed their names to the Confederacy of Targowica.

And Jan. Had he survived? This seemed less likely. He was the foolishly courageous type, willing to go at professional killers with a handsaw. But if both Anna and he survived, how long would it be before they found each other? The thought took hold of her, provoking a kind of panic. She wrestled with the counterpane and turned to the wall. When would she be well enough to return to Warsaw? How was she to get there? How far downriver had the current taken her?

And what would she find in the capital? Her thoughts and the helplessness of lying in a sickbed day after day were more than she could bear.

Why must life be so complicated? Her mind came back to Jerzy. How simple life would be if only she were sixteen and a pretty village maid being courted by him. She allowed the pleasurable daydream to play out in her head. She would tend a cottage garden, cultivating rue and rosemary for her bridal wreath and lavender to freshen the linens in her dowry chest. On her wedding night he would remove her wedding cap and take her into his strong, sunburnished arms. . . .

But a peasant? Zofia thought again. She looked about the bleak little room, pictured Danuta and her father in their pitiful clothes going about their tedious and grueling tasks. She thought of herself as part of their household, kneading dough, keeping the *bigos* pot at low heat for hours on end, feeding and killing chickens. And producing children like Lutisha turns out strings of sausages. She laughed aloud. *Not in this life,* she thought. The old attraction she had for the city, fine clothes, jewels, money, men—and power—sprouted up again, like a plant with intractable roots.

Still, at Jerzy's image she felt a tickling sort of warmth spreading through her. She stopped laughing. Surely there was some way she could repay the boy.

Jan paced the length of the reception room, fraught with worry. Each time he passed the window, he looked out into the bluish night, down the long curving avenue, high with snow and bordered by parallel rows of poplars and twin ponds.

Midnight had come and gone without a carriage from Warsaw. Had the departure date changed in the time that had passed since the letter came from Paweł? Had Anna been delayed? Turned back by the Russians? Or worse?

By the time most of the candles in the reception room had guttered, he sat in semidarkness, his body tense with worry. With the homecoming celebration suspended, he had sent the Szrabers home to their cottage for the night. From the rear of the house came the worried whispers of Marta and her daughters. Of course, they loved Anna, but Marta's mother, Lutisha, was the beloved matriarch of the little family, and their concern for her was great.

Jan Michał had refused to go to bed at midnight when hopes for his mother's arrival faded. It had been a mistake to tell the boy his mother was expected home, but who could have known? "No bed!" he told a frustrated Emma when she tried to coax him upstairs, "No bed!"

Jan had had to intercede. "Aren't you a little soldier?" he asked, lifting the brown-eyed youngster into the air.

"Oh, yes!" Jan Michał cried, thrilled by the motion.

"Well, soldiers must go to bed!" Jan said, setting him down. "They need their rest so they can do the king's work. You don't want to disappoint the king, do you?"

The boy's face clouded. "No."

"Then you'll let Emma bring you up to bed?"

The boy thought. "You bring me, Jan!"

The bargain was struck. Jan carried the boy upstairs. "Will *Matka* be here when I wake up?" Jan Michał asked before Jan could snuff the candle.

Jan kissed him on the forehead. "We will hope so. . . . Good night."

But his mother had yet to arrive. Jan sat now, despondent and frustrated. What should he do? What *could* he possibly do? He could not just ride off in the direction of Warsaw. He had no papers to travel, and his service under Kościuszko made him no friend of the interlopers. He looked at the bottle of good Gdańsk vodka that was to have supplied many a toast that night. He vowed not to touch it until Anna was safely home.

Jan struggled to stay awake, but the preparations for Anna's homecoming had exhausted him so that by two in the morning, sleep had overtaken him in the chair where he sat.

The clock was striking three when Jan came awake with a start.

Someone's hand was on his shoulder. He opened his eyes to find Walek's face staring down at him. The fire in the grate had gone out, and the room was dark and cold. "What?" Jan asked. "What is it, Walek? News?"

"Yes, milord."

Jan reared up in his chair, fear taking hold. "For God's sake, man, tell me!"

"Lady Anna's carriage has arrived."

Jan was on his feet in an instant. "Arrived? She's *here?*" Pulling on his frock coat, he broke for the front door.

"Wait, milord!"

"What? What is it?"

"The carriage has already been unloaded, milord. Passengers and baggage."

"Unloaded! Then where–?"

Walek allowed himself a smile now. "Lady Anna and Lutisha are in the kitchen with my wife and children."

Jan felt suddenly light-headed. And shamed that he had fallen asleep, that he was not the first to greet Anna. "What kept them?"

Walek shrugged. "That, Lady Anna can tell you herself."

Jan started for the kitchen, his heart beating erratically. He could hear the animated talk now.

He saw the back of her head first, the reddish tint of the brown tresses highlighted by the huge kitchen hearth at full heat. Lutisha, sitting across from her, saw him enter. She looked up and grinned. Her daughter and grandchildren fell silent. Anna turned in her chair to see him approaching and stood immediately to greet him. Her dress was gray and creased from traveling. The strain Jan saw in Anna's face lasted only seconds. She smiled widely. "Jan!" she cried, forgetting any formality.

Speechless, Jan moved forward and swept her into his arms. He was kissing her even before her face could fall into focus. It had been more than two years since he had seen her, two years that dissolved in a single embrace. The formality of kisses on either cheek was jettisoned aside as he held her, his mouth hard upon hers. She held tight to him, giving herself over. Forgetting present company, he drew back only to give her space for breath–and then kissed her again.

Pulling back at last, he saw her emerald eyes filling with tears. His love waxed full. It was only then that they realized how forward their behavior was in the company of servants—and that they held the rapt attention of everyone in the room. Anna's face flushed red.

"You must forgive us," Jan said, noticing that Lutisha and Marta were blushing, as well. Marta and Walek's two girls and young son were trying to suppress their giggles.

It was Lutisha's turn to surprise the group now. "Praised be God," she said, "that is the way every Pole should greet his love!"

Everyone laughed and gave assent, diffusing Jan and Anna's embarrassment.

"I told them not to wake you," Anna said, looking pointedly at Walek.

"Beggin' your pardon, milady, we figured he wouldn't have it that way."

"Indeed!" Jan cried. "Indeed!" It was all he could manage for fear his own tears would start. He suspected she had wanted their reunion more private.

"I'm sorry, Lord Stelnicki," Marta offered. "I should have awakened you as soon as Walek went out to direct the carriage into the stable, but I—I was too eager to see my mother, and I forgot. We all rushed outside."

"I understand, Marta," Jan said, dividing his smile between her and Lutisha.

Chairs were brought in, and everyone sat as if they were all of one class, one family. The occasion seemed to call for it, and no one appeared to mind. Anna told them of the journey home. "The delay at the *starosta*'s office was tedious and uncomfortable, but Lutisha had the worst of it, having to stay in the cold carriage. Thank God for her strength and patience!"

Lutisha's large face reddened, and her grandchildren chided her for it. She blushed all the more.

Jan sent Walek to the reception room for the bottle of vodka, and toasts were made all around for the health of everyone there, for Poland, for the king.

Later, just before sunrise, Anna and Jan sat facing each other in the reception room, alone for the first time. Jan had rekindled the hearth and found fresh candles. He studied Anna in the flickering light. "Why on earth did you tell them not to wake me, Anna?"

"I don't know. I was afraid, I think. Two years is so long . . . and your wound—you wrote so little about it—I didn't know what to expect."

"A shoulder wound—it's nothing." He shrugged. "A lancer knocked me off my horse."

"Is it painful?"

"No, it's well healed. I have a bit of a scar, though. He paid for his inaccuracy, I can tell you." He gave a nervous laugh. "I do hope a little damage doesn't affect our bargain."

"Bargain?"

He moved from his chair and sank to his knees near Anna. He took her hand in his. "You *will* marry me, Anna?"

She nodded. Color was rising in her cheeks. "It's been so very long. . . . Are you certain?"

"Of course, I'm certain!" Jan said, then paused, peering into the green eyes. "Are *you?*"

Her long-lashed eyelids sank slowly and retracted twice before she could summon speech. "Yes. . . . Jan, two years ago . . . at Halicz . . . you joined Kościuszko's army before I could tell you . . . that I love you."

Jan's very core seemed to melt away. "Oh, Anna, know that I love you."

"But I wished a thousand times that I had not allowed you to go off to war without having told you. . . . Had something happened—"

"Anna," Jan said, pressing her hand, "I knew. I knew! How could you think that I didn't know? Words weren't necessary then, and they aren't now."

Anna's eyes assessed him. It seemed that, rather than give herself over to tears, she laughed. "Then my worry was all for nothing."

He kissed her now, taking her by surprise and feeling her lips yield to his, her mouth to his tongue. He had not given her such a kiss since that day more than three years ago. Jan opened his eyes slightly to see that Anna's green eyes were open wide. He pulled back. "You were kissing with your eyes open!"

Anna smiled. "I had to assure myself it was really you, Jan, and no dream."

Jan returned her smile. "And your verdict?"

It was Anna who kissed him now, without reservation. His arms went around her. Her mouth was warm and sweet.

"We'll be married as soon as possible," Jan whispered, drawing back at last. "Next week—"

"Oh, Jan, there are conventions. The banns need to be read at church. . . ." Anna stopped speaking, and her face went as white as a Sunday napkin.

Jan laughed. "I know what you're thinking. That I'm of the Arian faith. Well, I have a bit of a surprise: I've become a Catholic."

Anna's deep-set eyes grew large.

"That *was* your concern, yes?"

"But when . . . why?"

"Last year, but I made up my mind to do it long before that—just after you asked me to be godfather to your son and I was unable to do so because I was not Catholic. I converted so that it would never be a concern again. But as far as other conventions, Poland has been reduced to nothing, so conventions be damned!"

"Jan, you meant what you wrote, about Jan Michał."

"About adopting him as my own? Of course. Although two Jans in the house may be confusing. Maybe you should call me *Janek*."

"No, I think not," Anna said. The reply came immediately and with a kind of abruptness.

"You don't like the diminutive?"

"No," she responded with a certainty meant to close the matter.

Her reaction to the diminutive was odd, but the lips that he longed to kiss turned up in a half-smile now, and he put the thought aside and kissed her yet again.

"As for the name," Anna said after the kiss, "we shall come to some resolution for what is the most happy of problems for me."

"Well, it's one you should sleep on. I must go and let you rest." Jan stood now. He did not want to leave. He wanted desperately to kiss her again—but he was afraid that another kiss would not be enough—

"Go?"

"Yes, I'm staying at the Szraber cottage."

"But there are two guest chambers here." Anna rose from her chair. "Haven't you been staying here?"

"Yes, but now it's hardly proper." Jan felt himself blushing. "Not until we're married, Anna." He attempted a laugh. "What would Lutisha say?"

Anna thought a moment. "Sometimes I do think it *is* the peasant class that sets the moral tone for the *szlachta!*"

"They do say," Jan added, "that the lining is sometimes better than the coat!"

They both laughed.

"Anna?"

"Yes?"

"The *starosta*—he treated you well, did he?"

Anna's eyes moved away. "Come to the window, Jan." She spoke as she walked, her hand in his. "Oh, he kept us waiting some time, but all's well now. . . . Look, Jan, the sun is just about to break!"

Later, as Jan walked to the Szraber cottage, his eyes fixed on the sky that was becoming tinged with red, but failing to bring it into focus. His thoughts inexplicably came back to Jan Michał and his elation was tempered just a little. He had vowed to adopt Jan Michał as his own, and he had meant it. Why, then, did the promise carry with it a weight that tugged at his heart?

*   *   *

Anna looked in on her son before going to her own room. The blond hair of his babyhood was more brown now, but the face was just as angelic. She dared not awaken him. Before retiring, she sat in her old window seat, watching the blue black of night recede. Below, a rabbit skittered across the snow, making for the bare acacia trees near one of the ponds.

Alone now, the memory of Grzegorz Doliński's face, voice, and touch returned. She had been kept waiting, listening to the ticking and pealing of those clocks for hours on end for no good reason. All on his whim. Then she was allowed to go. "I hope you enjoy your visit, Lady Berezowska-Grawlińska," he said as she left.

Anna turned around. "It is not a visit," she said dryly, "I have come home."

Doliński had smiled. "All the better." Those words, delivered in his gravel-like voice chilled her then, chilled her now, but Anna became determined not to permit this man—the man who had allowed the escape of her father's murderer—to haunt her.

Anna sat awhile longer. It was from that window seat in June of 1791 that she had watched in horror as peasants brought home the body of her father. Memories of the father she worshiped and that terrible time flooded her. The serfs on her father's land loved and respected him, all but one: the scoundrel who took his life, Feliks Paduch. The irony was that her father treated the families on his estate well and believed that the Third of May Constitution would bring the country closer to a full democracy.

Her father's death had seemed to initiate other tragedies. . . . Anna shook her head, hoping to clear her mind. . . . As tentacles of light reached up into the dark nave of the sky, Anna watched the snowy landscape glow pink, as if illuminated from beneath. She forced herself back into the present. She was to be married. She was to have the marriage she should have had nearly four years ago. With Jan's conversion to Catholicism, the last obstacle was set aside. She remembered how Jan had told her years before that he did not *disbelieve* the gods of the religions, that his was a personal god, one found in essence of the flowers, trees, and sky. He had puzzled her then, but in time she had come to understand. Oh, his conversion did not mean he had abandoned his iconoclastic beliefs, she knew. He had converted for her sake alone.

She smiled, warmed by the thought. He could not have known that his stand on religion would not have kept her from him. Nothing would have kept her from him. Not after all that had happened. And she would never call him *Janek*. That was a diminutive Zofia had used on occasion as a way of pretending some intimacy existed between her and Jan. Anna knew that Zofia had purposely set out to undermine her relationship with Jan. Oh, she had done her damage. But she would do no more, Anna thought. No more.

Anna willed away her fear of happiness. She *would* be happy.

A motion outside the window took her attention. She looked out now into the winter dawn to see a white eagle winging its way against a crimson sky.

3

Friday, 2 January 1795

"Zofia! Zofia!" Count Paweł Potecki's own broken cry brought him into consciousness. He lifted his head from the pillow, his face wet with perspiration. He had dreamt of her again. She had been so close, had seemed so real that he thought he could reach out and take her beckoning hand. But a step toward her did not bring him closer. Nor did any number of steps as her figure receded into a thickening fog.

It had been that way in their relationship, too, he thought. There was a closeness and yet a great distance between them, a distance that she controlled. A power that she possessed. How had he fallen so completely under her spell?

He threw back the covers now and pulled himself into a sitting position at the side of the bed. He remained there, trying to shake himself of the dream. A few minutes passed.

Finally, he rose and walked to his bedchamber window, as was his morning custom of late, to see what activity was afoot in the capital. Viewed from the second floor of the town house, Piwna Street was quiet enough. A peddler pushed a cart toward the Market Square. Here and there, passersby with serious faces braved the cold, their shoulders leaning into the wind that rose up off the River Vistula.

The bells at nearby Saint Martin's tolled eight. To look out at Warsaw, Paweł mused, one could not guess the city had fallen. Not a single building had suffered damage. Only Praga had been destroyed, and the Russians had made a good job of that. Only Praga, he thought bitterly—and the heart of the Polish people.

The physical well-being of Warsaw belied the political well-being. News had gotten out that King Stanisław proposed to the victor that he keep his monarchy while allowing himself to be tied to Russia by treaty. Paweł could well imagine Catherine's laughter upon hearing it. She would have jettisoned the French language of her court for colorful oaths in her native German idiom. The proposal was a wingless bird—too close to what Poland's status had been for years. And, by God—she had rewarded her General Suvorov with a golden baton for the Praga massacre! No, Poland was to be treated like what it was: the conquered enemy.

Those Poles who had taken part in the insurrection had been arrested and packed off to Russia. Somehow Stanisław had convinced—or bribed—Suvorov to be lenient in his dealings with Polish officers. Both Paweł and Jan Stelnicki had benefitted from that. He prayed their good fortune would hold. Paweł knew only too well fortune had not held—nor Suvorov's word—for the city's mayor, Ignacy Zakrzewski, who had been assured by Suvorov that he would be safe if he returned to the capital where his leadership skills were needed. He did return, but Catherine had different ideas, and he, too, had been provided with a ticket to a colder climate.

Paweł dressed—no uniform any longer—buckled shoes, breeches, a short waistcoat, cravat, and a frock coat. Then he went downstairs to scare up a servant and a cup of coffee. Both were scarce these days. And the house was quiet since he had sent Anna off to meet Jan. Anna and Jan—at least one good thing had come out of the tumult.

He looked into the coffee that his longtime servant Fryderyk had brought him, wishing to read the future of his country as a gypsy might tell his fortune. He saw nothing, only the liquid, dark as ink. What might be done? Poland was being pushed from the world map into obscurity, and there was nothing, nothing to prevent it. No one to help. Why was it that he somehow felt personally responsible for Poland's fate?

Oh, he had given good fight in the final hours. He had risen to the occasion. But he had come late to the party. He should have joined Kościuszko earlier, much earlier, just as Jan Stelnicki had done. It wasn't cowardice; he gave himself that. Or at least it wasn't what one usually thought of as cowardice.

It was ignorance. Ignorance of the plight of the common man, the peasant, in Poland and elsewhere on the continent. Joining Kościuszko's band of patriots had opened his eyes. He had witnessed firsthand the thousands of brave and simple souls who had left home and family to come fight for their Poland. Yes, the Third of May Constitution promised democracy and a better life, but Paweł doubted that was the true reason they turned out with scythes and other crude farm implements that had never been meant to harvest souls. He lived among them, fought with them, ate with them, slept on the hard ground with them, celebrated with them, cried with them. There was Franciszek, a grandfather of thirteen; Baltazar, with his faith as large as his girth; young Kazimierz, an idealist and newlywed. None of them lived to return to their loved ones. These and thousands like them cared more for their Poland and the threat from outsiders than for anything else. Centuries of invasions from Swedes, Turks, Tatars, Cossacks, and a half dozen other nations had steeled their marrow with patriotism.

And it was Zofia, too, he had to admit, who had kept him home and safe. For the longest time, he had been unable to bring himself to leave her. How she had mocked him when he spoke of Kościuszko with respect.

Much earlier, against his judgment, against his principles, she had managed to beat him down until he signed the Confederacy of Targowica. In doing so, he had become an accomplice with the magnates who invited Catherine into Poland so that their own powers would not be corrupted by the Constitution. It made him sick to think of it now.

In time he tried to make things right, to redeem himself by joining Kościuszko and his patriots. He thought back to Zofia's reaction, and the moment came back with cold clarity. Zofia had exploded into a rage that lasted nearly half an hour. He remembered little of what was said on either side, only her beautiful face made ugly by her anger, only her last words flung at him as he left. "You will die, Paweł Potecki, stupid man! You will die, and for what? For a map and its boundaries that shift year by year anyway, no matter what little people like you might attempt!"

But it was Zofia who had died. Paweł's despair, once nonexistent and now most often hidden deep within, bared itself. He drank down his coffee.

Anna had supplied the details. She told him how at the siege of Praga one of the brawniest of the Russians had swooped down on her, but Zofia had diverted his attention so that Anna could escape across the bridge to safety behind the Warsaw walls. Paweł knew that Zofia was too cunning not to know that doing so was placing herself in the very jaws of the enemy. So shaken with emotion, Anna had hardly been able to speak as she told Paweł of Zofia's falling from the broken bridge and being carried away by the River Vistula's cold and swift current. Zofia paid the ultimate price for her sacrifice.

At least everyone believed her dead. Yet there was some part of Paweł that would not accept it. Was it a presentiment? Or a fool's notion? He could only wonder how someone so vibrant, so alive, could be gone in the blink of an eye.

Oh, he had gone to search immediately, riding along either bank days at a time, stopping to inquire at villages or lone huts. Few victims had survived the river. Once he came across a team of peasants working at a mass burial site.

Time was of the essence, for the winter would soon harden the ground. He'd come away wondering if Zofia lay somewhere beneath the bodies he had seen thrown like drowned kittens into the makeshift hole.

He had heard of a few survivors, men and women given succor by the peasants and sent back to their homes in Warsaw and elsewhere, so that when he gave up his search of three weeks and returned to the capital, he did not give up on Zofia. She may yet appear, he thought, against all odds, against all reason.

He had proposed marriage a dozen times, and she had refused as many. His friends could not understand his fixation for Zofia. He maintained that they didn't know her, not really. They knew the gossip, some of which was based on fact. Paweł himself had witnessed her changeable nature, her selfishness, her unchecked sensuality. But there was a hidden side, too, one that told him she could be reclaimed. That side *had* come forward at last, propelling her to save her cousin's life. Now, however, Zofia was as inaccessible as the figure in his dream.

Paweł took his china cup and crashed it to the floor, where it shattered into a hundred pieces. Not even the optimistic Fryderyk would be able to glue the shards together. Paweł put his head in his hands and wept unreservedly.

He left the house an hour later, as the Saint Martin's bells tolled ten. It was but a short walk to the Royal Castle.

The royal sentries were Russians. He had tried four days running to gain an audience with the king, and four times he had been turned away. The king was not receiving, he had been told. He had no reason to expect the reaction today would be any different.

What good could come of seeing the king? he wondered. Why did he persist? What was there that could be done to make things right? He had no answer, but he was driven to go, nonetheless. Some faith, some spirit, had come of his experience with Kościuszko and his mighty band of nobles and peasants, and it was that mysterious force driving him now. He would not just sit back and watch Poland's dissolution.

On the previous occasions, he had gotten past the downstairs sentry at the Senators' Gate. Today the man gave a slight smile of recognition and waved him on. From the ground floor, Paweł climbed the curved white marble staircase to the first floor, his destination the Throne Room by way of the Great Assembly Hall.

"Potecki!" someone whispered sharply as he passed through the National Hall.

Paweł turned to the right to see one of the tall ornate doors partially open, the king's face, pale as plaster against the gold. "This way!" King Stanisław said, motioning Paweł into the Marble Room. "Hurry!"

"Your Highness!" Paweł bowed and quickly deferred.

"Come sit," the king said, pulling the door closed. "It is good to see you, Paweł. My manservant told me you've been here every day this week. Today I've been on the lookout for you. Imagine, me, a spy among spies in my own household!"

"You aren't able to see anyone?"

"Oh, they let a few bumbling fools in to let people think things are running normally. But even if they had allowed a proper audience with you, someone would have sat nearby taking notes. You can be certain of that."

The king must be seventy by now, Paweł guessed. He wore no powdered wig—seldom few did anymore—and his thinning gray hair was drawn and tied in the back. He had a simple face and birdlike eyes that betrayed the sadness beneath the smiles he affected. The two talked at some length of the December weather, the prospects of a long winter, and other mundane subjects. All was formality. Neither, it seemed, could bring himself to speak of the desperate situation of the country. At last, an awkward lull ensued, and with a great sigh, the king asked, "How goes it with the people?"

Paweł's lips tightened. "Well, there's been some improvement. The grain stores have been released, and that should shore up the cries of starvation. And soldiers are no longer being evicted from hospitals."

"Ah, is it possible there's a trace of humanity left in Suvorov? Has the golden baton softened him, I wonder?"

"It's just a phase, Sire. A fox may change his skin but not his habits. There will be other fields for his men to mow."

"Of course, you're right. People are slow to change, if they ever do. And what about the people, *my* people? What do they think of their king?"

"The people shall always stand with their king." It was the sort of thing a royal sycophant would say, but in this case, Paweł knew it to be true. Oh, the king had his enemies at home, and most knew his weaknesses, yet the country as a whole supported him.

"But he is not a Tadeusz Kościuszko?"

"No. Nor do they expect you to be." Now, Paweł thought, perhaps he *was* playing the sycophant.

"I have disappointed them. I continue to do so. The people appear on the castle steps daily hoping to see me, to ask me for help. I receive letters, hundreds of letters, Paweł! They just want the chance to live humbly. Some want no more than a plot for their war dead and a marker. It's heartrending. And it humbles me, I can tell you. I should have done more."

"But what could you have done?"

"I could have listened to that girl who came to me in October to tell me of the insurgents' plans. I might have tried to make them wait for Kościuszko. Then the rebellion would not have been so bloody that Catherine would unleash her meanest dog. Suvorov will pay in hell one day!"

"Why didn't you, Highness? Listen, I mean."

"Oh, I was certain that Kiliński and the other rebel leaders would not heed me, but I should have tried, just the same. I should have! What was the girl's name? Anna?"

"Yes, Sire, Anna Berezowska-Grawlińska."

"A brave girl, that one."

"Yes, Sire."

"Took some nerve for a young thing like that to come before a king and suggest he do something."

It did indeed, Paweł thought. He knew Anna's feelings toward the king had been tempered by that meeting. They were strong—and ambivalent. She had found him the quintessence of sophistication and culture, a true and ardent benefactor of science and arts and letters. But she deemed him weak and ineffectual as a leader of men.

"I might have done something then," the king was saying, as if in response to Paweł's train of thought, "but now I can do nothing for my people. Why, even when the city's mayor was carted off to the coldest part of Russia, what could I do for him? Nothing but give him a fur coat—and that's what I did. A fur coat! It is all so sad, Paweł, so sad."

"What is to happen, Highness?"

"Oh, I'm certain even peasants far removed from the city know that the country will be fully carved up now, like some prize cow. Word has it Prussia is hungry for Warsaw. And they want to see me removed. I would be an obstacle, they say. Of course, I would be, even if only a token one."

"Have you heard anything from—?"

"Catherine? Yes, just yesterday, as a matter of fact." The king sneered. "She wants me to go to Grodno. Lithuania! Can you imagine? To spend my last years in a guarded country castle—like I'm some cast-off English queen!"

Where Catherine was concerned, Paweł could well imagine. "And . . ."

"Will I go? I have conjured a number of excuses to keep me in Warsaw—bad health, poor carriages, the weather, an unfit castle at Grodno. I've made a list. My hope is that while I delay, Catherine and Prussia will somehow get into a squabble and change their plans."

Paweł could not fathom how a squabble between Catherine and Prussia might be advantageous for Poland, and so he chose not to press the issue.

The two heard movements in the adjacent Yellow Room. "They're probably looking for me, Paweł. I've been off the leash too long. Will you come back on Monday? I have something to discuss with you. Something important."

A servant led Anna into a small room in the church rectory. This was the one formality of the marriage arrangements that she had dreaded.

The balding priest entered, smiling. "Lady Berezowska-Grawlińska, it is indeed good to have you back in Sochaczew."

"Thank you, Father Łukasz."

"Don't be nervous, child. This is a mere formality. Please, sit."

Anna nodded and obeyed. Once they were both seated, the priest spoke in what must have been his tone in the confessional. "It is quite all right, however, for the bride to be nervous when speaking of her wedding." He chuckled.

Anna knew he was trying to make her feel at ease and so attempted a smile.

"Now then, my lady," he said in normal tones, "let's move to the matter at hand. Do you have a record of your husband's death?"

Anna had thought of lying, saying she hadn't, but somehow couldn't bring it off. She couldn't start a new life with a lie. She turned the document over to the aging priest, then watched his face cloud over.

"Antoni Grawliński died in a duel? Good God! Oh, pardon me, my lady, this is just such a surprise. I'm so sorry."

"That's all right, Father. Antoni was not a good husband."

"Oh?"

Anna knew the priest was waiting for her to offer more information, but she could not bring herself to do so.

"And the child that you and Antoni had?"

"He is well, Father . . . but he is not Antoni's child." Anna regretted the admission before it was out of her mouth. She had meant to keep things simple.

"Then . . . who–?"

Anna saw no way out, other than to go on with the story. "Father, the child is the result of an attack that occurred shortly after I arrived in Halicz . . . before the marriage."

The priest suppressed a gasp. "Oh, my dear, I see. Did you keep that from Grawliński?"

"No, he knew. He was marrying me for what I could bring to his family. For money, Father. And land. You see, he wanted to build a distillery here in Sochaczew on my family property."

The priest's mouth fell slack. "A distillery! And the–person who attacked you?"

"My cousin Walter."

"Your cousin! Holy Mary, Mother of God!"

"He is not my cousin by blood."

"Well, you were spared that, at least. But, still!" The priest took a moment to collect himself. "And Jan Stelnicki? Will he be a good father to little Jan Michał?"

"Oh, yes, Father, they've taken to each other as if they *are* father and son."

"Excellent, my child. I fear that in similar situations, the man might resent a child not his, and especially in this situation. . . ." The priest's face was reddening.

Anna tried to spare the priest embarrassment. "Jan is . . . a decent man." Anna found herself at a loss in describing Jan's worth.

"I'm certain he is, and I will find out for myself tomorrow when he comes to see me. If all goes well, the first engagement announcements will be read in church on Sunday. The banns will need to be read three succeeding Sundays."

"Of course, Father."

Anna left, thankful that Father Łukasz was a simple soul and that the twists of her story had deterred him from coming to the question hardest to explain, the question that would surely have given him pause in bestowing his blessing on the pair. He had not asked the identity of Antoni's dueling partner. To explain that it had been Jan who had challenged Antoni would not have been an easy thing. And impossible to explain that it was Walter—still obsessed with Anna—who had actually assassinated Antoni.

Were such omissions a form of lying? The better part of herself thought so, but for once she took stock in the maxim that only fools and children speak the truth.

She would warn Jan that on his visit to the priest he should tread softly.

The banns were read on the appointed Sundays. The Christmas holidays fell within this time period, and recent events notwithstanding, the *wigilia* celebration was the happiest Anna could recall. Tradition held that Christmas Eve was better observed and celebrated than Christmas Day. Jan, Walek, and Walek's son Tomasz went out into the forest to collect boughs of spruce and fir with which to decorate the manor house. Jan Michał had talked himself into being included, and when they returned, he sat in the sleigh high atop a little mountain of greenery, his smile showing every baby tooth. It was little Jan Michał, too, who had the privilege of searching out the first star of the evening, for it was only after its sighting that the *wigilia* supper could begin.

Although Jewish, Emma and Jacob Szraber joined Anna, Jan, and Jan Michał at table. They even shared in the unconsecrated *opłatek* that was offered after a short prayer by Jan. It was the first *wigilia* at table for Jan Michał, and he seemed mystified as the wafer was passed from person to person and individual wishes were made. Everyone called for a restoration of a true Poland and for prosperity in the fields, barns, and homes. Jan Michał was not to be overlooked. "I wish," he cried in a high voice, "for a horse of my own."

When everyone laughed, Jan Michał looked about him and quickly amended his wish. "Or a dog!" The laughter escalated.

After dinner, Lutisha and her family were asked to join the others in the music room. The happy group sang the old carols while Anna accompanied them on piano. Emma, her former governess and music teacher, claimed she had not lost her touch, but Anna thought differently. She would have to practice more.

As midnight neared, Anna, Jan, Jan Michał, and the servants climbed into sleighs and headed for Shepherds' Watch—Midnight Mass—waving farewell to the Szrabers. The night was clear, allowing the nearly full moon to brighten the snow and light their way. Along the route Anna found herself counting the roadside shrines with their carved icons sheltered beneath two boards forming an inverted *V*. This had been a favorite pastime as a child.

"Look, Mother," Jan Michał cried from beneath his scarf. His eyes were lifted to the sky. "So many stars now!"

Anna looked up. The stars, said to be the shepherds' fires of the first Christmas, were numberless. "Yes," she said. "So many!"

"Jan Michał," Jan said, "those stars foretell next year's harvest, and it looks to be a good one, indeed."

A good harvest and a good future, Anna prayed.

Anna and Jan were to celebrate their wedding day on 4 January 1795, the Sunday after the third reading of their banns.

On the wedding's eve, Anna sat at her dressing table while Marta combed her hair. Downstairs, Lutisha was directing Marcelina and Katarzyna in making the wreaths of rue that Anna and Jan would wear and exchange at the church ceremony. In the morning, Lutisha would rise before dawn to bake the *kołacz*. No wedding bread she had ever made, Lutisha claimed, had crust that cracked in the baking.

In case there was any truth to the notion that cracks in the bread presaged a bad marriage, Anna prayed that the good servant's skill would hold up. Anna's aunt had seen to the baking of the *kołacz* for her first wedding, and the crust had cracked.

"You have such beautiful hair, madame. Not brown, not red, but the best of both."

"Thank you, Marta. You know, as a girl I often wished for blond hair, like yours."

Marta giggled. "It's getting gray, little by little, what with a husband and three children. . . . Madame will wear the amber combs tomorrow, yes? They work well with the bits of amber in your green eyes."

"Do you think I should wear them? . . . Then I shall!"

Marta was pleased. "And you will cry tomorrow, at the church?"

"Cry?" Anna thought for a protracted moment. "I don't know."

"Oh, but you must, madame! You *must!*"

"Must I? Why?" Anna asked, teasingly. She knew very well the superstition.

"Oh, Lady Anna, if a bride doesn't cry at her wedding, she will cry all of her wedded life."

Anna laughed. She had not cried at her marriage to Grawliński, but she knew that no amount of tears could have salvaged that union.

"Did *you* cry when you married Walek?" Anna asked.

"Oh my, yes."

"Then you believe the saying?"

Brush in midair, Marta paused and thought for a moment, locking eyes with Anna's in the mirror. She shrugged. "A few tears?" she asked with great sincerity. "It hardly seems worth the risk *not* to cry, does it, madame?"

Anna let loose a peal of laughter, and a few seconds later, Marta joined in.

Some sixty guests, all *szlachta* from Sochaczew and the neighboring towns attended the wedding Mass, witnessing the exchange of Jan and Anna's wreaths of rue. The occasion afforded the minor nobility a show of extravagance.

Jan had dared to wear his dress uniform of blue, crimson, and gold trim. Anna had lost her best dresses when Praga burned, but Emma had saved the day by creating for her a French patterned dress in soft yellow. She stood in low-heeled yellow slippers facing Jan, bathed in the cobalt blue of his gaze, and she thought she could never be happier than at that moment. She would no longer fear happiness—she would embrace it.

Anna was too elated to cry, yet she knew it was expected. Still, by the end of the ceremony, her eyes remained dry. For too many years she had shunned crying in public. Oh, she held herself no braver than anyone else, but her tears had always been shed in private. She tried to think of something now that would induce the crying. She thought of the attack upon her in the forest nearly four years ago. She thought of her first marriage and what a trial that had been, what a scurrilous character Antoni Grawliński had proved. She thought of Zofia and her deception. . . . And still no tears came.

So be it. With Jan as her husband, she turned away from the altar and started for the far entrance, resigned to leaving the church dry-eyed. It was then that her eyes fell on brown-eyed, brown-haired Jan Michał, sitting like a little man with Emma and Jacob. It struck her at that moment that if her life had not taken the sometimes tragic turns it had, she would not have this wonderful child. It was that simple thought that unsealed a chamber of her heart, allowing a rush of tears—and bringing smiles of relief to many in the church. The news would please Marta, who was home preparing for the guests that were to eat, drink, and dance the entire night.

The supper and reception were splendid affairs. While Jan was landless, he still possessed considerable assets, the interest of which he contributed to the running of the estate, but Anna requested of Lord Lubicki, her family's longtime investment banker, a significant sum so that the celebration would be truly memorable. Her father had wisely invested in foreign markets, so that most of the family wealth survived the Russian interlopers.

Polish hospitality dictated that even Lord Doliński, the despicable *starosta,* be invited. Anna had seen him at the church, too—or thought she had—in one of the pews farthest from the altar. The sight sent a chill playing along her spine. Still, she was not about to let his presence ruin her day, so she put him from her mind—until the recessional commenced and she and Jan moved toward the door. Her eyes surreptitiously sought out his pew—but she found it empty. At home, as Anna welcomed several families that had been friends of her parents, as well as a few women she had known in girlhood, he crossed her mind again, but—thankfully—he did not darken their threshold.

Redolent Christmas greenery accented the white tablecloths. Candles gaily danced everywhere.

A small commotion arose then. Under the supervision of Jacob, two youths hauled a wine barrel into the dining hall. "What is this dirty old thing?" Anna asked.

Jacob's smile was as wide as the sky. "It is your wine, Lady Stelnicka—it is 'Lady Anna's wine'—purchased in Hungary in the year of your birth for the occasion of your marriage—as is the custom!"

Anna could only stare and mumble, "As is the custom." She watched dumbly as the keg was tapped and purplish wine began to fill up glasses. Her mind spun with thoughts. Her first marriage had taken place in Halicz, so far to the south and performed in such a hurried fashion that no thought had been given to this cask, so long buried in the cellar. How fitting it was that it survived to slake the thirsts at *this* wedding instead.

Jan handed her a glass. Her hand trembled as she raised it to the guests. If only her parents had lived to see this day. . . .

Her reverie fell away as toasts were made for Poland, for the king, for her and Jan. Anna and Jan then shared the prescribed bowl of *kasza;* the porridge had been cooked in milk to make it sweet, just as their married life was to be. Baked chicken was served to all, along with stewed cabbage, beet soup, and peas—symbolic of fertility. Then came the *kołacz.* Anna's heart swelled to see that the crust of the wedding bread was perfect. Not a single little crack. *God bless Lutisha!*

Toasts began again, more boisterous than before the meal and accompanied by the crash of glass upon the hearth. Then came the dancing that continued until well after midnight. It was at the height of the celebration that five young married women took Anna to her parents' room, the room—and bed—that was to be hers and Jan's. Had this been her first marriage, much show would have been made in public about the removal of the wedding wreath, the unplaiting and ceremonial cutting of her hair, and the placing of the *czepek,* the cap of a married woman. None of this had been observed in the marriage to Grawliński, however, because of the shame associated with the rape.

Now, at least, Anna was to have a *czepek* for what was politely called "the bedding down." One of the women, Halina, presented Anna with the embroidered wedding cap. "Emma made this for you, Anna."

Anna gasped. It was the most beautiful cap she had ever seen, all done in pastels and laced with semiprecious stones. Once the wedding wreath was taken from her head and the cap put in its place, the women cried out their sincere compliments as Anna assessed herself in the mirror. She saw herself as more than a beautiful bride—she saw herself as *happy.* This cap would be used only for the special occasions of her life—and at her death.

"A toast now!" one of the women—Sylwia—announced. She had brought up to the bedchamber a bottle and six glasses. She poured out the vodka, and the glasses were passed around. A naughty sparkle came into her eyes, and she cried, "A girl no more!" so used was she to the saying at weddings.

Embarrassed, the other women quieted, and when the stout woman realized her blunder, her eyes went large and the sparkle disappeared. She put her hand to her mouth in horror.

"I've been married before, Sylwia. I've not been a girl for a long time!" Anna laughed. "But come now, I'm not offended. You must laugh, too."

The tension was immediately relieved and the room rang with girlish laughter. Sylwia, however, still had a mouthful of vodka and as she released her laugh, the liquor was released, as well, spraying out and down her dress. The sound of their collective laughter now became shrill enough to break windows. Halina thought this called for a dance and led the other five in a spontaneous mazurka. They sang

> Everyone take a good look
> She was in a wreath and comes in a cap.

The dance ended with the other women climbing up onto the great feathered bed. Anna could only stare and hold her breath as the five jumped up and down, laughing and calling out rude things about the future of the marriage as they tested the strength of the bed. One by one, they collapsed onto it. By some miracle, the bed held.

Halina proposed another toast, but by the time she was ready to pour, a strong rapping came at the door. Anna watched the five turn their attention to her, their eyes ablaze with vodka and humor. Anna could read their silly faces like pictures in a child's book. Sylwia giggled. "They've come for you, Anna."

"Open up!" someone called. The door had been bolted.

"It's my husband!" Halina laughed. "Go away!" As was customary, the women refused admittance, playing at protecting Anna until the men threatened to take down the door. "Go away!" they cried. "Go drink yourselves silly!"

The revelers persisted. "Much is to be done before the night is over," someone shouted.

Anna watched and listened to all this as in a dream. She cringed to think that her union at last with Jan was to be so public, such a cause for hilarity. And yet she trembled with elation to think that she no longer had to love him from afar.

Halina opened the door at last, and the wedding guests crowded into the room, many carrying drinks to toast the couple's wedding night. Two of the groomsmen stumbled to the bed and fell upon it. One of them announced in a slurred voice, "We must warm it up for Lord Stelnicki and Lady Stelnicka!" His eyes rolled back into his head then, and he passed out. "Make way! Make way!" someone was calling, and soon another groomsman was pushing through the throng, pulling the husband into the bedchamber. Jan had his part to play, too: that of a reluctant groom. "Make way for Jan Stelnicki!" the groomsman announced. "Where is the Lady Anna? Ah, there she is! My lady, we have come to deliver the goods!"

That comment set everyone off on a bawdy tavern song that continued through a toast and many good wishes. The guests were still singing as they filed out and crowded into the anteroom. Many were having trouble with the lyrics, but the irreverent refrain—though raucously off-key—was delivered with great enthusiasm. The unconscious groomsman was slapped awake and set to, so that all three groomsmen could wish the couple the best and finish clearing the room.

When all the guests were assembled in the anteroom, Jan walked over and closed the door, bolting it securely.

He turned to face his bride. He smiled.

Anna's heart beat as if a sparrow were held captive in her chest. She walked to him now, her eyes on his—those cobalt blue eyes she had discovered that day in the meadow years before. She had wished for this day a thousand times, never fully believing it would come. But it had come. They were husband and wife. Whatever the future, they were as one.

When she reached Jan, he bent to kiss her. And the kiss held—oh, she had had her share of vodka, but it was some other unearthly elixir that lifted her now—transporting her. His mouth went to her ear. "Anna," he said in the same soft murmur he had said her name that fall day so long ago. Eyes tightly shut, she could hear the rustle of leaves that day, smell the very scent of earth, feel his body near hers. . . .

Outside, the revelry and singing continued, as if at a distance. "Now, don't be lazy!" someone was calling. Anna laughed.

"May God grant you descendants as plentiful as the stars," said another.

"At last!" It was a woman's voice this time that came through the door. Anna thought it Halina's. "The bedding down is complete."

"Oh, it is hardly that!" Jan called back, laughing, and the crowd beyond the door responded in kind. He bent now to lift Anna, scooping her up as if she weighed no more than a hummingbird.

"You've brought some of your carvings!" Zofia exclaimed, moving from the bed to her chair. "Come, sit."

Jerzy nodded. He had come to visit her several times, each time managing to do so while his mother and grandfather were on some business in the village. He carried to the chair next to Zofia's an armful of his wooden carvings, painted and unpainted.

Jerzy sat and started to hand them, one by one, to Zofia for her inspection. "Oh, my, these are excellent, Jerzy," she said, noticing that he was well-groomed and his hands scrubbed clean. "How long have you been carving?"

"Since I was five, I think. My grandfather taught me. His fingers are too bent these days for carving."

Zofia smiled. "So he carves now through you?" She turned over in her own slender hands the figures of a bird, a cow, a dog, a windmill, passing them then to the bed.

"What kind of wood is this?"

"Linden. It's best to use."

Zofia inspected now the wooden replicas of peasants, crudely hewn, but surprisingly evocative in emotions. She felt something for each likeness, something in their stance and in their faces that went to the heart. The people depicted were impoverished, but they were rich in spirit and character.

"Who is this one?" Zofia asked, for the bearded figure did not look like a peasant.

"John the Baptist, milady."

"Ah, I see the halo now. . . . And this one? Another saint?"

"Saint Barbara."

"Ah, some say that when one dies, the soul must spend a night with Saint Barbara. Do you suppose that's true, Jerzy?"

The boy reddened.

"Well, it is true. That some people believe it, I mean. But then, some people believe anything. . . . Oh, these are all wonderful! You've got one more. Let me see it."

Jerzy seemed uncertain and held back. Zofia reached for it, but the boy moved it out of reach, as if he were afraid for her to see it.

"What's so special about that one? You wouldn't have brought it if you didn't mean for me to see it." Zofia rose now, laughing, but quickly managing to pull it from his grasp.

"It's not finished," Jerzy said.

As if in slow motion, she took her seat again, turning over the figure in her hand, her eyes wide in amazement. It was the unpainted figure of a woman, not in village costume but in a modern western dress with a wide skirt. It wanted only a little splash of red paint. The almond-shaped eyes of the face stared out, eerily transfixed, as in death. "Why, it's me!" Zofia exclaimed. "Dog's blood! Did I look like that when you found me?"

Jerzy eyed Zofia cautiously. He was blushing to the roots of his hair. "Yes, milady."

Zofia stared at the carving. "Dog's blood," she murmured. He had captured an emptiness, the emptiness of death. But it was the emptiness she had also felt in life.

Jerzy pulled himself to his feet, as if to begin collecting the sculptures.

Zofia was at a loss. What was she to say to him? What did she mean to him—that he could create such a thing? Or he to her?

When he reached for the figure, Zofia held it away from him, teasingly. It was a childish reaction, she knew, but it was the only one that came to her. Jerzy leaned across her for the extended hand that held her likeness. Zofia reached up with her free hand, lightly touched his face, and arched her back so that her face moved near to his.

His face flashed surprise at her touch; then as she held her hand on his smooth cheek, fear suffused his blue eyes.

"Jerzy?"

"Yes?" His voice, cracking slightly, betrayed another reaction—arousal.

Zofia gave him her most generous smile. "Would you teach me how to carve?"

4

*A*nna was alone when she awakened. She pushed her arms out from under the counterpane, stretching. How long she had slept, and how deeply! The soft winter light in the room caressed her, whispering that it was already midmorning. She looked over to Jan's place, ran her hand over his pillow. He had roused her a few hours before, already dressed, saying he was going to tend to some things on the estate and that she should sleep. She thought she remembered murmuring something in reply, but she was quite certain of the kiss he had given her. She smiled now to think of it. *Now* the bedding down was complete.

Things to do on the estate, she thought. Oh, he had much in common with her father. Although Jacob had always been an excellent estate manager, in the old days, her father himself had done much of the overseeing of his modest estate and several serf families. Anna's mother had never approved of her husband's taking such an interest and let her opinion be known. No, she had never understood her husband. But the count had taught his daughter to love the land and how to grow things, beginning with a small garden that yielded an array of tulips and other flowers, as well as vegetables. Much to her mother's vexation, Anna wasn't afraid to get her hands dirty or tear a nail.

I will not make the same mistake as my mother, Anna thought. *I* will *understand my husband.* Her father would have been quite satisfied with the match she had made. She pulled Jan's pillow to her, held it, brimming with contentment.

A light knock came at the door. Then a soft, tenuous voice: "Madame?"

"Come in, Lutisha. I'm quite awake."

Lutisha entered, taking a tray directly to a little table near the bed. She seemed careful not to glance at Anna, who smiled to herself at the maid's modesty. "I've brought coffee, madame, with extra cream, the way you like it."

"Thank you, Lutisha. Good country cream—not like we get in the city, I can tell you." Anna sat up in bed and tucked Jan's pillow behind her. She watched as the servant started placing upon the tray the glasses from the night before. Anna interlocked her hands behind her head. "Well?"

Lutisha paused a moment but did not look up. "Well, madame?"

"Lutisha! Every day you come in and you say, 'How is Madame this fine morning?' And today you are silent."

The woman began to color and could say nothing.

"Lutisha, look at me. Yes, that's it. I can tell you I am *very* fine this fine morning." Anna laughed.

Lutisha turned crimson now. "I am . . . pleased, madame. . . . Will you be coming down to breakfast?"

"Yes, Lutisha, I will be coming down to breakfast." Anna put on a serious face. She enjoyed teasing the old servant, but thought it best to bring it to an end.

When another knock sounded, Anna, thinking it Jan, called, *"Entre!"*

Two blond heads topped with ruffled white caps appeared in the doorway. "Oh, pardon, madame," Katarzyna said. "Marcelina and I thought Grandma would need some help, but we didn't know you were still in bed."

"Didn't you?"

"Oh, no," Marcelina said, giving her sister a gentle push into the room. "We're sorry to bother you, madame."

"It is no bother. You may help your *babcia* by taking those bottles there and picking up Lord Stelnicki's sash from the floor. Katarzyna, would you bring my morning robe? The blue one—it's in the wardrobe."

The girl obeyed, managing to steal a look at Anna as she approached her. Setting the robe on the bed, she stood for a long moment staring at Anna's embroidered wedding cap that lay on the bedside table.

Anna smiled. "It's beautiful, yes?"

"Oh, madame," Katarzyna gasped, "I've never seen a *czepek* like it!"

"How old are you, Katarzyna?"

"Eighteen, milady. . . . I mean, madame."

"You're seventeen," Marcelina contradicted.

"Nearly eighteen!"

"But that's months away!" her sister said.

Anna turned to Marcelina. "That must make *you* sixteen this year, Marcelina."

She gave a little wince. "Not till October, madame."

"Well, it won't be long before you are *both* married off, I'm certain. Tell me now, have you prospects?"

"Oh no, madame!" Katarzyna cried. Marcelina shrank back, shaking her head.

"Very well," Anna said, "but I'm not sure I believe you. Two pretty girls like you! Katarzyna, you may try it on. Go ahead . . . look in the mirror now. Come, Marcelina, you may have a turn, too."

The sisters radiated their pleasure as one posed, then the other, before the mirror at the vanity table that had belonged to Anna's mother. Lutisha's expression, however, darkened by the minute. "Madame, they should not be in your chamber today."

"Shush, Lutisha. They only wanted to see if I am a changed woman, didn't you, girls?"

The girls' heads turned toward Anna, their eyes widening. They looked at each other then in guilty wonder to be found out.

"Perhaps you would like to try it yourself, Lutisha?"

"Oh, madame! What nonsense you talk." Lutisha looked as if she didn't know whether to give herself over to indignation or laughter. The servant tried to cover her toothless smile as laughter won out. Everyone joined in.

"Whatever you say, Katarzyna and Marcelina," Anna said, "it will not be long before the two of you will require caps." The sisters giggled, squirming in embarrassment. "I will see," she continued, "if I can't prevail on Emma to make your caps for you when the time comes."

Again the eyes widened. "You would do that?" Marcelina whispered.

"Yes, I would!" Anna laughed. "Now, time to leave me alone or I shall be certain to come upon you on *your* marriage morning! Out!"

"You heard Madame. Out!" Lutisha cried, shooing her granddaughters from the room. She turned toward Anna at the doorway, gave a little flustered smile, and made her own exit, closing the door behind her.

Before coming to serve at the Berezowski estate in Sochaczew, Lutisha and her family had been servants at Anna's aunt and uncle's larger estate in Halicz. Anna smiled to herself, remembering how these two girls had regarded her when she came to stay at the Groński home. Anna had questioned them about the garden that they kept, even commenting on the variety of an onion. They answered nervously, giving each other side glances, clearly aghast that a countess should concern herself with such things.

But Jan had understood her inherited love of the land. And he loved her for it.

As for being a changed woman, she was that, indeed.

* * *

The hard snow crunched under the highly muscled stallion's hooves. Jan was exploring field and forest, his head held high as he inhaled the frosty January air. He had tried to be of help to Walek earlier that morning, but everyone had his assigned Monday chores, and there seemed to be nothing in need of doing. For his offer he had gotten some odd, knowing glances—some, too, that perhaps questioned his absence from the wedding bedchamber. So he had gone riding instead. He had not ridden in days, and it felt good to have a horse beneath him again.

As he rode, he fell into his old habit of reliving the campaigns he had made with Kościuszko, reveling in what was done right, guessing how the mishaps and defeats might have been avoided. A true Pole sought glory, or so the saying went. He wondered if it were so. He had fought for democracy, fought against the allied forces. He did not bask in his victories, nor did he show off the shoulder scar rendered by a Russian lancer, the scar Anna had so delicately traced with her fingertips last night.

He found himself singing aloud a ditty about swordsmanship popular among the cavalry:

> Hungarians cut directly,
> Muscovites cleave from above,
> Turks whip roundabout,
> And Poles slash crisscross!

Jan's sword—nicknamed Jadwiga after Poland's saintly first Jagiellonian queen, for it was her sacrifice that made for the union of Lithuania and Poland into one commonwealth—hung now on the wall in the reception room, and Jan had to own up to a sadness that he carried it no longer.

Oh, there was excitement in war; he could not deny that. For most soldiers who had seen action, there was—in the moment—an incomparable thrill to it. Even in the killing—or was it *especially* in the killing? How many lives had he ended? He didn't know. He had seen death in the most nightmarish forms. Only the devil could have engineered so many excruciating ways to bring an end to life. Soldiers on both sides fell like so many papier-mâché dolls—to the lance, saber, carbine, and cannon. Allies and enemies, peasants and nobles, all bled equally. Battle was the ultimate gamble. A riptide of energy and emotion flowed through him on the field, a tide that excited his senses, and it was this experience that brought him low after the battles, brought him low now. How could he feel such bloodlust? Yet he knew instinctively that it was bloodlust that allowed him to survive. The thought chilled him.

Jan found himself in a pine forest now, its floor white as milk, the incredibly tall trees rising to the heavens. The lower forty or fifty feet of the trees were devoid of branches, sturdy as columns, so that he felt he was in a pristine and soundless cathedral. The forest *is* God's church, his father had told him. The memory soothed him. He tried to conjure up his father's face and voice, recalling with pride how he had helped give birth to the Third of May Constitution.

Jan dismounted and, leading his horse, slowly laid down his own path. Before joining Kościuszko, he had been content to live a good and full life, a noble on his family estate near Halicz. Now he had put off his uniform, taken marriage vows, and resigned himself to live the placid life of the *szlachta* on the Berezowski estate, his wife's estate. It seemed that life was asking him to forget that his own estate had been confiscated by Austrian forces, forget his father's dying wish that he fight for democracy, forget that brave men died at his side fighting for a Poland that people said no longer existed. A roiling tide of convoluted and unsettling emotions wore away at him.

In all of this, there was Anna. He had loved her from that first day so long ago. They had waited an eternity, it seemed, but they were together now. Their wedding night had not been a disappointment. Her hunger had equaled his, and he loved her for her passion. No man could have asked for more.

The marriage would be a good one—and yet Jan felt himself still some distance from any sense of peace or complacency. With the marriage ceremony he had become a parent, as well as a husband. Would he be a good father to Jan Michał, a child not his own? The boy was delightful, he had to admit. Anna worshiped him. And yet, to think that this was her cousin Walter's child somehow unsettled him. He could never allow Anna or Jan Michał to know this. He prayed he could bridge the distance he felt and do right by the boy.

Jan suddenly realized he had gone far into the forest, one unfamiliar to him. He turned around and began to retrace his steps.

An hour later, coming to where field and forest met, he mounted his horse again and gave good spur, hoping that the sharp blast of winter wind against his face would help to clear his mind. In no time, the great thatched roof of the barn loomed ahead. As he neared it, Walek saw him and waved. The door was open, and Walek stood prepared to take the horse. Jan knew that the loyal servant had served in Kościuszko's peasant army, taking up a simple but sharp and effective scythe against the allied forces.

Walek had come back, fitting once again into family and service, doing the tasks he had always done, albeit on a different estate. Jan wondered what Walek's thoughts about it were. Did he have dark thoughts, too? He would ask him one day, he decided. For now, Jan worried whether he himself would adapt once again to the traditional life of the *szlachta*. Or had he been a soldier too long?

Walek took hold of the horse and Jan dismounted.

"Walek, those big old sheepdogs they keep in the south, near Zakopane—do you know anyone in these parts who keeps them?"

"No, milord."

"Ah, well, ask around in town, will you? See what you can find out. I'll pay a good price for one. It's for little Jan Michał."

Realizing that the morning was nearly gone, Jan ran toward the house, hurried through the kitchen—aware of surprised faces in his wake—and raced up the servants' staircase just as Lutisha was descending.

He found Anna dressed and ready to leave the bedchamber. She gave him a disparaging smile. Was there a trace of real hurt in it?

"Fine husband you are," she said, "running off on our first morning!"

Jan bowed in exaggerated fashion. "I beg your pardon, Lady Stelnicka," he said. Her married name did not go without the effect in her expression that he desired. Any hurt she might have felt dissipated at once. "Or is it to be Lady Berezowska-Grawlińska-Stelnicka?"

Anna laughed. "Stelnicka. Only Stelnicka!"

Jan took her into his arms. Anna spoke before he could kiss her. "Speaking of names, I have a solution for having two Jans in one house."

"And what is that, Lady Stelnicka?"

"I will start calling my son by his second name, Michał."

Jan smiled. "*Our* son," he said. "So the problem is solved!" He kissed her now, felt her yielding. Then, drawing back, he said, "I have another apology."

"What? Are we to begin married life with apologies?"

His mouth went to her ear. "I am sorry for one thing only," he whispered, "and that is that you went to the fruitless task of dressing. I told Lutisha we would not be down before the afternoon meal. Why, the old girl's face turned as red as her apron!"

"You've heard?" King Stanisław asked. Paweł's second visit to the king came on Monday, 5 January 1795, just two days after Austria signed a treaty joining Russia and Prussia in the dismemberment of Poland. They met in the Monarchs' Portrait Room, a small chamber off the Throne Room, and all precautions were taken for secrecy.

"That Austria is to share in the spoils with Russia and Prussia? Yes, Your Highness."

The king sighed. "They say that 'Where one owl comes out, two others soon follow.'" He chuckled, but his face was pinched in bitterness. "Here, it's the other way around."

"Poland is no mouse, Sire."

"Ah, but we are in their talons, just the same."

The irony that they conferred in a chamber with portraits of all the European monarchs looking down on them was not lost on Paweł. "Have they worked out boundaries?"

"No. They'll take good time in that, you can be certain. As for me, my final day has been set, Paweł. No excuse to stay has worked."

"When, Sire?"

"The day after tomorrow."

"I'm sorry," Paweł murmured, his heart aching for the king, who seemed at once sad and resigned to his leaving. Perhaps he was relieved to be fully free of the yoke of leadership.

Paweł had come today, wondering what the king had wanted to speak to him about. What in matters of the state could *he* could possibly do? Especially now, with this news.

"Don't fret about me," the king told Paweł. "Don't pity me, either. I've had my time. I might have done better with it, God knows, but regrets will do no good now. Ah, I've been a ship's captain on a tempest-tossed sea." The king then told Paweł that while he held no hope that he would ever be restored to the throne, he did believe that Poland itself could be resurrected under a new, elected king. His reason for inviting Paweł back was to conscript him into a movement that would have as its goal the reestablishment of a Polish state with a democratic system working in conjunction with a monarch.

Paweł had waited patiently for a name to come up. Who was to be the rallying point for such a movement? While the king had not married, he had a number of children by several women . . . and there were other possible candidates, too—the king's nephew, Prince Józef Poniatowski, among them.

Paweł knew that the king had always worn a belt that bore symbols of the Masonic Brotherhood—the square and compass—but he thought it little more than a decoration, an ornament like any other given a king. Now, as King Stanisław spoke of a group capable of establishing a new order, a new line of succession, his forefinger lightly tapped the insignia. Paweł realized that the king, afraid of spies' ears, was silently relaying information to him. The Masonic Brotherhood was the group the king was entrusting to restore the monarchy.

It suddenly rang clear: King Stanisław was himself a member of the Brotherhood. Who could have imagined? But to think that the secret organization, powerful as the Brotherhood was, could somehow put back together what three powers had dissolved . . . Paweł thought perhaps the king had gone a little daft in the head.

"You're wondering how you might be of help," the king said.

Paweł nodded. *Daft but Argus-eyed just the same.*

"They," he whispered, "will find their uses for you. You came to me on your own to see what you might do, remember?"

"Yes."

The king pulled from his robes a folded sheet of paper. "Here is the name of a person you are to contact, so that work can begin. Odd, isn't it, that his surname is so close to yours?"

Paweł nodded, recognizing the name. He had gotten much more than he bargained for. While he was not committing himself to anything–especially anything harebrained–he would not leave without asking about the succession. "Your Highness, just who–?"

"Might follow me? Do you know, I would not wish this on one of my children. The throne carries a weight beyond your imagination. *They*," he said, "will know whom to nominate. I suspect it will be someone with a clean slate, someone with no connections to the great political families of the day. Someone not related to the Czartoryskis, the Radziwiłłs, the Lubomirskis–or the Poniatowskis, my own family."

"I see," Paweł said. In fact, he didn't see at all.

"My time has dwindled away," the king said as Paweł was taking his leave. He placed a slender hand on Paweł's arm. "And I don't want to be known as the last king of Poland." He attempted a smile. "Help me, will you?" he pleaded, his voice a whisper. "As for the future, trust in the Brotherhood."

Two days later, at nine o'clock in the morning, Paweł Potecki left his city mansion and fell into the flow of the crowd moving toward the Castle Square. The final date–7 January 1795–for the removal of King Stanisław from his beloved Warsaw and Poland had come. The streets were lined with Russian soldiers meant to preserve order. Paweł marveled at the sheer number of citizens, noble and peasant, come out into the bitter cold–with unmasked grief and sadness on their faces–to bid good-bye to their king.

Staying in the city had meant forgoing the wedding of his friends Jan and Anna. Paweł had sent a wedding gift of silver place settings and his deep regrets for missing the ceremony. What a lucky man, that Jan! When Paweł had joined Kościuszko's forces, he made it a point to search him out and to tell him of the great concern Anna held for him. He had only wished that Anna's cousin Zofia held such concern for himself.

Paweł and Jan had become fast friends on the battlefield and off, but events within the capital were unfolding too quickly now to get away, even for a day or two.

Paweł made his way to the arched opening that led into the Great Courtyard. People stood shoulder to shoulder. This was as far as he would get. He was glad for his height as he watched the door that held everyone's eyes transfixed.

Within a quarter of an hour, the king came into the courtyard. His breeches and cloak were brown, the cloak lined in crimson velvet that matched his cap. Crimson! Even at such a time, how proudly he wore Poland's color.

The servants of the Royal Castle were lined up to bid him farewell, some of their faces streaming tears as he passed by and allowed them to kiss his ring. Now and again he gave a consolatory pat on their bowed heads.

This done, Stanisław's eyes fastened on someone across the courtyard. Paweł stretched his neck and for the first time saw that it was General Suvorov himself. Paweł's blood grew hot. A flame of anger licked at the back of his throat. Here was the red devil that had overseen the Praga massacre. Twelve thousand innocent civilians—women and children among them—had died. Here was the man responsible for Zofia's death.

Suvorov was presenting before King Stanisław the Russian Guard of Honor. Paweł cursed to himself. Suvorov knew the military, knew maneuvers, knew novel ways of killing, but he did not know honor. The man was the lowest of shape-shifters.

The king, holding his head up with quiet dignity, turned then and reviewed his own Royal Guards for the last time. He managed a small smile of gratitude.

Here was honor, Paweł thought.

Without final words, the king climbed up into his carriage. One adjutant general, General Gorzeński, had been allowed to accompany him, along with the king's valet and doctor. Other members of his entourage, as well as wagons filled with favorite belongings, would follow later in the week. The carriage immediately began to move, mounted Russians at the front and back. The king waved sadly to the swarms of people as he passed. The carriage came very near to where Paweł stood, and he was certain the king caught sight of him, for there was a flash of recognition in the eyes of faded blue, the lifting of the veiled lids, and the slightest nod.

Paweł would remember that moment all of his days. It was as if in that split second some transference of power or responsibility was made. He was immediately reminded of his standing over his father's deathbed. Count Potecki had been rendered speechless by a devastating stroke, and just before he died, his eyes went to his fifteen-year-old son, wordlessly imploring him to take good care of the wife he was leaving behind. No words were necessary.

Here, too, something of an ethereal nature occurred, something of great import, linking Paweł to the king and the fate of Poland. His hand unconsciously moved to the pocket holding the little sheet of paper the king had given him. He had yet to act on it.

What might be done? *What?* Was there a way to save Poland, save the throne? Or was he bearing witness to the leave-taking of the last king of Poland?

Suddenly his thoughts were dislodged by the spontaneous cry of the people. "The People with the King!" they called. "The King with the People!" It was the old rallying cry used in fighting off the allied powers. Well, they had lost, Paweł thought, but their spirits had yet to be defeated.

"The People with the King! The King with the People!" The chanting went on as the little retinue wended its way down, moving like a church processional toward the city gates and river. Suddenly, the carriage was stopped by the masses, whereupon people sought to unharness the horses and retain their king. Stanisław was leaning out from his window attempting—his motions inplied—to discourage such actions.

Paweł's hand went to his mouth in a motion of pity and despair, for the Russians were already upon the insurgents—pistol shots ringing out—and in moments the carriage was moving down the incline toward the river at a healthy trot, a scattering of bodies in its wake, the people's chant silenced.

The area was clearing a bit as Paweł came out into the Castle Square. He stared up at Zygmunt's Column. At its top the bronze figure of the long-dead king held a cross in one hand, a sword in the other, like a warrior saint. Beneath it now, moving toward the river was another king—one of flesh and blood—this one being forced from his throne and homeland. Stanisław was neither warrior nor saint, but he was undeserving of this fate.

Paweł slowly walked to the city walls fronting the River Vistula. He watched as the king's carriage was ferried to the Praga side—it would be spring before work on rebuilding the bridge could begin. The carriage stopped and remained on the embankment of the ruined Praga. Paweł could see the king—the crimson cap unmistakable—alighting from his coach and coming to sit on a little folding stool provided by his valet. He sat facing the panorama of Warsaw—it was a sight Paweł had often marveled at from a window of Zofia's now destroyed town house.

The king was holding something up to his face. Paweł stared in wonder, then realized what it was. King Stanisław was surveying his beloved city for the last time through a field-telescope.

Time passed, and the pantomime of the Russian general now in charge of the king's journey to Grodno, Lithuania, indicated his great frustration and anger. The king remained impervious to his urgings. He would have his last look.

It began to snow. The citizens in the square and at the walls shivered in the cold and began to return home. Paweł left, too, after an hour, taking one last look at the lonely, sad man in the red cap. He could take no more—and he had been charged with things to do. What things, he had no idea.

Later, Paweł would learn that the king had sat there peering through the field-telescope at his capital for a full two hours.

King Stanisław II Augustus leaned forward on the little wooden stool, his shoulders sagging, his lips so thinned as to be invisible. He studied the Royal Castle that sat perched on the escarpment on the opposite side of the River Vistula.

Thirty years before, he had come to the throne through the machinations of his one-time lover, Catherine of Russia. His rule had initiated a new period in Polish history. As his eyes moved over his beloved capital—a city of thirty thousand that had burgeoned to five times that in the span of his reign—regrets he had held all morning for the sake of his subjects pummeled him now, like the stinging pellets of snow and ice that blew up at him from the river. Oh, he had overseen significant change for the good, a period of enlightenment in the law, education, and the arts. His dream to re-create the Polish world had had its successes, most notably the Third of May Constitution, the first written democratic document of its kind in Europe. Its aegis allowed for Poland to keep her elected monarch and at the same time respect the rights of the individual. The reforms were admired all over the world. But the peasants' rebellion in France had sent shock waves to Austria, Prussia, and Russia, where they shook and rattled the very thrones of the monarchs. Any seeds of democracy were to be stamped out like weeds. Ultimately the three powers brought about the third and final partition of Poland, all three partitions incurred under the king's watch.

The short-lived Constitution was but a memory now, yet the king prayed with the whole of his being that its memory would endure. He prayed, too, that he would not be known as the last King of Poland.

A motion caught the king's eye. He looked up. It was the Russian general once again approaching, his face screwed up against the cold wind off the river.

King Stanisław gave him the same gentle smile he would give to any suppliant. He had kept the man waiting long enough.

The monarch stood, tucking away his field-telescope and adjusting his crimson cap. Then he took his final look at Warsaw, sighed, and moved toward his carriage.

So slipped the scepter.

5

Late March 1795

*A*nna was awakened one morning by sounds on the roof above her. For a moment she thought someone was up there repairing the evergreen tiles. Then came the cries: *"Kle-kle-kle!"*

She sat up in bed, smiling to herself, then laughing aloud. "You are a bit tardy this year, Józef and Alicja!" she called out, laughing. "I might have done without you. Oh, but you are welcome just the same." For years the pair of storks had been returning from wintering in a warmer climate—Africa, it was said. Like clockwork, the storks sought out their fair-weather home. They would nestle into the huge awkward nest adjacent to the chimney and stay until September. They were thought to bring luck—and sometimes a child—to the owners of the house.

Anna remembered standing with her father and looking up at the pair, awed by the flurry of black wing feathers against the white plumage of the body and the red of the legs and bills. "Oh, they're fighting, Papa!" she had cried. "Do make them stop." Her father spoke gently, telling her they were merely playing. She must have been five or six and could not have known they were engaging in a rhythmic and nearly violent rite of courtship.

Anna became lost for the moment in the reverie of childhood. A few minutes later, Lutisha knocked and entered. "Will you be coming down to breakfast, madame?"

"Yes, Lutisha. Why shouldn't I?"

Lutisha brought a ewer of warm water for the washstand and had her back to Anna. "It's just that you haven't always come down, of late."

"Ah, that's true, isn't it?" Anna felt she could keep the secret no longer. "Lutisha, I think the storks have returned."

"Oh, just the one, madame," Lutisha said, turning around. "The male, I suspect. That's the way of it. He repairs the nest and gets it ready for the female."

"Why is that, I wonder?" Anna asked. "Do you imagine they spend the fall and winter months apart?"

"Some think so, madame, and the way they carry on when the female arrives, well, I do believe it!"

Anna laughed. "Well, I think I've beat them at their game, Lutisha!"

The servant understood, her smile lighting her large face. But it was not a smile of surprise. "Then it's luck to the whole house they're bringing."

"You *knew*, didn't you?" When the woman pursed her lips, Anna laughed. "I thought so."

Lutisha shrugged. "There's just something about a woman in the family way I've come to see."

"What is it?"

"Just a look, madame. A secret sparkle in the eye."

Anna laughed again. "I've always said servants know more of what goes on in a house than does the master."

Lutisha blushed. " 'Tis the case, sometimes, madame. Truly." She turned to go.

"I'll be down momentarily."

Lutisha rounded about at the door. "Are you looking for another boy?"

"Perhaps."

"It would be good for Jan Michał to have a little brother. And I expect Lord Stelnicki will be wanting a boy." The door closed on Lutisha's happy smile.

Anna's euphoria was immediately snuffed out. Her moods were volatile these days, and mention of Jan and the child brought her low.

Jan had gone out early again, hadn't been around long enough in the mornings these past weeks to realize she had the sickness. What was it he was always finding to do? The estate ran well enough under the watchful eye of Jacob; what could he possibly find to busy himself with? And why? Didn't he know she needed him? Oh, he was there in the evening, and at night their lovemaking was everything she could hope for . . . but in the morning . . . to find him gone . . .

Anna began to dress. Suddenly, a thought ran through her like an ill wind. She seemed to be thinking and behaving like her mother, who had so resented her father's desire to get out and about on the estate, directing and doing. It was as if Fate had somehow given Anna's mother's life to her. Here she was in her parents' house, in their bedchamber, and in a relationship that—for the moment, at least—possessed eerie parallels. The spectral thought chilled her.

Anna had understood her father and his love of the land, understood him more than her mother had. But now—as if she were in her mother's place—she seemed to understand *her* better.

Her mood still did not lift. Lutisha had cut to the core of another worry. *Would* he be wishing—expecting—a boy? Would he be happy with a girl? Anna was praying for a girl, but it was only now that she came to grips with the reason for her prayer. The truth was, she feared that delivering a boy now, just as the bonding between Jan and Michał was taking form, could somehow reduce the strength of that father–stepson relationship. As loving and open as Jan seemed to be with little Michał, Anna said a prayer that she bring a girl into the household.

Anna would tell him the happy news tonight. She had no choice, for the whole house would know in no time. Or perhaps everyone did already.

Paweł rode alone, the morning mist rising up around him. For the sake of secrecy, he had been told to avoid the road, and so he directed his horse through the dense forest, taking care to avoid fallen trees and low-hanging branches. Tired as he had ever been, he scarcely noticed the buds on the oak trees or the light green shoots on the pines. These trees that rose around him—like pillars in a Greek stadium, he had often thought—failed for once to incite within him his awe of nature. In time, he passed through a mile-long clearing, then drew up his horse at a bank of birch trees that stood like sentries at the clearing's edge. Before him lay a wide expanse that encircled a hill, upon the crest of which sat a large wooden hunting lodge, its windows like square, unblinking eyes.

He had slept little in the past week. With spring at hand, he had returned to the countryside, talking among the peasants, inquiring, combing the little hamlets along the riverbanks for some trace of Zofia. Hope died hard. But he had yet to upturn a single clue. Zofia had vanished. Lately he had seen only pity in the eyes of his friends, who had given her up for dead long ago. Anyone would have. And yet he could not give himself over to the thought that she lay among the many bodies that had been dropped by peasants and soldiers into pits like so much human refuse. Not Zofia . . .

He dismounted now, fighting off fatigue. He tied his horse to a shrub and took the brown robe from his saddlebag. With the robe in place over his clothes, he began to trudge across the clearing, his eyes on the lodge. Before he reached the halfway point, something flashed from one of the upper-story windows, a glint that quickly disappeared. Was it just the reflection of the quickly rising sun? The spectacles of someone at the window? A spyglass?

Paweł allowed his thoughts of Zofia to fall away. The sun was tempering the morning chill. He felt relief in thinking of other things. He stopped and drew the hood of the robe up over his head. Through the eyeholes, he took his bearings and moved toward the lodge. This was his fourth meeting, and he felt as silly in this costume as he had at the first, in Warsaw. How had he allowed the king to draw him into this little masquerade? He felt a fool. At the word of the king, he had taken up with a group concerned with power and shrouded in secrecy and ceremony. It was not a group to make him feel a true member or even welcome. And there seemed always an undercurrent of danger. But he continued his membership, thinking—at times—that King Stanisław had entrusted to him a quest, one that somehow held the fate of the nation in the balance.

This lodge, hidden away in the country, seemed no different from other hunting lodges owned by magnates. A morning's ride from Warsaw, the site acted as an artery of its main lodge in the capital, "Charles to the Three Helmets," where Paweł had been inducted, and where he had sworn to live according to the Rite of the Strict Observance. It was with more than a little hesitancy that he had vowed allegiance to the superiors in the order. But for the moment his promise to the king—who had belonged to this very lodge—stifled his second thoughts.

At the door he was met now with the familiar somber greeting of a short, stout member in a rumpled robe cinched beneath his overhanging belly. He was shown to the large, vaulted hall where some forty members of the Brotherhood, grouped in threes and fours, were speaking in serious tones. Was it his imagination, or had his arrival caused a subtle stir in the movements of the hoods, a lowering of voices? A few Brethren nearby nodded and mumbled hellos, addressing him as Piotr, the fictitious name he had been given.

Paweł was beginning to tell one from the other by their size, the drape of their robes, and, most especially, their voices. These were nobles, for the most part. They, too, had fictitious names, but the voices of some were familiar to him. Some were acquaintances; a few, friends. However, he had been sternly warned never to show a hint of recognition, and he obeyed.

The Grand Master approached him now. "Brother Piotr, you are a trifle late. But we had faith you would come."

"I was delayed. I'm sorry, brother." He could not imagine why *his* attendance should carry such importance.

"It is good that you are here."

The Grand Master's voice was deep and authoritative. Paweł knew his own identity was no secret to him. He wondered if everyone knew his identity. He instinctively felt that they did. Or did he imagine as much? The man to whom the king had sent Paweł had sworn that was not the case, and yet . . .

He had heard of the power of the Freemasons. Sometimes he felt it among them. Yet what did they think they could do to restore Poland as a nation? The king was gone. Not dead, but in the clutches of Catherine he had passed into history as surely as if he were stone cold in the ground. The Brethren knew—as did he—that there would be no resurrection, nor did they long for one.

Over the course of the meetings, he had learned of their plan, or parts of it. The Brotherhood was determined to see a new king seated, a new Polish banner of white and crimson waving once again. Poland would not be swallowed up. It would be reconstituted. The Brotherhood was prepared to wait . . . and to plot. Paweł himself could think of several likely prospects that might rally the nation. Yet names at these meetings—unless whispered in small groups—were avoided.

Members spoke of schooling, languages that would have to be learned, leadership traits inculcated in a newly chosen king. It was as if Poland's hope lay in a boy-dauphin or infant messiah—Paweł found it very strange. And when he pressed them for specifics—what man or child would suit their needs—they seemed to lead him down circuitous paths.

Later, Paweł dared to question the Grand Master: "Why is it that this smaller group meets away from the city, brother?"

The Grand Master paused before he spoke, and Paweł wished he could see through the hood to his expression.

"The Capital has too many ears and eyes, Brother Piotr, for what we have to say and do."

"Too many *Prussian* eyes and ears?"

The Grand Master nodded. "Oh, we may owe the existence of our order to the Prussian influence, but with our nation fully partitioned today—and no little part gone to Prussia—the interests of true Poles like you and me, Brother Piotr, will do battle with Prussian interests."

"I see." Paweł had hoped to draw more out of the Grand Master through his questioning, but hadn't learned anything he hadn't already figured out for himself. His efforts went unrewarded.

"Come, let us all be seated," the Grand Master announced, "so that we can discuss as one body. There is business to be done."

It was fully dark when Paweł returned to Warsaw. He walked from the carriage house to the rear door of his town house. Any real business that had transpired at the lodge escaped Paweł's notice. Thankfully, the return trip by road had made for a shorter one than the morning's trek through the forest. Still, he felt as drained as he had after battle. The thought of sleep quickened his pace up the stairs.

"My lord," his servant said, greeting him at the door, "you have a visitor in the reception room."

"Yes? Who is it, Fryderyk?"

The servant took Paweł's coat. He seemed afraid to speak. The pallor of the man put Paweł on notice. Rather than repeat the question, Paweł strode quickly to the reception room. The chamber was dimly lit, and had the servant not told him of a caller, Paweł would not have noticed the motionless figure at the far end of the room.

"Hello," he said, starting across the floor. The low fire in the hearth sent flickering shadows playing on the visitant's form. It was a woman, he saw now, in peasant attire, a mass of dark hair crushed under a kerchief. What business could she possibly have with him? How was it that his servant had admitted her?

To his surprise, she started to move toward him with assurance and familiarity. He immediately recognized—despite her costume—that her posture and gait were those of a woman of high birth. The hearth light fell across her face at that moment, shimmering on the arresting features. He recognized her.

His heart swung out in an arc over a void—and slowly, slowly—returned.

If God had given him the breath, he would say later, he would have gasped. As it was, he was struck dumb, and his legs threatened to fail. "Zofia," Paweł said at last. It was nothing more than a whisper, and he could say no more.

"Paweł," she replied, the old uninhibited smile playing under the dark almond eyes and aristocratic nose. She was in front of him one moment, embracing him the next. He could not tell which of them was trembling—he thought perhaps they both were.

After a long, long moment, Zofia drew back, appraising him, the smile teasing now. Her eyes were wet. He had never seen her cry. The moments seemed to draw into minutes. Paweł was afraid to speak, afraid that this was a vision or a spell or a dream and that the slightest noise would crack the illusion. That she would crumble into dust.

"Paweł," Zofia said, "you look as if you've seen a ghost!" She threw her head back in that old familiar way.

It was her laugh—like the tinkling of coins—that made him believe her real and alive.

"By the white eagle and all things holy, Zofia, I believe I have."

6

Anna decided to hold a little celebration for Jan Michał on his third birthday instead of 15 May, his name day. Although when that came around, she thought, another celebration might be in order just the same. As for the third, Anna knew that everyone's mood would be dampened by the thought of the Third of May Constitution and how it had been brought down by the allied powers—as well as by certain short-sighted and greedy magnates within the Commonwealth. A party would be something to divert darker thoughts.

While little Jan Michał took his afternoon nap, Jan, Jacob, and Emma gathered in the reception room that had been decorated with colorful *wycinanki* cut by Marcelina and Katarzyna. Anna longed for the day when she could teach her son how to make the papercuts like those that hung from the rafters and at the windows, but for now he was too young to handle the dangerously sharp sheep shears.

"Why is it," Emma asked, "that you named your son as you did?"

"Oh, I could have named him after Saint Antoni, whose feast day it was, Emma, but—" A sick feeling washed over Anna. She could say that Antoni was the name of the man who had married her for her estate, the man who had hired men to kill her—but they knew that. Everyone knew that. Instead, she finished by saying, "That name held little meaning for me." Anna's anxious tone engaged everyone's attention. "I chose Michał for his second name after my good friend Michał Kolbi, who quite literally saved my life. He was killed in Kościuszko's service." Now something must be said about the first name. She felt herself coloring in embarrassment, for there was no turning back, and she had never been a cool liar. "And as for the name Jan, well, as you know, King Jan Sobieski is one of our forebears on the Berezowski side of the family."

"I see," Emma said.

The answer *seemed* to satisfy. She wondered if they suspected she had chosen the name Jan to honor, not the legendary king, but the man she truly loved, Jan Stelnicki. Surely Jan knew, but they had never spoken of it.

"Tell me," Emma said. "With *this* child, will you go against tradition again?"

Anna felt a warm flush come into her face. She looked across the room to where Jan stood at the hearth, talking to Jacob. "Well, Jan and I have yet to discuss it, but I have my heart set on having a Barbara."

Upon hearing this, Jan turned and cast an inscrutable smile.

"Then you expect a girl?" Emma pressed.

Anna shrugged. "It will be as God wills," she said.

"As God wills!" cried Jacob. "This calls for a toast!" He poured vodka into four short crystal glasses. Everyone drank, expressing good wishes for the health of the child.

"What about you, Jan?" Jacob asked. "You'll wish for a boy, won't you?"

Jan walked over to Anna and bent to kiss her lightly. "It will be as God wills, but I know if it *is* a boy, we have too many Jans in the house already!"

Everyone laughed. "Another toast!" Jacob called.

"Not for me," Anna said, rising. "I should go wake the young man of the hour before his guests are laid out on the floor."

More laughter followed, and another toast was made as Anna climbed the stairs to Jan Michał's room. Her mind was trying to decipher her husband's reactions. *Did* he have his heart set on a boy? She had never asked his preference outright because she was afraid of the answer. *And what if it is a boy?* she asked herself, as if it were a challenge. Surely her worry that Jan would love him more than he would Jan Michał was only a worry—and nothing more.

"Is it time?" Jan Michał asked as she opened the door.

"Yes," Anna answered with a laugh, "it's time. Did you sleep at all?"

"I . . . I think so."

"Good. Now let's get you washed and dressed. Can you comb your own hair today?"

"Yes, Mama. Did Lutisha bake the *babka*?"

"Yes, Lutisha baked the *babka*!" Anna replied in a singsong voice. "It is downstairs waiting for you." As Anna helped him into his little breeches and waistcoat, she thought back to her own childhood and the cakes baked for her in the same kitchen. The fluffy *babka* with its hidden raisins had been her favorite, too.

"And what else?"

"What else, Michał? Here, comb your hair."

"What else for me?" he said, drawing the comb through his brown hair.

Anna pulled a face. "For me? *For me?* Is that all you can think of? Isn't *babka* enough?"

"Papa said there would be a surprise!"

"Oh, he did, yes? Well, then both of us will be surprised." Anna watched him, smiling at his efforts. "All right, you're ready. Let's go down."

At the top of the stairs, Jan Michał pulled his hand from Anna's grasp. "I can do it now."

"Very well, Michał. Be careful. Hold to the bars in the railing."

Anna watched her son descend the steps before her. He moved with a child's precision and pride. She thought how in no time another child would join the household, a child of Jan's. Her own hand moved now to her thickening stomach, and a radiant happiness—like sunshine—coursed through her.

At the bottom of the stairs, Anna had to step lively to keep up with her son's little legs. They moved through the reception room, Jan Michał's wide-eyed attention on the decorations, and into the dining room. All the servants had been invited in to celebrate—Walek and Marta, their daughters Katarzyna and Marcelina standing close by, sat at table with Jan and the Szrabers. "Michał! Michał!" they cried in chorus. "How old is Michał? How old is Michał?"

Jan Michał held up two fingers.

"Oh, no!" Marcelina wailed and fell into a fit of giggles. She had evidently been tutoring him for this moment. One look at Marcelina, and he held up another finger from his other hand. Everyone cheered then and clapped. "Michał is three!" they cried. "Michał is three!"

Jan Michał clapped, too, his eyes sparkling at the attention. He ran to Jan now and stared up in wonder at the huge *babka* on the table. "*Babka!* Eat?"

"But where is Tomasz, Michał?" Jan asked. "We should not cut the cake without your good friend Tomasz."

"Tomasz?" Michał asked, bewildered, the brown eyes searching.

Anna had not thought of Walek and Marta's twelve-year-old son, either. But she knew immediately that some little surprise *had* been arranged.

"Tomasz! Tomasz!" Jan called from his chair in his best stage voice.

The door to the kitchen swung open now, and Tomasz entered, a secret smile on his round face. In his hand he held what seemed a leather strap of some kind. Those with a better view than Anna's gasped and held hands to astonished faces. Anna had to step farther into the room and around the table to see what was at the end of the strap.

For the moment all she could make out was a bundle of white, but as she stared, she deciphered dark little triangles that were its ears and a tiny black disc that was its nose. All else about the animal was white as the whitest, fluffiest cloud.

Anna looked to her son. His eyes were as round as golden ducats, his breath taken from him.

"What do you think, Michał?" Jan asked, his arm around the boy. "Will you make friends with Borys?"

Jan Michał could not take his eyes off the creature that was sidling up to Tomasz's legs in fear.

Everyone seemed to be watching the little drama unfold with wide eyes and smiling mouths. All but Anna. She walked over to where Jan was sitting. "Jan, whatever possessed you—?"

"Oh, isn't he beautiful, Anna?" Jan bent to stroke the animal beneath its chin, causing it to look up, its button eyes trained on Anna. At that moment a long red tongue unfurled itself, and Jan Michał let go a shriek of glee.

"It's most beautiful, Jan, but it's an *owczarek nizinny!*"

"That it is," Jan said, his eyes still trained on the interaction between his son and the dog. "And he's a beauty!"

"But—a *sheepdog,* Jan. It's not meant to be in the house. It's meant to do herding!"

"It'll learn, Anna. It'll adapt."

"But will *we?* They get huge. It'll be bigger than Michał in no time. It'll be underfoot. Things about the house are bound to be broken."

By now Anna could sense that even if their eyes were elsewhere, everyone in the room seemed riveted to the discussion she was attempting with Jan.

"They're very smart, Anna, and very precise in their movements. Of course, who's to say Borys won't herd the lot of us into a cupboard one day!"

Anna chose not to compete with the laughter this comment stirred. She would talk to Jan later about the foolishness of having such a dog in the house. The issue would be reassessed.

Jan leaned over and picked up the puppy, stood, wheeled about, and—without warning—placed it in Anna's arms. "Here," he said, "he won't always be of a size for you to hold, and your arms will be holding something else come Christmas."

Anna blinked back her surprise while the velvet of the puppy's red tongue explored her face. She looked down into the dark little eyes. What good was there in discussing the issue, here or in private? She had been bested and she knew it. She might as well enjoy it, affording the group now a grudging smile.

Jan Michał put his arms out to Anna, imploring her to relinquish his gift. No sooner had she placed the ball of fur on the floor than it stood on one of

Jan's polished boots, letting go a little yellow stream. Jan Michał screamed with laughter. Everyone else joined in. Except for Jan. "Ah, you see," Anna said, wagging a finger, "there are consequences to hasty decisions."

Jan laughed, too. Then he clapped his hands as if he were a sultan. "All right, Lutisha! Time to cut into Michał's cake!"

Anna waited in the reception room for Jan, who had taken Jan Michał up to bed. She was making her way through the well-worn copy of *The Odyssey*. She had lost count of how many times she had read it.

In a little while, Jan joined her near the hearth. It seemed that his demeanor had become more serious. "Did he go peaceably?" Anna asked.

"He did."

"And Borys?"

"I invented a little makeshift pen for him."

"Oh? In the kitchen?"

"No—in Michał's bedchamber."

"Oh, Jan!"

"It'll be fine."

"Oh, don't worry," Anna said. "I'm not going to give you any more argument. Except maybe for his name. Borys—what a ridiculous name for a dog!" She laughed. "You've had your way. We'll all find out in time whether it can adapt."

"I'm sorry I didn't consult you, Anna, but I wanted it to be a surprise for you, too."

"Well, it was that! I suppose you're disappointed by my hesitancy to embrace the little beast!"

"No, I knew the *little beast,* as you say, would win you over."

"Am I so transparent?"

"In such things, yes. That's why I love you."

Anna shook her head in mock irritation. "You do know how to clinch the deal, too, Jan."

Jan did not reply. They didn't speak for a few minutes. Jan sat staring into the low fire, and Anna felt an uneasiness. She made no attempt to take up her book again.

"What is it, then?" she asked at last. "You've turned so very serious."

Jan cleared his throat, never taking his eyes away from the grate. "I've had a letter—from Paweł."

"Yes? Bad news? . . . The king?"

Jan seemed to be collecting his thoughts.

"Tell me, Jan."

Jan turned in his chair now, his cobalt eyes flickered black in the room's light. Drawing in a long breath, he said, "Zofia's been found, Anna."

"Zofia?" Anna repeated dumbly.

Jan nodded.

"Her body?"

Jan shook his head. "She's alive, Anna."

Anna felt the room begin to spin. It was as if the top of her head had been taken off and all her thoughts given such a stir, she could settle on no single one.

Jan went on talking, but his words were meaningless. They might as well have been in a language she didn't understand. Alive . . . alive! Zofia? Was it possible? After all these months? *Alive!* How had she survived the river? "Dog's blood," she heard herself whisper, using one of Zofia's oaths, "is it possible?"

"It's true."

"But . . . how? . . ."

"It seems some peasants picked her up."

The logical questions came to her; only later would the emotions come, unsummoned. "But Paweł searched for her! He said he talked to everyone in the vicinity of the river."

"Be that as it may, this family managed to keep Zofia's presence from the other villagers—at Zofia's own request, it seems."

"And she's only just arrived in Warsaw?"

"No, she's been at Paweł's two months."

"Two months! And not written to me? Not to have sent word before this? Was there a note from her included in Paweł's letter?"

"No, it seems she didn't want us to know yet. But Paweł felt duty-bound to tell us."

"Why should she want to keep it a secret? Why?"

Jan shrugged. "You know Zofia."

"No, Jan, that's the problem. I don't know Zofia. I never have. She's an enigma Oedipus himself could not decipher."

"Exactly," Jan said, standing. "I'm going to bed."

Anna realized he was waiting for her. "You go on. I'll come up presently."

Jan kissed her on the cheek and went upstairs.

Anna sat and stared. The fire died away to nothing. Her world had suddenly been transformed into something for the moment unfathomable. *Zofia alive!* The woman who had saved Jan Michał's life, protecting him from his father's influence, and the woman who had saved Anna's life, sending her off across the bridge to the safety of Warsaw and away from the cutlasses of the Russians as they swooped down on Praga. She was Anna's cousin, of Anna's blood. But she was also the woman who concealed things, destroyed letters, lied, and sent Anna into a hellish marriage with Antoni Grawliński. Had it not been for Zofia's scheming, Anna would have married Jan years before.

How was she to react to this news? Of course, she was happy. Surprised and relieved that her cousin had thwarted death and could live out her life. But with her good feelings came—what?—a threat? Why should Anna feel threatened? She had nothing to fear from Zofia now. Jan and she were married and expecting their first child. No interference from her cousin could change that.

Anna's thoughts came back to Jan. She replayed in her mind his telling of the news, considering his reactions. He had said little. In fact, it came to her only now how flat his demeanor had been, how emotionless. What could it mean?

Zofia stood in front of the mirror in one of her new gowns, her dark eyes assessing herself. Oh, it wasn't a Parisian import, but it was French in fashion—violet and cut to show off her bosom. The new French styles since the Terror were simpler and—with fewer layers, less corseting, and no scaffolding or bustles—scantier. Something good had come of the rising of the scum, she thought. And Paweł had been generous in seeing to it that her wardrobe was replenished, for almost everything she owned had gone up in flames when the Russians came down on Praga. *Very* generous, she thought. Thanks to foreign investments, Zofia had her own funds, considerable ones at that, but she had no wish to see them depleted.

Two months had passed since she had left the tiny cottage on the River Vistula clad in the simplest tunic. Jerzy had taken her to the Praga side of the river, where she insisted he leave her. It was not until he was gone that she looked up to the bluff where her family town house had stood. She was not one for tears, but she wept then. It wasn't so much the loss of the house and its opulent furnishings as it was the loss of her mother who had died on the eve of the Russian onslaught. Zofia had come to regret her many failings as a daughter. And as she cried, visions of the recent parting from Danuta and her father—and Jerzy—surfaced with a poignancy she seldom experienced. What would she have done without their peasant hospitality?

And Jerzy's innocent devotion to her? He had begged her to stay—and she had laughed at him. Still, at their parting, in gratitude Zofia had tried to press into his hand the diamond ring, knowing its worth could improve the life of the peasant family beyond all measure. Jerzy's face clouded, however, and he adamantly refused it, walking away. The thought of him taking his leave, shoulders sagging slightly, often came back to her.

Jerzy–Jan's peasant double! Was that part of her attraction to the boy? Well, both Jan and Anna were safe–and married! Now *there* was something to think about. Something not wholly pleasant.

Zofia shook herself free of these thoughts. *I am in Warsaw once again!* She pinched her cheeks to bring up the color and presently went down to supper. Paweł was already seated, a seriousness about him that put her on guard.

It was after the meal–while they were still at table–that he came up behind her chair, bent to kiss her, and whispered a proposal of marriage.

Zofia turned to him and smiled. She could not feign surprise. Before joining up with Kościuszko, he had asked her numberless times. "Paweł, you know how I feel about that. I care for you. I really do . . . but I have no desire to marry."

"Zofia, things are different now. You can't behave . . . as you once did."

"What does *that* mean?" Her defiant tone was meant to discourage his bringing up past indiscretions.

He took pause, too, seeming to recognize that her reputation was not a topic to take up. "The times have changed," he said, clearing his throat and standing erect. "I mean that you need a home. Oh, I know your claim to the Praga site has been favorably received, and you have the resources to build again, but you need a man to stand beside you, to protect you."

"Do I?" Zofia stared up at him. "Paweł, I am in no hurry to build. And I am in no hurry for a husband. Life can go on as it has for us here."

"Until when, Zofia?" Paweł demanded. "When? . . . And what are we to say to people? How are we to be received?"

"Ah, is that it? You're worried about the perception of things? Why, this is a new day, Paweł. We would not be the only unmarried couple in Warsaw living together. What's left of Polish society is too busy simply surviving to worry about shunning us."

Paweł sank into a chair at an angle to Zofia. "I'm not worried about what others think! I'm worried about you! Zofia, I love you."

Zofia let out a shallow breath. "You should know by now that I have a knack for survival. You are not to worry. I am like the phoenix–always have been." Before he could reply, Zofia said, "Paweł, I have something to tell you." The seriousness of her tone–sans her usual cavalier humor–immediately silenced Paweł.

The moment hung fire.

Zofia took a sip from her wine, her eyes above the glass holding his gaze. Setting it down, she said, "Paweł, I am to have a child."

It seemed to be the last thing he expected. His face reflected, in turn, complete surprise, wonder—and delight. Zofia instantly realized her mistake in telling him in such a way. He had misread her.

Paweł was smiling broadly, as a child might when, against the odds, he wins a game. He stood and then knelt at her side. "All the more reason, Zofia! All the more reason to marry—to have a family!"

Zofia sat silently, and something in her glance pierced his mask of euphoria, and she saw his smile fall away. *"What?"* Paweł asked. "What is it?"

"Paweł," Zofia sighed. "Oh, Paweł." His crushed expression indicated that he took her meaning immediately. Zofia sensed the sting she had inflicted, but she could say no more.

As for Paweł, Zofia was thankful that he could not bring himself to press her for the identity of the father.

7

Late October 1795

The autumn gathering at the country lodge was charged with voices and emotion. Paweł had missed a few meetings over the course of the summer and early fall, but he would not miss this one. Just a few days before, almost a year after the massacre at Praga and the fall of the Commonwealth, the partition had been signed by the three allies. Prussia had at last given up the territory of Kraków to Austria in exchange for Russian-held Warsaw. It seemed official and final: Poland was no more. Warsaw fermented in its despondency, and yet there was more bad news.

"Catherine is pressuring the king to abdicate!" the Grand Master announced.

A tremor reverberated among the Brethren gathered in the vaulted meeting room. The Grand Master paused, long enough for the agitated conversation to build for a full minute and then diminish as they turned to him for further details.

Paweł was as concerned as anyone. While most did not expect Stanisław to return, few had foreseen talk of an abdication.

"What does it matter?" Brother Dymitr called out. A few Brothers echoed his reaction.

"It matters!" the Grand Master shouted. "It matters greatly!"

Paweł had not seen the angry side of the Grand Master before. The group quieted and the Grand Master continued. "The King of Poland has no right to abdicate! Some of you here in this room, some of you as old as I, *elected* Stanisław. Not without pressure from Catherine, you will say, but nonetheless, he cannot abdicate. He must know that! Only we, the electors, can release him from the *Pacta Conventa* that binds him!"

The Grand Master paused. "Ah, your silence underscores Brother Dymitr's question. What does an abdication mean? My brothers, it means this: to abdicate is to vindicate—yes, *vindicate!*—the violent dissolution of our land done by three neighbors. It would say to Europe and to the world that this terrible and insufferable violence was justified! No, he must remain as king, as symbol of what has befallen us."

The brothers sat like monks sworn to silence.

At last, Paweł spoke up. "Grand Master, is it likely Stanisław will bow to Catherine?"

The long sigh beneath the hood of the Grand Master was audible. "Stanisław is a good man," he said. "Even now he thinks of others, writes to the allied heads on behalf of his subjects who have lost so much. He has given attention to thousands of requests insofar as he is able. His heart is big. But his strength is small. You've met him, Brother Piotr, can you not answer your own question?"

Paweł kept his silence. It was, of course, a moot question.

Anna became so heavy with child that she had to take to her room two weeks before the birth. Each day she checked her calendar for the saints' feast days, wondering on what day the child would be born and what name she would be given. Some of the names fast approaching were Ireny, Ursula, and Teodora. Of these, she rather liked Teodora, but she still preferred going against tradition—as she had with Jan Michał—by choosing a name other than that of the feast day saint. She wanted to name her child Barbara, whose name day would not come until the fourth of December.

She never looked to the list of male saints. To do so would allow for the possibility the baby would be a boy—and she would have none of that.

The days went slowly. On the night of 26 October, sleep would not come until long after midnight, and so it was that she was slow to be roused in the morning when she heard a disturbance in the room. Jan had long since risen.

Certain it was Lutisha or Marta checking in on her, she kept her eyes closed, wishing them away. The room remained quiet for a long time, but still she could not fall back into sleep. She sensed that someone remained in the room.

Anna opened her eyes. She lay on her back, her condition such that she had no other option. The curtains were still drawn, and the day was overcast, it seemed, for the room was cloaked in grays. Anna's eyes scanned the room ahead of her and to the right, unable to make out anything in the dimness. Her eyes moved to the left now. Her heart caught as she discerned the outline of someone sitting in a chair brought up just a foot or two from the bed. The figure remained silent and motionless. Anna stared, wondering who it could be. She thought for a foolish moment it was the spirit of her dead Aunt Stella. Then she heard the faintest suppressed laugh.

Anna's head rolled on the pillow. "Who is it?" she whispered.

"Who is it?" mimicked the voice.

Anna became lightheaded. She could not mistake that mocking tone.

A hand reached across the blanket and took Anna's. "It is I, cousin. Zofia! Is it so dark in here, you don't recognize me? Let me go pull back the draperies."

"No!" Anna held on to the hand. "I–I just couldn't believe it. I thought for the moment it was your mother."

"Well, have I aged so much?" Zofia lifted Anna's hand and kissed it. "Come to think of it, I *feel* ancient. What a ride it was getting here! I'm all aches and pains. It comes with getting older, I suppose."

Anna laughed. "Good Grief, Zofia, you're only twenty-two–a year older than I!"

Zofia laughed, too. "But I've lived a lifetime in that year's space."

"No doubt. Especially if you're talking about this past year!" Anna pushed herself up against the pillows behind her. "Oh, Zofia, I thought you dead."

"And I thought so, too, for a while."

Anna had held on to Zofia's hand, and she squeezed it now. "I have so much to thank you for."

"Nonsense." Zofia's hand slipped away. "I really don't wish to talk about that day–or the past."

"Then we'll look only forward! Why, when we heard from Paweł that you had been rescued by peasants–what news!"

"Indeed–plucked from the river like a drowning lamb."

"My God!"

"*Someone's* God, I guess–I'll have to tell you all about it–another time."

"When we heard that you were in Warsaw, I wrote. Did you not get–?"

Zofia sighed dramatically. "You know I'm not one for writing. Not like you with your diary. Forgive me."

"Of course. And Pawel–has he come, too?"

"No."

"Oh." Anna's surprise was momentary. Zofia had always been one to forge her own way. "How are things in Warsaw?"

"Tedious as an English tea from my perspective, I must say. But Pawel keeps busy with some kind of political group. He's very closemouthed about it–disappears for a day or two at a time going off to clandestine meetings."

"Having to do with what?"

"I don't know, Anna, and I can't say I much care. You know I have no stomach for politics. Oh, but I do have an amusing story to tell you about Lord Kubacki!"

Zofia went on to relate how the Kubacki family took in a French count, his wife, and three children, all refugees from the revolution in France, explaining with glee and in great detail how the arrogant little family put the Kubacki children out of their own bedchambers, ate through the pantry and storehouse, insulted their friends, and incurred even the disdain of the servants. All of this went on for six months, it seemed–until a French duke arrived in Warsaw and exposed them as commoners and parasites.

Anna listened to the story with but one ear. She was still trying to grasp the fact that Zofia was here–and that her own feelings toward her were as ambivalent as ever. Anna owed Zofia her very life–in that, there was no exaggeration. Zofia had diverted the attention of a Russian so that Anna could make it to safety across the bridge that connected the walled city of Warsaw with the suburb of Praga. She had put herself at great risk, staying on the Praga side with the maddened Russians swarming down upon innocent civilians, most of whom met death that day.

She should feel happy that Zofia had lived to tell the tale, happy to see her. And–despite her cousin's past scheming, she did feel happiness. It was the other feelings that came into the mix now that she grappled with. Waking up to find Zofia in her home, she felt–what? Awkward? Uneasy? Fearful? She could not help but wonder how the meeting between Zofia and Jan had gone. How had Jan reacted? She tried to bury the notion that she had awakened to an enemy within her room. After all, it was *she* who had won Jan Stelnicki, not Zofia–*she* who was expecting his child, not Zofia.

By the time Zofia had finished with her story, Anna had come to terms with her divided self and shored up her confidence. Zofia was not to be feared. The past was the past.

"And do you know," Zofia was saying, "this is not just a singular incident.

There are as many French commoners in our capital claiming noble birth as there are rats in the gutter. Now let me go let in some light. It's dark as Tartarus in here."

"No, please don't! I'm not ready to receive anyone. My belly's as large as a pumpkin, and I know I must look a fright."

Zofia ignored the plea and went to the windows and pulled back the draperies. She returned to the bedside, her dark figure silhouetted against the gray light, like a *wycinanka*. But as her cousin neared the bed, the likeness to a papercut fell away, and her face and form took on texture and definition. Anna gasped, her mouth falling slack.

"My God, Anna, you should see your face!" Zofia laughed, her head going back in that old familiar way. "You see, I'm as big as a manor house, too."

Anna couldn't think what to say.

"Just imagine, Anna, we may deliver on the same day."

"Zofia—have you—?"

"Married? Good God, no!" She laughed. "Better a cholera on any husband of mine!"

"Oh." Again, Anna should not have been surprised.

"Not that Paweł didn't ask. It's just that I'm not ready. Remember, once I told you that old saying that one should live wildly for three years before marrying?"

"Yes, but that was *more* than three years ago!"

"*Was* it?" Zofia let loose a peal of laughter. "Well, perhaps I'm not meant for marriage at all."

"What does Paweł say?"

"What does that matter? Anna, Paweł is not the father."

"I see." Anna's surprise at this admission did not easily dissipate. She could think of nothing more to say.

"It happened while I was recovering," Zofia said, filling in the silence.

"Then it was an . . . attack?"

"No, and that's all that I will say on that subject."

Anna's head reeled. Zofia would give birth to a fatherless child—and yet she seemed so blasé.

"Anna," Zofia said now, "I've come to Sochaczew to have my child."

"But—why?" Anna was suddenly afraid that Zofia planned to stay with her. And with that fear came no little guilt.

"I'm going to ask the greatest favor of you, cousin."

Anna stared at the beautiful face, waiting for her to continue. The dark, almond eyes were uncharacteristically serious.

"Anna, I would like you to . . ."

"What, Zofia?"

Zofia took in a long breath, then said, "I would like you to raise my child."

"What?"

"Oh, Anna! You of all people should know I would not be a good mother. It wouldn't be fair to the child."

What seemed a full minute passed before Anna finally found her voice. "But, Zofia, I'm about to give birth to my own child—and I have little Jan Michał."

"True, but you are *fit* to be a mother. You have it in your nature. There is an able staff here to help you, some of whom came from my family's estate, I might add. And you would certainly be able to find a wet nurse nearby."

"Zofia, you are most welcome to have your child here. Lutisha and Emma and the others will see to everything. But I cannot for one minute—"

"And you have Jan. You have your happiness, I can see that! Please help me find mine."

"It's impossible, Zofia. Impossible. I'm sorry that you've come all this way. You really should have written."

"Ah, it's just that I didn't think you could say no to me."

Anna felt hot tears beading in her eyes. "I must, Zofia. I *must*." Anna searched Zofia's face for emotion, but it was beyond deciphering. "Listen to me, Zofia, keep your child, please do. Mothers should not give away their children as if they were puppies. You will *thank* me one day for refusing you." Anna's words brooked no discussion.

A dark expression fell like a curtain over Zofia's face. She stood. "I should let you rest. I'm sorry to have upset you." She bent forward and kissed Anna on the forehead, a false smile hanging on her lips like a half-moon.

"Zofia, I—"

Standing erect, Zofia interrupted: "You're happy here, yes?"

Anna nodded. "Yes."

"Good."

Zofia walked across the room to the door. Turning around, she fixed her eyes on Anna. "And Jan—is Jan happy?"

Anna was dumbstruck. What intent was there in such a question? Zofia's face was still inscrutable, but it was no innocent question, she was certain. Had he in some way indicated his feelings to her? Said something? The thought that Jan might speak his feelings to Zofia brought on a sick dizziness. The thought that Jan was not happy threatened to break her heart.

A long moment passed; then Anna said, "We are very happy, Zofia."

Zofia smiled enigmatically, turned, and left the room.

*   *   *

"May I have a word with you, Brother Piotr?" The Grand Master asked. "Will you walk the grounds with me?"

Paweł agreed and together they left the social that followed a regular meeting.

The weather was warm for October. Paweł wished he could remove the hood—after all, he knew the Grand Master's identity, just as his was known—but all formalities were strictly maintained on the premises of the lodge.

They moved away from the lodge and along a field path. "As you know, Brother Piotr, the greatest desire of the true Polish patriots among us is that one day Poland will be restored—led by a worthy noble, one capable of being king."

"But discussion varies greatly as to who that might be. Which of the families—"

"Discussion, yes. Ah, yes, the Lubomirskis, the Poniatowskis, the Czartoryskis, I know. Arguments is more like it. Feuds. No one can agree. And each family carries with it its history, often proud—and justly so—but often negative, too. The competition among them is great, and to choose one family over the others makes for bitterness, jealousy, and divisions."

Paweł shrugged. He knew all this and could only wonder where this was leading.

"The chance to install a new monarchy may be years away," the Grand Master said. "You know that we've been considering educating a *child* and preparing him for the throne."

"But not from one of the families?"

"No."

Again, Paweł waited.

"Brother Piotr, you are close friends with Lord Jan Stelnicki. You know also that just before Warsaw fell, King Stanisław saw to it that Jan's wife—then Lady Anna Berezowska-Grawlińska—was named a princess of the Commonwealth."

Paweł caught on at once. "And that would make a son of hers eligible for election?"

"Exactly. And the fact that the Groński line can be traced to King Jan Sobieski clinches it."

"But I should tell you that the lineage of her son Jan Michał is—well—"

"Questionable. We know that. We've had people looking into this matter, I can assure you."

"Then why would you—?"

"We have no interest in Lady Stelnicka's first child."

"Ah! But a son she and Jan might have together *would* be considered?"

"Absolutely," the Grand Master said, nodding. "The Stelnicki lineage may be of the *szlachta,* but it is not to be questioned. His father worked to implement the Constitution."

"I see."

"We know—as I'm sure you do, too—that the princess is in her final weeks of confinement."

"She is."

"We would like you to let us know when she delivers. And, naturally, whether it is a boy. Will you do that?"

"Yes."

"Good! We'd better go in now for the closing ceremony."

Paweł wanted to ask what plans would be put to work should Anna deliver a boy, but the Grand Master was already loping toward the door that led into the main hall.

By the time Paweł had set his horse on a canter toward Warsaw, his amazement that the Brotherhood was considering for king a child of Jan and Anna's had worn off. After all, with Poland's being held in three pieces by Prussia, Austria, and Russia, the likelihood of such an event occurring seemed remote.

In time, his thoughts returned to Zofia. It was she he had been thinking of when the Grand Master took him out of his melancholy. He was certain that Zofia had gone to Sochaczew. Why? Would she return? When? He worried— not only was it unseemly to be traveling in her final months, but it was also dangerous to her health and that of the baby.

Paweł pressed his horse into a gallop now. He was angry with himself. When Zofia had refused marriage, he should have put her out of his house. She had her own money. She would survive—she always had. He knew now that he and his home were merely conveniences to Zofia. But he had stowed away his pride and bowed to her terms. He knew he loved her too much. The road beneath him flew past in a blinding blur of hope that when he reached Warsaw he would have some word of her.

Anna's emotions were many and strong and as tangled as the tendrils of Medusa's hair. She remained close to tears all morning.

It was enough for Zofia to show up, releasing in Anna a thousand emotions, each at odds with the others. All the old insecurities came to the fore.

And now, to ask Anna to take on the responsibility of yet another child—it was unthinkable!

Still, as the morning wore on and her reservoir of tears dried unspent, she *did* think about it. The child of her cousin deserved a good life. Would Zofia be able to provide that? Anna doubted that she had the capability. She certainly didn't have the inclination—that was evident. By noon, when Marta came into the room carrying a tray, Anna had reversed herself, deciding that she *would* parent Zofia's child. Somehow, she would make it work.

"Will you be able to eat a bit, today, Lady Stelnicka?"

"Not now, Marta. I wish to see my cousin, Lady Zofia. Will you go down and tell her?"

"Oh, madame," Marta said, placing the tray on a nearby table, "the Lady Grońska went off in her carriage this morning."

"For a ride?"

Marta's eyes waxed large. She seemed not to know what to say.

Anna grew impatient—and fearful. "What of her portmanteau?"

"She had with her a trunk, madame."

"Where is it?"

"Oh, it was still lashed to the top of the coach when the carriage drove off. I think she was returning to Warsaw, Lady Anna."

On the morning of 28 October, Anna went into labor. Jan stood at the side of the bed, holding her hand while the women whirred like worker bees about her, making the necessary preparations. Anna knew he would soon be shooed from the room.

"Jan?" she asked.

"Yes?"

"Have you been happy?"

His face folded into a question. "Happy?"

"If anything happens to me—have I made you happy?"

He smiled. "Every day, my love. Today is no different. Nothing will happen to you! Everything will unfold as we would hope."

"And you won't mind if our child is a girl?"

Jan laughed, squeezing her hand. "No, I won't mind, but she will have a ways to go to be as pretty as her mother."

Anna smiled through her pains. "Not today she wouldn't."

"It's time now, Lord Stelnicki," Lutisha announced. The master of the house was to be ruled by the servant in this one matter. Her tight smile seemed to say, *You are to wait downstairs.* Jan bent and kissed his wife now. Anna watched him leave the room and prayed that she would live through the ordeal, if only to see him again.

A second prayer came at once. *A daughter, dear God, grant me a daughter.*

Jan wished he could go out to the far field and split wood to vent the tension within, but he dared not venture out of the house. And so he paced from the reception room to the music room, back and forth, sat for the space of five minutes, then paced again. Back and forth—and again.

He worried for Anna and for his child. And her words kept coming back to him. *Have you been happy?* What had made her ask the question? he wondered. Had he given her reason to doubt it? Had she seen through to his restlessness?

At three in the afternoon, Lutisha came into the room, her old, large frame straight as a rod, her toothless smile ear to ear. "It is a son you have, Lord Stelnicki, a strong and healthy son!"

Jan bounded up the stairs, two at a time, heart pumping with joy. When he entered the bedchamber, Anna was still in a state of discomfort, but she braved a smile. He moved quickly to her side, taking in her expression even as he sized up the bundle in the crook of her arm, its pink face in repose. "What is it, Anna? Is something wrong?"

"No, nothing's wrong, Jan." She pulled herself up a bit against the goose feather pillows. "He's got all his fingers and toes. You may inspect."

"No need for that." Jan bent and kissed Anna, and then the forehead of the child, who did not stir.

"I—I thought it would be a girl," Anna said.

"Ah, is *that* it? You wanted a girl? Well, the next one will be!"

Anna tried to smile. "From your mouth to God's ear. You're pleased with a son, yes?"

"Of course, Anna! What man wouldn't be pleased? What are we to name him?"

"I don't know," Anna said in a tentative way. "We have two Jans in the house already."

"And that's enough, I quite agree. Whose feast day it is today?"

"I don't know, Jan. I've been looking only at the girls' names for the days around my birthing time. I was so certain. . . . Lutisha, whose feast day is it today, do you know?"

The servant, who had just come in with a fresh ewer and basin, set them down. "Saint Tadeusz," she said.

"Tadeusz!" Jan exclaimed. "Tadeusz! What could be more perfect—the name of a saint and the name of my great patriot friend, Tadeusz Kościuszko! Little Tadeusz Stelnicki!" He kissed Anna again, on the mouth this time. "Let me go find Jan Michał," he said, drawing back. "He is to meet little Tadek. They will be great friends." He turned to leave.

"Brothers," Anna said in a strange voice. "They will be *brothers*."

Jan pivoted, facing Anna again. He didn't know quite how to interpret her correction. "Yes, brothers, Anna," he assured her, "and great friends, too." He moved off now to locate Jan Michał.

Three weeks later, the little family was sitting at the afternoon meal when a letter arrived from Paweł. Jan read it to himself, then announced that Zofia had given birth to a girl, Izabela. "*Your* girl," Jan teased.

Anna affected a good laugh while thinking, *It might have been so!* She had never said anything to Jan about Zofia's request. Neither had she written to her cousin, thinking that best, hoping Zofia had had a change of heart.

Jan lowered his voice. "It says nothing here about marriage, however."

"Did you really think that Zofia would consent to marriage?"

Jan looked at his wife and shrugged. "Poor little Izabela," he said. "What chance does she have?"

Late into the night, Anna lay sleepless, thinking back to his comment. Her heart ached. Zofia's asking her to take on the responsibility of her child had been too much. It really had been. Yet, Anna regretted not agreeing to Zofia's request. Had it been a mistake?

What would become of the child?

Part Two

Everyone will get in where
the fence is low.

–POLISH PROVERB

8

February 1797

Hold your spoon steady, Tadeusz," Anna said. "The *kasza* is spilling onto your vest. There that's it! The cinnamon makes it just right, yes? Good boy. One more bite, and you can get down from the table."

Anna worked at finishing her own meal while tending to Tadeusz. Michał had finished his porridge and gone out to see what mischief he might get into. As was often the case, Jan was late for breakfast because he was out seeing to things on the estate.

Tadeusz thrust out his arms for Anna, miming for her to let him down. Freed from his chair, the boy's quick little steps took him to the window, where he dropped to the floor and resumed play with his carved wooden soldiers. Anna watched him. The winter sun shone in on his blond head, creating a halo effect. His perfect features and cobalt blue eyes made her think him a replica of his father. He would grow to be just as handsome. Michał was handsome, too, but his looks contrasted greatly with his little brother's. His tousled hair was a very dark brown now that matched his almond-shaped eyes, and his features had become more prominent, his complexion almost olive. He reflected, no doubt, the fact that his father's bloodline carried some Tatar blood. That was often the way of it in southern Poland, where Anna's aunt and uncle had adopted Walter as an infant. Zofia, too, possessed a dark beauty and the same almond-shaped black eyes that might be traced to the incursion of Tatars centuries before.

His face red from the cold and wind, Jan entered through the swinging kitchen door and made his familiar apology for being late. Anna smiled at him, her irritation dissipating. She would tell him later about the letter that awaited him in the reception room.

Marta came in and went to the sideboard to prepare a plate for him. Anna studied him as he ate his *kasza,* scrambled eggs, and ham, listening as he commented occasionally on the line of Polish-bred horses he had taken to raising. It had been some little while, she noted, since he had touched upon politics. She could not escape a sinking feeling that something was happening to him—or to them. A distance had opened up between them, little by little. What was it? Oh, he worked harder than the lord of an estate need do, he found time to play with his children, and he made love to her into the night. But he had become quiet, thoughtful, reticent to open up his heart to her.

Anna was not blind to the fact that he had lost his own estates and that his current status depended in a large part upon her. It was only their marriage that had spared him from becoming one of the myriad landless nobles. He still held significant funds, but the situation would sting anyone's pride. And she knew his love for Poland could only make him seethe at its demise. She felt the same.

She was certain that he brooded and railed against the fate that had brought low his own fortunes and that of the fatherland. But his pride was such that he spoke not a word of it to her. She sensed that beneath his taciturnity, resentment festered.

And Anna could not help but recall Zofia's question to her from so many months before: *Is Jan happy?* The implication that marriage to Anna had not made Jan happy had hung over her like the belly of a cloud—darker, more threatening, and more real than any past scheme of her cousin.

A commotion arose in the kitchen, and moments later Michał appeared in the doorway. Pushing past him, his dog—full grown now—came bounding in.

Tadeusz stood up, his eyes enlarging. He had a great fear of the huge and shaggy animal. Pausing to shake the snow off his fur, the dog fixed his eyes on the toddler now and happily loped toward him. Tadeusz screamed, unaware the dog meant no harm.

"Borys!" Jan shouted. "Halt!"

Too late. The boy was already knocked off his feet. He lay on the floor, shrieking and striking out at the animal, whose tongue and slobber covered his face. In an instant, Jan pulled the dog off Tadeusz and with a smack on its behind sent the animal out into the kitchen. Jan turned now on Michał. "You know Tadeusz is afraid of Borys, and yet you behave so carelessly!"

Michał's brown eyes went wide in fear. He couldn't speak.

Jan took a step toward Michał.

"Jan!" Anna cried.

Jan turned to Anna, his face like thunder. Had he meant to strike Jan Michał? She couldn't imagine his doing so, and yet he was so angry.

Jan went to Tadeusz now and picked him up. "There, there, Tadek, no need for tears." Continuing to shush the crying child, he carried him into the reception room.

Anna sat stunned by the turn of events. Her gaze came back to Jan Michał—almost five now—who stood like a stick, his face reddening by the minute, his eyes brimming with tears he attempted to hold back.

"Come here, Michał," she said, holding out her arms. "Come to Mother."

The boy stood a few moments more—and then could resist no longer, running to Anna and hiding his face in the folds of her dress.

In another situation, Anna might have lightly taken her husband to task for thinking a sheepdog an appropriate choice for a house pet. She had often chided him on the subject. But the way things had just unfolded—with Jan seeming to place one son before the other—she kept a bitter silence.

Had he come to love Tadeusz more than Jan Michał?

She held her son to her, remembering that she had not told Jan about the letter from Tadeusz Kościuszko. All morning she had agonized over what it might contain—and how it would strike Jan. Her deepest fear was that one day such a letter would arrive, calling Jan to some duty, and he would be taken from her.

Anna had every intention of speaking to Jan at bedtime about his treatment of the two boys, but after the evening meal, Jan lay on the floor with the two boys playing with the wooden soldiers, delighting them both and providing equal attention. Her fears seemed unfounded after all, so she chose to remain silent.

"How is the boy?" the Grand Master inquired.

"Tadeusz is fine," Paweł said. "Fifteen months now."

"You've not mentioned the interest of the Brotherhood in him to the Stelnickis?"

"No, Grand Master, I have not."

"Good. Secrecy is the best course, Brother Piotr. As quickly as events are unfolding now, it's only one of several options open to us. And the fewer people to know about it, the better."

Paweł watched the Grand Master move away. It was true—he had not told

Jan. The subject of Jan's son made him uneasy. What would come of it? Might the Brotherhood actually put him forward one day as a candidate for a reinstated monarchy? How would Jan and Anna react to such a plan? Or to its actual implementation, should it come to pass?

Paweł walked to his usual bench in the hall. A brother was lighting the candles atop the three decorative columns that represented the trinity of Beauty–Strength–Wisdom. What news would be revealed today? He dared not miss a meeting because word of anything of import happening on the continent was spoken of here long before surfacing in the newspapers or in the reception rooms of Warsaw.

The signing of King Stanisław's abdication document in late 1795 had placed a pall on the nation, but a succession of events recently breathed life into those who believed Poland still lived and possessed a future. Catherine of Russia had died in November of '96, and her death seemed to ignite a little light in the dark prison Poland had become. No love had been lost between her and the son that succeeded her, so much so that Tsar Paul I immediately began to undo certain actions of his mother's reign and to redress what he saw as wrongs. Of chief interest to Poland was the tsar's decision to release those prisoners of war held in Russian prisons for two years–General Tadeusz Kościuszko among them.

Rumor had it, too, that the tsar met frequently with King Stanisław and that–dared anyone believe it?–a plan was afoot to restore the Polish Commonwealth.

And yet the noose around Poland tightened not long afterward, when the three powers–Prussia, Austria, and Russia–came to an agreement on the disposition of the Commonwealth, signing a protocol that bound them to expunge from all future records the very name of Poland. If they were to have their wish, this country with its long, proud history would to be relegated to a mere footnote in the chronicle of nations.

At a subsequent meeting, the presumption by the rest of Europe that Poland was fated to vanish from the continent's map brought the blood of the collective Brotherhood to a boil, and for the first time, Paweł felt as one with them. "We have no allies," the Grand Master had declared at the news. "We have only our sweat and our blood and our faith! It is enough. We will prevail. We will swim against the current until our arms and lungs give out–and then we will swim some more." He concluded in the prescribed way of the Brotherhood: "I have spoken."

The response of the Brethren had been strong and spontaneous–they fell into the old chant: "The King with the People! The People with the King!"

The Grand Master quoted then the patriot Stanisław Staszik: "A great nation may fall," he cried out, "but only a contemptible one can be destroyed!" Paweł would never forget those words. He thought about them now as he watched the flames of the candles flicker and dance. The Grand Master stepped up onto the dais. Paweł could not have guessed that what he would hear today would change the course of his life.

Zofia appraised herself in the full-length mirror. Her pulse beat faster at the sight. Set off by an emerald necklace and earrings, the high-waisted gown of green silk, light as gossamer, scarcely covered her breasts and draped beautifully. It was worth every ducat. Ringlets of her black hair peeked out from an orange turban with feathers at the front. She smiled.

She felt as if she were starting afresh, as if she had been given a life to start over. To look at her, no one today would guess that she had nearly died at the hands of Russians and then of a fever—or that she had given birth some fourteen months earlier. Her color and figure had come back. Her black eyes sparkled in the reflected sunlight. True, she was twenty-four, but she would give any sixteen-year-old a good race.

Her self-satisfaction vanished as she turned from the mirror and her gaze fell upon the trunk that held her carving materials. She walked over and picked up the figure she had been working on most recently. It was supposed to be Jerzy, but she saw now that it was a very poor likeness. No likeness at all, in fact. Her finger lightly touched the face. The night before she had dreamt of him again, dreamt of the humble little cottage that for months had been her home, a refuge that had restored her to life. She could smell the baking bread and simmering *bigos,* hear the voices of the happy little family. Jerzy came to her so vividly in her dreams, every feature perfectly defined, as in the best of the Dutch portraits. But, strangely, in her waking hours when she went to carve him, attempting to conjure the handsome face in her mind, she could not see him. It was as if the portrait painter's model had excused himself and walked away. What did it mean?

Out of frustration, Zofia would put aside the figure for days or weeks at a time.

A knock came at the door. *"Entre!"*

Elza entered and curtsied. "The carriage has arrived, madame."

"Very well. The princess can wait a few minutes." She pushed Jerzy from her mind. "Help me into my silver slippers." Downstairs, the dwarf belonging to Princess Charlotte Sic stood in attendance at the door. Lifting the end of Zofia's ermine cape, he followed her to the carriage and helped her up into the coach.

"My God, Zofia, you look divine!" Charlotte exclaimed.

"As do you, dearest." Zofia sat on the bench across from her. With wigs quite out of fashion, Charlotte had her own hair—pitifully thin these days—powdered and set in curls. Zofia noted that her friend no longer could be called merely plump. Here was one woman who should have decried the decline of corseting, for she appeared quite fat in her white muslin. But the three-tiered diamond necklace would no doubt deflect negative attention at the Nieborów Palace. It was magnificent.

The carriage began to move toward the West Gate. "Your headpiece is divine, Zofia!" Charlotte cried, giggling. "It serves to bring out your Tatar blood."

"Does it?"

The French princess was not aging well. Zofia didn't know her true age. To hear Charlotte tell it, she was actually shedding years. Zofia was certain at least that she would not see the sunny side of forty again.

"How have you fared under the occupation, Charlotte?"

"Oh, I've managed. Money oils the wheels of any government. But everything's been so dull these many months. And you! Keeping yourself under wraps, too. It's so wonderful to see you. And I'm so glad that social events are staging a comeback, aren't you?"

Zofia nodded. "I tried playing at domesticity, Charlotte. But I've lost interest."

"How is Paweł?"

"Oh, he's fine—off at one of his meetings."

"The Brotherhood?"

Zofia's jaw fell slack. "You know?"

"What other meetings go on these days?" Charlotte gave a little wave of her hand. "Oh, these men think they are more secretive than they are!"

Zofia laughed. "Well, I've only just learned about it myself."

"And how is little Iza?"

"Izabela is fine but quite a handful. I thank God Paweł procured an able governess for her. Even so, she's always underfoot."

"She's beautiful, I suppose?"

Zofia shrugged. "She's hardly more than a baby. A real nuisance some days."

"Oh, I remember how those two children of that French maid you had—I can't recall her name—my God, they got on your nerves."

"I wasn't meant for motherhood, Charlotte."

"I should say not," the princess said, a certain naughtiness in her tone. "I don't know why you don't send her into the country—after all, it's healthier there. The fresh air and all that. Why, maybe Anna would take her! Isn't she out in the country?"

"Sochaczew. And I already asked her."

"Oh?"

"She said no."

"Really? That doesn't sound like the little Ania I met."

"Well, she's not the same."

"She had another child, didn't—?"

"Charlotte, you are depressing me! This is my first venture out on my own since—since—"

"The Russians?"

"Yes, so let us truly enjoy ourselves. How long is the ride?"

"I don't know—a few hours west of Warsaw."

The two lowered the shades against the cold flurries of snow and fell to gossiping. They had not seen one another in many months and had much to say.

In time, the carriage slowed and turned into a drive, falling into a line of arriving coaches and sleighs. Zofia and Charlotte raised their shades and had to blink at the sun-kissed whiteness. Set against the snowbound landscape, the stone Nieborów Palace did not fail to impress, its many windows glinting like the facets of a diamond.

"Oh, my," Charlotte cooed, "it's lovely!"

"Well, it's no Wilanów, but it will do. How *did* you manage to fetch an invitation, Charlotte?"

"I have managed to make a *few* connections since you bowed out of society. I'm not totally helpless without you and your intoxicating beauty, you know. Besides, with the overabundance of phony French nobles in Poland, every good party needs a *true* French aristocrat."

Zofia resisted a retort. Instead, she said, "Speaking of personas, Charlotte, I am about to take on a new one myself."

"What do you mean?"

"Now that I know I'm not meant for dull domesticity, I have to get serious."

"Oh, Zofia, you're on the prowl!"

Zofia smiled impatiently. "Not as in the old days, my dear."

"What do you mean?"

The carriage had moved up to the entryway now, and the dwarf jumped down from his perch atop the coach to open the door and set the stool.

Zofia gave Charlotte a quick smile and prepared to alight the carriage. Soon they were walking toward the main entrance. The crush of vehicles and people costumed in lively attire brought a flush to Zofia's face. How she had missed this! She could hear Charlotte puffing in her attempt to catch up to her. "*How* are things to be different, Zofia?"

Zofia slowed, turned, silently critiquing Charlotte's canary yellow wrap, and whispered: "I mean to get married."

"To whom?"

Zofia walked on. "I haven't the slightest notion."

"But what about Paweł?" Charlotte became breathless in her attempt to keep up.

"Poor as a pauper."

"No!" Charlotte's arm drew Zofia to a stop.

"All right, I exaggerate. But he's lost his estate in the southeast to the Russians."

"Like Stelnicki?"

"Yes, exactly. Oh, he has the town house and some funds—but that's not enough."

"Still, he worships you, no?"

"*That's* not enough." Zofia tossed off a tight smile. "Charlotte," she said through clenched teeth, "all these months I've tried to be what he wants—I really have! But it's no use."

"Ah," Charlotte trilled in a consolatory tone, "everybody knows best where her shoe pinches."

"Thank you for that," Zofia said, laughing. They left their wraps with an attendant and moved into a reception hall where the Radziwiłłs—Prince Michał and Princess Helena—stood receiving their guests. Introductions were brief, for the arrivals lining up to be greeted by the hosts were many.

Zofia and Charlotte explored the ground floor, commenting on the sculptures, Roman sarcophagi, Etruscan vases, and the like. The little servant trailed. "Now *here* is a magnate family," Zofia said, her eyes moving over the family portraits that spanned several centuries. "They say the Radziwiłłs own half of Lithuania and great chunks of Poland."

"That they do."

"And their forebears were of the *minor* nobility," Zofia said.

"Yes?"

"Yes. Don't you see? The leap can be made! Marrying forward, I mean, from mere *szlachta* into the magnate class."

"If only King Stanisław had given *you* the title of princess, instead of Anna."

"Indeed!" Zofia turned on Charlotte with a sharp voice. "What good did it do *her?*" She could feel her temples pulsing. "Anna would have had her happy little marriage to Jan Stelnicki with or without it. Whereas, the title would have meant much more to me."

"Marriage to a magnate?"

"Exactly! But I'll marry a magnate yet." Zofia noted Charlotte's narrowed eyes. "Just watch."

They walked the length of a long glittering hall lighted by ornate gold sconces.

"This place is beautiful, but more like a museum," Zofia said. "All these funeral urns! Who would want funeral urns in their home?"

"They're relics, my dear," Charlotte said.

"And they belong in the ground." Zofia gave a little shudder.

Charlotte laughed. "I see your point."

"Now who is *that?*" Zofia asked.

"I don't know."

"Not the painting, Charlotte, you goose egg! The incredibly tall man at the end of the hall. The one in the turquoise frock coat."

"Him? Oh my, he *is* tall. Well, he's not a Radziwiłł, if that's what you're thinking. But he is a magnate. And *unmarried*. Come, I'll introduce you."

Before Zofia could respond, it was done. Prince Ryszard Podolski's long and narrow but handsome face was trained down at Zofia while the three made small talk. The more he stared and smiled, the more assured Zofia became that she had not lost her allure.

The moment became awkward as the hall filled with people wishing to pass through. Before making a cordial good-bye, Lord Ryszard elicited from Zofia the promise of a dance later in the afternoon.

"Let's go upstairs," Charlotte said, pulling her through the throng.

Near the foot of the stairs, on a tall, slim table stood the marble head of Niobe.

"So this is what all the fuss is about," Zofia said. "All Warsaw is talking about the acquisition. Charlotte, just who *was* Niobe?"

"A mythological character, Zofia. I'm sure Anna could tell you about her."

"Indeed, no doubt *more* that I would wish to know."

They began to climb the sweeping stairway, marveling at the blue tiles that covered the walls from the first floor to the ceiling of the second.

"Well, it just seems to me," Charlotte joked as she followed Zofia in tandem, "that magnates like the Radziwiłłs could afford the entire statue."

Zofia let out a good laugh and was just about to make a comment when her smile vanished. Coming down the stairs in front of her was Lady Dorota Driedruska.

Zofia almost suffered a misstep, recovered, and continued, keeping to the right and conjuring up a smile for the woman. The hems of their dresses touched in passing.

Charlotte was out of breath at the top of the stairs. "Did you see who that was?"

"I did."

"And she saw you, Zofia. What a look! It could have frozen summer. If looks were lethal, I'd be stepping over your body."

"Your humor is getting tiresome, Charlotte."

"Well," Charlotte puffed, "you did alienate her from her husband, if I remember correctly."

"You remember all the wrong things. This is a new day. Besides, he proposed to me, pretending he was unmarried." Zofia had to laugh to herself. The Driedruskis owned a castle on the cliffs of the Carpathians, and before they purchased a town residence, Lord Branko Driedruski visited Warsaw—and Zofia—on occasion. Zofia had feigned pregnancy and collected several good sums of money over two years—until the poor man discovered the child was imaginary.

"Driedruski," Charlotte said, drawing out the word. "The name hardly sounds Polish."

"No, it doesn't, does it? And I often wondered about his title. Branko was always quite coarse. It wouldn't surprise me if he and his wife are merely pretenders."

From the second-story salon, they looked out through the rear windows at the perfect snowscape formed by the English-style gardens below. From downstairs wafted strains of a polonaise from the orchestra and wonderful aromas of the food being prepared. "You see, Charlotte, the way they live here, rather breathtaking, isn't it? A perfect sort of world."

The French princess sighed. "As it was in France, once upon a time."

This go-round, Zofia told herself, she would play things differently. She would think less about immediate pleasures if they didn't suit her larger motive. She was determined to marry into a magnate family—and not one of those newly impoverished by the wars, either. There were a good number of families who had held on to their estates and wealth despite the shifting political winds. "Look, people are starting down to take their seats," Zofia said. "Let's go down."

In the great hall, the two friends took their places at one of the many large round tables, and Charlotte sent the dwarf off to find the company of other servants.

Presently Prince Podolski came up to the table, bowed, and asked if there was a vacant seat. The little group of five or six assured him he was welcome, and the gentlemen stood to greet him. He took a seat across from Zofia, his clear blue eyes lingering on her. Zofia silently cursed the stout gentleman who had taken the seat to her right, certain that had it been vacant, the prince would have chosen to sit next to her. She returned his gaze, her blood quickening. How long she had been away from society, she thought. It was good to be back in the game.

Conversation and wine flowed as tardy guests found their seats, and attendants started to move in with the first courses. Beautifully molded aspic, spicy marinades, and bowls of borscht were laid before them. Someone commented then on the lush and romantic gardens Lady Radziwiłł had created. "Have you seen them in the summer, Lady Grońska?" the prince asked, his eyes fixed on Zofia. "Lady Radziwiłł calls them Arkadia."

"This is my first visit to Nieborów, Lord Podolski."

"A winter promenade can be as nice as one in summer, if you don't easily take a chill."

Zofia nodded and smiled. "I'm immune to the cold weather, my lord."

His laughing eyes affirmed an assignation for later. A little thrill—long frozen—unthawed within and coursed through her like a summer brook.

At that moment Zofia became aware of Charlotte's elbow in her ribs. She looked at her friend's stricken face, then followed her line of sight to a woman taking the last vacant seat at the table, two to the right of Lord Podolski. Zofia felt the blood from her face draining away. The woman in the midnight blue dress was Lady Dorota Driedruska.

The gentlemen stood and introductions were made, the man next to Zofia presiding. When it came to Charlotte, Lady Driedruska nodded in a perfunctory manner, but when her eyes locked on to Zofia's, she said, "Yes, I am familiar with this woman."

Zofia smiled in return, all politeness and ice. With roast quail, rump of boar, and hare in cream sauce, the long meal progressed peaceably, and Zofia regained her inner composure. After all, she was certain she had secured not only a dance but also a snowscape promenade in the Radziwiłł gardens with the magnate across the table. She could afford to quietly bide her time—and once she had Lord Podolski away from the table, she would make certain they kept a good distance from Lady Driedruska.

She quietly chatted with Charlotte, and both were now and again brought into the larger conversation for a brief comment. The eyes of the prince would occasionally catch those of Zofia—and she would allow herself to briefly return his glance. Then, into the second course, at precisely one of those flirtatious moments, something made her glance at Lady Driedruska.

The woman returned her look, turned to the prince and back again, taking in everything. *Damn!* Zofia knew instinctively she had given the enemy an opening. The woman would somehow try to spoil the flirtation. Zofia declined to cast her eyes at the prince again through the remaining courses—though some voice inside her told her the damage was done.

Nearing the end of the meal, a lull in the conversation ensued. Lady Driedruska had been waiting for just such a moment, it seemed, and she spoke up. "Lady Grońska, I was sorry to hear of the destruction of your home in Praga."

Zofia nodded. "Thank you."

"Why, you haven't been seen about all these months, and some people—well, they thought you might have been among the twelve thousand lost."

Zofia affected a smile. "No, I survived, Lady Driedruska. It's nice of you to have been concerned."

"Oh, I wasn't. I didn't believe for a minute that you wouldn't survive. In fact, I thought perhaps you had accompanied our good King Stanisław to Grodno."

The woman next to Charlotte gasped at the snide allusion to the affair Zofia had had with the king.

Zofia felt a sick sensation in her stomach. "No," she said. Knowing the woman expected her to ask why such a thought came to her, Zofia said no more.

Lady Driedruska's face did reflect disappointment—but she wasn't about to lose the thread of conversation. "Well, he fawned over you so, they say. Had Catherine allowed it, I'm certain he would have appreciated the company."

Zofia's face flushed with anger and embarrassment. "You overestimate my influence with the king, Lady Driedruska."

"Do I? Well, I couldn't overestimate the influence of your salon in Praga. Everyone was welcome there, including the *Russians* during the occupation."

"I *did* entertain Russians, Lady Driedruska," Zofia said, summoning up a half-truth. "I did so in order that my cousin could hold patriot meetings with impunity in the same house."

"A well-rehearsed answer, I must say."

The table went silent for a few moments. The gentleman next to Zofia tried to end the awkward moment with a political question directed at the prince. Before the prince could reply, Lady Driedruska continued: "I hear, Lady Grońska, that the fact is there was no end to the comings and goings at your town house."

"You seem to rely on hearsay to a excessive degree, Lady Driedruska." Zofia was losing patience.

Before the woman could reply, Charlotte chimed in: "I can tell you something that's not hearsay." All eyes went to the princess. "I must bear witness," Charlotte trilled, "that your *husband* certainly enjoyed his visits to Praga. How *is* the dear man?"

Zofia could have kissed Charlotte.

But the moment quickly went sour. Lady Driedruska put her knife down with a clatter as color rushed into her gaunt face. She grew flustered as she searched for words. At last, she cried, "He's dead!" She threw down her napkin and stood. "And I won't have you speak of him in that way. Why, you're despicable—the both of you!"

"You're not leaving, Lady Dorota?" The deep voice commanded everyone's attention. It belonged to Lord Radziwiłł himself, who was moving table to table, playing the perfect host.

"I've been subject to insult, Michał!"

"Have you?"

Prince Podolski stood now. "Lord Radziwiłł, the matter is not so serious. Lady Driedruska made comments about our king that I'm certain were sincere on her part, but others at this table may have thought them slanderous."

Lady Driedruska's dark eyes went wide.

"We will not have that, Dorota," Lord Radziwiłł said, attempting to make light of the matter. "Polish hospitality does not extend to guests speaking ill of the king. But I'm certain you meant no such thing. Surely!" He paused, clearly expecting a defense in harmony with his tone.

Lady Driedruska's reddened face turned to Lord Radziwiłł. For a moment it seemed as if she was about to reply, but finding no defense that would not lead dangerously close to the disclosure that her husband had had a brief affair with Zofia, she excused herself and left.

Lord Radziwiłł bowed to those at the table. "An emotional type, Lady Driedruska. I trust otherwise you are all enjoying yourselves. Ah! Here comes the dessert—from my own hothouse, I might add." He moved on as everyone assured him that his party was a great success.

Servers brought in plates of pineapples, figs, and oranges.

Zofia waited to catch the prince's eye so she could communicate her thanks, but the man next to him kept him involved in conversation.

The music started, and a few of the guests at the table excused themselves, saying they were going off to dance or take a walk about the palace.

Prince Podolski stood now. "I regret that I must leave the party," he said, his eyes passing over everyone at the table, and lingering on Zofia no longer than on the others.

There would be no dance, no promenade. Zofia attempted to keep her face devoid of emotion. *Damn him—and damn Lady Dorota Driedruska!* She had triumphed, after all, spoiling Zofia's chances with Prince Podolski. Zofia held her composure, praying Charlotte would not say anything–trivial or not–for a good long time. She reached for her glass of wine, watching– seething all the while–the prince make his good-bye to the Radziwiłls. *A cholera on him!*

Not very long ago, she would have run after him–and she would have triumphed in one way or another, either winning him over or venting her spleen. Not now, she thought. Not now. Different times called for different measures.

Zofia felt Charlotte nudge her. "Darling, if you're not going to eat your fruit plate, may I have it?"

Zofia tossed a scathing glance at her friend and pushed the plate toward her.

Other men danced with her that afternoon and into the evening, but her first attempt at finding a new niche in Warsaw life had been sabotaged by her own past.

"You shouldn't feel so bad, Zofia," Charlotte said as the carriage wended its way back to the capital.

Zofia turned her head to look out the window. The night was dark.

Charlotte seemed to feel compelled to continue: "You know, they say one should never paint a brick building."

Zofia turned back to Charlotte, her face folding into a question. She thought the wine must have gone to her head. "A brick building?"

Charlotte smiled. "Once a brick building has been painted, *ma chère,* there's no going back. You'll never get *all* the paint off."

Zofia stared at Charlotte. Her first instinct was to reach over and strangle her fat friend.

9

Anna sat quietly in the reception room. Jan was out on the estate, and the boys were in the care of Emma. She regretted not broaching the topic of Jan's treatment of Michał. Just this morning she had heard him speak sharply to Michał, who had asked to go out into the fields with him rather than stay and study with Emma. When the boy begged a second time, Jan seemed dangerously close to using a curse word. Was it his temper? Only the week before, she had overheard Marta telling Lutisha that he had given her husband Walek a tongue-lashing for leaving something undone in the barn. And Anna remembered, too, that day in Halicz when Zofia's lies incensed him so that he left her and Zofia alone in the forest. The attack on her would never have happened but for that. His temper had cost them both so much.

Was it that event that caused him to feel differently toward Michał than Tadeusz? No, she told herself. But then it occurred to her he might harbor feelings he was not truly aware of. Michał might very well be an unhappy reminder of ugly events. Or, it could be that Jan cooled toward him, now that he had a son of his own blood.

Anna rose and walked into the library. It was warm here. Both the fireplace and more modern tiled stove radiated heat. This had been her sanctuary as a young girl. Her father had so treasured his books, many of which she had read. Emma had been *her* governess, too, and had been a good teacher, but much of her education had been inculcated here, directly from these books. Even though most peasants could not read, the servants—knowing that the books made for the essence of Polish culture—had kept this the best maintained room in the house. She could feel her father in the room, amidst the writing desk, endless rows of books on varnished shelves that smelled of fresh beeswax, and ancestral weapons that hung over the fireplace.

After the deaths of her parents had left her depressed and alone, Anna had at last received her dearest wish—a home and a little family. She tried to rejoice in that thought. Against all odds, her marriage to Jan had come to be. It was a better story than any of those on the shelves. A voice inside her told her that she was *afraid* to broach the subject of Michał with Jan. Afraid that there *were* thorns that could tear at the tissue of the life she had wished into being and settled into. She shut out that voice.

Marta came into the room and curtsied. "There's a rider coming up the drive, madame."

"Is there? Thank you, Marta."

As cold as it was outside, Anna could not resist going out onto the little portico with its two columns, the very symbol of Polish hospitality. This was not the magnificent manor home the Grońskis had had in Halicz, but it meant everything to her. Anna put her hand up to shade her eyes from the brightness of the snow in sunlight. It wasn't until the rider pulled up on his reins and shook off his snow-laden hat that Anna recognized him.

"Paweł!"

Tomasz hurried from the barn to take the brown stallion just as Paweł dismounted. "Hello, Anna!" He dashed up the three steps and kissed her on either cheek.

"It's been so long, Paweł."

"Too long! My God, it's good to see you! But you shouldn't be out here. You'll catch a chill."

"Come into the house, then." Anna took his arm and led him into the reception room. A guest brought up her spirits immediately. She could remember her father saying that a guest in the house was God in the house. "You've ridden all the way from Warsaw in this storm? You must be cold through and through. Will you have some hot coffee? Wine? Vodka? A cordial?"

"I *am* thirsty. Coffee's so hard to come by these days—you have some?"

"We do."

"I'll have a glass of vodka."

Anna laughed. She called Marta and asked for coffee and vodka. Turning back to Paweł, she said, "Sit, sit! There, near the fire."

"You look splendid, Anna!"

"And you, just as handsome." Anna sat opposite Paweł. "What a wonderful mustache! You look like a general."

"Getting older all the time. A few hours in the saddle like today, and I'm done in. And the cold does invade the bones, too. Not like in the old days. But I will have to retrain myself, I guess."

"I don't know why you should. There comes a time when men like you should enjoy riding in carriages and sleighs rather than on the back of a horse."

"Don't go painting my coffin portrait, Anna. Not yet, please God." Paweł made the sign of the cross. "Where is Jan?"

"Out in the fields, I suppose. Hunting, maybe. He always manages to find something to do. Oh, he'll be so delighted you've come. He'll enjoy the two of you going over the war years—well, the battles won, anyway."

"I haven't seen him since we were discharged. I've missed him."

"And Zofia—how's Zofia? I write, but she doesn't answer."

Marta entered now with the refreshments, and Paweł held back his response until she made her exit, leaving a cup of coffee, two glasses, and a bottle of vodka. Anna poured only one glass of vodka and brought it to Paweł.

"Just coffee for you?" Paweł asked, standing and taking the vodka.

"Just coffee."

"A toast, then!" Paweł raised his glass.

"Excellent!" Anna said. "A toast."

"To Poland!"

Anna raised her cup. "To Poland!"

Paweł stood and took the few paces to Anna so that their cup and glass could ring. And while Anna sipped at her coffee, Paweł, still standing, drank down—in military fashion—the considerable amount of vodka.

He sat now—quite satisfied and warmed, it seemed.

"You were about to tell me about Zofia just before you drank us out of good vodka."

"You make me laugh, Anna! Oh, if only Zofia could make me laugh! She's the same as ever, and you *know* she's not one for writing."

Anna recalled the journal that her cousin used to keep—one that detailed every aspect of her romantic interludes—evidence to the contrary, but kept her tongue. "And her child? Izabela?"

"Iza? A beautiful child with a wonderful spirit! I love her as my own."

The comment struck Anna. "Do you?" she asked, attempting spontaneity.

"I do! I would do anything for her—she's that precious."

Anna stood and walked over to refill Paweł's glass.

"Thank you. I'll sip this one, I promise."

"Oh, drink it down!" Anna cried, laughing. "You know it's the Polish way."

"At your insistence, Lady Stelnicka," Paweł replied, a glint in his eye.

"You'll stay over, of course," Anna said as he drank. "I'll have a guest bed-chamber prepared."

"No, I can't, thank you. Too much to do in the city."

"I see," Anna said. Her hope that he would elaborate went for naught.

After a while, he stood. "My horse has had his rest, and my blood is flowing again. I think I'll ride out and look for Jan."

Anna suggested he stay and wait, but he was insistent. Throwing on a cloak, she led him to the barn, and Walek gave him directions for where he was likely to find Jan. Anna waved him off and walked back to the house, not knowing what to think of his behavior. He seemed on a mission.

His comment about loving Iza as his own stayed with her. She could not help but wonder, Did Jan love Michał as *his* own?

Jan was chopping wood in a far field on the edge of the forest. It was his secret activity, although he suspected both Walek and Jacob knew about it. Chopping his own wood on the grounds of the house would not have been proper. That was done by other people. For that matter, all the occupations on the estate were done by others. Oh, Jan performed well as an unofficial overseer, lightening Jacob's load a trifle, and he regularly worked with a string of Polish mounts he was raising, but at frequent intervals he felt he had to put his body to work. He had to *do* something—other than playing wooden soldiers with the boys.

The size of the woodpile had started to grow very large—until one day the summer before when he caught a peasant boy pilfering a few pieces. Jan scolded him harshly, so harshly, the boy's face went white as Death herself and his knees began to buckle. Afraid the boy would piss himself and die of shame, Jan reversed himself then, telling him he could take five pieces a day if he swore himself to secrecy. Jan would not take his masculinity from him. The turn of events startled the boy, and he nodded uncertainly. Occasionally now, they found themselves on the site at the same time, and Jan spoke civilly.

Chopping wood allowed for a great release of energy and emotion—and often, thought. There was much to crowd and cloud his mind these days, much to consider, and at times he thought he would go mad because his head was so full of thoughts. He felt as if he were a plant uprooted from the south of Poland and transplanted here in Sochaczew where the soil was different, where everything was different, where it was not meant for him to take root and grow. There were Anna and the boys, of course, whom he loved with everything in him, but he had left behind the confiscated family estate in Uście Zielone and town house in Kraków, friends, travel, his years in the light cavalry, the blood rush and lust of war, battling for Poland. He feared nothing in those days, not even death at the hands of the Prussians or Russians, for it was death on the field of glory, his death for others, his death for Poland.

He had cast aside his sheepskin coat today, despite the bitter cold. But he worked at his chopping even longer and harder than usual, lifting and striking, striking and lifting. Somehow the task felt even better in the cold, the release more rewarding, more exhilarating.

The rider was almost upon him before he took notice. "Jan! Jan!"

He looked up, his mouth falling slack. "Paweł?"

"Yes, Paweł, man! Who'd you think it was?" Paweł swung down from his horse. "If it was a bloody Russian, you'd be knocking at Heaven's Gate right now."

Jan held up the ax in a menacing but mocking way. "Not likely, my friend. I'd mince you like a mushroom first! How are you?"

"Excellent!" Paweł came and hugged him. "My God, you're soaked in sweat! What are you doing chopping wood out here in the middle of nowhere?"

Jan felt himself going red. "It's something I do."

"Something you *do?*"

"Yes." He tried to collect himself now. "I don't want to get to be some old, cranky lord of the manor with a paunch and gout, you know."

Paweł laughed. "At this rate and in this cold, you'll die long before suffering such indignities!"

"This is a shock to see you! What in Hades are you doing here?"

"I had to see my partner-at-arms, Jan. That's all. Oh, and I've brought some vodka. Good Polish stuff! It's in my saddlebag."

"Get it out with you and let's sit over here."

Jan cleared the snow off the woodpile and structured it so that they might sit.

Paweł returned with the bottle. "Sorry, no glasses."

"Like the old days. Drink, man!"

"You first."

Jan took down a good swig.

"Oh," Paweł said, "I've brought news, too."

"News? Ah! I expected as much."

"Yes—there's still breath left in Poland. You know that the tsar has freed Kościuszko and sixty thousand other sons of Poland?"

Jan nodded.

"I thought as much. But what you can't know—what I've only just learned—is that France's Directory has enlisted our General Dąbrowski to form his own legion in Italy to protect Lombardy."

"From whom?"

"From Austria mostly. Last month he published a proclamation calling for Polish recruits. Think of it, Jan—a Polish legion!"

"I see."

"You *see?* Where's your excitement, man?"

"I would have preferred a Polish *army.* Why should we do work for the Directory?"

"Because, damn it, France was the only nation that spoke up as Prussia, Austria, and Russia took their places at our tables year after year and drank Polish blood! Believe me, French action against the three is in the cards. And in the doing, France can help us get our country back. Jan! Why are you laughing at me?"

Jan stilled his laughter, but a strange smile remained.

"What?" Paweł demanded. "*What?* You knew this? You did! I've been jawboning you for naught!"

Jan nodded, laughing. "I had a letter from Kościuszko yesterday."

Paweł's eyes waxed large. "How is he? *Where* is he?"

"His wounds still bother him. He's in Sweden."

"*Sweden?*"

"He can't return to his homeland—ever. He promised the tsar."

"No, I don't believe that!"

"He did! Oh, it wasn't for his own safety. He had to swear an oath in order to secure the release of those sixty thousand. And you know he's a man of his word."

"Too much so! Good God!" Paweł cried in disgust. "And Dąbrowski's legion? Kościuszko knows about it?"

"He does. And he supports it. Tentatively, I think. I suppose he thinks a small chance is better than none."

"It *is*, Jan! Don't you see?"

Jan shrugged.

"You must!"

"And you've come here in the dead of winter—?"

"For you, man. For *you!*" The dark eyes were intense. "Ride with me again, Jan. We've been given a second chance!"

"By the Directory? I can't, Paweł."

"It's not so much the Directory that's empowered Dąbrowski, Jan. It's their General Bonaparte."

Jan nodded. "Napoléon Bonaparte—the little Corsican prodigy, I know."

"Exactly! Listen, it'll be like old times for us. There'll be time enough for you later to sit on your portico watching the freezing and thawing of the Vistula."

Paweł touched on something with that image, something that went to Jan's core. He groped for words, finally turning away and feeling hot tears come into his eyes. "You don't know how I want to come! But how can I?"

"*Why* can't you?"

Jan shrugged, staring out at the snowy fields.

"Anna?"

Jan nodded. "And the boys."

"They will do fine, Jan. The estate is well-manned. And look at you—chopping wood—to what *purpose?*"

"There's something else." Jan felt blood coming to his face. "How do you think we've managed to hold on to Anna's family estate once the Prussians were given control of the Mazovian province?"

"I've wondered."

"Bribes, Paweł, bribes!" Jan shouted. He stood now, facing Paweł. Anger had crept up on him "They could take it away from us in the blink of an eye. I pay it for Anna. Losing her parents' estate would crush her." He left unsaid the fact that *he* had suffered that very fate.

"Who takes the bribes?"

"A Pole, damn him! A wretched bureaucrat in Sochaczew named Doliński. Had it been only me and not Anna, I would have killed him on the spot and proudly gone to my own hanging! Of course, I've kept this from Anna."

Paweł stood, one arm gesturing. "All the more reason you should go with me! Dąbrowski promises we'll get the opportunity to regain our country. That would mean the end of the bribes, the end of your insecurity. And you could claim back your own town house in Kraków and estate in Galicia."

Jan turned toward the flat, white fields. Paweł wasn't saying anything he hadn't thought of already—and yet he could not come to a decision. It wasn't just his fear of Anna's reaction—the fear of breaking her heart—it was also his fear that he wouldn't be here when his family needed his protection.

"Jan," Paweł said now in a strangely quiet tone, as if he were laying down a winning hand at cards, "there's to be a lancers' regiment. And nobles who join the legion will be allowed to choose their regiment. With or without experience."

Jan turned about, his eyes widening. "Is this *true?*"

10

A guest in the house is God in the house," Lutisha said.

Anna smiled, attempting to put aside her uneasiness by helping Lutisha, Marta, and Katarzyna prepare the dining room for a fine supper of venison stew. On occasions like this she especially missed Marcelina, who had married and now lived with her husband in a cottage nearby. Katarzyna presently had no prospects, but she seemed happy enough—especially when she was allowed to help with the boys.

At last supper was ready. The enticing aroma of the stew blended with the sweet smell of freshly baked rye bread. Emma and Jacob were seated, as was Tadeusz, and the food was being placed on the table when she heard Jan entering through the rear of the house.

"Come in—come in, Jan! We're going to have a glorious supper."

Jan walked into the well-lighted and warmed dining room.

"Where's Paweł?" Anna asked.

"He's gone back to Warsaw."

"What?" Disappointment set in at once. *"Why?"*

"He said he had to get back and told me to extend his apologies." Jan walked over and kissed Anna on the cheek. "There! That's from him."

"But he hasn't eaten!"

"He's had a nip of vodka to stave off hunger until he gets home."

"And you smell as if you've had *more* than a nip!"

Jan shrugged and smiled. "Ah, perhaps, but I'm hungry as a bear just the same." He kissed her again. "That one's from me. I'll call Michał."

In her nightgown, Anna sat at her vanity, brushing her hair. Her disappointment at Paweł's disappearance had not lasted through the whole meal—but it did not transform into any positive feelings, either. Despite the wonderful food and the company of Emma and Jacob at the table, Anna could not shake some indefinable sense of doom.

Jan, still dressed, came up and stood behind her, placing his hands gently on her shoulders. When she looked up into the mirror at his reflected face, she knew the moment had come. "You have something to tell me, Jan."

"Yes, Anna."

"What?"

Jan drew in a long breath. "You know that I love you."

"Are you asking or telling me."

"I'm reminding you, I guess."

Anna didn't reply. Her gaze—by way of the mirror—held his.

"I'm to go away, Anna. To Italy."

Heart pounding, Anna stood and faced him. "Italy!" she rasped. "For what?"

"I'm called back to duty. A Polish legion has been formed there to help buttress French interests."

"You're going to Italy for the French! I don't believe what you're telling me, Jan. You can't do this!" A feverish heat was rising into her face.

"It's for Poland, Anna. In the long run, we believe that France will support us in our cause against the usurpers."

"In the long run! *Who* believes? Paweł? And now you?"

"General Dąbrowski—who's organizing the legion. And even Kościuszko supports the cause."

"But you aren't *called* to duty, as you say!"

"I am."

"You're lying to me—it's voluntary!"

"My call to duty comes from here, Anna." Jan took Anna's hand and held it to his breast.

Anna pulled away. "And what about *my* heart, Jan Stelnicki? You've *done* your duty. How many times do you think you can escape death? There are others now, younger ones whose turn it is. You have a family, Jan!"

"It is for my family and this home that I must go."

"Your family needs you here. And there is no threat to the estate. The Prussians have let us be."

"The Prussians—" Jan seemed to think better of his reply and stopped in midsentence.

"What—what is it? They've been fair, yes?"

"They'll be a lot fairer when they're back within their *old* boundaries."

She stared into his eyes, blue as a darkened sky. "You're set on doing this?"

Jan nodded.

"And you waited until the house was asleep to tell me, so I can't even raise my voice against you and what you're doing to us, Jan Stelnicki!" Her hands were suddenly fists then, striking at Jan's chest. "You can't do this, Jan. You can't!"

Jan's powerful arms encircled Anna now, immobilizing her. One hand reached up and forced her head upon his shoulder. "I must," he whispered. "I must."

Her mind went numb. She felt as if she were falling through space, as if her spirit had pulled itself free of her body. Unknowing, she had had her last day of happiness for a very long time—perhaps forever—and it had come in the form of an unannounced friend.

Later, she would remember on her neck a faint wetness that could only have been Jan's tears.

Zofia's carriage trundled along the riverfront street just as the pink of the new sun was breaking on the horizon, shimmering on the rippling and plashing waters of the River Vistula. She was exhausted.

The vehicle turned onto Piwna Street, the click-clacking of its wooden wheels on the cobblestones breaking the silence. Churchgoers were making their way to Saint Martin's for weekday Mass as Zofia alighted the carriage. A few turned to stare at her.

Wishing not to awaken the servants, she used her key and entered quietly through the front door. She crossed the front hallway and was about to ascend the steps to her room when she thought she heard Pawel's voice. She halted in her tracks, thinking she was mistaken.

"Zofia?"

It *was* Paweł's voice. She turned and walked slowly to the adjoining reception room. In those split seconds, she recalled having been caught by her father in a similar situation and so now resigned herself to a similar confrontation. She immediately dispelled the fear that rose up within her. She was an adult now.

"Is that you, Paweł?" she called, her voice spun sugar.

Paweł was pulling himself up from a winged back chair. He had only just awakened. He stood, still orienting himself, seeming to notice the light at the windows. "Are you just arriving home, Zofia?"

Zofia steeled herself. "Yes."

"You've been out all night?"

"I stayed at my friend's. Charlotte Sic. I've talked about her a hundred times."

"Yes, the French princess, I remember. But I didn't know you had revived your friendship."

"I did—only last week when she took me to that party at the Radziwiłł palace. You were at one of your meetings. Didn't I tell you it was she who invited me?"

"Perhaps—I don't recall." He walked over to Zofia and kissed her on either cheek. Taking a closer look, he said, "Your hair's come undone."

Zofia smiled, praying *she* wouldn't be undone. "Well, it is morning, Paweł, and I haven't been to bed yet. Charlotte and I sat up all night talking and talking."

"I see," Paweł said, looking into her eyes. "So much to say?"

Zofia ignored the question. "I thought you would be staying overnight in Sochaczew."

"I changed my mind."

"But to ride there and back on the same day and in such weather—Why?"

"I don't know—it was awkward."

"I would expect so. I don't imagine Anna took too kindly to your recruiting her husband. As if *one* Don Quixote isn't enough?" Zofia's blood began to stir. It always felt better to lead in a conversation that threatened volatility.

"Jan had already had the news—from Kościuszko himself."

"Really—and his response? Is Jan to go, too? As if enough Poles haven't died?"

"I don't know. He was uncertain."

"Ah ha! You planted the seed but didn't want to wait around for Anna to see what grew from it."

"It's a chance for Poland, Zofia."

"Poland! Poland! Dog's blood! I'm sick to death of hearing of it. How many times have we seen the boundaries on all sides shift and shift again? It's the way it's always been, for God's sake. And always men going off to be mowed down liked sheaves of wheat—all for the *glory* of it!"

Paweł sighed. "Not merely glory, Zofia. Honor."

"Honor?" Zofia snapped. "How does the saying go? 'Honor buys no beef at the market'!"

"We won't ever agree on this matter, Zofia."

"No, we won't. Good night, Paweł. I'm tired. I'm going to bed."

Paweł caught her arm as she turned to leave. "You stayed at Charlotte's—is that the truth?"

"Paweł, you're hurting me!" Paweł released her. "It's absolutely true! Where do you *think* I was?"

"I—I don't know."

"Well, with you in Italy, I guess you will have to start placing *some* trust in me—unless you plan to evict me before you leave?"

"No, of course not."

"Maybe you'd like it if I became a camp follower, a concubine following you and the regiment from place to place."

"Zofia!"

Zofia laughed. "I do have my own money."

"This is your home—yours and Iza's!"

"Good night, Paweł. Please don't allow anyone near my room until the afternoon meal."

"Not even Iza?"

"Especially not Izabel."

In her bedchamber, Zofia pulled the remaining stays and diamond combs out of her hair and peeled off her clothes, dropping them to the floor. She shook with cold—the fire in the grate had been out for hours, and no servant was up and about to place coals in the bed warmer. She fell into the goose down mattress, pulling covers atop her.

She shut out thoughts of the conversation below, the lie she had told. Warming her now were thoughts of Prince Ryszard Podolski, how his long, lean body held her to him, how he kissed her.

His letter and invitation to supper had come several days after the Nieborów party. In it he apologized for leaving so abruptly. Zofia had waited two days before sending a response. She would not appear too available. For the assignation, she suggested the day that she knew Paweł would be going to Sochaczew. She knew that by that time the prince would be more than eager. In person, Podolski admitted that he had been unnerved by Lady Dorota Driedruski's accusations at Nieborów, but he assured her that no sooner had he climbed into his carriage than he regretted his leaving. It seemed that in the days following he had been unable to exorcise the thought of Zofia. A little investigation on his part revealed that after the fall of Praga, Zofia had been taken in by a family friend, Lord Paweł Potecki. He wrote to her at once.

The room was indeed cold. Zofia let out a little voiced sound, more a sigh than a shiver. The prince had real possibilities. So strong was his link to the Russian court that he spent much of his time in Saint Petersburg.

Zofia smugly settled into sleep, imagining herself possessing the kind of wealth and prominence he had, imagined herself being welcomed to Saint Petersburg by Tsar Paul, imagined herself being announced before a hall of Russian nobility as the Princess Zofia Podolska.

She hadn't meant for the evening to go so far. However, the opulence of his apartment, the rich food and wine, the little orchestra he had hired, and the hangdog eyes under a shock of black hair had proved irresistible. Still, she had pretended to fight him off, crying out, watching his excitement increase, knowing that he thought himself the master.

The seduction scene replayed itself in her dreams that night and in a way that it was more sensual, more exciting than it truly had been. How odd it was, Zofia thought, stretching out her arms upon awakening, that a dream could be more pleasurable than life itself.

Tethering his horse, Paweł started toward the lodge. His thoughts remained on Zofia. He could remember once interceding in her behalf to Anna. He had told her that Zofia was like a wild tropical bird. Anna had quipped back, "An *untamable* bird."

Paweł had thought for many months that he had tamed Zofia. How had he dared? Anna was right—Zofia *was* untamable.

Paweł entered the lodge.

"And the child?"

He was taken off guard by the abruptness of the Grand Master's question. The Stelnicki child had not been mentioned in months. It was suddenly clear that they knew he had just been to Sochaczew. A chill played along the length of his back. "He's fine. I didn't actually see him. I stayed only long enough to speak with Jan."

"About your going to Italy?"

"Yes."

"Is Jan Stelnicki likely to go with you?" The question came from a Brother close by. The hood Paweł wore precluded good peripheral vision, so he could only wonder if the man had been purposely eavesdropping. Paweł turned to him. It was the one with the gravel voice. Brother Fabian, he was called. He had attempted to engage Paweł in conversation a few months before, but he seemed to be seeking more information than he was providing. The man made Paweł uncomfortable.

"I don't know whether Jan will go," Paweł answered. It was the truth.

"You made the suggestion?"

"Yes."

Why was this man interested? Paweł wished he could see behind the hood. He turned back to the Grand Master. "Are there plans regarding Tadeusz?"

"It's unlikely that they'll come to anything, Brother Piotr. You're not to worry. There are other plans that will likely take precedence. And if Dąbrowski eventually marches into Poland—well, the story will begin anew."

"I see."

"Remember, though, your vow of secrecy. To violate it—even to your brother-in-arms—carries with it the ultimate penalty."

Those were words hard to get out of his mind as he rode home. He was forbidden by penalty of death to tell Jan. In that he felt traitorous, but he arrived at the conclusion that perhaps that was the best policy. The whole business might come to nothing—probably would come to nothing. It was nonsense to think otherwise. And then again, if the Brotherhood *did* somehow manage a coup, bringing to a revived throne Tadeusz Stelnicki—what could be the drawbacks in that? Jan's son would be king!

Jan brought out from his trunk his old army raiment, the day uniform and the one for dress. He had no idea whether the Polish uniform would be used or a new one would be expected. He would take as attendant Lucjan, a young man from those attached to the estate. It was the minimum expected of the landed *szlachta*. He supposed, however, with so many landless these days, many nobles went without even one. His little retinue would include five of the horses he had been raising: one for himself, one for Lucjan, and three to spare. These were the smaller and more maneuverable horses Poles had taken to war for years. They were well suited to the demands of a lancer.

Jan stared at the blue-and-crimson uniform—the *kurtka*, pantaloons, and for his head, the four-cornered *czapka*—thinking how the mention of a lancer regiment had sealed the bargain. He had always admired the skill and daring of the lancers. He knew them from stories, legend, and history. But he had seen

them in action, too, when he had fought as part of the light cavalry for
Kościuszko. In 1794, when Warsaw had attempted to hold out against the
Russians at Praga's ramparts, Jan's horse was killed by a Russian cutlass to its
neck, propelling Jan to the ground. He stood in time to see the Russian's horse
turn—the reddened weapon glinting in the sun—and bear down on him. Jan
raised his saber, ready to give good fight against the significantly longer
lance—but ready to die. It was then that a Polish lancer—on a small Polish
mount—flew at the Russian, puncturing him in the middle of his chest and
sending him flying to his death. Jan had decided then that if one had to fight,
if one had to kill, the lancer was the ideal Polish soldier to become.

The preparation and packing did not take three days, but he gave it that
just the same, wishing to remain with his little family as long as possible,
hoping that Anna would come to understand. Would she see him off with a
smile?

The day came. Everything was in readiness. Lucjan and the horses
awaited Jan in the barn while he forced down a little breakfast. He had sent
word to Paweł to expect him by afternoon. Anna busied herself feeding
Tadeusz and admonishing Michał for something or other. Her eyes continued
to avoid Jan's. Did she understand? Could she understand the ways of men?
The ways of soldiers?

Jan tried to speak of events they had in common, some trivial, some not,
but in each case the gravity of the imminent parting seemed only greater.
Eventually he fell silent. And then came the time to leave. Jan stood, went
around the table to kiss Tadeusz and then Michał. "Take care of your mother,
Jan Michał," he said.

Anna stood. "You've begun your mustache once again, Jan. Does a mustache make the soldier?"

He knew looking into her sweet heart-shaped face would weaken his re-
solve. He did so nonetheless, a thrumming at his temples. "I hadn't thought
about it. I suppose that it's the other way around."

Anna's amber-flecked green eyes remained dry. A smile was painted on
her lips, a smile to take with him. He thanked God. He kissed her now, a kiss
she yielded to.

"You come back to us, Jan Stelnicki," she whispered, a little catch in her
voice. "You come back."

"I will, Anna. I promise."

Anna reached up and guided his face to hers, kissing him hard and long.

Jan drew back, braved a smile, and made for the kitchen and rear of the
house.

* * *

Anna retreated to her room. The day passed slowly, as if the clocks had wound down. How had it come to this? It had taken years for the love she had for Jan to be realized, and now, after two short years of marriage, they were separated again. For how long? How many months or years of not seeing him, not knowing how he was? If he still lived? For the past three days, Anna had packed ice about her heart, dreading Jan's departure. Oh, she had smiled and talked and welcomed his embraces, but that was another person doing those things. It was almost like the time she had been left exposed to the wintry elements after her carriage had broken down. She had been close to dying of exposure when her spirit separated from her body, rising high into the air, hovering over the scene, watching her physical actions from a safe distance.

Jan knew she had distanced herself, too. He was too smart and sensitive not to have known. She wished that she could weep away the regret she felt, but the tears would not come. She paced her room, refusing trays of food that Lutisha brought to the door, failing to notice that the grate in her fireplace had gone cold. She would stop at the window, wipe away the frost, and peer out into the darkening snowscape. She would imagine a figure on horseback coming up the drive of bare and dark poplars to the house, the frozen ponds on either side. A blink of her eyes and the seasons would turn like a wheel. Spring–summer–fall. When would he return to her? *When?*

Standing at the window, her breath visible now in the cold, she moved a hand down to her slightly rounded belly. I didn't tell him, she thought. I didn't tell him.

By God, I should have!

It was fully dark when Anna emerged from her bedchamber wearing an old-fashioned, heavy brown dress. She moved quickly downstairs into the dining room, where supper was being cleared. She sent orders out for Walek to harness the sleigh.

Michał ran to Anna, wrapping his arms about her skirt. From the reception room, Emma came chasing after him, Tadeusz in her arms. "Oh, Anna, the children have been asking for you! Are you well?"

"I'm well, Emma. I'm going to Warsaw."

"Warsaw?"

"Don't look like that. It's not Moscow. I'll be back within a day or two. I trust you completely with the little ones."

Emma nodded. "Katarzyna will help." Anna knew the woman wanted more information but didn't dare ask.

Jacob came into the room now. "Walek said he is to hitch up the sleigh?"

"Yes," Anna said, turning to him. "I want him and his son to take me to Warsaw."

"Anna," Jacob said, "I must advise you against doing so. The sky is dark with snow. It's halfway to the knee already."

"I can stand a little cold and snow."

"But the road will not be visible. A trip tonight will be very dangerous, even for a skilled driver like Walek."

Anna walked to the window and looked out, her self-assurance splintering. Michał still clung to her, dogging her every step. She turned back to the concerned faces of Jacob and his wife.

"You would be putting all your lives at risk," Jacob said in his strong but quiet way.

Tadeusz squirmed in Emma's grasp, reaching out for his mother. Anna walked over and took him into her arms. Turning back to Jacob, she asked, "And tomorrow?"

Jacob nodded. "Tomorrow, yes," he said, his relief visible. "First light."

Anna stood in the entry hall of the Potecki town house watching Zofia descend the stairs. She wore a slate-colored day dress, her black hair—shorter now and curled—complementing the dark, almond-shaped eyes.

"What a shock this is!" Zofia cried. "I thought the maid must have gone daft." Zofia kissed Anna on either cheek, then drew back, appraising her. "You look tired. What in heaven's name are you doing here?"

"I've come to see Jan and Paweł before they depart."

"You're so white. Come into the dining room. When did you last eat?"

"Yesterday morning." Anna allowed herself to be led to a dining chair. It was true—she felt faint. And a terrible presentiment was setting in. . . .

"You'll eat something at once." Zofia hurried into the kitchen, and Anna could hear her putting a servant to work.

When Zofia returned, Anna looked up at her. "Jan—where is Jan?"

Zofia dropped into the chair next to Anna. She took Anna's hand into hers. "He's gone, Anna."

"Gone?" Anna could barely voice the word.

"Yes, he and Paweł left first thing this morning. They're well along the road to Lombardy by now."

It was as if Anna had heard the words before, as if she had known exactly what Zofia would say. Her own reply seemed scripted, too. "But I thought they were to leave on Thursday."

Zofia shrugged. "They were too anxious to play soldiers again, I guess."

"It can't be," Anna said, her breaths becoming very shallow. "It can't be. It can't be." A servant came in now and set a plate of potatoes and sliced breast of duck before Anna. She stared at it a few moments and pushed it away.

"You'll have to eat something, dearest."

"Not now."

"Why did you come, Anna?"

Anna remained silent a long time while her cousin waited. At last she said, "We did not part with everything settled between us."

"You sent him off in anger?"

Anna shook her head, holding back the tears.

"What then?"

"It's hard to explain. I didn't fight it. I didn't cry."

"You were silent?"

"No, it was much more subtle. You wouldn't understand. Jan and I are so close that he would see my resentment in the smallest action, the tiniest change in my voice."

"Ah, so you think I've not had such a relationship."

"No, I didn't mean to imply that—"

"That's all right—Anna, you mustn't worry. Jan knows how you feel—subtleties or no." After a little while Zofia coaxed Anna to eat. "And I insist you stay over," she said. "I have plans tonight with Charlotte, but I am free all day tomorrow."

Mention of Charlotte Sic brought back unhappy memories. "You're still friends with the princess?"

"We've only just resumed our friendship."

"Zofia, may I ask you something?"

"Of course, darling."

"How did you and Paweł part?"

Zofia gave a little shrug and a wince. "We kissed and he left."

"That's it?"

"Oh, I wasn't about to waste my words on him, like I did a few years ago when he joined Kościuszko. He knew what I thought of it . . . and then I think our relationship has reached a plateau, too. In fact, I was going to start re-building in Praga—before this happened."

"And now?"

"Now there's no real need to rush. One day."

"I see."

"You keep at that plate, and I'll go call Jagoda.

"Jagoda?"

"Izabela's governess."

Zofia soon returned and presently a middle-aged woman with sharp features appeared in the doorway, Zofia's daughter holding her hand.

Izabela was a striking child. She had Zofia's black hair and perfect bone structure, but her eyes were as blue as the sky. Her skin was lighter than Zofia's, too, and the combination of dark hair and light complexion and eyes was disarmingly pretty.

Zofia introduced Anna to the two. "Go and say hello to Lady Anna, Izabela," Zofia said.

The child hugged herself to the dark folds of Jagoda's skirts. When a second entreaty met with a similar response, Anna rose and went to the child. "Hello, Iza. What a pretty blue dress!" Anna dropped down and smiled into the little girl's face. "May I have a kiss?" The girl gave the slightest nod and Anna kissed her. "You're very beautiful, do you know that?"

There was the slightest hint of a smile, then a glance to her mother and it vanished.

"Izabela is no doubt in need of a nap," Zofia said, nodding to the governess.

As Anna stood, Jagoda curtsied and led the child away. "Good-bye, Iza!" Anna called.

The girl gave a quick glance back and was gone. It was in that moment that Anna realized she should have accepted responsibility for the child nearly two years ago. Her home at Sochaczew would have afforded the girl the warmth in which to flourish.

"She's beautiful, Zofia."

"I've seen beautiful turn to plain in some children as they grow. So we shall see before I start making plans for her."

Anna turned back to Zofia. She could find no words. Surely she loved her daughter.

Zofia fixed her eyes on Anna. "Now, why did you come to Warsaw?"

"To see Jan."

"I know that—and I know what you told me."

"It's the truth."

"Come, come. You were afraid, weren't you? Afraid to have him sleeping in the same house as I?"

"No!" Anna felt a sudden dizziness.

"Admit it."

"I will not!"

"Then why? There's something more—something else."

"I'm expecting."

"Good God, Anna!" Zofia's long black lashes flew back. "I hope you're not going to be producing babies like Lutisha produces dumplings."

"Zofia!"

"I'm sorry." The apology came in tandem with a little tinkling laugh. "So Jan doesn't know?"

Anna shook her head.

Zofia's eyes narrowed in suspicion. "You could have written, given him the happy news that way."

"I wanted to tell him in person."

"To make him stay?"

"What?"

"To fill him so with responsibility and guilt that he would put down his saber for a safe life."

"No!"

"Oh, Anna! It's just as well you missed him, don't you think?"

Anna drew herself up. "I think I must decline your invitation to stay. I would like my sleigh made ready."

Zofia smiled smugly. "As you wish, cousin."

Later, as the sleigh wended through countryside and forest for home, Anna tried to make sense of her feelings and the thoughts than flew through her head like Tatar arrows.

She had left angry with Zofia—and yet her cousin's questions haunted her. *Had* she been afraid to have Jan in the same house as her cousin, the woman who had schemed for so long to keep them apart? Had she hoped that news of a new baby would make Jan think twice, that his concern—and, yes, guilt— would keep him home? She searched deep within her soul now, and realized— to her own horror—that there was some truth in Zofia's observations.

As the sleigh glided smoothly on, the snow-laden pine and fir trees flying past her, she realized that she was glad she had not caught up to Jan.

Godspeed you, Jan!

11

A nna went into labor earlier than expected, sending the house into an uproar.

Walek and Jacob had carried her up to her room, leaving her then to Emma, Lutisha, Marta, and Katarzyna. Although she had some experience at birthing, Emma deferred to Lutisha and her midwifery experience.

Anna prayed as the pain came and went, came and went, increasing all the while until she lost hold of her rosary. She prayed directly to God then for a healthy baby who would survive even if she did not. A second prayer went out that she would live to see Jan again. She pictured him in a new uniform riding home to her, coming down the poplar-lined drive, coming up the stairs. The door would open. . . .

"Push now, Lady Anna," Lutisha cried, the other women's voices echoing. Emma's voice was at her ear: "Push now, child, push!"

Anna pushed and pushed again, perspiration rolling away from her face. The vision of Jan stayed with her. The vision of his homecoming. She held to it. She would do this. She had to!

The pain endured for an eternity—and then—at last—Lutisha announced, "It is here, Lady Anna, the baby is here!"

Katarzyna's voice came to her now, the marveling voice of a person witnessing birth for the first time. "It's a girl, Lady Stelnicka, a little girl!"

"Not so little," said Marta, "but beautiful just the same."

Anna could hear its cry now, high and piercing. She fell back into her pillows and waited for the baby to be cleaned and placed in her arms. As she took the chubby-faced girl into the crook of her arm, she saw that Lutisha had already wrapped a piece of red yarn around its little wrist, a protection against the evil eye.

The next day Anna awoke to the sound of a horse in the drive and voices below. She was too weak to rise and go to the window. She knew not to think her vision had come true. Jan would come back to her, but it would be many months—or even a year.

Soon, she heard the closing of the door and the retreat of the rider's horse.

Later, when Emma looked in on her, Anna asked who the rider was.

"An insistent man, I'll tell you that. And rude, too!"

"Who?"

"The *starosta* from town."

Anna's heart leapt in her chest. "Doliński?"

"Yes, Lord Doliński. Wanted to see you. Seemed quite surprised you had just given birth."

"I imagine he was."

"Why it would concern him," Emma continued, "I have no idea. What is it, Anna? You've turned as white as your sheet! Are you bleeding again?"

"No, no, I'm fine. It's just a passing weakness."

Emma insisted on checking to make certain. When she left, satisfied Anna was recovering, Anna pulled to her the child she had named Barbara Anna. "Sweet Jesus, protect us all," she whispered.

Zofia lay naked, facedown on the wide, soft mattress. She shivered slightly, not against the cold because the chamber was lighted and warmed by the flames of the fireplace. Rather, she trembled at the touch of Lord Podolski, who was tracing with his fingers the curve of her shoulder—slowly—through the valley between her shoulder blades, moving down into the small of her back, rising over supple flesh, and then returning.

"Ryszard?"

"Yes? You wish me to stop?"

"No, do continue. When you go to Petersburg next week—"

"Yes?"

"I wish to go."

His hand stopped moving. "To Saint Petersburg? For what?"

"To see it! The great Russian city. I've not been out of Poland."

"Ah, I thought you were going to tell me it was for love of me—that you couldn't bear to have me away for any length of time."

"And if I had?"

The fingers began again. "I wouldn't have believed you."

Zofia laughed, her head coming up from the pillow. "Well, I *would* miss you."

"About as much as you miss your Paweł?"

"Don't be mean. I would miss you. But I want to see the palace. And the Hermitage. Perhaps you could arrange for me to meet the tsar, who knows?"

"And—what else?"

"What else?"

"Yes, what other reason?"

"Well . . . there is a Pole there whom I would like to meet—Czartoryski."

"Adam? Why?"

"It's not what you might think. Don't be jealous. The prince has the tsar's ear. It's about my sequestered property."

"In Halicz?"

"Yes."

"I'm afraid you should forget such notions, Zofia. It's the Austrians who took that province. It will not be coming back to you."

"It's not impossible. The tsar could bring pressure to bear on Austria. My friend Anusia Tyszkiewicz told me that years ago her father had so impressed Catherine in some little way she gave him back their estate. And they say the tsar has a fairer mind than his mother."

"He hated his mother."

"You see!"

"You have enough, Zofia. You have money, the property in Praga where you can rebuild. What would you do with an estate so far in the south of Poland? You said yourself the Russians burnt the house to the ground."

"I would rebuild."

"For what? To live in the country? You despise the country, and you certainly don't know how to run an estate—even if you had the inclination."

"Well, I have Anna's interest in mind, too."

"Anna?"

"Yes, her husband's estate there in Uście Zielone was taken, as well."

"This Stelnicki fellow you told me about?"

"Yes, his estate should go to their children."

"And should you regain it for them, they would be in your debt."

"I suppose—"

"Look at me, Zofia."

Zofia obeyed, propping her head on her hand.

"Something distant comes into your eyes when you speak of this Stelnicki. What is it?"

"Nothing."

"Are you finished with him?"

"Yes."

"Certain?"

"He's Anna's husband, Ryszard." Zofia rolled onto her back now, her arms reaching out. "Now, my lord, will you take me to Saint Petersburg?"

October 1797

Anna sat waiting outside the *starosta*'s office, Emma at her side. After Doliński's call at the house, she had known she would hear from him again and had worried about it these three weeks following Barbara's birth, but she had not expected a *summons* to appear. He did not keep her waiting long. The door opened, and Doliński stepped out. "Lady Stelnicka," he said, bowing slightly.

Anna stood and moved past him, into the room. Closing the door behind him, Doliński motioned for her to sit. Anna obeyed. The tickings and movements of the many clocks in the room were all too familiar, as was the sense of vulnerability she had felt when he had interviewed her nearly three years before.

"Who is your companion out there, Lady Stelnicka? A friend or in your employ?"

"She is both. Her name is Emma Szraber. Jacob's wife."

"Your estate manager? The Jew?"

Anna nodded. "She is governess to my children."

Doliński thought for a moment, then asked in his graveled voice, "If that is the case, Lady Stelnicka, what is she doing here?"

Anna stiffened in her chair. "I asked her to accompany me."

"Indeed. Not out of fear of me, I hope. Well, well. Three children now. You hardly look any worse for wear."

Anna held her anger at bay. "If that is a compliment, Lord Doliński, I thank you."

"Indeed. You may take it as such." He smiled solicitously. "Your husband has joined Dąbrowski, yes?"

"Yes, in Italy."

"Who's to say how long he will be gone, Lady Stelnicka? I hope that we can be friends. You see, you may be in need of the *starosta*'s protection, come one day."

"I think not. My estate is self-contained; my people very loyal."

"Yes, yes. Very true, I'm sure. But things here have changed—what with the Russians yielding the province to Prussia."

"How does that change things?"

"In one way it doesn't, Lady Anna—may I call you so? It doesn't change in that I am still *starosta*. With the Russians, without the Russians. And now with the Prussians." Doliński stood, pushing his chair out behind him.

Anna watched as he walked about the room, feigning to examine one clock or another. "As hard as the Russians are, the Prussians can be harder," he said, his tone artificially casual. "Nothing and no one under them is *too* secure." He droned on about the latest occupiers.

Anna kept her eyes fixed on his desk although in time she could hear his boot steps moving up behind her.

"I have endured and triumphed because I am clever, Lady Anna, as I am certain, are you."

Afraid that he was about to touch her, Anna stood and faced him. He was but a step away. "Are you saying my estate is at risk?"

"No, not at all. I am merely saying that in the absence of your husband, you may find you have need of the *starosta*."

"I see. Thank you, Lord Doliński. May I go now?"

"I meant to ask after your children."

"My children? They're fine."

"Healthy? All healthy?"

"Yes."

"Good! Now I ask one thing from you—when I next invite you to come into town, I will send my carriage. There will be no need for a companion. Let the governess do what you pay her for."

Anna's throat closed up. *Invite,* indeed. She could only nod and make for the door.

Jan sat in the tent reading over a letter from Anna that had been forwarded from Milan to their camp in what was now an Austrian province—but what had been part of southern Poland.

He had a daughter! A daughter—a little thrill ran through him as he reread the words. *Barbara.* He counted the months on his fingers and realized Anna must have known at the time of his departure. His emotions broke away into two pieces. On the one hand, he wished she had told him, and on the other he was touched that she let him go without adding to his reservations. He wished he could snap his fingers and find himself home in Sochaczew, if only for a little while.

And yet he was supremely happy to be where he was. And proud. He was a lancer at last! The lance was Poland's weapon, it seemed, had been for two centuries or more. His own great-grandfather had carried a twenty-foot lance as part of the legendary Husaria, the winged cavalry that stood at Vienna in 1683, effectively protecting all of Europe from the formidable Ottoman Empire that had declared a jihad against the West. It was a supreme irony, Jan thought, that Poland—the least military power in Europe—dealt the decisive blow in saving Europe—and yet, a little more than a century later Poland was carved up by its neighbors. A *bitter* irony.

Well, Napoléon would indeed benefit from Polish lancers. They performed well against infantry in square, for their lances—while not twenty feet anymore—were longer than infantry bayonets. They were also excellent in small conflicts, or skirmishes. There was the legend of invincibility attached to them, too, one that inflamed fear in many an enemy. While lancers no longer wore the wings—impressive wooden arcs of eagle feathers attached to their shoulders or saddle—of his great-grandfather's day, the sight of the dual color pennant—red over white—on a Polish lance still struck sheer panic into enemy ranks, often enough to rout them without the delivery of a blow.

Paweł entered the tent now. Jan quickly replaced the letter in his leather pouch. He looked up at his friend, eager to tell him the news of his daughter. But Paweł's face was dark. He seemed to be searching for words. "My God, man, what is it?"

"Disaster, Jan. We're to go back!"

"To Milan?"

He nodded and dropped to the side of his cot. "Yes."

"Why?"

"France signed a treaty with Austria a few days ago at Campo Formio."

"Damn the French! Men of straw and sons of bitches—all of them! What does Denisko say?"

"The man's dumbfounded, but he got the word from Dąbrowski. He says we'll go back quietly and bide our time. The opportunity will come again."

"But we're here now, damn them! We're *here!*"

Later, in fading October light, Jan walked the length of several fields in an attempt to work off his anger. From the time of their arrival in Milan, it had all seemed too good to be true. Too damn good! Yes, they had taken on Italian epaulettes and French cockades, but they kept their Polish cavalry uniforms and marched to a song written by a Pole, Józef Wybicki. They were given strong Turkish horses and addressed by both General Dąbrowski and the commander-in-chief of the Army of Italy, Napoléon Bonaparte. Jan was moved to discover that the motto on the Lombardy epaulettes translated to

"Free men are brothers." It made him think that leaving his family and joining the legion had been the right thing to do.

He and Paweł were currently accompanying Joachim Denisko on an expedition into Austria's newly acquired provinces in order to buttress an underground movement there aimed at overthrowing Austrian rule.

Jan climbed a steep hill and looked out over the River Dniestr. He was so close to his own family estate at Uście Zielone that the rose of the sunset and strong whiff of mown fields brought back memories of his happy childhood.

And now he stood not far from the home burned by Russians, the land stolen by Austrians. A tide of bitterness surged within him. Only his thought of Anna and a new daughter kept his heart from breaking. Some part of him was glad that he would not bear witness to what remained of the house and grounds—this time.

But the day would come. He would be patient. The day would come.

After all, treaties often didn't outlast the drying of the ink. He wondered who had negotiated the agreement at Camp Formio. France's Directory? Napoléon? He felt certain that if it was Napoléon, the treaty meant nothing. In the little time that Jan had observed the machinations of Napoléon Bonaparte, he concluded that the man responded to his own inner drive—not to the wishes or boundaries of other countries—or even the orders he received from France's Directory.

He stayed awhile in the fading light, the smell of autumn thick in his throat, thinking of his boyhood home, his parents—long dead now—and a life never to be retrieved. "Napoléon," he muttered aloud, "whore's son."

It was dark when he got back to camp.

12

January 1798

Despite severe winter weather, the prince, Zofia, and their retinue entered Saint Petersburg in mid-January. Zofia was appropriately impressed by the city.

She had gotten her way. Prince Ryszard Podolski had gone to Saint Petersburg the previous October, leaving behind an angry and brooding Zofia. When he returned a month later, she refused to see him or answer his daily messages. But at the theater one night, she put herself in his path in such a way that it appeared accidental. It was only after profuse apologies on his part—as well as the promise she could accompany him to Saint Petersburg on his next trip—that Zofia forgave him and took him back into her good graces.

On the day after their arrival, Ryszard asked Zofia, "What strikes you most about the city, my dear?"

"Well, there is the architecture, it's so very distinctive and Eastern—but more than that, there is the huge number of Polish voices I hear."

"There *are* many Poles about, I grant you that. I guess it was quite a sight when King Stanisław arrived from Grodno. Every Pole this side of the steppes rallied to see him!"

"He's here *now?*"

Ryszard nodded. "He's been lent what they call the Marble Palace."

"Not as a prisoner?"

"Oh, he's a prisoner, but one treated like royalty. The tsar himself welcomed him to his new residence. He's a bit of a trophy of war, I think. How is it you didn't know?"

"Oh, Ryszard, you know I don't follow politics."

"And there's something else, too. They say Paul suspects that Stanisław may be his real father."

"*Really?*" Stanisław's long-ago affair with Empress Catherine was well known. *This* was not.

Zofia got another wish. It was at court supper that night that Ryszard introduced her to the handsome Prince Adam Czartoryski, who sat across from her. She worked at listening to the highly charged political discussions, smiling when his eyes would look her way. Later, after she had consented to a polonaise with him, she told him about her desire to see her family estate returned.

"And you think I have enough sway with the tsar that I can put your petition forward."

"Yes."

"Perhaps I do, Lady Grońska. But I would never allow my relationship with Paul to deteriorate to a gift-giver arrangement."

The dance was ending. "I don't understand."

"The kings of old were known to be gift-givers to their thanes, Lady Grońska. I do not consider myself a common thane. Would you care to dance again, my dear?"

Through the detailed steps of a German cotillion, Zofia's mind worked feverishly. How was she to turn this around? She could not play the coquette with this man with Ryszard breathing down her neck—and she had the feeling that Czartoryski was too smart for that. She had thought of nothing by the time he led her off the floor.

But *he* had. He suggested she meet with the Polish king.

"Stanisław?"

"Yes. You know him?"

Zofia shrugged. "Not really," she lied.

"Put your request to him. He may be a prisoner of Russia, but he's highly favored by the tsar."

"It is an idea."

"And your best one—unless you want to go directly to the Austrian court—and I don't recommend that. It so happens I am to dine with the king in a fortnight. I think that I can gain for you and Ryszard an invitation." Prince Czartoryski's forefinger lifted Zofia's face to his. He was smiling. "I could not bear to disappoint you completely, Zofia."

Count Adam Czartoryski proved successful in his endeavor.

Zofia was struck by the luxury in which King Stanisław and his entourage had been installed at the Marble Palace. It had taken thirteen carriages to bring them here. A host of family members included Michał and Stanisław Grabowski, the sons he had fathered with the married Elżbieta Grabowska, who herself had been given a house nearby. Among a complement of personal servants, his doctor had accompanied him, as well as Paolo Tremo, his renowned chef.

"Zofia!" the king called out, moving toward her. "Zofia Grońska! How marvelous this is!"

Zofia shot a sideways glance at Ryszard, whose eyes waxed large at the king's show of familiarity. Ryszard bowed and Zofia curtsied. "Your Majesty," she said.

"Stand up. Let me catch sight of you. Sweet Aphrodite, you're as beautiful as ever. Why, under the Prussian rule, you've flourished like a hothouse flower! And is the lord here your latest love? You've not *married?*"

"No, Sire. In that, you and I are alike."

"Ah ha! You still have that Grońska wit, I see. Lord Podolski, you must watch out for this vixen."

Zofia had not expected a greeting like this. She looked to Ryszard, whose smile seemed forced.

"And your cousin, Anna Berezowska? What a beauty—and a patriot *par excellence!*"

"She has married."

"Good for her! I suppose you think I should have conferred a title on you, too."

Zofia shrugged, for once at a loss for words.

"Maybe I should have." He laughed merrily, his little gray eyes glinting. "You might also have found a husband by now."

Zofia's lips widened into a lifeless smile.

"Come, come, child, let's take a tour, and you can tell me all about what's transpired since I saw you last." The king took Zofia by the arm and started moving toward a hallway that served as a gallery for some of his artworks. Zofia cast a look of helplessness back at Ryszard, whose own expression was one of bewilderment. No doubt he was recalling the afternoon at Nieborów and Lady Driedruska's gossip about Zofia and the king.

The supper was elegant. The notable dignitaries sitting at the table with Zofia and Ryszard included the Marquis de Riviére, the English ambassador Lord Whitworth, and the portrait painter Élizabeth-Louise Vigée-Lebrun. It was only after the sumptuous meal that Zofia cast her net, asking to speak to the king alone.

The king ushered her into the library, its shelves filled with Stanisław's books from home. Zofia didn't know what to think. It was eerie—here was a king forced to abdicate, who had been able to move the trappings of his monarchy into another country's capital. And yet—as comfortable as his new residence was, the king was a prisoner.

"I'm afraid I have a petition to make," Zofia said.

"A petition of me? Oh, my dear, I am a king without a country."

"You've been welcomed here."

"It would seem so. You know, if there's anything I can do for you, I will."

"Thank you, Sire. It's the matter of my property in Halicz."

"Ah, Halicz."

"Yes, Sire, it's been in the family for ages. And there is Anna's husband's property nearby in Uście Zielone"

"Ah, the one lucky enough to marry my little princess with the green eyes!"

Zofia felt a twinge of jealousy. "You have a good memory."

"Too good sometimes." The king paused, and his eyes grew glassy. "I wish I could help you and your cousin, Zofia. I really do."

"I thought you could exert some influence with the Austrian court."

"With the Austrians! Oh, dear Zofia! Do you know what's going on now—at this very moment? My own properties are being confiscated. The Prussians were demanding that my Ujazdów castle and even the Little White House in the park be sold to them. When we held them off, they declared that my properties were acquired while I was king—and they designated them properties of the Prussian State." He paused, his hands trembling. "And, as it is, who knows how long my welcome here will be? The thought of not being able to go somewhere—being so dependent on a tsar." His voice dropped to a whisper: "A tsar who changes from one day to the next."

Zofia didn't know what to say.

"Kings are not meant to be poor, Zofia, and neither are beautiful creatures like you." He took her hand. He could see that she was crestfallen. "I am not completely without resources, however. And a little manor house or two may be of little interest to the Austrians. I'll see what I can do." The king stood. "I will. Are you ready to dance?"

The king danced with Zofia, then with several others, finishing with the Madame Vigée-Lebrun. Much later, Zofia sat with Ryszard and the other guests after the orchestra had finished. She felt buoyed that there was at least a little ray of hope to win back the estates, but—more than that—she also felt touched by the sad irony of the king's position. She vowed to herself anew that *she* would not want for money or position in her twilight years.

The king excused himself, encouraging his guests to stay on. His gout was bothering him, he said. "It is more than gout," Madame Vigée-Lebrun said in a soft, confidential tone once he was out of earshot.

"What did you say, madame?" Lord Whitworth asked.

"I have painted faces all my life, Lord Whitworth," she said, "some living, breathing souls—others for their coffin portraits." She paused, nodding at the king who was at some distance, making polite good-byes. "The look of the latter is on Stanisław."

"Surely not!" pronounced the Marquis de Riviére.

"You think he is ill?" Ryszard asked.

The portrait painter nodded. "The king has the mask of death upon him."

"Dog's blood," Zofia muttered.

The little group grew unsettled, conversation strained, and soon they disbanded.

Zofia said little on the way back to the apartment lent to Ryszard by the Czartoryski family. She feared the presage Madame Vigée-Lebrun had pronounced.

Late the next morning, word came that the king had suffered an attack. The tsar's doctors were in attendance, administering medicines and bleeding the monarch. By early afternoon, the last rites were given. Tsar Paul stayed by his bedside throughout. All day and into the night, the king clung to life; some would later say he did so with more tenacity than he had clung to holding Poland. But it was to the same end.

Early on the second morning following the supper, King Stanisław died.

The death—unexpected by everyone except Élizabeth-Louise Vigée-Lebrun—aroused suspicion, and an autopsy was ordered. The physicians examining the body declared in due time that the king had died of a stroke. Zofia, however, remained convinced that the stress relating to his displacement and the loss of his homes in Poland had done him in.

As for her hopes for the reclamation of her own estate and Jan's, the trip to Saint Petersburg had proved wholly unsuccessful.

March 1798

With Michał and Tadeusz in the care of Emma, Anna sat in the reception room nursing Barbara while reading in the *Monitor* the full account of King Stanisław's death and funeral. Death had come for him on 12 February.

His embalmed body had been dressed in the Polish cavalry uniform and laid out for view first in the Marble Palace, then, on 22 February, it was placed in a grand public hall decorated in black silk, white crepe, a throne, and Poland's white eagle. Tsar Paul and two grand dukes placed a crown on his head in a solemn ceremony. For four days, mourners streamed past. On the twenty-sixth amidst much pomp and overseen by the tsar himself, the body was placed in a coffin. People—Poles and Russians alike—continued to come for days on end. Finally, on 5 March, in a cortege led by the tsar—walking—and a knight riding in effigy, according to Polish tradition, the coffin was delivered to the Church of Saint Catherine. A great and elaborate funeral Mass was held on 8 March, after which the body was entombed in a lower vault of the church.

Anna said a prayer for the repose of his soul—and that one day his body would be returned to his homeland. If only, she thought, Catherine in her lifetime had afforded King Stanisław—and Poland—the kind of respect given him at his death.

And she wondered, as others did these days, if Stanisław *was* the tsar's father.

Anna heard now a carriage on the graveled drive. It passed the house and moved around to the back. Standing, she laid the baby in the cradle, then closed the bodice of her dress. Her heart beat fast with foreboding. In a little while, Jacob entered from the rear. "Lady Stelnicka, the *starosta* has sent a carriage for you. You were expecting this?"

"No, Jacob," Anna said.

"Emma can go with you. Katarzyna will look after the little ones."

"No, Jacob, I will go alone. I'm going up to change. Tell the driver that I'll be out presently."

* * *

Lord Doliński stood waiting for Anna at the threshold of his office. "Good day, Lady Stelnicka. The roads were not too slushy, I hope."

Anna nodded. "The ride was smooth enough, Lord Doliński."

"Come in, Lady Stelnicka. I have a new clock—would you care to see it?"

Anna nodded and followed him over to the mantel, where it had been given a place of honor in the center. It was an elaborate affair of dark wood, brass, and glass. Beneath the white face with its black Roman numerals were little doors, one on the right, one on the left. "It's English," he said.

Reaching up, he moved the minute hand forward a half hour to 3 p.m. Immediately bells began to chime, more raucous than melodious, and the figure of a peasant emerged, his legs in a running pose, mouth open and fear painted on his face. As the mechanism moved him forward in fits and jerks, the likeness of a peasant woman appeared, anger on her face, an oversized spoon in her raised hand. The two circled the front of the timepiece, retreating then into the workings of the clock—only to repeat their dance for two more revolutions. Doliński laughed, turning to Anna. "Isn't it marvelous?" He moved the minute hand back.

"Indeed," Anna said. "It would be more marvelous if she caught up to him."

"Ha, ha, you are a wit today, I can see, Lady Stelnicka." When Anna gave no reply, he motioned for her to sit. With the desk between them, the *starosta* seemed to study Anna. "You are especially beautiful today, Lady Anna, as well as witty, may I say? Only a smile could make you radiant."

"I have no reason to smile."

"I see—what with your husband away, and so many new widows in the making. Who can blame you? But I'm sure Lord Stelnicki will return safely."

"So am I."

"Of course—ever the hopeful wife at home. Until he does return, I am at your service."

Anna sat, silently watching him. She knew desire when she saw it. Her fear increased, moment by moment. But it was as if he were reading her, as well. "You needn't be afraid of me, Lady Anna."

"Just what is it you wish, Lord Doliński?"

"I have been instructed to look after you—and little Tadeusz."

"What? Instructed by *whom?*"

"That must remain a secret. I will just say that there is an interested party— a group of people who wish no harm to befall you."

"And what does Tadeusz have to do with this?"

"I will come to that. Think for a moment, Lady Anna, if you will—you were granted the title of princess by Catherine through our king."

"How did you know that?"

"When we met in '94, we inspected your papers right here in this office."

"There was no mention of that in those papers."

"No? Well, I guess I learned of it in other ways. It wasn't to be a state secret, was it?"

"No."

"Well, then, back to the reason for my—concern—for you. As a princess, a son of yours is a possible candidate for the throne of Poland."

"What are you talking about? There is no throne of Poland. The last king of Poland has died recently, in case you have been out of touch."

Doliński smiled. "There are those who are working to restore the monarchy."

"And they have *Tadeusz* in mind?" Anna thought the man crazy. "*My* Tadek?"

"They do."

"He's a mere child!"

"So he is. And all the more malleable."

"But there are the king's own sons."

"Bastards."

"There are magnate families aplenty that would welcome the opportunity—the Poniatowskis, the Czartoryskis, the Potockis—any number!"

"And each family with its own agenda, it own greed, and its own abuses."

"And *my* family?"

"You and Stelnicki are of the *szlachta,* like me. Your ambitions are more earthbound."

"What you mean to say is that we can be manipulated."

He shrugged. "If you wish to burnish it with that term." The wolfish eyes moved over her. "But I shall warn them that you have pluck."

"The Brotherhood! Is that whom you mean? It is, isn't it?"

Doliński's lips thinned into the facsimile of a smile.

"Why my *younger* son?" Anna pressed. "He's three years old, for God's sake!"

"Instead of Jan Michał? Did you really need to ask, Lady Anna?" The man harrumphed. "Jan Michał is your son by your cousin. Walter, wasn't it? Rape, too, or so you told people. Anyway, you killed him for it. So you see, Jan Michał would hardly be the better candidate."

Anna had the strange sensation she was falling into some great abyss. How did this man *know* these things? She drew herself up. "And if Jan and I were to refuse?"

"That could prove most unwise for you both. In point of fact, however, you are forbidden to tell your husband of my group's interest. Not by writing. Not by spoken word, should he return."

"This is an outrage! *Why?*"

"A precaution. If not for your own self, think about your husband and your children's safety. Your tongue could put them all in jeopardy."

Anna paused at this blatant threat. "What now, then, Lord Doliński?"

"Nothing for the immediate year or so. There will be instructions down the line regarding his schooling. At some point, he will have to go to a boarding school."

Anna stood. "No! I won't have it!"

"You *will* have it, Lady Stelnicka." The *starosta* slowly got to his feet and moved around to the front of the desk. "Resign yourself. Besides, how terrible would it be to be the mother of a king?"

"Is that all for today, Lord Doliński?"

"It would seem so." He stood very close to her now.

Anna held her ground although she felt the blood draining from her face.

"I like your fire, Anna," he said, lifting his closed hand and very lightly brushing her cheek with his knuckles.

Anna stepped back.

"Don't worry—my job is to *protect*, Lady Anna."

Anna felt the slightest twitch at her upper lip, and she saw at once that he noticed it, too.

"My, my, there's fear beneath the fire, isn't there? Why, I would wager that when my carriage arrived at your manor house you ran for your rosary!"

"I did not!" Anna effected an exit without further words. As the carriage moved out of the Market Square, she pushed her hand into the full skirts of her dress, searching for something. She had not run for her rosary earlier in the day. She had gone upstairs for the pistol she kept in a locked wardrobe—the pistol she had used to kill Walter. Anna held it now, wishing—God forgive her—for the first time since that day that she could kill again.

13

Jan had only the light of the campfire to aid him in cleaning and salving the wound in Paweł's shoulder. The Lombardy sky was moonless and dark but for a scattering of stars. The night had gone quiet.

"How deep is it?" Paweł asked.

"Not deep. You'll live to die tomorrow."

Paweł grimaced in pain. "You were right, Jan."

"About what?"

"The Treaty of Camp Formio—it didn't last long."

"Anna's tulips at Sochaczew last longer."

Paweł managed a little laugh and fell silent, his eyes closing.

Jan thought how he and Paweł had seen action—serious action—but none that brought them again to Polish lands. They stood with France to maintain control of Lombardy. It was a formidable job by now, for those allied against them were England, Austria, Russia, Turkey, and Naples.

That morning, 17 June, Dąbrowski's Polish Legion, one of seven divisions led by General Macdonald, had moved down from the Appenines onto the Lombardy plains to contest the encroachment of Russo-Austrian forces. The French-Polish numbered thirty-nine thousand and the enemy—in two groups—was estimated at twenty-five thousand Austrians, thirty-five thousand Russians. Battle lines against the Austrians were drawn on the western bank of the River Tidone.

The French forces fell upon the Austrians. As the battle progressed, two French divisions ran low on ammunition, and the threat of full encirclement became real. The third, Dąbrowski's, moved in, extending the flank and routing the Austrians. Dąbrowski directed the cavalry and lancers—with Jan and Paweł fighting stirrup by stirrup—toward Castel San Giovanni. Success seemed well within reach when Russian regiments of cavalry descended in huge numbers. The French dragoons—in a panic now—were slaughtered, and Polish chasseurs, formed into a square, were cut down by Cossack lances that outreached Polish bayonets.

Dąbrowski was unable to come to their aid, for an Austrian regiment cut his battalion off from the rest of his division. The general called for a retreat into the mountains. Jan and Paweł, *chefs d'escadrons,* reluctantly passed the order on to the men of their squadron. The rest of the French troops were forced behind the River Tidone, and the enemy chose not to pursue them because it was long after dark. Macdonald collected his forces, withdrawing farther—and made camp beyond the eastern shore of the shallow River Trebbia, leaving the field between the two rivers unoccupied. They counted at least six hundred dead—and more wounded or captured.

Jan knew the morning would bring more bloodshed. "Where is our Napoléon now?" Jan asked, fully unaware he had muttered it aloud.

"On campaign in Egypt. You know as well as I."

"Off playing Caesar, you mean. I'm almost finished with the bandaging. Then you can sleep."

Paweł scowled. "He'll return when he gets wind of these changes."

"Maybe," Jan said with a chuckle. "Maybe not, if he's found his Cleopatra."

"Listen to you—and not a scratch on you! Ouch!"

"Sorry. Sometimes I wonder what we're doing here, Paweł."

"You miss Anna."

"Here. Swallow down this brandy. It'll help you sleep."

Jan extinguished the lantern and lay down upon his mat. He tried to remember how old his daughter was. The daughter he had yet to see. She would be two in the fall.

Soon Paweł's steady breathing indicated he had fallen asleep. Jan could not turn the thoughts out of his head. Word had circulated through the camp that the Russian general across the river was Catherine's old warhorse Aleksandr Suvorov. The thought stung worse than any wound he had suffered. This was the red devil that had come down on Praga in '94, slaying twelve thousand in his path, mostly citizens. He had been the one to deal the death blow to the nation. Jan would give anything to confront him on the field—to deal *his* death blow.

It was a long time before Jan gave himself up to sleep.

Against Jan's advice, Paweł was mounted and ready the next morning.

Suvorov's troops formed on the other side of the River Trebbia at nine o'clock. The battle lasted three days. At one point Dąbrowski found his forces attacked on three sides. After a valiant effort, he called for a withdrawal and in its execution was hit again by Austro-Russian cavalry. His third battalion was all but slaughtered, its standard and fifteen officers captured. Jan and Paweł, despite staying close to the general, were unable to keep him from suffering a light wound to his thigh. Impervious to the bleeding and pain, he stayed mounted and—together with his officers, lancers, and infantry survivors—slashed and cleaved through the enemy line. In the end, however, the French forces were overcome and Dąbrowski moved his division out and regrouped.

On 20 June, the extended battle at an end, Dąbrowski's division was named rear guard for the entire army as it moved toward Castel Arquato. They suffered several engagements in the process, and Dąbrowski would have been captured were it not for the increasing prowess of Jan and Paweł's lancer squadron. The tattered Polish company, standards waving, sang Józef Wybicki's song as they entered Castel Arquato.

> Poland has not perished yet
> So long as we still live.
> That which alien force has seized
> We at sword point shall retrieve.
> March, march Dąbrowski!
> From Italy to Poland!
> Let us now rejoin the nation
> Under thy command.

Months followed, with regular skirmishes on a lesser scale. The legion remained at Castel Arquato.

On an overcast afternoon, Paweł burst into the little outbuilding that he shared with Jan. The open door became for the moment a valve allowing into the single room—with its little stove, two cots, two chairs, and a small table—a great gust of November air that lifted and blew to the floor several papers from the table on which Jan was writing. The modest flame in the stove flared up momentarily.

"Sorry!" Paweł said. "Did the post rider come through? Did you get the letter from Anna you were looking for?"

"No, but I got a long letter from Kościuszko. A real dissertation. He's in Paris." Paweł dropped into the chair opposite Jan's.

"Really! Well, don't keep me waiting, man! What does he say?"

"I'm not sure you want to hear. His thoughts may knock Napoléon off that little pedestal you've set up for him. It seems Napoléon went to see him unannounced."

"Ah, the little general meeting the little corporal," Paweł exclaimed.

"Your little corporal did everything but beg for his support."

"And?"

"Kościuszko didn't commit."

"Well, that makes sense, I suppose," Paweł said in defense of the hero. "He probably has spies from Russia, Austria, and Prussia nipping at his heels. He's got to watch himself."

"That's true, no doubt, but not the reason. Kościuszko found Napoléon arrogant and opportunistic."

Paweł shrugged. "It's how he got where he is. Maybe that's what it takes."

"Look at Kościuszko, Paweł—have you ever run across a more sincere person, one more interested in the lives of the many?"

"You're right, Jan. But look at his current position—not an enviable one. It's one of impotence. A man who can't return to his homeland."

"*Touché*. But I haven't given you the biggest news about your Napoléon. You know, the leader who foresaw a new egalitarian order for the common man in Europe? I imagine the whole camp will be full of it later today."

"What?"

"Within a week of his visit to Kościuszko, he staged a coup in Paris. He forced the Directory to resign and has set up a neat little triumvirate of which he's First Consul of France."

Paweł took some moments for this to sink in. He sighed finally. "Such ambition."

" 'Ambition, thy name is Caesar!' Isn't that how it goes?"

"Something like that. But, Jan, we've been robbed of our *homeland*. If a man comes along and says to you he can restore it to you, what choice do you have?"

"You're right, my friend, no choice. But it doesn't mean I have to like it."

"Just wait, you'll see! The ambitious little corporal will help us take back Poland. There was no letter for me?"

"No."

Paweł stood and walked over to his cot. "Time for forty winks," he said, lying down. He closed his eyes, but he somehow sensed Jan watching him. "You don't like her, Jan—Zofia?"

"No."

"Well, that's to the point. That's why you've never talked about her, asked about her."

"She made things difficult for Anna and me—before you knew her."

"How?" Paweł opened his eyes and pulled himself into a sitting position on the side of the cot. "I'd like to know."

Jan looked over at Paweł, a grim expression on his face. Paweł's own un-flinching expression commanded a response. "Before Anna went to live with Zofia and her parents," Jan began, "Zofia got it into her head that a marriage to me would keep her from having to marry the man her parents had chosen. When Anna happened on the scene and Zofia saw that we were falling in love, she became obsessed."

"And?"

"And she did things to separate us, Paweł. Her interference led to Anna's being attacked—and then to having her married off to Grawliński. And you know how that ended."

Paweł thought a long time. "But she saved Anna's life at Praga."

"That she did."

A few more minutes went by. "You think me a fool, Jan?"

"No, Paweł, no friend of mine is a fool."

Paweł sighed. "Oh, I know Zofia's not staying home every night caring for little Iza. But a flying fish cannot stay in the air forever, you know." Paweł straightened his shoulders. "I know her better than you might think. Do you know she carves?"

"Carves? Carves *what*?"

"Figures, little figures made of linden wood."

"You must have a fever, man! You're talking through your head."

"No, really! Once I came home from—oh, I don't recall now, but it was late. Zofia had gone out. When I checked her room, I found a trunk open near her vanity. In it were carving tools and all these little figures, most of them rather crude, but a few weren't bad."

"Well, I'll be damned!"

Paweł chuckled. "Me, too."

"What did she say about them?"

"I never told her I found them. I closed the trunk—actually it was her dowry chest—and she just didn't know. I suspect one of the peasants who took her in taught her."

Jan smiled. "Did she carve one of you?"

Paweł laughed, shaking his head. "Nor you—unless it was that thin ugly one with the crooked nose!"

Jan laughed, too, and threw his *czapka* at Paweł.

It came back to Paweł later that night how he had almost let out the secret that he belonged to the Brotherhood. The night he discovered the carvings he had been returning from a meeting. Had he let it slip, Jan would have been full of questions. It had been a close call. Paweł had been sworn to secrecy un-der pain of death, and even though the Brotherhood was quite capable of eliminating traitors of any kind, it wasn't that fear that kept him from speaking of it to his friend. It was that the Brotherhood had plans—*possible plans,* they said—for Jan's son Tadeusz. Paweł hadn't a clue about how Jan would react should he find out—but he instinctively knew the revelation could be dangerous to everyone involved.

14

January 1800

Zofia descended the interior staircase of the town house just as Princess Sic was making her entrance. "I'm so glad you're on time for once, Charlotte. My goodness, you've worn your silver-blue gown! There was hardly need for that. We're staying in."

"Well, your note was so cryptic. What's the little surprise?"

Zofia kissed Charlotte on either cheek. "I wanted to do something interesting and amusing to start the new year."

"They're calling this the grand century! The prince is in Saint Petersburg, I take it?"

"Yes, but he wouldn't take me this time."

"And—I hesitate to ask—what of Paweł?"

"Ah, Paweł!" Zofia took Charlotte's cape and passed it to a servant. "I do wonder how he can keep up a war and find time to write so many letters."

"No talk of marriage from the prince?"

"Ryzsard avoids it. But tonight I may get a clue. Come in to the dining room."

"Good! I'm famished."

"You may eat later, if you must, Charlotte. The surprise is in there. As is my friend Anusia Tyszkiewicz."

"Oh my, the king's niece! You *are* traveling in *haut monde* these days, aren't you?"

"My relationship with Ryszard has been good for that, at least. Those who knew me before Praga seem to have shortened their memories of my *colorful* past and warmed a bit."

The dining table had been moved to the far end of the room, and Lady

Tyszkiewicz was sitting at a small table used for cards. She stood to greet Charlotte.

Zofia made the introductions and they sat, making small talk until Lady Tyszkiewicz spoke of Napoléon Bonaparte. "I was just telling Zofia, Madame Sic, that I admit to be taken by the buzz that surrounds your fellow Frenchman."

"Frenchman, indeed!" Charlotte trilled. "He's Corsican—and short to boot."

"That does nothing to lessen my admiration," Lady Tyszkiewicz said. "Such victories! He seems another Caesar or Alexander."

Charlotte shrugged. "I don't take much interest in such things."

"Nor I," said Zofia. "But I should like to meet him and take the measure of the man myself."

Charlotte giggled naughtily at this, and a confused look came over Lady Tyszkiewicz's face.

"Now just what is this surprise, Zofia?" Charlotte asked.

"Yes, do let us in on it," Lady Tyszkiewicz urged.

Zofia smiled. "Actually, it was you, Anusia, who gave me the idea for it."

"I?"

"Yes, when you told me about the astrologer that visited the Poniatowski family when Stanisław was newly born."

"Ah, yes, it is a well-known story, but my aunt actually knew someone who was in the room."

"What happened?" Charlotte asked.

Anusia needed no further prompting. "It seems that years ago the Poniatowskis invited in an astrologer for an evening's entertainment. On that very night Lady Poniatowska went into labor. While the birthing was taking place, the astrologer cast the horoscope of the Poniatowski children—there were four at the time, I think. He declared glorious futures for them all, boys and girls alike. It was all the elder Poniatowski could do to maintain Polish hospitality when it was so clear he thought the man a complete charlatan and his proclamations a hoax. Throughout the reading, an ironic smile persisted on Lord Poniatowski's face. The astrologer could do little to convince him. I'm abridging the story considerably, but to get to the end—just as the astrologer was about to take his leave, the midwife came into the room with the newborn. Without missing a beat, mind you, the astrologer turned to the infant, little Stanisław, still bloody from birth, and declared, 'I salute you, King of Poland!'"

"Goodness!" Charlotte exclaimed. "It makes my skin pimple."

Lady Tyszkiewicz nodded. "The unbelieving Poniatowski admitted years later that at that moment a chill ran through him to the very marrow of his bones."

"An excellent story, Lady Tyszkiewicz. Now don't keep us in suspense, Zofia," Charlotte cried. "What is to happen? Have you found this Swedish astrologer? Is he *here?*"

"He's too old and probably dead, my sweet." Zofia said. "But I hear he went to school in France. You may have been schoolmates. Your ages are in alignment, at least!"

"Why you little—" Charlotte caught herself before taking up the name-calling game she played with Zofia. In present company, such an epithet would have been inappropriate. She gave a tight smile.

"But you *have* found an astrologer?" Lady Tyszkiewicz pressed.

"No, dearest—a fortune-teller!"

"Really?" Zofia's friends cried in unison.

"Yes, she's in the kitchen stuffing her mouth as if she'd never tasted good food."

"Oh, I should like to have a bite, too," Charlotte said.

"Later," Zofia said, giggling, "after we find out if you even have a future." She rang a little bell, and presently a maid escorted a small gypsy woman into the room. The fortune-teller was perhaps in her mid-fifties.

"Come and sit down, Zinia."

The woman came forward without any air of subservience and sat, wiping at crumbs about a mouth that puckered like a purse drawn closed. Underneath a bright red headcovering, the eyes—like ebony stones—considered her three customers.

"Who is to be first?" the woman asked. The evening went along splendidly as the gypsy read for each the women's present, future, and past. Charlotte seemed delighted with the reading, as was Lady Tyszkiewicz, who was promised a sterling marriage to a man of the Potocki house. It was only when Zofia declined to have her past told that the mood changed—at least for Zofia.

The gypsy would not be deterred from a full reading. "Once I begin your fortune," she said, in her husky voice, "I must finish. It is the way, milady." Without delay, she laid out the prescribed seven cards: Queen of hearts. Five of clubs. Jack of hearts. Queen of spades. Two of spades. Ace of diamonds. Four of hearts.

The gypsy took in a long breath, then said, "Two young women—one dark, one light—one young, light-complexioned man—a triangle. The five is Ride. The two is Lie and the ace of diamonds is Letter. And the four of hearts, Change." The woman sighed, as if something had come through clearly. "You have competed with a lighter complexioned woman, yes?" When Zofia said nothing, she continued. "Somehow, a ride on horseback, a lie, and a letter never opened are involved. The result of these things was change—change having to do with marriage."

After the gypsy left, Charlotte and Lady Tyszkiewicz enjoyed a little meal while going over their respective readings. Zofia sat at table, but her mind had blurred. She had brought the woman in for a little fun. She believed in none of it. And yet the gypsy had seen into her past with incredible precision. There was the introduction of Anna into Zofia's life and the plans Zofia had for Jan Stelnicki, the fateful ride in the forest, the lies she told and the letter from Jan to Anna explaining why he had been unable to return to the pond that day—the letter Zofia destroyed. And then there was the change of brides for Antoni Grawliński—from Zofia to Anna. These were things Zofia cared not to think about, and she seethed that the woman had channeled her into the past. Upon being forced to look back, she burned with—what?—a sense of defeat? Shame? But then again, she wondered whether, if having it to do over again, she would change anything.

That night the gypsy woman came again, entering Zofia's dreams. The specter forced the king of hearts card into her hand. Zofia looked at it and seemed to see the face of Jan Stelnicki. She attempted to give the card back, but the woman snarled and declined. For some time, the two argued over the card. Then suddenly the woman disappeared, as people often do in dreams. But the card remained in Zofia's hand.

As she looked down at it, she saw that it was not the likeness of Jan at all. Staring up at her, so real that breath seemed to be coming from his lips, was the handsome face of Jan's look-alike, Jerzy.

February 1800

Anna thought she would go mad. The house was in an uproar. All three children had come down with a severe winter fever. The first weeks of the new century were ruined, but that paled considering the risk at hand. A number of Sochaczew citizens and peasants had been carried away with the sickness, including a child belonging to a milkmaid on Anna's estate.

"Well?" Anna demanded.

Jacob Szraber stood in the hall, snow still upon his shoulders and fur hat. He had gone to town to bring back a doctor. "No, luck, Lady Anna," he said, his head hanging slightly. "The old physician is ill himself, and the young one has gone off to join Dąbrowski in Italy."

"Damn them," Anna said, forgetting herself. "What business do Poles have in Italy, I ask you." It was more a statement than a question. "A cholera on them." Anna turned and hurried upstairs. Softly, she walked into Barbara's bedchamber. Lutisha looked up from her place at the two-year-old's bedside. The child had at last fallen asleep, but beneath the yellow halo of hair, a frown, like an old woman's, bore witness to the body's struggle with the fever. Then she took up her own post in the boys' bedchamber. Jan Michał, nearly eight now, had come down with it first, but he seemed to be past the danger. He opened his eyes slightly at the sound of his mother. Anna put her finger to her lips, shushing him in case he was about to speak. On the floor at the end of Jan Michał's bed, Borys lay faithfully in a great furry heap, one eye on Anna. Like the children—even Tadek—she had come to love the dog.

Anna sat in a chair between the boys' beds. The dog came over and sat at her feet. She looked from one boy to the other. With time, the three-year difference in their ages had become less of a divide. They learned together, played together—and now they were weathering this sickness together. Tadeusz was Anna's chief worry now. He was very ill. Even in sleep, he gasped for air. A rattle sounded from deep within his lungs. Lutisha had done everything she was able to do, tried all her herbs. "Keep the covers piled high, madame," she had warned Anna. "The fever must burn itself out."

A day went by with little change. On the next, Anna was called downstairs, where a visitor awaited in the reception room. As she entered, the stranger rose. He was a large man with thinning hair, small dark eyes, and a wide nose. He immediately started speaking in German, telling Anna he was a doctor who had come to tend her children.

"Thank God! Thank God!" she cried, leading him upstairs almost immediately.

He first gave the three a cursory look, then returned to Tadeusz's bed. "The other two are past the crisis," he said. "This one is not yet out of danger."

The tears came to Anna's eyes, and her throat closed. She couldn't speak. How could she face the death of this child? How could she face Jan upon his homecoming?

Tadeusz was moved into another bedchamber so that he could be attended without disturbing Michał. The doctor stayed with Tadeusz through the night, applying and reapplying hot compresses, forcing medicines down his throat. Katarzyna sat on a chair in the hall so that she could fetch anything the doctor might request. Once, during the night, Michał's head turned on his pillow to Anna. "Is Tadeusz going to die, Mama?"

Anna steeled herself, stifling the emotions that question called up. She was about to tell him she didn't know—until she realized the boy was putting his faith in her and she could not fail him. "No, Jan Michał, little Tadeusz is not going to die. He'll be back in this room with you in no time."

Michał accepted her words and soon fell back to sleep. *Dear God, you must make him well now,* Anna prayed. *I've given my son your word.* The night crept by. Anna stayed at her place next to Michał, sleepless, helpless, afraid. Only once before had she faced this kind of fear—when as a baby, Jan Michał had nearly died of a fever. If only the end of this trial would be as happy. What terrible pain was bringing children into the world, she thought. And afterward, every pain, every sickness, every heartache of each child was there for the mother to take on and share and try to remedy.

Michał stirred just after dawn. "Is the doctor coming in again?"

"I don't know." Anna felt his forehead. It was cool. "You're getting well, Michał. It's Tadek who needs the doctor's attention. Now, don't be disappointed. You want your brother well, too, yes?"

"Yes." A little later, Michał fell back to sleep.

Katarzyna knocked lightly on the door at midmorning. "Madame Stelnicka, the doctor wishes to see you."

Anna hastened past her to the guest bedchamber. The doctor stood just inside the door. Even as she greeted him, Anna's eyes tried to see past him for sight of Tadeusz. He stood in her way, however, high as a wall. "Tadeusz?" she asked fearfully. "How is he?"

The doctor gave a thin smile. "He has made it through the night, my lady." He stepped aside. "Your son is out of danger now."

"Oh, thank God! Thank God and you, doctor!" She rushed to the sleeping boy, her hand reaching for his forehead. It was smooth and dry now, finally cool.

An hour later, the doctor stood in the front hall, preparing to leave. "Have you been given something to eat?" Anna asked, coming down the stairs.

"I've been well fed. Now I'm on my way."

"Have you far to go?"

Pulling on his greatcoat, the doctor named some Prussian town she had not heard of before.

"However did you hear of my children's illness?"

He smiled enigmatically. "I heard."

She could tell he wasn't going to say any more about it. "What about your fee, Doctor?"

The smile widened slightly. "I have been paid."

"By whom?"

"Good-bye, Lady Stelnicka."

Anna watched him pull the door closed behind him now, a sick feeling rising up within her. She suddenly knew who had sent for the Prussian doctor.

15

December 1800

News of a mighty battle at Hohenlinden arrived in camp in mid-December. Both Jan and Paweł listened in awe to the stories. The Polish Danube Legion, serving with France's Army of the Rhine, had stood near Hohenlinden with its force of one hundred thousand engaging the Austrian army. In two separate units, the Austrian army totaled 120,000.

Engagement occurred on 3 December under an iron-gray sky that spattered dry snowflakes. One of the first to attack was the Second Batallion under Józef Drzewiecki. The bayonet charge proved effective, but losses were many. The battle broke down into many smaller skirmishes then because of the weather and because of the terrain, which was wooded and laden with marshes. The story came back how a young brigadier, Jan Pawlikowski, spied enemy in the shrubbery and—accompanied by a French chasseur—charged the Austrians, calling out orders to nonexistent fellow soldiers. He took down two officers with his lance and took a third into custody—along with fifty-seven soldiers! When Pawlikowski was offered a promotion to lieutenant, he declined, admitting he could neither read nor write, qualifications of an officer.

By the end of the day, the Austrians were in full retreat, having lost at least twenty thousand men. The French lost twelve hundred, of which Poles numbered fifty dead. Toasts were raised in the Lombardy camp that night for the brave soldiers of the Danube Legion—and for Jan Pawlikowski.

Just two months later, with the treaty of Lunéville, France made peace with Austria and her allies, dashing the hopes of thousands of Polish soldiers. The Polish legions were for the moment an embarrassment to the French government. What to do with them?

Dąbrowski's legion was to become the army of the new state of Lombardy. Some units were disbanded. One force of six thousand was to be sent, under the French aegis, to put down a rebellion in Santo Domingo. "What about Santo Domingo?" Paweł asked.

"Are you crazy?" Jan sat on his cot, his spirits crushed. They had been twice fooled by Napoléon's machinations. "That's not our war!"

"Won't you stay with Dąbrowski, then?"

"This wasn't our war, either. What did we gain? Scars and medals and dead on the field—and for what? For *what*, Paweł?"

"I'm sorry."

"You're sorry? Why should you be sorry?"

"For encouraging you to come."

"I think I'd be here in any case. And I'm still alive. And so are you, my friend. Forget Santo Domingo. Forget Dąbrowski—God bless the man! But come home. Come home with me!"

Paweł fixed his eyes on Jan but said nothing.

He would not come home, Jan knew. And he knew not to insist.

February 1801

"How old is the boy now?" the graveled voice demanded. "Four?"

"Not till the end of the year." Anna found herself once more sitting across from Doliński, the desk between them.

Doliński smiled. "I appreciate your coming, Lady Anna."

"What choice did I have?"

"Your dress is very pretty. Green suits you. Do stand and let me see it."

"Lord Doliński, I did not come here to show off a dress. You have not had me come here for a very long time. You must have your reason."

He fixed his eyes on Anna. "Humor me."

Anna stood and was told to turn about. "Lord Doliński—"

"Turn. Slowly."

Anna bit her tongue and turned. Before she could complete the revolution, she heard the legs of his chair grate against the floor as he stood, moving quickly around the desk. It was his strong hand on her arm that brought her to a stop in front of him. His face was very near hers. She stared into the milky blue eyes, her heart accelerating. Her first thought was that she had not brought the pistol, and she cursed herself for it.

"I can arrange for you to keep Tadeusz a little longer. Maybe a year."

"What?" Anna grew dizzy trying to understand his words.

"I said that I could hold the Brotherhood at a distance until he's five."

"If?"

His mouth was on hers then.

Her head reeled. Based on previous meetings, she did not expect him to act on his attraction to her. Pulling her head back, she opened her mouth to scream.

Doliński's right hand covered her mouth while his left arm moved around her waist, pulling her to him. "You will not call out, Anna. And if you do, it will not matter. I made certain no one is in the building today."

Slowly, he removed his hand, and when she didn't call out, he attempted to kiss her again.

"No! Take your filthy hands off me!" Anna struggled to break free, but the man's grip was tight. His appetite had been whetted too long for him to let go of his prey.

Anna's arms were bound by his. She started to kick out and, despite the thick fabric of her dress, found her mark several times. Instinctively she called out for help.

Doliński laughed. "No one can hear you."

"You will regret this!"

"Who will see to that? Your husband? Your *absent* husband?"

"Yes!"

His grip tightened, and his eyes lost the passion for a moment, reflecting anger instead. "Listen to me, Anna, and listen with your heart and ears. To reveal anything to Stelnicki about the Brotherhood will bring death to your entire family." He was breathing hard. "About this, too," he said, pulling her closer so that she felt his arousal.

"But the Brotherhood—"

"What of the Brotherhood?"

"If they find out—about *this*."

"They won't."

"But if they do."

He stopped. He was thinking, taking in her counterthreat. It seemed that the civil penalty for rape—the ax, assuming it could be proved—did not worry him, but the Brotherhood's reaction did give pause. The many clocks around the room ticked away the seconds. She could feel the desire going out of him.

Doliński's wolfish eyes looked at her despisingly. Suddenly he released her.

Anna moved to collect her cloak, amazed at herself, amazed that mere words had somehow stopped him. Was she free to leave? She pulled on her cloak and turned to face him.

His attitude had changed. "It's best that you forget this incident, Lady Stelnicka. You will do so?" He seemed almost apologetic. Anna was certain she had found a leverage with the *starosta* that would keep her safe, for a time.

"They will come for Tadeusz before his fifth birthday," Doliński said now. "You will have no choice but to let him go. Do not do anything foolish. Should a democratic monarchy be realized, one with Tadeusz as king, you and your family will only benefit."

Anna took in Doliński's words but avoided looking at him. Was it his way of asking forgiveness? Without speaking she pivoted away from him and walked out the door.

Climbing up into the sleigh that would take her home, she recalled someone saying once that Poles were known for dramatic exits. Amidst the feelings of repulsion that boiled up in her came a bitter little laugh for the exit she had just effected.

16

March 1801

Paweł had gone off to play cards with some of the other officers, so Jan retired early, luxuriating in the quiet. The letter had gone out earlier in the day. What would Anna think when she read that he would be coming home? Would she read it to the children? He was to leave in three days.

Jan was asleep when the door opened and a wintry gust blew in. The door stayed open a full minute it seemed. Lifting his head, he shouted, "Close the damn door!"

The door banged shut and the air became still. "Are you drunk, Paweł?" Jan looked toward the figure at the door. The room was shrouded in shadows, the only light fluttering from the stove, but he knew immediately it was not Paweł. Swift as quicksilver, he jumped to his feet. "Who is it?" he demanded, reaching for his saber. "Who the hell are you?" Jan had his saber unsheathed and was ready to advance.

But the intruder had moved near the stove. "Jan?"

Light flickered on the man's face, and Jan dropped his saber. "Oh, my God—a thousand pardons, sir!" Jan's midnight visitor had never been here before. Their exchanges had been limited to the field.

The man removed his hat. "May I light the lantern, Jan? I have something to talk to you about."

Jan's head was spinning. "Yes, of course, General Dąbrowski."

* * *

"Your father's coming home!" Anna announced at the evening meal.

Michał's eyes came alive. "Papa's coming home?" The nine-year-old got off his chair and came around to Anna. He put his head on her bosom. "Your prayers have been answered, Mama."

"Indeed they have!" she said, kissing him on his curly brown head. She sent him back to his seat. "And you, Tadek? Ah—of course you were too small when he left. Well, what do you think?"

"Papa?"

"Yes, Papa's coming home!"

Tadeusz gave a little shrug and a tentative smile.

"And Basia, you weren't even born yet!" Three-year-old Barbara Anna sat at attention in a chair, the seat of which had been raised so she could reach the table. She was pulling at a strand of her blond hair. She had Anna's green eyes, and as if even she sensed something important was happening, they were wide with wonder now.

"Will he be wearing his uniform?" Tadeusz asked.

"I don't know."

"Will he be going to war again?"

"No, I don't think so. Thank God."

"Don't you like war, Mama?"

"No, Tadek, I don't."

Later, with the children in bed, Anna sat alone in the reception room, deep in thought. Three years Jan had been away. Three years of doing and managing for herself and her family. Three years of living as if she were not married. But Jan was coming home now, and the peaceful family life they had known for such a brief time after their marriage would resume. When she went to bed, her mind was so full of thoughts, so full of Jan, that she could not sleep.

For long days Anna could think of nothing else but the return of her husband.

The time came at last. Jan arrived at the manor home on a Saturday in late March, drawing up reins on his small black stallion. Everyone rushed out onto the pillared portico to greet him. He wore the blue-and-crimson uniform of his Polish legion. Jan Michał ran to him, little Tadek trailing behind. He hugged them both, then moved toward the steps where Anna stood, Barbara at her side, clutching the folds of her mother's dress.

"Don't be afraid, Basia," Jan said, reaching down and scooping up his daughter. "You are a real beauty, you are!" He hugged her tightly for a few moments, then set her down. His eyes came up to fix on Anna's now. He removed his *czapka* from his head.

Anna's breath went out of her. Here was the man she had fallen in love with so long ago. Older now—thirty-five—but no less handsome with his long, blond hair, fine features, and dimpled chin. Anna noticed that his mustache was flecked with gray and that the cobalt blue eyes brimmed with moistness.

"Anna," he said, taking her into his arms.

Anna lay awake while Jan slept beside her. She felt like a married woman once again, and her heart was full. He lay there, his naked side touching her, the scent of him upon her. They had explored each other as if it had been the night of their first bedding down. But no vodka was needed this time to lift them to a dizzying height. Despite separation, their love, their desire, had not waned, but grown.

Yet the sight of his body had shocked her, the scars on his shoulder, his back, his arms. She found that he limped slightly, too. He had held the boys spellbound earlier with his tales of spies and sorties and engagement. Even in his understated way, it all sounded so full of heroism and glory and excitement. Only she was privy to the damage done to his body. Only she could appreciate now the fact that he still lived—and had come home.

War was not glorious—it was hideous.

In time, Anna slept. She didn't hear Jan rise, sometime before dawn.

Anna's heart went out to Michał, who sat at the table, eating little of the afternoon meal. He was despondent. Jan had gone out early that morning, taking little Tadeusz but leaving Michał behind.

Halfway through the meal, Tadeusz burst into the dining room from the kitchen. "We hunted! We hunted!" he shouted in his little voice.

Anna smiled. "Did you catch anything?"

Tadeusz held up two fingers. "Two wabbits—two! And a deer! A big one!"

Anna saw tears coming into Michał's eyes.

Jan came into the room now. "It *was* a big deer, wasn't it, Tadek?" He came around and kissed Anna on the cheek.

Jan sat and began to prepare plates for himself and Tadeusz.

"Michał would have enjoyed the adventure, Jan. He's been brooding all morning."

Jan looked to Michał. "I tried to wake you this morning, Michał. I did. But you didn't stir."

The boy's face went white as porcelain. "You didn't," he said.

"I did, but I thought maybe you were up too late and needed your sleep."

Jan Michał stood, tears ready to spill. "I would have gone!" he shouted. "I would have." He ran from the room.

Anna didn't know what to say. She wished Jan would go after him and at-tempt to console him, but he seemed busy preparing Tadeusz's food.

"Michałek is a very sensitive child, Jan," she said, using the boy's diminutive.

"Evidently." Jan pulled at a piece of sweet rye.

"He *is* a heavy sleeper, Jan. Sometimes I have to push him out of bed. Maybe tomorrow you can take him."

"Can't. I've got business in Sochaczew."

"Well, one day soon."

"Can't."

"Why?"

Jan stopped chewing and looked at Anna. "I have to go back."

The moment hung fire while Anna attempted to sort through his words. "Back? Not to Italy?"

Jan nodded.

Anna was shocked into silence. It was clear to her that he had not meant to tell her here at the dining table, but that did nothing to assuage the sudden pain and terrible hurt that came over her like a fever. Just as her son had done, she hurried from the room, lest her tears start to spill.

"I'm sorry, Anna," Jan said in the privacy of their bedchamber. The words were shopworn and weak, he knew. "I really am! I had every intention of coming home for good."

"And you should! Why are you defending French interests in Lombardy? Tell me!" Anna turned her back to him and began to undress.

"Because Dąbrowski asked me to. Personally."

"It seems to me you saved his life more than once. He owes *you*, Jan! Not the other way around."

"Anna, he's been assured by the First Consul that in time France will go against our enemies, and if we help, we'll have our nation back."

"When, Jan? When is this to unfold? How many more years of our lives are to be spent apart?"

"Not long, Anna. I'd like to have my estate back—and I want yours to be secure."

"Secure?" Anna pivoted to face him. "Is it not secure now?" She looked at him for a long moment.

Jan became momentarily unnerved. How had he managed to let slip the comment? Did she suspect something? "Well—yes, of course, but we are still behind the Prussian cordon."

"Oh—but I thought you had doubts about this Bonaparte fellow."

"I do, but as long as there's even a chance of evicting our enemies here—I have to take it."

"No matter what?"

Jan gave a hesitant nod. "No matter what."

A while later, he tried to make love to her, but—for the first time—it ended with neither of them satisfied. He lay awake, certain that she, too, remained sleepless. He thought of telling her what his business was in Sochaczew. How he had to set up the continuance of the monthly bribe to the scoundrel Doliński. Without that bribe each month, Jan and Anna's family would join the ranks of the myriad landless Polish nobility. Doliński was making his fortune on the backs of his own countrymen.

But Jan would not tell Anna. He would not have her live with that kind of insecurity. One day, he prayed, the Prussians would be driven out and Doliński exposed as a traitor. He longed for that day.

Two days after Jan's departure for Italy, a carriage arrived. The note the driver handed to Anna was from the *starosta*. The time had come.

Anna had one hour to pack a trunk for Tadeusz and send him off to Doliński, who was to send him on to a military boarding school in Warsaw. To disobey the Brotherhood would mean death for her entire family, he had said. Her own limited knowledge of the secret organization told her not to doubt the threat for a moment.

"But why is he to go?" Jan Michał demanded. "Why Tadek? I am the older. *I* should be going!"

"It's something I can't speak of. It's to be Tadek."

"Let me go, too. He's so young. He'll need me to watch out for him!"

Anna shook her head. "I need you here, Michałek. I do."

"You mean they only want *him!*"

Anna could not deny it. Her heart was torn in two. She knew Michał remembered well the night the physician tended only to Tadeusz. And there was the slight he received only a few days ago, when Jan took Tadeusz hunting. How hard *had* Jan tried to wake him? And now this. How could she explain it to a child? How to make it right?

* * *

The trunk was lashed to the top of the coach. Jacob lifted Tadeusz up into the interior bench. The boy was dressed in his best. His eyes—cobalt blue like Jan's—were wide but tearless.

"Ready?" the driver asked.

Anna kissed the inside tips of her fingers and reached up, placing them on her son's hand. She drew back from the carriage now.

"Be a good little man, now, Tadek," Jacob said. He shut the door, and the carriage began to negotiate the curve in front of the house, then make for the poplar-lined drive and the main road.

My husband and now my son! Anna retreated into the house. She found Jan Michał in the reception room. "It's you and me and Basia now, Michał," she said.

He looked up at her, his dark eyes intense with rage—and for a moment they were his father's eyes. The eyes of her cousin Walter. Her attacker. She tried to read his expression. "Michał, I know you're hurt. And you're angry."

"I want to be a soldier, too!"

Anna drew in a deep breath. "I need you here, Michał. I need you to be *my* soldier." She saw the tears welling up in his eyes. Rather than let her see them fall, he ran off to some other part of the house. Anna recalled how in her own life she had always done everything she could to keep from crying in public.

The boy was Walter's. There was no denying that. But he was hers, too.

17

June 1801

Anna was shown into the office of the headmaster at the cadet's academy of the *Szkoła Rycerska*, the military training school founded by King Stanisław. The man rose from his desk. He was obese and officious in manner. "Ah, Lady Stelnicka, you've been to see your son. Did you have a nice visit? Was everything to your expectations?"

"I notice that Tadeusz is the youngest boy here."

"Is he? I suppose that he is. But let me assure you he is adapting well."

"He cried to see me go."

"And that is as it should be, don't you think?"

"Captain Spinek, I have a request."

"Do you? If it's possible for me to grant it, rest assured, I will."

"Tadek has an older brother, Jan Michał. We call him Michał. I would like very much for you to take Michał into the academy."

His fleshy face indifferent, the man expelled a long sigh. "We are full, Lady Stelnicka. Filled to the rafters, as they say. It is an honor for one child out of a family to be chosen. A second one is *very* rare, indeed."

"Except for those with connections. Boys from magnate families?"

The captain shrugged. "Occasionally such is the case."

"It is Jan Michał's dream to come here."

"If we were to fulfill everyone's dream, Lady Stelnicka, we'd have an army of all officers and no infantry."

"I speak for one, Captain. I would feel better about having my youngest here if Michał is here to look after him."

"I understand, my lady. But there's really nothing I can do."

"And if I were to withdraw Tadeusz?"

The man's face darkened. "That is something I would not recommend."

Anna took in a deep breath, readying herself to play her highest card. While there was no one trait about the man that gave him away as being a member of the Brotherhood, she had become convinced that he was indeed a Freemason. "You know, Captain, I am well aware of the purpose that has brought my son here."

The man paled instantly. It was as Anna suspected. In his effort to make her beholden to him, Doliński had told her too much. Anna spared him from answering. "*Any* mother would investigate when her five-year-old son is conscripted, Captain."

"I see," Spinek said.

Anna wondered if by speaking out she had put Doliński into shark-infested waters. She hoped so. "I am not here to create a scene or place anyone in a bad light. After all, if dust were to be stirred up, who knows where it would settle?"

The man harrumphed. "Do I understand you correctly, Lady Stelnicka? Are you threatening—?"

"Oh, Captain Spinek, I'm the last person to engage in threats. I merely want to have my son—Tadek's brother—enrolled here. It's that simple."

The captain pulled his large frame to his feet, tipping over his chair behind him. He put on a false smile. "Very well, Lady Stelnicka. It will be done."

Anna left the castle-like structure, her head dizzy with victory, her pulse still racing. She had done it! Jan Michał would be so pleased to hear the news.

"Anna! Anna!" someone called.

Anna looked up to see a carriage drawing to a halt. Zofia was at the window. "Anna!" her cousin cried. "What are you doing in Warsaw?"

"I came to see Tadeusz."

"Your son is here? At the academy? My God, he's only—what? Six!"

"Not quite." Anna gave a tight smile. "Never too many soldiers, they say."

"So they say. Shame on you, Anna! You had no intention of stopping while you're here in the city? Well, now that I've caught you, you're coming home with me!"

"I need to return to Sochaczew soon."

"And so you will—but I won't take no for an answer. I really won't. We'll have supper together, just you and me."

Anna didn't have it in her to argue. "What about Iza?"

"Oh, Izabel usually eats earlier than I—with her governess. You know the house well enough. Come directly."

Upon arriving home, Zofia rushed to her bedchamber and stood before her full-length mirror. She gauged herself from a few paces away first, her dark eyes moving up and down over her figure. The silver-pink gown did her justice. Then she drew in very close to the glass, examining every shade and nuance of her face. Was there some new blemish, the beginning of just the tiniest new wrinkle?

Anna had looked so fresh and lovely, her green eyes sparkling in the sunlight. Zofia's cousin was only a year younger than she—twenty-seven now. And yet she looked as if she had not aged at all in the last five or six years! Could it be that, like a crab, Anna was going backward while Zofia advanced in time?

Am I showing my age? There were those little lines at her eyes. What could be done about those? A wide smile worsened them, so Zofia affected a more moderate smile before the mirror. *Better.* Zofia decided, all in all, she was holding up well. There were years left to be spent—like gold ducats, as she used to say.

She pinched her cheeks, drawing up the color, and went down to welcome Anna.

"So you came to visit Tadeusz and enroll your other son?" Zofia asked at table, raising a glass of wine in a toast. "Then you and Barbara will be all alone at Sochaczew."

"We'll hardly be that," Anna said, sipping at her wine.

"Oh, I know you have the Szrabers and your servants. What I meant was that of your family of five, there would be only you and your daughter."

Anna smiled weakly.

"I didn't mean to make you sad."

"I'm not sad. It's a temporary situation."

Conversation lagged for a while as the meal continued. Zofia talked of other things, but her mind kept returning to Anna's "temporary situation." It was over dessert that the conversation took a dramatic turn. "Anna!" Zofia blurted. "I have an idea."

When Anna looked up from her apple cake, Zofia cried, "Come live here!"

Anna set down her fork. The green eyes blinked in surprise. "Here? Zofia, I couldn't possibly."

"Of course you could. It would do you and your daughter good to be in the city. Barbara is only two years younger than Izabel. They're cousins! It's only right that they should get to know each other and become friends, too, just as you and I did." Some dark glint in Anna's eyes brought Zofia up short. "Oh, I know I didn't always *behave* like a friend, Anna. I'm sorry for that. I came between you and Jan." Zofia fixed her eyes on Anna's. "Can you find it in your heart to forgive me?"

"You saved my life, Zofia. How can I not?"

Zofia smiled. "All's well that ends well, yes?"

"Zofia, this is not your house. It's Paweł's and I would feel—"

Zofia interrupted. "It's as good as mine. Paweł wants what makes me happy. And I'd like for you to come and stay. Really!"

Anna shook her head.

Zofia noticed again a darkness in her eyes. "My life is not what it was when we lived in Praga, Anna, if that's what you're thinking. I am not nearly so reckless. The scandal-mongers will starve these days for any juicy tidbits about Zofia Grońska. Why, I shouldn't be surprised to find myself married by thirty!"

"To Paweł?"

"No. Paweł is very dear to me, the tried-and-true type, you know, but—well, I'm looking for someone to lift me off my feet. Your eyes are laughing at me. Oh, *will* you come live here, Anna? The whole second floor will be given over to you as a separate household. Let me make up for my past indiscretions. Let us become friends once again."

"We are friends, Zofia. But I can't. I'm sorry."

"Give me but one reason."

Anna paused for a moment. "Jan Michał has given his dog Borys over into Barbara's care. She wouldn't leave him behind."

"And she doesn't have to. A dog would liven things up around here. Izabel would love it! If that's the biggest of your concerns—"

"Big? The dog is *huge,* Zofia."

"So?"

"And there's Jan." Anna gave a valiant smile. "He'll be coming home soon."

"For good?"

The smile proved fugacious. "I hope so."

"You are too hopeful, I fear. He is not so different from Paweł. Do you know what Paweł told me?"

"What?"

"That he would put up his sword when Poland is Poland again. Can you imagine? This century will be ground to dust before that happens."

Anna stood now. She had gone white as a nun's bib. "Zofia, I appreciate your offer. It means much to me. Really. But I can't accept. I should be going now."

Zofia rose. "I'm sorry—I put you on the spot. Just do one thing for me, Anna. Just go home and think about it. There's so much life here in the city, so much more for Barbara to do and to learn. And you'll be a stone's throw from your boys should you wish to visit, or should they need you. Just tell me you'll think about it."

Anna sighed and gave a smile meant to mask her heartache.

Part Three

Two suns cannot shine
in one sphere.

—POLISH PROVERB

18

October 1805

Before the mirror, Anna adjusted the amber combs in her upswept auburn hair.

"Anna!" Zofia called from below. "The carriage is waiting! What's keeping you?"

"Coming!" Anna responded, frowning at her reflection, then smoothing the folds of her slate-blue gown. She pulled on a wrap and made for the stairs. Once inside the coach, she made her confession. "I wish you didn't insist I come to the Potocki party, Zofia."

"Oh, don't be silly."

"I'm not capable of being civil to the Prussian commandant. Prussia is no friend to Poland."

"One has to be pragmatic, darling. All right, then, you don't have to speak with General Kalkreuth. But it wouldn't hurt. You may need a favor sometime, and he's in charge of all of Warsaw."

"I don't care! You should have brought your friend Charlotte to this reception instead."

"Charlotte! My God, no! She's *French!* And she'd be sure to say the wrong thing and have us all arrested. She can be a rattlebrain at times."

Anna laughed, settling back for the drive to the fashionable Wilanów district, where Zofia's friend Countess Anusia Potocka lived out the winter months with her husband, Aleksandr, and his parents. Anna had deferred to come along because Zofia had treated her with great warmth and generosity since she and Barbara had come to live in Warsaw. That was four years ago, she realized with a start. Four years! And in that time she had seen Jan only once. Once! Twin emotions of longing and sadness—held at bay most of the time—began to stir at the thought.

Four years. Ten years of marriage in all. But so few days spent with Jan. Marriage was not what she had dreamed of, hoped and prayed for. A guest at her wedding had said that husband and wife are two windows, each letting light into a home, light that seemlessly blends, brightening and sanctifying the marriage. But for years now, there had been but one lone window. And every day the worry that Jan would be wounded or killed preyed upon her, the worry that a letter would arrive saying he would not be coming home at all.

She had received a letter from Jan a fortnight before. "Both Jan and Paweł are well and off on a new assignment," she had told Zofia, who received fewer letters from Paweł these days. "Once a soldier," Zofia clucked, "always a soldier," failing to inquire about the nature of the assignment. It had become her stock phrase, and its stinging effect on Anna never lost potency. Zofia seemed not to miss Paweł and did little commiserating with Anna on Jan's absence.

Nonetheless, coming to Warsaw had been the right thing to do. Here Anna was able to see her sons more frequently and provide a life for her daughter that was more varied and rich. Barbara and Izabel had become like sisters. If only it had been like that for her and Zofia years before—

"What are you thinking about, Anna?"

"Me? I was thinking I should thank you—for bringing me to Warsaw."

Zofia's eyes fixed on Anna's. "My judgments are not always so very wrong. Anusia is a Tyszkiewicz and grand-niece to the former king, as you know. Look! We're coming to their drive now. You should have seen her wedding, Ania! It was splendid. Did I tell you that a gypsy once predicted she would marry a Potocki? And who would have believed, she did! Now you are to enjoy yourself today."

"Thank God you're here at last, Zofia," Lady Anusia Potocka called as Zofia and Anna alighted the coach. "Hello, Anna! Come in, come in!"

The house was warm and alive with music, conversation, and delicious aromas. Anna had met the Countess Potocka on two or three occasions, but only now was introduced to her in-laws and her uncle, Prince Józef Poniatowski, nephew of the late king. She could see the resemblance—although the prince was much more masculine and handsome.

Twenty guests were scattered about the huge reception hall, talking in little clusters. General Henryk Kalkrueth sat ensconced in a cushioned high-back chair, speaking German in low tones with several other Prussian officials—sycophants—standing nearby. Anna thought he hardly seemed a military man. Were it not for a strong nose, his fleshy face and simple smile would remind one of an elderly aunt. Anna could not fathom why he and his companions had been invited. After all, Lady Anusia Potocka's father had supported the Constitution, and the whole household favored a *free* Poland.

Seated in a chair at the east end of the room—opposite to the Prussians—was a man in Russian uniform. He seemed to be staring at Anna. "Who is that, Zofia?"

Zofia, not always one to lower her voice, did so. "That's General Bennigsen—one of the five assassins who murdered Tsar Paul."

"Tsar Paul!" Anna blurted. The assassination of the Russian tsar—rumored to have been at the hands of officers bribed by British agents—had shocked the continent in 1801.

"Shush! You'll be heard."

He had looked away, affording Anna closer observation. He had glittering, deep-set eyes and a protruding chin. His gray hair was drawn and tied at the back of his head. He seemed genteel enough. "It was a British-instigated assassination, wasn't it?" Anna asked, holding her fan to her face.

"Yes, and he'll talk freely of it, too, if you bring it up. The tsar fought off the five with more valor than they expected. As for Bennigsen, he's quite proud of his part in the murder. Considers himself a modern Brutus. You know what they say," Zofia intoned, giving a flick of her hand, "the doorstep of the palace is slippery. Our own Stanisław also learned that little lesson."

Zofia's comment was said in passing, but the words came to haunt Anna every time she thought of the Brotherhood's scheme to make Tadeusz king.

The meal was delayed and delayed again. It soon became apparent that other guests were expected. "Who are we waiting for, Zofia?" Anna asked at last.

"Lord Adam Czartoryski."

"Oh?"

"And a surprise visitor."

"Who? Tell me!"

"You'll see." Zofia pulled one of her smug faces.

Anna didn't have to wait long. Within half an hour, a young, handsome man in a shimmering Russian uniform, tightly tailored, entered the Potocki home, followed by Prince Czartoryski and others. Everyone's obeisance to the Russian made it clear that he was no mere officer. He was Russia's Tsar Aleksandr!

Anna felt a heat come into her face. Zofia had played her a dirty trick. Her cousin had certainly known that Anna would not have attended had she known the Russian tsar was to be entertained. Despite the passage of years, her memories of Catherine and of Russians in Warsaw were still raw.

Anusia's father-in-law, Count Stanisław Potocki, introduced the tsar to his guests, eventually directing him to where Anna and Zofia stood. Anna attempted to wipe her face of any emotion as she curtsied before him. Zofia smiled, her eyelids sinking seductively. "I am honored to meet you, Your Highness."

Tsar Aleksandr's eyes widened slightly. He mumbled like a schoolboy and moved on.

At the earliest opportunity, Anna pulled Zofia aside. "Why didn't you tell me?"

"Because you wouldn't have come! Isn't that so?"

"Yes. But it should have been my decision to make. I'm leaving now!"

Zofia grasped Anna by the arm. "You can't, Anna!" she whispered. "Anusia has you seated at his table. It would be an insult."

"And what was it when Catherine sent her legions down on Praga massacring everyone—and I might add, burning *your* home to the ground? Did that not rise to the level of insult?"

"It was, Anna. I *agree*. But one must think about *today*."

"Just what's going on here, Zofia?" Anna disengaged herself from her cousin. "The Prussian commandant—and now the Russian emperor—under the same roof?"

Zofia smiled. "Aleksandr is rather good looking, don't you think?"

"Yes, in a doll-like sort of way. But what is he *doing* here?"

"It's as I told you earlier, cousin. Pragmatism is the best course. You see, while we have Polish legions fighting with the French against a coalition of our longtime enemies, Adam Czartoryski has worked his way in at the Russian court. Aleksandr is said to be about to give us our country back—but with himself as King of Poland."

Anna shrugged. "I've heard rumors to that effect. The thought does not thrill me. Now that hardly explains Kalkreuth's presence here."

"It's a precautionary measure on the part of the Prussians. They're not allowing Aleksandr to pass through the city unescorted because they're afraid the people would become too enthusiastic for the idea of him as king. They fear a coup. Kalkreuth and his detachment are here to see him *safely* through the Prussian cordon."

"Is that what some of the Russians are snickering about?"

Zofia nodded. "Of course, the Prussians don't think it's too funny, what with this little enterprise coming at the same time as Napoléon's threats from the west. But they need Aleksandr as an ally."

The late afternoon meal commenced. To her amazement, Anna was seated next to the tsar. He seemed irritated that too much room was left on either side of his place at the table, so he moved his armchair a pace to the right—next to Anna's chair.

"I have no communicable diseases, my dear," he said, "and I don't bite."

Anna feigned a smile. It was enough to make her heart race with an ambivalent mixture of emotions. She held in her bosom deep bitterness for Russia's past treatment of Poland—and yet fought off a sense of awe at sitting next to the tsar of all the Russias. His handsomeness and offhand attitude were disarming. In fact, he seemed rather ordinary in speech and manner, with no sense of hubris about him. One could easily forget that he was an emperor. And he talked like a magpie—in stentorian tones because he himself had poor hearing.

Most of the talk was in French, a language Anna had learned as a child and one widely used by the nobility across Europe. How odd it was that Poles, Prussians, and Russians sat at table, and their language in common was the same as that of a little French general who was moving—even at that moment—toward Poland and the East.

"Have you been to Russia?" the emperor asked, turning to Anna.

"I have not," Anna said. "However, my husband's estate was not so very far west of your borders, near Halicz. But it fell behind the Austrian cordon when Poland was carved up. The same fate befell my cousin's estate."

Anna saw Zofia—who sat directly across the table—wince at the boldness of the comment, but Aleksandr seemed not to take in the meaning, or chose not to.

"Have you no wish to travel the steppes?" the tsar asked.

"Should I?"

As the tsar rambled on in a litany of Russia's strengths and sights, Anna glanced down the table and realized that General Bennigsen's hooded eyes were fastened on her, a slight smile playing on his lips. She turned back to the tsar.

He made no mention of the plight of the Russian peasant, and Anna thought she might play devil's advocate by bringing up the Polish proverb that people behaved "in Russia as one must, in Poland as one will." But then she realized that Zofia was still closely following her little tête-à-tête with the tsar. Almost as if her cousin could read her mind, Zofia tossed her a glance that cautioned her to be more affable.

The truth was, Anna could scarcely believe her own nerve. She could not help but wonder, though, if it *was* possible for Aleksandr to intercede with Austria in behalf of the lost estates. She remembered that before the meal, Anusia's mother-in-law had joked about asking the tsar outright for all of Poland back, then noting in a whisper that one didn't ask for something a monarch had not already deigned to grant before the asking.

The tsar finally wearied of reciting Russia's virtues without inciting more than a raised eyebrow from Anna. He fell silent and used his fork to put his mouth to better use. Soon another topic at the table took his attention.

During the course of the evening–to every patriot's disappointment–Aleksandr only alluded in the vaguest way to his purpose regarding Poland. But in the reception room, the after-supper wines and cordials prompted his bolder and flirtatious generals to ask the women what trifles they might wish from Paris, so presumptuous were they that their victories would one day soon take them to the core of Napoléon's power.

"Now, aren't you glad you came?" Zofia asked on the return trip to the capital's center. "Remember, you're the one who has always loved politics."

Anna had been listening passively to the clattering of the wheels on the cobblestones. "I only wish to know those politics that pertain to my country."

"Anna, I do appreciate your bringing up my estate at Halicz. What nerve–sometimes you surprise me."

Anna shrugged. "Do you think it will come to pass–that Aleksandr will declare himself King of Poland?"

Zofia gave her characteristic flick of her wrist. "Not if Napoléon finds his way into Warsaw first. He undoubtedly has similar intentions."

"Ah–so we will be a prize fish over which they'll contend–the East and the West." Anna spoke with a sharp edge. "Why can't monarchs be content with what they have? Why must they always meddle with Poland?"

"It's their way, I suspect."

"What did you think of Aleksandr?" Anna asked.

Zofia smiled, then winced. "He's nice-enough looking, but a bit too–too elegant–for my taste. And fidgety rather than frisky, if you know what I mean. I like a leader to be, well, more in command. He was kind enough to you, though."

"Those who seem always kind may not be kind always."

Zofia laughed. "Too true! Now, Napoléon Bonaparte–there's an emperor I want to meet."

"Why is that?" Anna asked. "What intrigues you about him–his new title?"

Zofia shook her head. "His power, cousin," she pronounced in a languishing drawl. "His power."

Late into the night, Anna sat in a chair before a window that looked out on Piwna Street. For the second time that night, she took stock of the Warsaw years. At the time Zofia's invitation to come live in Warsaw had been extended, Anna had inwardly laughed. The idea of once again living with her cousin seemed ludicrous. They were too much at odds.

But her mind had changed in a moment that very day as her carriage came into Sochaczew on the return trip to her estate. They were stopped by Prussian guards, and Anna found herself once again in Lord Doliński's clock-filled office.

While he made no overt move toward her, something had changed in his demeanor. She sensed something had shifted in the balance of power, and she was learning to trust impulses of this kind. Did he doubt Jan would ever return? Did he no longer care if the Brotherhood got wind of any action taken against the mother of a possible candidate for the monarchy? Whatever it was, she drew in the scent of imminent danger, especially when he hinted he might send a carriage for her, as before.

It was in that room and at that moment that she made her decision to leave Sochaczew. The next day was spent in preparation. In the dead of night, she hurried Barbara and Katarzyna into the carriage where the sheepdog, placed there by Jacob, happily waited, tongue slobbering over each one entering.

Anna made certain that the driver knew what country roads to take to avoid the main district of Sochaczew. Emma offered to come along, maintaining her position as Barbara's governess, but Anna would not hear of separating her from her husband, who had the estate to manage. At the last moment, Lutisha came puffing out of the house with a pitiful valise. "You'll not leave me behind, Lady Anna. Please allow me. I'm old now, but not without value. And I would die sooner in an empty house." She was in her seventies now, her frame less corpulent and a bit bent, and although she moved slower, she seldom stopped moving. Anna nodded and motioned her forward, tears filling her eyes. She was family. Soon there were tears all around as the good-byes were made, no one forecasting that four years would pass—and still no end in sight.

19

General Dąbrowski's promise to Jan that the peace of Lunéville would not last and that the French would move against Austria and other coalition members took good time to play out. Napoléon Bonaparte had been too busy in Paris bullying the French senate into declaring him Emperor of France. Even the pope was present at the ceremony the previous year to give his benediction. Jan wondered what Machiavellian undercurrents made *that* possible. The French people acquiesced but were less enthusiastic about a revived monarchy than was the growing army that regarded the Corsican an idol.

Then came the new emperor's preoccupation with a planned invasion of Britain, an attempt that dragged on for two years. When a series of misadventures ended disastrously as the French–Spanish armada met with the English at Trafalgar, Napoléon's dream vision of the tricolor flying in London dissolved like a sugar cube in hot English tea. So as he turned his attention to the continent, the legionnaires took heart that Poland—too long the wallflower—would be given the attention she deserved. Her old enemies, the Austrians and Russians, were now aligned with the English against the French upstart while Prussia claimed neutrality.

Jan and Paweł caught their first glimpse of the emperor when he arrived in Lombardy and had himself crowned Emperor of Italy in a ceremony of great pomp.

"So much for a new order," Jan said at its conclusion.

Paweł chuckled. "The mapmakers will have their work cut out for them. Boundaries are going to be shifting time and again, like wiggling snakes on a hot stove."

Jan didn't laugh. It was said the emperor had a kingdom planned for each of his many brothers. He bristled at the thought. Poland would not suffer such degradation, he told himself. *Not Poland.* And then came the bitter thought that to the rest of the world Poland did not exist.

Leaving the legionnaires behind, the French moved on Austria, quickly taking Vienna. While the neutral Prussians dithered about joining the enemy coalition, Napoléon—with his growing Grande Armée of 350,000—met the Austrian–Russian forces at Austerlitz, a hamlet east of Brunn in Bohemia. Like every other Polish legionnaire in Lombardy, Jan and Paweł were held spellbound by the story of Napoléon's military prowess that sent the Austrian and Russian monarchs in full retreat. Removing his forces to Poland with great dexterity, Aleksandr even sent the French emperor a letter of congratulations. Jan recalled Anna's letter of months before detailing the Potocki party and the arrogant presumption of Aleksandr's generals in promising Parisian tokens to the Polish women. He chuckled to himself, wondering if they dared even stop there on their return route—or rout—tails between their legs.

"The little Corsican is lucky," he would tell Paweł, more out of mischief than conviction. "It's mere luck!"

"His brilliance is in his choice of generals," Paweł would say. "They're *young!* Their commissions are based on merit, Jan, *merit*. They're not the doddering old fools his enemies have for generals, men who have by chance or cowardice stayed alive—or the pink-faced young noblemen still wet behind their ears." And he would continue in that vein until Jan raised his hand in surrender.

The map of Europe did change. Jan had to admit Paweł had been right about that. After Austerlitz, the emperor destroyed the Holy Roman Empire by fusing a number of central states and principalities into what he called the Confederation of the Rhine, with its seat at Frankfurt. Jan took comfort that Poland's longtime enemies—Prussia, Austria, and Russia—would never come to terms with France while its vassal state—the Confederation—sat like a watchdog among them. And as long as Poland was tied to France, there *was* a chance for the phoenix to fly.

Prussia did take to the field and for a time fought alone but was outfoxed by Napoléon at every turn. The French occupied Berlin and went on to claim great victories at the twin battles of Jena and Auerstädt. The occupation of three-fourths of Prussia and decimation of her army did not bring full surrender, however. Queen Louise insisted the fight would go on and—with a band of partisans—took to the east to join Aleksandr.

Rumor had it that the French people wanted Napoléon to fall back, that a continuing war, its cost and casualties, was quite unpopular in France. Instead, he followed his own drumming pulse and continued east. Anxious for allies, he set his sights on Poland.

The news buoyed Jan and Paweł. They sensed their days of defending a foreign kingdom—mostly inactive now—were numbered. Poland was coming into the equation.

They were right. Early in November, Dąbrowski entered their quarters with the news. Jan and Paweł were to accompany him to Poznań to prepare for the entry of Napoléon Bonaparte into the city.

Anna stood at the window of her bedchamber's anteroom, the room that served as her reception room since Paweł's second floor was given over to her and Barbara. She was watching for the crowd to disperse from Saint Martin's early morning Mass.

The city was profoundly quiet. Only days before it had teemed with the reverberation of marching boots upon the cobblestones as the Russians retreated from Napoléon, allowing a brief respite for Warsaw's citizens. Anna wished she could see what had become of Aleksandr's strutting sycophants—surely those who had survived moved back toward the steppes with less swagger than they had demonstrated on their way west.

Her eyes darted from person to person as the faithful below bundled themselves up and made their sorties into the cold winter wind. It was but a Tuesday, and yet Barbara had insisted on attending Mass. What a little saint she was becoming at the tender age of nine! She had taken the sacraments of Holy Communion and Confirmation so very seriously and now took advantage of their close proximity to the church by attending Mass almost daily. The present for her recent name day that she liked the most was a little pamphlet on her feast day saint. And she was already looking forward to her twelfth birthday, when she would attend convent school.

Anna smiled to herself, recalling how Jan's faith was in a God found in nature. Would he be surprised by a daughter so devoted to church and ceremony?

Anna caught sight of Basia now, descending the stairs, the purple wool greatcoat well fastened. The wind pulled back the white veil from her head, whipping the blond hair into a motion that from a distance made it look like a glowing halo.

Ignoring the errant veil, Barbara leaned into the wind and began navigating the few hundred paces to the house. She moved along on the opposite side of the street and drew very near to where she would cross over. Anna was just about to go downstairs to open the door when she saw a man step out of an entryway and detain her daughter. *As if he had been waiting for her.*

Barbara looked surprised at first, but then she smiled at something he said. The man pointed across to the house and asked her something. Barbara nodded. Another question. This time she shook her head. He continued to talk to her.

Anna drew as close to the window as possible and wiped at the frost, an alarm ringing in her head all the while. She stared, a sickness rising within her. Much of the man was covered by his hat and coat, but the nose and mustache—and something about his manner—revealed his identity. Her hand went to her heart. *Good God! Doliński!*

Anna turned and made for the stairs. One hand grasping the folds of her skirt, the other the banister, she fairly flew down the long flight. Rushing to the door, she pulled it open, certain that her worst fear would be realized—that her daughter would have vanished.

"Mother!" Barbara stood in the doorway, momentarily stunned by Anna's breathless intensity.

Anna looked from her daughter to the vacant entryway across the street—and back again.

"What is it, Mother?"

Anna reached out to her daughter's arm, drew her into the house, cast another glance across the street, and closed the door.

Anna found herself going to the window several times during the course of the day to assure herself Doliński was no longer there. In the evening she was still very much unnerved. Since coming to Warsaw, she had put the man out of her thoughts, as if he didn't exist. But now he had brought himself into her life again. Barbara had confirmed that the man did indeed have a gravel-like voice. Why was he stalking her family? *Why?*

Was it in connection to Tadeusz? Anna had never given any real credence to the notion that her son might actually take the throne of Poland, even if it were restored. It was just that—a notion—and far out of her family's star. In truth, she did not wish for it to happen. In her short life, she had seen too many tragedies befall monarchs. It made quite a list, she thought now: Louis and Marie Antoinette; Catherine's husband, Peter, and her son Paul; and, of course, Stanisław. *The doorstep of the palace is slippery.*

If only her family could be reunited—that would be enough for her.

The Brotherhood was educating her child with an eye to his becoming king. She had obeyed Doliński and kept the secret, even from Jan—not only because of his threats, but also because she never believed such a thing could happen. That morning Doliński had asked Barbara her name, where she lived, and with whom. He had complimented her on her hair and eyes, too. The thought that he was attracted to her chilled Anna to the marrow.

"He was a very nice gentleman," Barbara had said, curious over Anna's concern.

"He's *not* a nice gentleman, Barbara Anna!" Anna's hands grasped hold of Barbara's upper arms and shook her. "He's *not*, do you hear? And you are not to talk to him—or any stranger again. If there is no one to go to Mass with you, then you're not to go. Is that understood?"

"Yes," Barbara said, her green eyes round with wonder.

After Barbara left, Anna was drawn to the window. What did it all mean? She worried, staring down into the street, cursing her husband's absence.

Jan was not surprised by the friendliness of the crowd as the Polish forces under Dąbrowski entered Poznań, one of Poland's great cities. Those who turned out seemed as like-minded as he in hoping Poland would be raised. French squadrons had arrived two days before, and preparations were well under way for the arrival of the emperor.

The Polish forces were billeted in the inns, homes, and outbuildings of a single neighborhood. Jan and Paweł found themselves toasting each other in a particularly nice inn, where they had been allotted commodious lodging.

Paweł looked about the vaulted dining hall. "Ten to one, when the city really starts filling up, our rooms go to some brass."

Jan lifted his glass of vodka. "Let's toast it while we can, then!"

"You're right," Paweł said, lifting his glass. "In war, you live for the moment. As if each day is your last. To life!"

"*Sto lat!*"

Paweł laughed. "*Lucky* the soldier who *does* live to be one hundred." They drank down the mediocre vodka, and Paweł called the girl over to refill their glasses.

A few days later, they rode a good distance out of the city. Coming to a bluff, they sighted the arrival of the French infantry. It hardly looked like an army at all. To avoid the thick mud of the roads, the men held to no formation but crossed the fields haphazardly as they searched out dry paths, their muskets held in no particular way, their greatcoats of every imaginable color painting the landscape like a crazy quilt.

As they came within sight of Poznań, however, their drums commenced, and the scene was transformed. Within moments, coats were removed to reveal uniforms, and the men fell into formation, muskets in proper position, and the bicornes on their heads perfectly straightened. Jan and Paweł marveled at the sight. The two rode back to the city in time to see the infantry's arrival in the Market Square. These men who had been trudging the roads for days stacked their weapons and began cleaning the mud from their shoes. Camaraderie was loud, friendly, and full of fun.

"It's as if they've just marched in a parade," Jan said, staring.

Paweł shook his head. "Good God, what spirit, down to a man!"

"I won't be too quick to trade in my horse for an extra pair of boots, but I can see now why it is the infantry that wins the battles. The cavalry works the infantry to their advantage and often claims the credit, but here's a sight that reminds one where the glory truly belongs."

When Emperor Napoléon Bonaparte himself crossed the old Polish western borders, General Dąbrowski and his legionnaires went out to greet him. Napoléon assigned the legionnaires to ride both before and after the carriage, a clear indication of his faith in Dąbrowski. The general, sitting straight in his saddle, rode parallel to the carriage, and when the mud made the going painfully slow, he and Napoléon would converse through the carriage window.

The nighttime arrival into Poznań precluded a grand entry. The emperor's entourage was billeted at a Jesuit mission, where the legionnaires stayed, as well, four to a room. For three days, the emperor employed a contingent of the Polish legionnaires—including Jan and Paweł—to ride with him on exploratory missions. In the evenings, the two friends returned to their more capacious and comfortable rooms at the inn.

"It's as if he's sight-seeing," Paweł said on the third day, as they waited in a courtyard while the emperor was made welcome at a palace in Kondrzew.

"He *is* one who enjoys getting the lay of the land, as they say," Jan replied. "Gives everything—every field, every windmill—a damn good look. But did you notice he almost never looks you in the eye? Did you think that odd?"

"I did. Doesn't look at you, and yet he's so full of questions—like a newspaperman! Wants to know your lineage, place of birth, schooling, ambitions, attitudes of the peasants and gentry. By God, a talk with him is exhausting."

"Exactly." Jan looked toward the little palace. "And now, he must have the poor Lady Treskowa cornered in her own home."

"Well," Paweł joked, "you did say 'lay of the land.'"

Jan chuckled. "It could be he is inventorying Poland's treasures. He's reputed to have an incredible memory."

"If you mean to say Lady Treskowa might herself be a jewel of some sort, I caught a good look, and as far as I'm concerned, he can cart her off any time."

"Ha, ha! Where's your sense of chivalry?" Jan intoned in mock seriousness. "No, the lady in question is Poland herself. Her lands and castles."

"Pessimist!"

A ball was held that night in the emperor's honor. The hall was so choked with festive souls, one could hardly imagine that war was being carried on elsewhere. Gaggles of women had shown up in their finest to have a look at the famous conqueror—and no doubt to be looked at. Jan watched with some interest as the emperor moved among the clusters, smiling, nodding, and talking. Sometimes, when Napoléon found an especially pretty woman, he lingered awhile, unleashing his litany of questions. He wore two or three women out in that manner. One swooned and fainted dead away. The emperor retired about midnight, allowing his Polish honor guard to end the night, as well.

On the fourth day, General Dąbrowski summoned Jan and Paweł to his makeshift office in a nearby home. "What do you suppose it's about?" Paweł asked.

"I suspect we're to give up our rooms. The other legions from Italy have been streaming into Poznań all day, as you know. We've got rooms good enough for generals, and I can tick off the names of four or five old Polish warhorses arriving today."

"Maybe it's just new orders."

"That won't happen until the general parley with the emperor."

Ten minutes later, General Henryk Dąbrowski stood and moved around the desk to greet Jan and Paweł. "May I commend you both on your service to the emperor? It's because of your prowess the other day that the man didn't lose his horse and himself in the mud."

"The man—" Jan paused, correcting himself. "Rather, the emperor—has his share of derring-do, General. It's a wonder we didn't lose one or two of *us* out there."

"Indeed, indeed!" The general harrumphed. "Now, to the matter at hand. . . . I have to first admit that this course of action was suggested to me by the emperor himself, but please don't think that I haven't harbored the idea myself for some time."

What seemed a long moment passed. General Dąbrowski cleared his throat. "You have both been excellent *chefs d'escadron*."

"Thank you, sir," came the tandem reply.

"It is my intention to appoint the two of you majors tomorrow."

Jan felt himself flushing with pride as he and Paweł mumbled their appropriate and formal expressions of gratitude.

Outside the house, Jan and Paweł congratulated one another. Their enthusiasm lost its vigor, though, as they walked back to their rooms in silence.

Each knew that the new commission meant they would be placed in separate squadrons, for there was but one major per squadron. They would no longer ride spur by spur, fight side by side. And their squadrons might be attached to different legions and sent to different locations.

"A toast?" Jan asked as they entered the inn.

"No thanks," Paweł said.

Jan put his arm around Paweł's shoulders. "Just one. A bittersweet one."

Paweł's smile was just that: bittersweet.

Two days later, Napoléon's favorite, Prince Murat, came from Warsaw, declaring that city taken. Napoléon wasted no time in making preparations to depart for the former capital of the Commonwealth. Jan heard him tell Dąbrowski that this time his arrival would not be by night and that he looked forward to an enthusiastic welcome. On the day of Napoléon's departure, the legionnaires gave his retinue a good hour's safe conduct on the Warsaw Road, then returned to Poznań to ponder what orders might come.

20

December 1806

Anna walked downstairs and found Zofia preparing to go out. "I've had a letter from Jan," she said. "Both he and Paweł are in good health."

"Of course they are. You worry too much, Anna." Zofia pulled on her wrap and made for the door.

"He says Napoléon is likely to come to Warsaw."

"I've heard that."

"There's more," Anna blurted.

Zofia turned around.

"They've both been promoted to major."

"Oh. Good for them! I suppose they're thrilled to the top of their *czapki.* Ah—but I see you're not, are you?"

Anna shook her head.

"You think Jan may be making a career of soldiering?"

Anna's answer caught in her throat.

Zofia's eyes narrowed. "How many years has it been, darling? You *know* that's what he's doing. That's what they're both doing. The army has them, and they'll grow old in it."

Anna looked at Zofia and tried to hold her tears in check.

Zofia went to her and put her arms around her. "There, there, where's your old patriot spirit, Anna? You're the one who held illegal meetings in *my* house, putting us all at risk, are you not? The minx who minced her way into the Royal Castle, impersonating me in order to gain entrance?"

Anna wondered if her cousin wasn't mocking her. Still, there was truth in what she said, so she chose to laugh. "I was quite the actress, I admit."

Zofia released Anna. "Maybe I'm wrong, dearest. Let us hope the emperor puts everything to right and both Jan and Paweł can come home. Well, I must fly." She kissed Anna on either cheek and made her exit.

Climbing the staircase, Anna went to her little reception room and reread the letter. Was Jan to grow old in the army?

Barbara came into the room and sidled up to her mother. "Is that from Papa?"

"Yes, dear."

"What does he say?"

"He says he loves you."

"What else?"

"He's been made a major."

"Is that good?"

"Yes, Basia, it is good. It's a promotion. Now run and get ready for supper. Lutisha's making your favorite."

"Plum pierogi?"

"Yes, plum pierogi."

After Barbara left, Anna fell into a reverie. She found herself staring at her treasured crystal dove where it sat on a table near the window, wings extended and enlivened by a nearby candle. Zofia had reminded her of the days before Warsaw fell to the Russians in 1794 when Anna held meetings at the Groński town house for her patriot friends. Now that the bonds of Prussia were loosened, she could do the same, she thought, and her spirits were immediately lifted. But then, as she went over in her mind the list of those people, she realized most had taken up with the legionnaires or moved away, breaking contact. Or had died. No, it was not a group that could be reconstituted.

While she had received much of the political news of the day through those friends back then, she was not without a source of information in the present. The Countess Potocka had taken a liking to Anna and extended invitations to her, whether or not Zofia was to be included. And the Potocki household seemed to be a little headquarters where policy was discussed and leaders entertained. Anna would often read in the *Monitor* something she had learned at the Potockis' a week earlier.

Anna's eyes fell on the paragraph in Jan's letter detailing Prince Joachim Murat's arrival in Poznań and the prince's news that the Prussians had been put out of Warsaw.

Anna smiled to herself. Warsaw was free, indeed. In fact, Murat, Grand Duke of Berg, had been the houseguest of the Potockis prior to his departure for Poznań.

In an attempt to put aside her emotional reaction to Jan's letter, Anna went to her desk now, took a sheet of paper, and put quill to a letter to Jan. After the congratulatory paragraph regarding his appointment, she described just how peacefully the Prussians had left. With the French bearing down, General Kalkreuth, Warsaw's commandant, picked up and moved out, bags, baggage, and every musket in the city. He left to the sounds of women and boys making catcalls from windows, taking his men across the Vistula and joining forces with the Russians. The French, led by Murat, arrived on 21 November, and the city erupted in celebration. Tables laden with food and drink were set up in the streets, and a carnival atmosphere prevailed. Citizens fought one another for the right to billet the infantry, even though most of the Polish citizenry didn't speak French—and the soldiers certainly didn't know Polish! Shunning the Hotel Raczynski, Murat took up lodging at the Potockis'. It was there that Anna met the prince, brother-in-law to the emperor and general in his army.

Anna had been less than impressed. Oh, he was young—twenty-two on the outside—forthright, elegant in accent and manner. However, he talked like a parrot, but unlike a parrot, did little listening. His lectures on war could easily exceed an hour, tedious stuff in mixed company. Lady Potocka said later how he seemed to be playing the part of a king, for he was constantly alluding to the legendary King Sobieski. Anna wondered if he didn't imagine himself Poland's king. Did he see his own future in Poland? Perhaps it was not out of the question—after all, he was said to be a favorite of Napoléon, who seemed to be finding or making kingdoms for his newly royal brothers.

Anna asked Jan his opinion on the Murat question and closed off her letter, choosing not to end with more personal commentary, not to write of her fears.

"Well?" Zofia demanded even before Charlotte could take her seat in the reception room.

Charlotte's blue eyes, appearing smaller than they were because of the weight a predilection for sweets had inflicted, sparkled with teasing delight. "Oh, I've talked to quite a few fellow French wayfarers—those in the know," she said. "I'm a veritable cornucopia of information on Napoléon's love life."

"I knew I kept you around for something." Zofia laughed. "Here, take your tea."

"*Merci*—biscuits, too—how delightful!" Charlotte began to prepare her tea, mixing in two teaspoons of sugar. "Well, he was engaged when he met Joséphine—to some chit a decade younger than himself. He all but jilted her for Joséphine—and after compromising the chit, I might add."

Zofia's mouth fell slack. "And then to marry someone a decade older than he!"

"Well, not quite—but six years, at least. What was the man thinking?"

"Maybe he thought her exotic. She's Creole, isn't she?"

Charlotte nodded. "From Martinique. But exotic? The bloom was off the rose, you can be sure. They say even then Joséphine's teeth had blackened so that she learned to smile without showing them. She'd been married before and has two children—grown now—to remind her."

"Divorced?"

Charlotte chuckled, wiping away the crumbs of a biscuit from her rouged lips. "You might say so! By the big knife. Her husband went to the scaffold during the Terror. Just five days before Robespierre's downfall. Fate, I guess. She was in prison and would have had the headache cure, too, but ten days after the coup, she was freed."

"Fate again."

"It's rumored she was quite active in the prison—Les Carmes—if you know what I mean. Seems the place was a den of iniquity where the aristocrats shamelessly cavorted as a way of denying their fate and showing their disregard for the new regime."

Zofia shrugged. "Understandable, I suppose."

"Well, after her release, she stalked Napoléon, they say. She wanted someone powerful and wealthy. He was coming into power, but wasn't wealthy. In fact, he thought *she* was a woman of property in Martinique. Ha! No such thing!" Charlotte fell into a fit of the giggles now. "It seems that on their wedding night, Joséphine had her pet dog in their marriage bed, and it bit the little man! Mind you, the dog's name was Fortune."

Zofia exploded into laughter, too. "How apropos! Good heavens, Char, I didn't expect this kind of detective work. You're quite amazing."

"Oh, there's more. After the wedding, Joséphine complained to friends about Napoléon's performance—said if it were a play, it would be only a one-act!"

Zofia's eyes narrowed. "Now you're embroidering."

"I'm not, I swear!"

"Is their marriage as bad as all that?"

"Worse, if you can believe it. Neither has been faithful from the beginning. Joséphine's carnal appetite is voracious, and what with the many and long separations, she has had ample opportunity to indulge it. And Napoléon seeks out women wherever he goes . . . or vice versa. On his Egyptian campaign, he took the wife of one of his lieutenants as mistress. Broke up their marriage, he did, and led this woman—Pauline—about Cairo as if she were Cleopatra to his Caesar."

"How old was *she?*"

"Only twenty."

"Ah, a change from Joséphine. Did it last?"

"Only as long as the Egyptian campaign. When it was done, he dropped her as if she had the cholera. In fact, he has a reputation for cruelty to women—in word and deed. Then there was this Italian opera singer he carted back to Paris and set up in a house. That ended when she met a young musician and tried to balance two lovers. Napoléon ejected them both from the city. And so it goes—wherever he travels. Oh, he writes to Joséphine regularly and has spies report back to him on her indiscretions."

"While he pursues his own indiscretions."

"*Précisément!* But the marriage somehow endures."

"And now he hopes to find something out about the essence of Polish women?"

Charlotte was about to respond when she caught Zofia's meaningful stare and realized a response was unnecessary. She laughed instead and reached for the last biscuit.

Barbara and Izabel sat on a couch across from Anna, their eyes alive with excitement. They could scarcely contain themselves. Outside, despite a continuing rain something short of a deluge, the streets of Warsaw swarmed with people and buzzed with noise and activity. Fireworks were being prepared, triumphal arches created, and not a door or post in the vicinity went without a wreath. Vendors were already setting up, and street entertainers were laying claim to spaces in the square and its adjoining avenues.

"Now you two must be serious for the moment," Anna said, her eyes fixing on her daughter's green irises, then on Iza's eyes of sky blue. She glanced back at her daughter in time to see her rolling those eyes in impatience. "I'm serious, Basia—and you must be, too!"

"Oh, Mama, if this is another caution—"

"It is, indeed. And you're going to listen! Tomorrow is going to be wild with celebration. This street will probably be impassable, and half the citizens will be drunk. Do you understand?" Both girls nodded. "I'll not deny you your fun or the chance to see the French emperor arrive, but I don't want one of you to part from the other for a single moment. Not one! And you are both to be accompanied by one of the servants."

"If it's about that man, Mama—"

"It's not just about him, but if you do come across him, you're to come home immediately. It's about any number of people who might do you harm on a day like tomorrow."

Barbara jumped up and kissed Anna on the cheek. "Don't worry, Mama. We'll be careful." She effected an escape then, calling Izabel. "Come, Iza, help me select something to wear, should I catch the *emperor's* eye."

"A big chance that," Iza called back, and stood.

Anna reached out and took Izabela's hand. "You're the elder, Iza. Please don't let Basia out of your sight."

"I won't, Aunt Anna. I promise." Iza leaned over and kissed Anna lightly.

Anna knew that she meant it. How strange, Anna thought, once she was alone. Zofia's daughter was sensible and serene, so unlike Zofia, while Anna's own daughter had just a touch of Zofia's unpredictable and wild nature.

Anna's caution for the celebration proved unnecessary, though, for on 19 December 1806, Emperor Napoléon Bonaparte arrived in Warsaw at four in the morning on a sad specimen of a horse he had gotten at a posting house. His retinue's carriages had been left behind, mired in the mud-filled roads. For the arrival of the French messiah, the city slept—even the sentinel snoozed at his booth and had to be shaken awake by the emperor himself.

Had the weather been better in the morning, the street festivities would have gone on anyway, but once it got about that Napoléon had already slipped into town and was slumbering nicely at the Royal Castle, few people braved the December rain and winds.

Barbara and Izabel were crushed with disappointment.

Two days later, Anna arrived at the Potockis' in Wilanów at seven in the evening. Lady Anusia Potocka had sent an invitation earlier in the day, and certain she would hear firsthand impressions of the emperor, Anna was most eager to go.

Anusia's father-in-law had been one of the Polish nobles delegated to meet with Napoléon that very evening at the Royal Castle, so he was absent from supper.

After the meal, some of the guests played cards while others conversed quietly. Still, the activities could not dispel a keen sense of anticipation for the count's arrival.

It was fully ten o'clock, and Anna was thinking of going home when Count Stanisław Potocki returned at last from the meeting with the French emperor. He sat down in the reception room, seemingly drained and tired, while everyone drew up chairs as if he were a patriarch about to read a fable to his grandchildren. That he did not seem jubilant concerned Anna. He took a sip of wine to refresh himself before beginning. Then he looked at the anxious eyes all about.

"Tell us," his daughter pleaded, "what of Poland? What did he say?"

"Of Poland, Anusia?" He sighed. "Precious little. First, he talked of his deeds in Prussia. Went on for some time, pacing before us with his hands in his pockets and his chest puffed out like a parrot's. When he paused long enough to take a drink, we made our presentation. I spoke, as did the Prince Poniatowski, on behalf of the reconstitution of our nation."

"And?" the count's wife asked.

"The emperor did say that France had never recognized the partitions of Poland. This, of course, did our hearts good. He went on to say—between pinches of snuff—that independence brought with it sacrifice of every kind, of life and limb. He called for unity among all Poles. He called for provisions for his army, money for its maintenance, and men to form it."

"And in return?" Anna spoke up now, giving voice to what she thought was everyone's question.

Stanisław looked at Anna. His smile belied his message. "Napoléon made no promises, Anna. No promises."

No one said a word for the longest moment. The count shrugged. "That didn't keep the bulk of our delegation from a heady enthusiasm. They assured the emperor of complete unity and the silver plate from their tables if he asked for it."

"And he was satisfied?" someone asked.

"Oh, I think he was. Yes, indeed. But catching just a glance from Poniatowski, I realized there were at least two of us in the room who were not. There was nothing from the emperor's lips to even suggest a commitment to us." The count took a long gulp from his wineglass and surveyed the intense faces around the room. "But who knows?" he questioned. "Promises from monarchs we have learned over the centuries and in recent times have been only that—promises!"

* * *

It was not long before Warsaw society got its first look at the emperor. As Anna prepared for the reception at the Royal Castle, she could not help but think of her visit there when she saw King Stanisław for the first time—and then a second time, in 1794, when she had encouraged him—unsuccessfully— to abort the rebels' uprising against the Russians. How might things have been different had they waited for Kościuszko's forces to free the city in a more bloodless way? Would Poland have been preserved? Would they be entertaining tonight a self-made foreign emperor in hopes that their country could be reclaimed from their three inveterate enemies: Prussia, Austria, and Russia?

Lines of vehicles snaked from several directions to the arched opening of the castle's Great Courtyard, where they were dispersing the partygoers. "Pull into that opening!" Zofia called to her driver. Then, pantomiming a request from her coach window to the driver of a nearby carriage, she successfully carried out the cut in line. Even so, the wait lasted nearly half an hour.

"We should have walked," Anna said. "We live but paces from the castle."

"And how would that have looked to all these people—the sight of us trudging along through the snow?"

"We'd at least be inside by now enjoying a bit of champagne."

"Yes," Zofia snapped, "with sopping slippers and wet hems!"

Anna was taken aback by the sharpness of Zofia's reply, noting now that her cousin's demeanor had been intense all day. The two waited silently until the footman opened the door for them to alight the carriage. It was already nearly nine o'clock, and Anna thought perhaps they would miss the emperor's entrance.

Anna and Zofia had to pass through the middle of two lines of soldiers that led from the Senators' Entrance—where their wraps were taken—up the winding white marble staircase and into the Antechamber to the Great Assembly Room. The soldiers stood at attention, but Anna noticed that many of them could not help but steal glances at Warsaw's women, who had turned out, resplendent as possible. She had worn a blue gown; Zofia, red. "Wait," Anna said. "I'd like to wander around a bit before we go into the Great Assembly Room."

"A splendid idea, Anna! We'll see just who's come out for this little *divertissement*."

The Royal Castle's interior was unchanged from the last time Anna had seen it. They walked through the Marble Room, where there hung portraits of more than twenty past Polish kings. Anna drew in a long breath. Knowing that it was indeed possible there would never be another Polish king, she was filled with an immeasurable sadness.

Entering the National Hall, she felt an even deeper melancholy in this room that was a veritable pantheon of Polish history, its massive canvases displaying richly important scenes from the interconnected past of Poland and Lithuania. Passing into the Throne Room, Anna relived in just a few seconds the day King Stanisław had surprised her—and hundreds of others—by naming her a princess. She looked up at the king's dais now, a hundred carved eagles flying against the red velvet backing of the canopy. There the gilt throne stood shimmering in the light of a score of the best beeswax tapers—empty and forlorn.

"Are you all right, Anna?" Zofia asked.

"What? Yes, fine."

"You look a bit pale. Charlotte is supposed to be here. Do help me keep a lookout for her."

Everyone of the slightest importance in Warsaw and beyond had been invited, and judging by the thickness of the crowd, no one had declined. After about fifteen minutes, Anna and Zofia came across the Potockis in the Great Assembly Hall and were welcomed into their party. Compliments to the women's appearances were made all around. Anna was particularly taken by Anusia Potocka's black velvet gown, a perfect foil for the Potocki diamonds.

"There's Charlotte now," Zofia said, waving across the room. She immediately excused herself and melted into the crowd.

"Bring her over," Anusia called after her, but it was unclear whether Zofia heard because even though people were speaking in low, anticipatory tones, the muffled drone in the hall obscured any one voice. In but a few minutes, a loud voice boomed out from a doorway that had been closed previously, crying, "Make way! Make way!"

An opening appeared in the middle of the hall, and Anna could see the gentleman who was speaking. "That's Monsieur de Talleyrand," Lord Potocki whispered to Anna, pointing out the Grand Chamberlain and Minister of Foreign Affairs.

At that moment two words reverberated through the hall: "The Emperor!"

A palpable thrill passed through the room, leaving no one impassive. Anna, too, had heard and read too much about this man not to be impressed.

Emperor Napoléon Bonaparte stalked into the room, stopping in the large circle that had been made, and came to stand like a self-satisfied bull in his pen. He neither bowed to the crowd nor lowered his eyes. In full military regalia, he paused, as if to allow everyone to take in his appearance, seeming to revel in his own reputation as a prodigy.

What seemed a long moment of awe played out now, a moment in which protocol was forgotten and little gasps were audible. Then, as if a collective memory tapped each guest on the shoulder, the men began to bow and the women curtsy.

Anna felt a profound sadness, for this foreigner's presence filled the room, filled the Royal Castle, filled the onlookers with a substance both to be admired and feared, in a way that the presence of the former mild and meek King Stanisław had not.

Hat in hand, the emperor began to make the rounds of the room, chatting briefly with an individual or group, and then moving on. By the time he was half-finished, the guests' awe seemed to wear off a bit, and the wines being served sparked conversation and gaiety.

Soon it came their turn to meet the new Caesar. Lord Potocki introduced the emperor to his little group. Anna curtsied nicely, realizing to her surprise as she stood that his gray eyes were just slightly below the level of her own. This mighty figure on the continent was not quite as tall as she.

A softness had come into his eyes as they moved from the men to Anusia, then to her mother-in-law, and then to Anna. "What pretty women!" he declared before moving on. "Sweet as peaches!" And although they had heard him employ the same epithets on others before he reached them, they were nonetheless flattered. Anusia even blushed.

Within an hour, the formalities were done with, and the guests seemed to be enjoying themselves. Anna looked about for Zofia. Across the room, near the dais that supported the throne, Zofia and Charlotte were chatting and laughing with the emperor. Anna watched as the conversation went on for no little length of time.

"My cousin's husband is one of your legionnaires," Zofia told Napoléon. Her spirit soared. She had held him in conversation longer than anyone else that evening. The trick had been to allow him to lead the conversation while being concise and witty in her responses. He had a vast storehouse of questions.

"Ah, the legionnaires are invaluable," Napoléon said. "You must thank your cousin for sparing him. They are all heroes."

"Of course," Charlotte said, "the legionnaires hold out hopes for a quid pro quo, as do our leaders here in the city."

"Do they, Princess Sic?" What had been a sincere smile was immediately transformed into one as false as a player's mask.

But Charlotte did not pick up on his shift in expression. "Indeed, they hope you will restore the nation to what it was before '95."

"Shush, Charlotte," Zofia said, attempting to blunt the faux pas. "Politics are not for women. And you know I can't abide them."

"The princess here is only voicing what everyone is thinking here tonight, I suspect," the emperor said, the edge in his voice sharp. "That I am the new messiah, yes? But only she is naïve enough to mention it."

Realizing the sensitivity of the emperor to her comment, Charlotte looked from him to Zofia and blushed deeply. "A thousand pardons, Sire. I only meant to advise you."

The emperor turned on Charlotte. "You think because you are French you can tell me what the Polish want? That you have the right to confide in me? To *advise* me? Madame, your time would be better spent readying yourself to meet the public. While your diamonds do deflect from your dullness, *Princess Sic*, yellow is no color for a woman of your figure."

Charlotte's mouth fell open in shock. She studied the emperor's face, thinking perhaps he was joking. He was not.

Zofia braced herself, startled by the turn the conversation had taken. The emperor's reputation for cruelty to women was suddenly fully validated. Charlotte stammered an apology and, managing an awkward curtsy, hurried away.

"Your friend may be French," the emperor snarled, "but she is not noble, I can assure you."

"Then you have that in common." Before she could think, Zofia had blurted out the cutting words in defense of Charlotte. Only after they were out of her mouth did she realize the full extent of the insult to the Emperor of France. But she could not take it back.

He stared at her, the gray eyes round in surprise. He looked as if he had been slapped. Zofia became certain her comment had stifled any hope to snare the man. The very notion that she could capture him suddenly seemed vain and foolish. She thought she should make an exit herself but could not induce her feet to move. Her heart caught and seemed to be held between beats as the emperor stepped back, his eyes moving over her, from her slippers to her emerald combs. She waited.

The corners of his thin mouth began to twitch and quiver. And then—he laughed. Long and hard enough to catch the attention of those around them. "And I thought Polish women were merely pretty!" he cried. "They are bold, as well, I might add. Bravo!"

Zofia did not know how to react. Relief that he had not made her a target poured through her.

"Please extend my apologies to your friend," Napoléon said with a little bow and wave of his hand. "I'm certain that in her day she was a fully packed little turnip. Tell me, Zofia Grońska, in what other ways are you so forward?"

Forgetting the insult done to Charlotte, Zofia's mind worked quickly. "I know the Royal Castle quite well, Your Highness. If you have yet to see it all?"

"A tour guide! How excellent. You knew the former king?"

Zofia nodded. "Yes, I knew Stanisław."

"Stanisław? How well?"

Zofia turned back a blush at the insinuation in his words and smiled. "You know, Charlotte *is* noble."

Napoléon shrugged. "A bluestocking of the old days is no better than a pretender."

Zofia repressed the desire to suggest that he was himself a pretender. That would surely be pressing her luck. Instead she said, "Have you seen the little Portrait Room?"

"No, I don't think I have."

"It's a little room the king used for meditation or extremely delicate policy negotiations. On its walls are portraits of all the heads of Europe."

"Surely not *all?*"

"I do suspect it's missing a very important one."

"No doubt!" Napoléon gave a light laugh, his eyes moving to the scant red tulle that covered Zofia's breasts. "I'm certain that in due time the situation can be remedied."

"I would be happy to show you the chamber. It's just off the Throne Room."

Napoléon tossed off an intimate smile. "Not now." He seemed to enjoy the chase as much as she. "Shall we say in an hour or so—at midnight?"

Before Zofia could reply, however, Monsieur de Talleyrand approached the emperor, who turned and wordlessly moved away with him.

Zofia went in search of Charlotte.

"Well, Anna," Anusia Potocka asked, "what is your opinion of the man?"

Anna studied the emperor, who was passing near to them, Talleyrand at his side. "My impression is that he thinks a great deal of himself."

Anusia laughed. "That goes without saying. Great men have great pride."

"I suppose you're right. But pride isn't everything, Anusia. King Stanisław had pride and tonight a Frenchman sleeps in his bed."

"What was he lacking, Anna? You met him."

"Decisiveness, perhaps. And determination. But he was a good man."

"Father says that one good man can be undone by a majority of lesser men."

"And what about one good woman?" Zofia said, inserting herself into the Potocki circle. "Has Charlotte come this way?"

"No," Anna said. "The last we saw of her, you were both in heavy discussion with the emperor."

"Well, she managed to say just the wrong thing, and he insulted her. I think she may have left."

Zofia chatted with the group for a space of time but appeared distracted. After twenty minutes, she excused herself, first pulling Anna aside. "If you don't see me when you're ready to leave, dearest," she whispered, "go ahead and leave without me."

21

Zofia awoke in a sweat. The room was insufferably hot. She picked her head up and turned to see him adding more wood to the fire in the hearth. How could he? Dare she say something? He turned around now and approached the bed. He wore only his shirt, open at the front. "It's not yet dawn, but I sleep little. Did I wake you, my sweet?"

"It's *very* warm in here." *Hot as hell,* she thought.

"And so it should be. A bedchamber—any room of mine—must be well heated!"

Zofia lay on her stomach. As she started to pivot to her back, pushing back the covers at the same time, the emperor placed a hand on her side to restrain her. "There, stay as you are, Zofia. I'll pull back the covers if you're warm."

Zofia obeyed, feeling now the smallish fingers of his hand feathering lines over the exposed rise and fall of her back and buttocks.

He sat on the side of the bed. "There is nothing like a woman's backside, my dear. Nothing like it. No artist could reproduce it." Forward and back, his fingers moved, slow then slower.

Zofia fought off a chill the sensation was inducing. "Why do you say that?"

He applied more pressure. "Because it's true."

Zofia didn't reply. She thought the comment eccentric. No one had ever told her such a thing.

"Tell me," Napoléon asked, "how long since you've lost your virginity?"

"What?"

"You heard me."

"A gentleman doesn't ask such things."

"I'm an emperor, my sweet, not a gentleman."

Zofia peered up at him. The man was indeed odd—boldly so. "And are you *commanding* an answer?"

"Would you tell the truth if I said I am?"

"No."

Napoléon guffawed. "I thought not. Never mind. You do know your way about the castle, my petite bird. You knew right where the king's privy was, too, didn't you? You've slept here before! Don't even try to deny it."

When Zofia turned her gaze toward the pillow and gave no answer, Napoléon slapped her hard across the buttocks. It was the last thing she expected, and it hurt like the devil! Instead of crying out, she twisted in the bed, turning to her side and trying to cover herself. Napoléon grasped her wrist. "You have, haven't you?"

"What if I have?" Zofia wanted to spit the words out at him—but instead she reverted to an innocently flippant tone. "It was years ago."

"He was an old man even then, wasn't he—Stanisław?"

Zofia shrugged. "In his sixties."

"You like them old? You couldn't have been out of your teens. Isn't that odd?"

Zofia thought. She remembered her exhilaration at pleasuring the King of Poland. "No odder than liking backsides."

"*Touché,* my little vixen. They do say an old lover is like an old stove—much smoke but little steam. What say you about the old king?" He punctuated his joke with a laugh and another slap.

Zofia masked her pain. "Stanisław was gentle."

"Unlike me?"

"They say your wife is older."

"What?"

"They say—"

"You're not to speak of my wife, do you hear?" A pinch to Zofia's upper arm served as an exclamation point.

"Ouch!" Zofia's cry was at once one of hurt and surprise. He had pinched her the night before, too, she suddenly remembered, when she had left the door to the anteroom partially open. Couldn't tolerate open doors, he had screamed, loud enough to truly scare her. What a strange duck he was! Besides women's backsides and roaring fires, he liked to slap and pinch. *Oh well,* she thought, *when the time comes, I can give as good as I get.*

Zofia managed at last to pull free and turn over onto her back. He was staring down at her, his glass-gray eyes seeming to take on color at the sight. There is more to a woman than her backside, Zofia longed to say. Instead she smiled, reached up, and pulled his face toward hers.

For a time she made him forget Joséphine. For a time *she* was empress.

Anna was breakfasting with Barbara and Izabel when the door knocker sounded. The two girls lunged toward the front hall. Anna sighed in defeat. They knew to let one of the servants answer the door, but their youthful curiosity usually got the best of them.

Shortly, they ran back to the table and Anna took them to task, relaying to them manners and etiquette appropriate to their upbringing. The girls bowed their heads with the requisite degree of shame. They had forgotten, they said. Anna could not help but smile secretly at the scene. She was not so very far removed from their place in life, or so it seemed. And yet, years were ticking by like the movements of a clock's minute hand.

"Don't you wish to know who it was, Mother?" Barbara asked.

"Very well, who?"

"A soldier!" Barbara said.

"A very handsome one!" cried Izabel.

"A soldier?" Anna's first thought was a fearful one. Her pulse fluttered. Had some message come regarding Jan? "What soldier?"

"He didn't say," Barbara said.

"Was he an officer?"

"I don't think so," Izabel said. "No medals or ribbons, but good looking, just the same."

"What did he want?"

"He asked for the Countess Grońska," Barbara said.

"We told him she was out," Izabel chimed. "Aunt Anna, *where* did Mother go?"

Anna smiled and gave the answer she had prepared. "Your mother went out very early this morning for a gown fitting." Lies, even little ones with good intentions, still came with difficulty.

"She usually has the woman in to the house for that," Izabel said, less than convinced.

Anna returned to the subject of the caller. "Just what did this soldier say?"

"He asked how old we are," Barbara said.

"Why would he ask that?" The girls gave blank stares. "And you told the truth? No pretending to be older than you are? That's one of *your* tricks, Basia."

"We told the truth," Barbara said.

"Yes." Izabel sighed. "Actually, we didn't think fast enough to add a few years."

"There will be none of that," Anna said, thinking all the while how strange this was. She was immediately put on guard. What was this man about—and why would he be asking the ages of Basia and Iza? Was there some connection to Doliński? "Did he leave a card?"

"I asked if he had one," Izabel said. "He said that he didn't."

Moments later, the knocker sounded again. The girls stirred in their chairs, but Anna stood, shooting them a glance that kept them rooted to their places. She moved into the hall and opened the door to see for herself the young Polish soldier, an infantryman. The handsome blond man stood nervously, shifting from one foot to the other, his *czapka* in his hand. Anna guessed his age as twenty-seven or twenty-eight.

"Beggin' your pardon, milady. I came a bit ago to speak to the Countess Grońska."

"She's still not at home," Anna replied crisply.

Izabel and Barbara joined her at the door now, one on each side.

The soldier was blushing. "Your girls told me so."

"This one is mine," Anna said, her arm going around Barbara. "And one day she'll listen to me when I tell her something."

The soldier looked to Izabel, as if he expected Anna to say who she was. She thought that strange—and inappropriate. She resolved that he should be provided with no more information. Anna waited for his blue eyes to return to her, then said, "Is there a message for Lady Grońska?"

He put his head down and pulled from his pocket a little folded paper. Handing it to Anna, he said, "I have no card."

Anna took the paper. After speaking to the girls, he must have gone off somewhere nearby to write something—or have someone do it for him. She doubted the man could read. It was somehow touching. Perhaps he was harmless.

The soldier's boots came together as he stood at attention and bowed. "A good day to you, ladies." His gaze went again to Izabel and stayed a beat longer than Anna would have liked. Her sense of caution instantly flared to high heat.

"And to you," Anna said, shooing the girls back to the dining room and closing the door. Before she herself went in, she walked to the window and watched the soldier move down the street toward Saint Martin's. She looked then at the little scrap of paper.

On it, in awkwardly written letters, was a single name: *Jerzy.*

Just ten minutes later, Anna had no sooner excused the girls from the table than the knocker sounded a third time. Anna sighed. The soldier certainly was insistent. She rose and went to the door.

But it was not the soldier named Jerzy she found on the other side of the door. Still, it was a soldier, an officer. Anna had to catch her breath. "Paweł!"

"Hello, Anna!"

"You're knocking at your own residence?"

"I thought it best. I didn't want to just walk in and scare everyone to death." Anna quickly cast a look one way down the street, then the other.

"I'm alone, Anna. Jan's not with me. His orders took him elsewhere."

Anna attempted a smile. "I thought as much. Oh, do come in, Paweł!"

"Thank you." Paweł stepped up to the threshold and embraced Anna, kissing her on either cheek. "It's good to be home—even if it's just for a few days."

"So little time!"

"I know. Is Zofia at home?"

"No, not at the moment. Do come into the dining hall." As she led the way, she felt her face flushing hot. Lying to Paweł about Zofia's whereabouts was vastly different from lying to Iza. Would she be able to carry it off?

Once he sat, Anna prepared a plate for him from the dishes on the side-board. As she did so, they chatted about small, mundane things: the weather, muddy roads, and difficulty traveling. Anna passed him a plate of boiled eggs, sausages, and rye bread. She sat down and, to her amazement, the conversation continued without his asking Zofia's whereabouts.

He told how he was accompanying a messenger who was bringing documents and war maps to Emperor Napoléon. He was to return within the week with written responses from the emperor. Paweł had only just left the Royal Castle.

Anna felt the heat rising to her face again. If her suspicion about the night before was correct, Zofia was probably there at the very time Paweł was discharging his duty.

"You're very quiet all of a sudden, Anna. Forgive me, I've been rattling on, and I'm sure all you're thinking of is your Jan."

"How *is* he, Paweł?"

"Last I saw of him, he was fit as a fiddle."

"Thank God. You are both to be congratulated on your promotions."

"Thank you—although knowing they meant we would be attached to different squadrons, we would rather have declined them."

"But one doesn't do that sort of thing."

"Decline a promotion?" He shook his head. "No soldier would do that."

"And what of *his* orders?"

"As of two days ago, he was to move toward Gdańsk as part of an expeditionary and occupying force."

"So there's to be resistance? There will be fighting?"

Paweł's face softened. He no doubt wished he had said less. "There could be. But Jan can take care of himself."

"I liked it better when you were there with him."

Paweł smiled, as if to say he agreed. He finished his breakfast and took a second cup of coffee. "This is such a treat! I'm so tired of tea—and very poor tea at that. This is delicious! How do you manage getting coffee?"

"Anusia Potocka's father-in-law sent this over. He has all manner of connections. You wouldn't believe the personages coming and going at their home!"

"Yes, I would. Stanisław Potocki is in the thick of things trying to get some commitment for Poland out of the emperor."

"Tell me, Paweł, do you think we should be placing trust in this Frenchman?"

Paweł shrugged. "I'm quicker to do so than Jan, I can tell you that. He's quite a doubting Tomasz. But without placing trust in him, where are we? There's only one road for us to take, and take it we must."

"But will it take us to our destination—a free and independent Poland?"

"Ah! That is the question of the moment."

A small commotion arose in the kitchen, and in a few moments, Zofia came flying through the swinging door and into the dining hall. She halted abruptly at the sight of Paweł. "Good God in Heaven!" she shrieked happily. "Paweł!"

Paweł stood as Zofia sailed over to him. They embraced. Anna could see Paweł's eyes filling up. Zofia pulled up a chair next to his and began to ply him with questions.

After a while Anna excused herself, saying she was going upstairs to work on her morning correspondence. She had not yet made it to the second floor landing when she heard Zofia and Paweł moving toward their bedchamber, their tones low and loving.

She sat now at her writing desk, unable to write. Even to Jan. She just couldn't figure Paweł and Zofia. Her cousin's appearance could not have been more transparent. Zofia had arrived home wearing a ball gown from the night before, her hair and makeup less than presentable. And yet Paweł chose to look past the obvious, look past the imperfections—mighty as they were—in Zofia. He certainly loved her—had done so for years. Had he long ago given up the notion he—or anyone—could change her? And yet how could he reconcile himself to her behavior? To her other affairs? Did he think so little of himself? Or was his love so great—so unconditional—that he accepted her as she was? Was such a godlike love possible in this world?

It seemed that Zofia would always be both the snake and the snake-charmer.

Paweł and Zofia stayed in their bedchamber some hours before Izabel's knocking prompted them to partake in a meal. In the excitement of Paweł's arrival, neither Anna nor the girls thought to mention the other morning caller—the infantryman Jerzy.

The *wigilia*—the Christmas Eve meal—and Christmas celebrations were happy ones with Paweł there and Michał and Tadeusz home on holiday. The only person missing was Jan, and Anna acutely felt his absence. The boys returned to the academy on the twenty-sixth, and with Zofia and Paweł spending time together for the next few days, Anna became drawn to the Potockis' home in Wilanów, where she was always warmly welcomed. The elder Potockis nightly entertained a number of the French, it seemed, including Prince Borghese and Prince Murat, brothers-in-law to the emperor, as well as Monsieur de Talleyrand. Napoléon, occupied in war plans, spent nearly a week away from the city, visiting his forces to the east. But Anna was certain that sooner or later he, too, would show at Wilanów.

And he did. On New Year's Day, 1807, the feast of Saint Sylwester. Anusia met Anna at the door, her face pink with excitement. "Oh, Ania! He's come."

"Has he?" Anna didn't have to ask the identity of the visitor. That her friend's family was entertaining the Emperor of France in their home was something to marvel at.

"Yes, and he's brought some of his orchestra. We're to have a concert!"

"How delightful," Anna replied.

"Of course, it will be Italian music. That's *all* he allows them to play. He's brought the entire orchestra from Paris, can you imagine? A pity our music room isn't larger—we could have dancing."

The emperor bowed upon being reintroduced to Anna. "I do remember, Lady Stelnicka," he said. "We met at the Royal Castle."

Anna felt herself blushing. She smiled. "You're being polite, Your Highness."

"With eyes so green, how could I forget?"

He passed on, and Anna pondered whether she really had made an impression. The man knew how to flatter.

During the concert, Anusia passed on gossip that she had only just heard. It seemed that the emperor had already marked out the Polish woman whose heart he would break. "Who is it?" Anna whispered at supper to Anusia, who sat at her right.

Anusia held a napkin to her face, as if someone might read her lips. "No one knows—no one here, anyway. But it is fun to wonder, isn't it?"

Indeed, Anna thought. Of course, her first thought had been that her own cousin Zofia had been the favored one to capture the emperor's imagination. She didn't doubt it—even though Paweł's visit had recently compromised much of Zofia's time. However, Paweł was to leave in two days—soon enough for Anna's curiosity to be sated.

After supper, tables were set for cards. The emperor was partial to whist, and for his table, he chose Anusia, Anna, and Lady Potocka, Anusia's mother-in-law. In time, Anna found out it was his habit to play with three women, whether young or old. Anna wondered if this was because he had his fill of men in the war room and on the battlefield. As the game progressed, she suspected that he felt he was gifting the opposite sex with his playing. While the elder Lady Potocka seemed to play an indifferent game—intentionally, Anna thought—Anna and Anusia held their own, and Anusia even fell into a banter with the emperor about the stakes, daring to cleverly imply they play for an unnamed kingdom. "What kingdom?" Napoléon pressed.

Anusia seemed to sense, as did Anna, that to name Poland would invite something unpleasant from the emperor, who was known to be volatile when put on the spot. Anna came to her rescue then, saying, "Surprise us, Your Highness. Poles dearly love a surprise."

"Do they, Lady Stelnicka? Do you know what I love?"

"What?"

"Lovely and lively ladies who play cards—and who do not try to lose to a man!"

"Not even to an emperor?" Anusia asked.

"Not even!" He turned to Anusia's mother-in-law, maliciousness glittering in his gray eyes. "What say you, Lady Potocka?"

An uncomfortable half-smile came to Lady Potocka's face, but her silence and sudden blush spoke volumes.

Paweł passed up a ball at the Royal Castle to attend the Brotherhood meeting at the lodge in the countryside. He noted to himself that the group there seemed much concerned with avoiding any Prussian influence. The roots of the Polish Brotherhood that traced to Prussia's lodges, as well as to the recently ousted Prussian regime in Warsaw, were reason enough to be wary of motives not truly Polish.

Paweł was not surprised to find the group diminished in numbers. A few of the elders had died or become infirm, but a great many had joined—as he had—Napoléon's Polish legionnaires. Still, the twenty or so robed and hooded figures were animated this night. It had just come to light that one of their members—Brother Fabian—had been a spy for the Prussian crown. Paweł remembered the man, too, from years before, because he had felt an immediate aversion to him. All the talk was about a saddlebag of documents lost by Brother Fabian that had led to his unmasking—and what might result from the compromising of the Brotherhood's secrecy.

When the group was assembled, the Grand Master called for quiet. "It will do us no good to overreact to this news. We must keep our wits about us. With the Prussians now out of Warsaw altogether and at the mercy of Napoléon, I don't think we have much to worry about. Any information Brother Fabian took with him cannot be of much value."

"What about the location of this lodge?" someone asked.

"Yes, there is that," the Grand Master admitted. "We shall have to meet elsewhere in the future. This will be our last meeting here. But, listen, my Brothers, with Kalkreuth gone and Poles in line for power, why not meet right in Warsaw? Surely a place can be found." The notion of not traveling so far elicited a loud round of approval.

Later, Paweł took the Grand Master aside. "What about Tadeusz Stelnicki?" he asked with an air of urgency.

"Tadeusz? He continues his education at military school. He's seven now and doing quite well from what I hear. His brother is there, too."

"Then the plans for him—"

The Grand Master shrugged. "The plans have not changed—or should I say they have not been formulated. Who's to say what this French emperor has on his mind for Poland? Right now he seems to be toying with us. He may not know himself. With or without Napoléon, it may be that we will need a king on which to hang a new kingdom. Tadeusz is a fine specimen—good at his studies, good at the sword."

"Some say Napoléon may choose one of his brothers-in-law for king."

"God help us. He does give away kingdoms like bonbons. It is sad that circumstances put us at his mercy."

"To return to Tadeusz, Grand Master, shouldn't we be worried for his safety? Brother Fabian knew of the plans for him."

The Grand Master's head tilted slightly, as if in agreement—and as if he had thought of it for the first time. His shoulders sagged forward a bit. "That much is true, Brother Piotr, and if Kalkreuth were still commandant of Warsaw, I would be concerned. But the Prussians are gone, and I expect our spy has flown, as well."

"Tadeusz is the son of dear friends, so I am *most* concerned, Grand Master."

"And I can assure you that the school has the boy under good security."

"Good. That's important. Grand Master, only you know every Brother's identity. Can you tell me the identity of Brother Fabian?"

"I wish I could. But he wouldn't have been much of a spy, then, would he? He came to us as one of the newly landless *szlachta* from Opole. When he disappeared after the saddlebag discovery, we sent someone to Opole, hoping to locate him. But it seems that particular count, whose identity he provided me with, had died two years ago at the age of eighty-three."

"You saw his face when he applied, did you not?"

"Of course, I did, Brother Piotr, but I'm not good at remembering faces of people I've seen only once."

Paweł sighed. "Ah, all we have to identify him with is a voice."

"A voice?"

Paweł nodded. "Yes, that irritatingly raspy voice of his."

"You're right there, my friend. Brother Fabian sounded as if he spoke with a mouthful of stones."

While riding back to Warsaw, Paweł debated whether to tell Anna of this occurrence. Was there any real need? Why raise fears in her if there was not? The Grand Master was probably correct: any danger to Tadeusz was unlikely. Napoléon had negated the Prussian interest in Poland. And the spy may have followed in the wake of Kalkreuth and the Prussians as they abandoned Warsaw to the French.

And yet, Paweł thought, with his true identity still unknown, the spy could have remained behind and still be of service to the Prussian crown. Brother Fabian could be anywhere. Suddenly, he recalled an incident at the lodge years before. When the Grand Master was questioning Paweł about the Stelnickis, Brother Fabian had interrupted the conversation, seeming unduly interested. What had he asked? Paweł could no longer remember, but he did remember being taken aback by the man's interest. It had seemed so odd. Best to err on the safe side, Paweł thought. He would warn Anna.

22

January became a crush of receptions, parties, and concerts. The first significant ball for the French emperor was held at Monsieur de Talleyrand's. Napoléon's orchestra was already assembled and playing Italian songs when Anna arrived. Anusia waved her over. "I want you to meet a friend of mine, Anna. This is Lady Maria Walewska."

"I am pleased to meet you." Anna thought the young girl a vision, so very pretty in her white muslin gown and demure in manner.

"Anusia has said so many good things about you, Lady Stelnicka."

"I'm glad to have arrived before she came around to the bad," Anna joked.

Lady Walewska's laugh, like her voice, was musical. The woman's blond hair, falling in a mass of curls, and her alabaster complexion provided perfect complements for her sparkling eyes, blue like cornflowers. "You are not from Warsaw, are you?" Anna asked.

"No, my husband and I live at Walewice in Bronie, a rural province not far. But we do have a home on Bednarska Street here in the city."

"I see," Anna said. "Tell me, have I missed much?"

"You missed Talleyrand's delivering Napoléon a lemonade upon a gilt tray," Anusia said. "He's playing quite the servant when everyone knows he thinks the Corsican an upstart. My father-in-law says in his youth Talleyrand was quite successful among the ladies and that he's become embittered and jealous."

"Oh? Where *is* your father-in-law?"

"Both Lord Potocki and my husband are at a meeting." A knowing nod to Anna confirmed that it was a meeting of the Masonic Brotherhood. Anusia had only the week before confided in Anna that the two were members of the secret group.

In a little while, their conversation stopped when Napoléon approached Anna. "Ah, one of my favorite whist partners! Would you honor me with a dance, Lady Stelnicka? I've ordered up a quadrille. It's what I do best."

Anna curtsied and accepted. As he led her out onto the floor, the fact that she was a bit taller than he seemed to her all the more conspicuous. Knowing many eyes were upon her, Anna smiled while at the same time trying to keep up the small talk he insisted upon as they danced. Napoléon danced with a mechanical precision but a minimum of grace. It was as if he thought the music should, like his soldiers, follow him.

After the dance, they returned to where Anusia and Maria stood. "Were you watching?" he asked Anusia. "How do you think I dance?"

"In truth, for a great man, your dancing is divine."

"Is this a compliment, I ask?" the emperor said in a nasal tone, one eyebrow arching. "Or is it a clever Polish insult?"

Anusia's face colored immediately. "It is a compliment, Sire."

"Good!" Now he turned to Lady Walewska. "And who is this quiet creature?"

Anusia introduced them. Napoléon bowed toward Lady Walewska. "Perhaps the silent observer would suffer me one dance?" It was Lady Walewska's turn to blush, and she accepted silently, giving her hand over to the emperor. Napoléon led her away.

"I watched you out there, Anna—you poor thing," Anusia said, putting her fan to her face. "*Ma chère,* the man is as clumsy as a corpse."

Anna laughed. "When a woman is clumsy, she can blame the skirt. Not so with a man." They watched the emperor and Maria dance now, as did nearly everyone.

"Anusia, I didn't realize he had not met your friend Maria, or I would have introduced them."

Anusia put her fan to her face again and lowered her voice. "All is not as it appears, Ania. He was making a show of the introduction. He knew who she is—and that she would be here tonight."

"But—"

"Shush now." Anusia hissed, closing her fan with a tap. "We'll talk later. Ah, look! Zofia and Charlotte are arriving." Anusia waved the two over.

Charlotte steered through the crowd—her large bosom leading—as if she were a figurehead mounted on the prow of a Spanish galleon. Zofia, dressed in a low-cut amethyst-colored gown, followed in her wake, garnering lingering looks of the men and coldly polite glares of the women.

After the exchange of greetings, much talk was made of the ballroom, orchestra, guests, and apparel. Through it all, Anna noticed that Zofia's dark eyes kept going back to the emperor and Maria Walewska. When their dance had ended, the two did not return, but instead repaired to the refreshment table and then to two chairs across the room.

At last, in the middle of one of Charlotte's sentences, Zofia's patience expired. "*Who* is that woman?"

"What woman?" Anusia asked.

"*That* woman with Napoléon—the one in vestal virgin white! Who *is* she?"

"Maria Walewska, a countess from Bronie," Anusia offered. "My father-in-law arranged for me to bring her." At that moment, Talleyrand himself asked Anusia to dance, leading her away before she could explain further. Anna and Charlotte were left to attempt conversation, both knowing that Zofia was seething over the emperor's attention to the girl. And she was just that, Anna thought: a girl.

In a while Anusia returned, having endured two dances with Talleyrand. "His bad dancing is exceeded only by his breath, I can tell you."

Only Zofia did not laugh, her attention still diverted by the seated couple across the length of the room. Anna caught Charlotte's eye. Like her, Charlotte had been watching Zofia. In a wordless exchange, Anna and Charlotte—who had so seldom experienced a like thought—shared now a foreboding. Neither could imagine the evening's outcome. Zofia seemed to be moving toward some unseen precipice.

Zofia's heart beat with a fury. She had come with such high expectations. Lady Fortuna had smiled when Paweł had told her of his meeting, and that he would be unable to attend the ball. And so she had prepared for the ball the whole day, rehearsing how she would continue—and solidify—her affair with Napoléon. But she had taken too long with her preparations, it seemed. She had wanted to make a late entrance—perhaps make Napoléon doubt she was coming at all. She stared at the French emperor now as he went through his endless litany of questions for this woman she had never seen before. Emperor or not, he was so damn predictable.

Anna, Charlotte, and Anusia continued chatting, but their words had no meaning for Zofia. She could concentrate on nothing else but the little tableau across the way.

At last, Napoléon stood, bowed before Lady Walewska, and excused himself. He moved off to the left and became lost in the crowd. Zofia felt some of her anger and frustration go out of her. Her pulse beat more slowly. It had been a mere flirtation; that was all. Lady Walewska continued to sit, alone and unattended.

A servant came by with glasses of champagne. Zofia reached for one, turned back to her group, and joined in a toast followed by comments about those now dancing a mazurka.

A little while later, Zofia caught a movement out of the corner of her eye and swiveled slightly to look back to where Lady Walewska sat. The crowd was thicker now, and she could catch only brief glimpses of the woman. Suddenly, she saw Napoléon again at her side. He seemed to be placing a wrap around her shoulders.

By the time the crowd cleared a bit as people filed onto the dance floor for another quadrille, the emperor had disappeared again.

Zofia stared for the longest time at Lady Walewska, her pulse once again ratcheting upward. And then she began to strut across the room, ignoring Charlotte, who was calling out some question. She came to stand directly in front of Lady Walewska. "Pardon me, but allow me to introduce myself. I am Zofia Grońska."

The woman rose to her feet, smiling. "I am Maria Walewska."

"I am Anna Stelnicka's cousin."

"Oh, Anusia's friend, Anna! I am pleased to meet you."

Zofia had an express purpose in approaching Lady Walewska, but she put that off for the moment while she asked her about her hometown and lineage.

In time, though, her questions and patience ran out. She dropped the mask of camaraderie for one of sterner stuff. "I must tell you, my dear Lady Walewska—"

"Oh, do call me Maria."

"I must tell you, Lady Walewska, that the shawl you are wearing is *mine.*"

"What?" The woman was at first taken aback and confused.

When Zofia repeated herself, Lady Walewska's face went white as porcelain. "There must be some mistake," she said, her voice tremulous.

"I'm certain that there is, Lady Walewska, and that the mistake is not mine."

"I—I don't know what to say." The woman looked faint. "It was just given to me by—"

"So—you have met Anusia's friend, Zofia!" Charlotte chimed, inserting herself and surprising them both. "Will you introduce me?"

"I will not—but you have come in good time. Will you please vouch for me that this shawl is indeed mine?"

Charlotte looked at the woman, at the shawl, then back at Zofia, who could almost see wheels turning behind her friend's furrowed brow.

"It is indeed like yours."

"Like mine! It *is* mine!"

"Will you excuse us, Lady Walewska?" Charlotte said, taking Zofia by the arm and leading her away.

"What are you doing?" Zofia said through clenched teeth.

Charlotte maintained her grip and moved them toward an unoccupied corner of the room. There she released Zofia's arm. "I am trying to keep you from creating a scene."

"Scene or not, it is *my* shawl, Charlotte!"

"Come, Zofia. You've worked hard these last years to overcome the reputation you had in the old days. Don't undo it over a *shawl*. And Maria is a mere girl."

"*Girl!*" Zofia cut short her response because the emperor and Talleyrand were moving in their direction. Both seemed in good humor. Zofia turned to face them, staging a curtsy and a smile as they neared. Monsieur de Talleyrand gave a slow long-practiced nod of the head. Napoléon's gray eyes met Zofia's, but he did not so much as nod as the two proceeded out of the Great Assembly Hall through a nearby door.

Zofia stared in disbelief. "He cut me," she murmured. She turned to Charlotte. "He cut me!"

"He did at that. Our emperor is known to be rude and crude and insensitive. Not to mention fickle. I could tell you a hundred stories."

Zofia remained silent. How could this man whose bed she shared only days before walk by as if she were a nobody? *A cholera on him!* No man dropped her like that. She dropped them when she was ready. But she suddenly remembered there had been one who had dropped her . . . so many years ago . . . a lifetime, it seemed. Jan Stelnicki. He had thrown her over. And then, before she could remedy the situation, Anna had happened upon the scene. So much had happened since then.

Forcing her thoughts back into focus, Zofia realized Charlotte had launched into one of the stories about the emperor. "Madame Regnault was a lovely woman," Charlotte was saying. "Beautiful and charming. It was at a ball not unlike this one, I imagine. Hundreds of people. As the emperor came upon Madame Regnault, he paused to look her over. Her dress and hair arrangement were flawless, but he was in a foul mood, and as the music came to an end he said to her, 'Do you know, Madame Regnault, that you are aging *terribly?*' "

"And *was* she?" Zofia asked, ready to make light of the anecdote.

"She was twenty-eight," Charlotte said.

Zofia fixed her eyes on her friend. "And what is your message in this?"

"It is only that the emperor's temperament is more volatile than any woman's I know—and that he has no social skills."

"How did I then perceive a different message?"

"What do you mean, Zofia?"

"What I mean, Charlotte, is that you tell me this *aging* Madame Regnault was twenty-eight. And you know that I am all of thirty-three and that Lady Walewska is, as you said, a *girl*. You are alerting me to the contrast."

"That was not my intent. You are still so very beautiful, Zofia."

"Am I? It's time for me to go home, I think. Will you be so good as to make my excuses to Anna and Anusia?" Zofia turned and made an exit before Charlotte could reply.

At home, Zofia went immediately to the wardrobe in her room. She was hanging up her cape when something caught her attention—the dowry chest she had not thought about in some time. It had sat unopened in recent years, her carving for the most part put aside when she realized she was not suited to a domestic life. She opened the chest. Inside it were the several carved figures Jerzy had given her—including the one of her—as well as a few she had created herself. Withdrawing the tools and a piece of linden wood, she sat—still in her ball gown—and began carving. She would make one of Napoléon, she decided, already visualizing the wooden representation of a soldier with wide eyes under a bicorne, a rounded paunch, and short legs.

She set to work. Her aptitude had not diminished. In time, her pulse slowed and a certain serenity she had not felt in a long while settled over her. Here, at least, she thought, were figures she could create and control without interference. She laughed aloud at the notion. Only later did thoughts of the shawl come back to her. She had left the shawl at the Royal Castle the night she had won over Napoléon. How had it come to be at Monsieur de Talleyrand's residence? And why? It was a mystery.

In the early hours of the morning, she heard Paweł come in from his meeting. She returned the tools and work-in-progress to the chest. "Hello, Paweł," she said as he entered the bedchamber. That she was glad to see him caught her by surprise.

Anna's appointment at the academy had been set for noon. Even though she appeared early, the headmaster received her at once. Captain Spinek seemed more obese than ever, but his manner was less officious. Anna tried to determine whether his friendlier attitude was genuine.

"I can assure you, Lady Stelnicka, that Tadeusz—that both your boys—are quite safe here. I am well aware of the security breach regarding Brother Fabian that you mentioned, and actions have been taken." He smiled now.

"What actions?"

"Please, accept me at my word that we will do all we can. How did you come by *your* information?"

"I cannot say." Anna could be as evasive as the captain. "Have you no way of finding this Prussian spy?"

The captain shrugged. "That's where the Brotherhood's code of secrecy works against us. We're doing our best. Truthfully, Lady Stelnicka, not many of the group's members put much store in the notion of cultivating a child to be king. I doubt that our Prussian fellow did, either."

"And you, Captain Spinek?"

"Me?"

Anna knew his question was a stall for time while he sorted his thoughts for an answer. "Yes, do you not put much store in such a plan?"

His bulky form twisted slightly in his chair. "I suppose stranger things have happened in our history, Lady Stelnicka. But I doubt that this design will come to pass." His small, hooded eyes seemed to look past his guest. "Tadeusz *is* being groomed as a leader, and I trust he will be one, some day. In what way that will come to fruition, I can't say."

Anna could tell he was deliberately discounting the Brotherhood's scheme. She pressed the matter: "But even if the Prussians, who have long wished for the end of Poland, *think* you are cultivating, as you say, a future King of Poland, wouldn't they wish to put an end to such a hope?"

The captain's face colored. "We *will* protect Tadeusz."

"Whatever measures you have taken to protect both of my boys, Captain, I want you to increase them."

"Done."

Anna had to keep from blinking at the immediate and positive response. "I will check with them upon my next visit."

"And if they complain to you they are a bit less free, you'll know we are conforming to your wishes. Tadeusz will be the unhappier, I think, because he enjoys going beyond the confines of the academy and exploring nature. Jan Michał is quite at home inside a fencing hall."

Anna smiled. "And just how are they doing, Captain Spinek?"

A faint shadow fell across the headmaster's face. "Generally, quite well, as we discussed a few weeks ago."

"Generally?"

"Well, they both have tempers, and a few days ago they fell into an argument that came to blows. They had to be pulled apart."

Anna stiffened in her chair. "Over what?"

"They wouldn't say. Even under threat of punishment, they maintained it was a private matter."

"Why wasn't I informed?"

"That kind of thing does happen here from time to time. Boys have little jealousies, just as do girls."

"Are you treating Tadeusz differently? As if he *is* the hope of Poland?"

"Absolutely not! He hasn't a clue as to our *possible* purpose. But, may I ask if they are treated equally at home?"

"Of course! And you know how few and short in duration their home stays are."

"Well, I wouldn't worry. Jan Michał is the protective one, and Tadeusz may think much of himself—not an altogether bad trait for a leader—but he nonetheless seeks the approval of his older brother."

"What of their studies?"

"Tadeusz is the scholar, as you well know. We're quite pleased there. He takes to languages like a beaver to water."

"And Jan Michał?"

"Michał lives in his body rather than his head. He's a better fencer than those three or four years older. Strong and agile, he'll take risks but only after an instinctual analysis. As for the books, they take second place to his physical activities. In his studies, he manages to get by."

"I'll talk to him."

Later, Anna awaited her two sons in a small reception room off the main entrance of the academy. It came to her now that in the discussion of jealousy she had immediately assumed it was Jan Michał who was jealous. *Was* he the jealous one? Did he harbor old resentments dating back to their few years at Sochaczew? To those few occasions where he may have thought—rightfully or not—that Jan was favoring his natural son, Tadek? Or had she herself somehow given him reason to think his brother better loved?

The boys entered the chamber like the soldiers they were becoming: tall and erect in their perfectly pressed blue uniforms. But their eyes were most unsoldierly: wide with wonder at the prospect of a weekday visitor.

"Mother!" Tadeusz said, pushing past his brother and heading toward Anna.

Anna stood and bent forward for the kiss. She hugged the boy, simultaneously motioning Jan Michał forward. There was a hesitancy in his walk now. That he was the elder by three years was becoming more and more evident. "It's not visiting day," he said.

"They made an exception. Just come and give me a kiss!" As her right arm encircled Michał, she was startled by the realization that she did not have to bend for his kiss. He was already her height—and a full head taller than Tadeusz.

The boys allowed her to hold them for several seconds. "You are both so big!" she said, finally releasing them. They fell into conversation then, topics coming and going randomly and with spirit among the three. But once talk of Napoléon Bonaparte came up, both boys radiated real interest. "You *met* him?" Tadek asked.

"I've danced with him, and I've played cards with him." Anna enjoyed watching their stunned reactions.

"You haven't!" Michał said. His voice was different, deeper. He would be fifteen on the third of May. He was becoming a man.

"But I have!" With her thumb and forefinger, Anna gave a twist to Michał's nose. "Do you doubt your mother?"

"What was he like, Mother?" Tadek asked. "He's to restore Poland, my professors say."

"Do they?"

Michał was nodding. "In my strategies class, we are studying his new methods. He's invincible!"

"I guess he is—or at least he's *told* me so. He's not so very tall. I had to look down at him."

Both boys denounced her statement—in wonder and good nature. But Anna held firm in the assertion. They talked for some time about the French emperor and future prospects for Poland. Anna could scarcely believe she was speaking with two children, so knowledgeable were her sons on current politics. They were patriots in training, it seemed, and thoroughly indoctrinated with admiration of the emperor.

"I'm late for my Swedish class," Tadeusz said, suddenly noticing the clock on the mantel. "We're coming home in a fortnight, yes?" His voice, light and musical, was still a boy's.

"Yes," Anna answered, demanding a quick kiss before he fled the room.

She turned to Jan Michał. "And you? No Swedish?"

He shrugged. "I'm not so good at language. Russian, French, and German are all I can handle. *More* than I can manage, to tell the truth. But they're the important ones."

"No Lithuanian?"

He shook his head.

"It's an important one, too, if the Commonwealth is to rise again. What is your favorite class?"

"Fencing and Military Strategy. I have an hour before Fencing."

"I see. You must try harder at your other studies—Michał, the captain tells me you fight with Tadek."

Michał's shoulders sagged forward, and his glance went toward the floor. "Sometimes. It's not serious."

"You're bigger and much stronger, I think."

"I know."

"What do you fight about?"

"Nothing. Little things."

"Little things?"

A long moment passed. Anna waited.

"It's just that—that Tadek thinks he's the center of the world sometimes."

"And you feel you have to put him in his place?"

Jan Michał shrugged.

"What did you fight about the other day when you had to be pried apart?"

"Nothing—he called me a name."

"What name?"

"It doesn't matter."

"It *does* matter, Michał. What *name?*"

The boy's lips thinned, as if he were tightening his mouth.

Anna took his upper arms in hand, firmly but without force. "Jan Michał, tell me."

Jan Michał's face screwed up into a twisted and ugly expression as a storm seemed to rise up from deep within his body. "Bastard!" he raged. "Bastard!"

Anna's hold tightened for a moment, but he pulled away. The tears were coming now as he looked up to face her. "Am I, Mother? Am I a bastard?"

Time stood suspended as Anna took in the words and their meaning. The room and its furnishings blurred. Finally, she spoke: "What made Tadek say such a thing?"

"We overheard two teachers late at night—in the hallway. One of them used the word."

"About you?"

Jan Michał nodded.

"Do you know what it means?"

"Yes, of course!"

"Does Tadek?"

"No—I don't think so."

Anna lifted her hand to push away Michał's tears, but he pulled back, his brown eyes—Walter's eyes—staring her down. "Am I?" he demanded.

Anna had known the moment would come one day but could not have expected it today. Not like this. She had long thought about how she would reveal the circumstances of his birth—but all the rehearsals seemed to fall away. A long moment passed.

Anna drew in a deep breath and began, not knowing the turns the telling would take. "Michałek, you know that Jan is not your father. You've always known that."

"Yes."

"And that I was married to Antoni Grawliński when you were born. You are not a bastard, do you hear? Until Jan adopted you, you had his surname."

"Then he was my father?"

Anna's felt a tightening in her stomach. She was already at the moment of decision. She could say that Grawliński was his father and the subject would pass. The boy would be appeased. For now. But what about some day in the future when the truth would come out, as it had a way of doing. What then? He would start asking questions about Antoni. What was he like? Did Michał look like him? Act like him? And the thought of gilding Antoni's memory sickened her. If she did not reveal his true father, could she live with herself, having lied to her son? Anna drew in a long breath. What would the truth, convoluted as it was, do to this young man—her firstborn? "Come and sit down with me, Michał. Here on the couch."

The boy obeyed. Anna sat at an angle to her son, and as she started to speak, her gaze became fixed on the far wall. She made no attempt to touch her son. "Jan Michał, you were inside me when I married Antoni Grawliń-ski." Michał's body tensed. "Let me tell the story while I have a mind to," Anna said before he could speak. "Your father was Walter Groński. I know you call Zofia 'Aunt' Zofia, but she is my cousin—and Walter was her brother."

"He knew?"

"Antoni?" Anna nodded, turning to her son. "He knew I might have a child. What he wanted was my estate and my money."

Jan Michał took this in, giving his mother an adult expression. After a while, he asked, "Why didn't you want to marry my father?"

There were lurid twists in the story that she still hoped to avoid—but not this one. It had to be told. She turned to her son. "With your father—when you were conceived—I was not willing." The moment drew out. She could see his eyes lose focus. "Do you understand?"

"He—forced you?" Jan Michał's words were deceivingly soft for the meaning they carried. He stared some moments. "Then you didn't want me," he choked out. "I was a mistake and a *burden* to you. You didn't *want* me!"

Anna reached for his hands, but he pulled away from her. "Listen to me, Jan Michał. You ask adult questions, and I'm telling you the truth as I would to an adult. You need to know I wanted you from the moment I knew you were inside me. I *did!* Aunt Zofia can tell you as much. You're my firstborn, and don't think for a moment I could love Tadek or Basia more than you.

Never! I love my children *equally,* do you hear?" Anna caught one of his hands and pulled it to her. "Look at me, Michał!"

Jan Michał looked at his mother as if with disgust.

"You're my child, and you're soon to be a man. One I know I will be so proud of. Oh, Michał, how I love you."

"You don't. How could you?"

"I do!" Anna put a hand to his wet cheek. "I wouldn't change a thing, Jan Michał. Believe that."

"What happened to him—my father?"

"He was a Russian soldier, a mercenary. He died on the day Praga fell."

He took a few minutes for this to settle. "Do I look like him?"

Anna had to nod. "You do—more so as you get older. The brown eyes and hair, the darker complexion. They say he had some Tatar blood."

"Me, a Tatar?"

Anna immediately regretted the revelation. He would not have been taught good things about the Tatar tribes. "Maybe that's where you get your liking for military strategy," Anna said with a laugh, trying to make the best of the situation, but her son did not find it funny. "Oh, many Poles in the south have Tatar blood, Michał. Aunt Zofia does. It's nothing to be ashamed of."

"I don't want Tatar blood!"

"Our births are not things we can choose." They talked awhile longer, and Anna dared to hope Jan Michał was beginning to come to terms with his lineage.

When she stood to leave, she hugged her son. "You're the elder and the stronger, Michałek. I want you to look after Tadek. He's your brother."

He stood silently staring ahead.

"Michał!"

"I will."

It was grudgingly said, Anna thought. "No more fights?" she pressed.

"No."

"Good." Anna kissed him on either cheek. "Go now, or you'll be late to your class."

In the carriage, Anna wrestled with her guilt over the parts of the story she had omitted. Of the several facets she had skipped, one eclipsed the others: How could she tell her son that it was she who had killed Walter, his father?

As it was, he had not returned her hug. It would take some time for his thoughts and emotions to disentangle and settle. If ever they would.

By the time the carriage was nearing Paweł's town house on Piwna Street, however, her mind was taken up with the whole of her family. Another year was opening with Jan in the service, but—more than that—her two sons were fast becoming men whose lives also seemed destined for the military. She had only Basia with her.

Sweet Jesus! This was not the life she had envisioned.

23

February 1807

Clouds hung heavy in the late-morning sky when Charlotte, a light bundle in her grasp, alighted her carriage on Piwna Street. Zofia watched her from her bedchamber window. In a few minutes, a maid knocked and announced the Princess Sic's arrival.

Charlotte was still standing when Zofia entered the reception room. "What a surprise, Char," she said, approaching her friend and kissing her. "I thought I wasn't to see you until tonight."

"I—well, I thought it best to speak to you in confidence first."

"Why? I'm very busy at the moment getting ready. Napoléon has returned to Warsaw after seeing to his troops. I intend to look my best. Luckily, Paweł has returned to duty."

"Where's Izabel? I haven't seen her in a week."

"She's at convent school. The nuns are trying to undo the spoiling of her you've done. Really, that cameo you gave her was too much. I pray she doesn't lose it."

"Well, someone needs to pay the girl some attention."

"And what does that mean? Why, she's beginning to think of you like a *grand-mère.*"

"Oh, *does* she?" Charlotte's shoulders lifted.

"Leave Izabel to me. Now we've gone off subject. What brings you around in the afternoon, dearest?" Zofia took closer notice of the item in Charlotte's hand. "Ah, something for me? A gift?"

"No, Zofia," Charlotte said, giving over the parcel. "It's not a gift."

Zofia tore at the wrapping. "My shawl!" she cried, her dark eyes questioning. She unfolded the shawl and set it aside without inspection. "You recovered it from that twit—what was her name?"

"Lady Maria Walewska."

"Yes, that one. I *knew* it was mine. There is no other shawl like it.–Tell me, has she gone back to . . . to–"

"Bronie."

Zofia pulled a face. "The hinterlands! It's where she belongs."

"Well, Bronie is in the provinces, but it's hardly the hinterlands. Anyway, you have it back now."

"Damn it, Charlotte!" Zofia cried, retrieving the shawl and dashing it to the floor.

"Ah, it wasn't about the shawl then, was it?"

"Of course not! Not the shawl itself. But I *would* like to know how my shawl was transported from the King's Bedchamber at the Royal Castle to cover that *girl's* bony shoulders at Talleyrand's. You haven't solved that little mystery, have you?"

Charlotte nodded. "I have. Come, let's sit down."

"Will this take long? I still have a lot to do before tonight. I've not given up on the little corporal."

"It depends on how many questions you ask. Shall we sit?" They seated themselves in high-backed chairs, facing each other. "Well," Charlotte began, "it seems the Lady Walewska stood among a group of well-wishers at Bronie when the emperor passed through on his return to the capital on New Year's Eve. In fact, Napoléon gave her one of the bouquets that had been tossed into his carriage. Even though she could speak French quite well, he thought her a peasant girl."

Zofia sneered. "She looked the part, no doubt. Everything but a rainbow skirt!"

"She's *not* a peasant. Anyway, he was struck by her innocence and looks, so that when he arrived in Warsaw, he issued orders she be found."

"I'm not going to enjoy this story, Charlotte, am I?"

"Turns out she's eighteen and was married at sixteen."

"Ah! She's married!"

"To a count who's seventy-seven."

"Good lord! I *do* like what I hear."

"And she's given him a son."

"Better and better–not so virginal, after all."

"But the emperor's intrigue with her didn't lessen. He let a number of our men know he wanted her to attend Talleyrand's ball. In fact, he said he wouldn't go unless they procured her for him. An entire delegation of the patriotic party descended on the Walewice, the Walewski manor house, and actually managed to win the husband over before Maria relented."

"Polish fishmongers, the lot of them! Relented?"

"It took some convincing. Her patriotism ultimately weakened her stance."

"Oh, please! You mean to say she went to the ball out of some patriotic fervor? *Please!*"

"Yes. You see, her father died fighting for Kościuszko when Suvorov and his Russians came down on Praga."

Zofia gave out a stage sigh. "Charlotte, I was there—I nearly died myself."

"Well, Maria *abhors* the Russians and longs for the day when France will help reestablish Poland."

Zofia waved her hand dismissively. "Little Maria and the rest of the city. Returning to the subject of my shawl, let me guess: Napoléon needed a unique gift on the spur of the moment, so he took to Talleyrand's *my* shawl to present to the silly girl."

"I expect that was the scenario."

"And since then? Has she returned to her husband?"

"She has. But that has not slowed the would-be Emperor of Europe. He has showered her with impassioned letters and jewels."

"And the old goat of a husband?"

Charlotte gave a shrug. "It's a well-worn story. An affair with a monarch advances the family. He's positively preening at the attention. Not a goat but proud as a peacock."

"Stupid as a cuckold, you mean. . . . And she . . . has she . . . delivered the goods?"

Charlotte nodded.

Zofia gasped. "The damn fool!"

"He wants to bring her to Paris."

Zofia felt her face burning. "Ah, the Caesar–Cleopatra syndrome. I wonder how Joséphine will take to that."

"I'm sorry, Zofia. I really am."

"For what?" Zofia gave another wave of her hand. "I won't have you or anyone pity me. A cholera on them both!"

"It's hard, I know. When I met you, I still had remnants of my beauty. But no more, no more. Only my diamonds sparkle as they did in those wonderful days in Paris before the rising of the scum."

Zofia tilted her head at her friend. "So you think I have only remnants of my looks left?"

"No, no, child! You are still *very* beautiful. But you'll be thirty-four this year, yes?"

"Yes, thank you for reminding me."

"And Maria is eighteen."

"And a twit."

"A patriotic twit. She's to be Napoléon's 'Polish conquest.'"

"It makes me ill, Charlotte. *I* was to be his conquest."

Charlotte reached across, placing her hand on Zofia's. "No, Napoléon Bonaparte was *your* conquest, Zofia. And that's what made all the difference."

Zofia thought for a long moment, then gazed at her longtime friend as if for the first time. She was right: her own aggressiveness had done her in. Her own hunger. It seemed she had been short-changing Charlotte's intelligence for years.

"You still have the love of Paweł," Charlotte said. "Why, I haven't a notion."

"I do have that. And do you know what? I can't figure it, either."

"Will you still go tonight?"

Zofia's eyes iced over. "And see the twit?" She thought for a long moment. Did she really want to stay home? Her back straightened. "Dog's blood! Why shouldn't I go? There will be other men there besides the illustrious Caesar and his nubile whore." She laughed then, her eyes targeting Charlotte. "Taller men and men who take more than five minutes to make love to a woman!"

Napoléon Bonaparte, so they said, somehow deluded himself into thinking his affair with the married Lady Maria Walewska went unnoticed in the nation formerly known as the Commonwealth, but by early February and far removed from Warsaw, Paweł caught wind of the French emperor's Polish conquest.

Napoléon had had to tear himself away from his newest passion to join his forces assembling near Eylau. The Russians, it seemed, were impervious to winter's wrath.

No Polish forces were included in the French formations; nonetheless, because of his knowledge of the terrain, Paweł—and a dozen of his squadron—had been attached in a special assignment to Prince Murat's forces. And it was at Eylau that Paweł would learn that Napoléon Bonaparte was not wholly invincible.

The Russian General Bennigsen had initiated the winter action in the Polish lakeland region that drew Napoléon from the warmth of the bedchamber to the theater of war. Napoléon's initial decisions, solid as they seemed, were thwarted by mishaps, intercepted orders, and the hostile eastern Prussian lands rife with snow, frigid cold, and quicksand. A game of cat and mouse with Bennigsen ensued for four long days, nightfall alone bringing down the curtain on the fighting.

Then, on 7 February, a skirmish evolved into battle at 2 p.m. and continued for eight hours, the flash of artillery holding back the dark. The night temperatures dropped to thirty degrees below zero, so few of the combined four thousand French casualties survived the field. The battle raged the next morning despite constant snowstorms. One French corps ran against the pelting snow straight into a Russian seventy-gun battery and was cut to ribbons. When an opening occurred in the French line, Bennigsen took full advantage, and six thousand Russians overran Eylau. For one precarious moment, disaster was a mere heartbeat away because Napoléon had been issuing orders from the town's bell tower when the town was taken—and were it not for his heroic personal guards, he would have been taken, as well.

Riding with Prince Murat, Paweł witnessed the most telling event of the day. At a little before noon, the Murat cavalry crashed into the Russian center, commandeering the Russian guns and at last turning back the enemy. And yet fighting continued until ten at night. The snowy landscape, lighted by the moon, was laden with corpses as far as one could see. Tens of thousands. It was a sight Paweł would never forget.

The days-long battle ended in a standstill with the French leaving the fields of Eylau to the Russians. It would take more than an emperor's word to burnish the engagement as a victory of any kind. Prince Murat released Paweł with commendations for the extraordinary work of his lancer squadron. Paweł made his way back to accept further orders from General Dąbrowski. He had lost four good men.

The true winner, Napoléon would say, was General Winter.

A few days later, Paweł learned the emperor had moved his headquarters to East Prussia. Much later, critics—and there were many—would say that as a result of the battle at Eylau, Napoléon's military prowess suffered a lasting loss of surety. In any case, Maria Walewska—*ma petite Marie,* Napoléon called her—joined him at Schloss Finkenstein to console him, and their tryst continued in style.

Jan Stelnicki joked with Lucjan as the servant packed the portmanteau. Lucjan was true and loyal but no replacement for the camaraderie he had shared with his friend Paweł.

The cavalry was preparing to move out. A few days earlier, General Dąbrowski had apprised the officers of the orders. A siege of the Prussian-held city Gdańsk was the ultimate objective. The infantry had already moved out of Poznań with orders to neutralize any and all villages and towns along Gdańsk Road. The mud-laden highways hampered travel so that the days passed slowly. Agonizingly so. Rumor had it that Napoléon Bonaparte—still snug at Schloss Finkenstein with his Polish conquest—claimed to have discovered in Poland a new obstacle to his brilliant war strategies: mud.

The cavalry followed in the infantry's wake through Gasawa, Bydgoszcz, Świecie, catching up to the infantry at Gniew and then moving past Ciepło. They expected significant opposition at Tczew and so halted not far away, the officers gathering around Dąbrowski as he laid out his plan of attack on the Prussian-held town. It would be executed in the early morning.

The men settled in for the night. The homes in the suburbs of the town were owned by Poles who saw to it that the forces were well fed. Planks were brought out so that men could avoid sleeping in the mud. In the morning, Jan's squadron preceded an infantry battalion, moving past the suburban houses toward those nearest the Vistula Gate. Dawn brought into focus mounted Prussian hussars on the heights. Marksmanship on horseback was a dicey thing, and few shots of either side found their marks. Jan halted his horse, took careful aim with his carbine, and felled one of the Prussian hussars who were now disappearing behind the suburban houses to wait for their chance.

Jan's men moved into position on either side of the entrance, drawing fire while the infantry and grenadiers made for the gate. The houses nearest the wall were occupied by Prussian foot soldiers, and a volley spat out now from what seemed every door and window. Its effect on the Poles was deadly, wounding a number of the infantry, killing an officer, and sending the unit into disarray, with many fleeing. House-to-house fighting was the worst kind of warfare.

Jan saw a young friend of his, Lieutenant Dezydery Chłapowski, stand up next to the body of his fallen comrade and rally his men. "Stay for the cannon!" he called. "Don't fall back now! For Poland!" The young man had a true Polish heart! His effort was well rewarded, for within minutes, a French squadron could be seen rolling their cannon up the street that led to the gate.

The rallying troops, the lumbering cannon, and the approach of an additional battalion had its effect: a second Prussian volley did not materialize. Instead, the Prussian infantry, covered by their few hussars, retreated, running pell-mell into the walled town and slamming shut the gate.

Fire was exchanged while the cannon were being set up, and a number of men fell, French and Polish. It took three shots from the cannon for the gate to collapse. Buoyed by this success, the infantry, accompanied by Jan's lancers, burst into Tczew. A second battalion had been sent to the Mill Gate and additional cavalry to the Gdańsk Gate, which was, Dąbrowski had said, a likely escape route. The enemy fell into a full rout, and within an hour the

Prussian commander, General Roth, surrendered in a church where he had found sanctuary. With him were eight hundred men. A number of Prussians had attempted to escape across the delicate ice of the River Vistula, but few escaped drowning.

Jan came through it all physically unscathed, but the price had been high. One hundred fifty Poles had been lost, a half dozen from his own squadron. And it was only after the battle that he learned that General Dąbrowski himself had been wounded.

So when they moved out of Tczew, it was with General Kosiński in command.

24

Princess Charlotte Sic's sleigh stopped in front of Paweł's town house at midnight. Anna and Zofia were handed down by Charlotte's driver amidst the hard-falling snow. The three friends had spent the evening at the Potockis' and were still in good humor. "Farewell!" Charlotte called as the sleigh pulled away. It was the only vehicle on Piwna Street.

"Farewell!" Anna called.

Zofia had already proceeded toward the front door. As Anna turned to follow suit, she caught a movement out of the corner of her eye. Another sleigh was pulling out of the adjacent alleyway. It did so in almost total silence because the street's thick layer of newly fallen snow muffled the hooves of its horses and hiss of blades. Anna blinked at the strange sight. Two men sat in the front. The driver was on the far side of Anna's view. The passenger turned for a moment in Anna's direction, either to glance down the street for traffic—or because he sensed Anna's presence. For the briefest of moments his face was bared by the moon and reflecting snow. He immediately turned his head, and in moments the sleigh was moving quickly away, into the vortex of the snowstorm.

Anna thought she recognized the face. Was it possible? Could it have been? Her mouth went dry as she tried to call to Zofia. She couldn't speak.

"What is it, Anna? Hurry in! You'll catch your death out here."

"Zofia! Did you see?"

"See what?"

"That sleigh!"

"What sleigh?" Zofia descended the few stairs to Anna. "*Charlotte's* sleigh?"

"No, there was another."

Zofia glanced in either direction. "I don't see another. Just a sheet of snow. Come in the house now."

The sighting had been most peculiar, and Anna felt sick to her stomach. Had she imagined seeing Doliński? "Zofia, it came out of the alley leading to the coach house."

"Paweł's coach house? That seems unlikely, Anna. Come in now."

In the downstairs hallway, the sense of urgency did not dissipate. Without removing her wrap, Anna rushed the stairs.

"Where are you going?"

"To Basia's room! You must check on Iza."

"But—why?"

Anna paused and turned. "Just do as I say!" she screamed, then raced to the second floor. Her heart beat frantically against her chest as she pushed open the door to Barbara's bedchamber. It was completely dark. And cold— no one had seen to the hearth before bedtime. She moved into the room. "Basia?" she whispered. "Basia?" She fumbled for the candle on the bedside table. Her hands trembling, she lighted it. "Basia?"

"Mother?" The sleepy voice sent relief flooding into Anna's body. Barbara sat up in bed. "Oh, Mother, I fell asleep."

Anna sat on the side of her daughter's bed. "That's as it should be. It's very late."

"But I wanted to stay awake for you to come home!" Barbara seemed suddenly fully alert, her voice effervescent.

"Why, dearest?" Anna's hand sought out Basia's.

"Because they're home!"

"Who's home?" The terrible sick feeling surged again.

"The boys, Mother. The boys have come home!" Barbara withdrew her hand and flew from the bed. "Let me go get them. I'll bet they're not yet asleep!"

"No, Basia!" But the girl was already out of the room and heading for the stairway to the third floor. Anna took the candle and followed. On the landing, she nearly collided with Zofia, who was just coming up from the first floor, candle in hand.

"Izabel is sound asleep downstairs. What's all the commotion up here?"

"Basia says the boys have come home!"

"Did you expect them?"

"No!" Anna knew at her core that something was amiss. Before she and Zofia could turn to mount the stairs to the third floor, Basia's scream rang out, long and loud, and then came a refrain of several more, staccato and piercing. Anna looked at Zofia and saw her own fear reflected there. Shielding their candles, the two rushed up the stairs.

On the third level, ahead in the shadows, Anna could make out Basia's crouching body and a form lying prone on the floor. The girl was crying hysterically.

Fear rose up, clutching Anna at the throat. She moved closer. Then both she and Zofia saw it. Barbara knelt weeping over the body of their beloved sheepdog, Borys. A crimson sash lay nearby the lifeless dog. Anna took no time to examine the dog or console her Basia. She moved to the boys' room. Why was it Basia's screams had brought neither of them out? She opened the door and peered into darkness. As she walked in, her candle shed light on Jan Michał's bed. He seemed to be in it—with the covers pulled over his face.

Anna leaned over and pulled back the bedclothes. What she saw made her gasp. Michał had been tied with a sash and cravats. His mouth had been gagged so tightly that he could scarcely breathe. "Jan Michał!" she cried.

By now Zofia had come into the room. She moved toward the other bed, candle in hand. Anna started at once to remove Michał's gag, but she looked up as Zofia's candle lighted the area around Tadeusz's bed.

It was empty.

"Dog's blood!" Zofia cried.

In less than an hour, Anna and Zofia bundled themselves into the open sleigh that Jan Michał had hitched. "Make for the western gate, Michał. Fast as you dare!"

"I shall," he called back from the driver's seat.

His story had spilled out with his tears. A note had come to the academy, ostensibly from Anna, hinting at some family tragedy and requesting the boys' presence at home. Arriving home, they had been greeted by Barbara and Izabel. Not long after they had gone to their bedchamber, taking the sheepdog with them, Borys began scratching at the door, as if wanting to get out. Assuming that he preferred sleeping near Basia, as had become his custom, Michał opened the door and shooed him out. A minute later, he heard a low growl and the sounds of scuffling. He went to the door, opened it, and stepped out into the hall. At that moment something hard came down on his head. He went out like a snuffed candle.

When he came to, he was bound and gagged in his bed, the covers reaching up over his head. He lay very still, listening intently to sounds in the room.

He could hear Tadeusz's muffled voice in protest. There were two men in the room, he realized. They spoke German. While German was not his best subject, Jan Michał did manage to understand them. They had been instructed to bring Tadeusz to some Prussian town Jan Michał had not heard of. The one who seemed to be working for the other kept asking about payment, but he was told to keep quiet.

"Are we to bring clothes for him?" the underling had asked. No, he was told, the boy would be needing no change of clothes where he was going. The intimation had been clear to Jan Michał, and then, upon the retelling, to Anna and Zofia. Tadeusz had been kidnapped and would likely be killed in Prussia upon his delivery.

Zofia had gone white. "Why on earth would anyone wish harm to sweet little Tadeusz?"

Anna could see that her question stood for Jan Michał's thoughts, as well. "There are reasons, Zofia, but for now we must search him out."

"How?" Jan Michał asked, wiping away the last of his tears.

"Tell me, Michał," Anna asked, "did either of them use the other's name?" When he said no, she asked, "Did one of them have a rough, raspy voice?"

"Yes! Mother, he did! The one who was the boss. Like gravel it was."

It was as Anna had thought when she saw the sleigh move noiselessly out from the alleyway leading to the coach house. It *had* been Doliński's face she caught just for a second in the light of the moon. Her fear for Basia had proved wrong. He had been after Tadeusz. Her son was a captive in that sleigh and at the mercy of Doliński!

Anna remembered Paweł's warning and concluded that Doliński must somehow be connected to the Polish member of the Brotherhood who had infiltrated the group on behalf of some Prussian interest. Or—perhaps he was the spy himself!

They passed out of Warsaw's western gate. "We'll have to make a decision soon, Mother," Jan Michał called back. "Which way now?"

Anna leaned forward. "Take the Sochaczew Road, Michał!" *What am I doing?* Anna asked herself. *What?* Flying through the night in a sleigh—two women and a fourteen-year-old boy—chasing down a criminal who could easily kill them all without a wrinkle to his conscience? She sat back against the cushion. *What have I gotten us into?*

But there had been no time to tell authorities, authorities who would likely find her story incredible. No time to seek help from the Brotherhood, even though they were likely to believe her because of their interest in Tadeusz. No time. She had to act. Tadeusz's life was at stake.

Iza had been as distraught as Basia over the dog's death, but she collected herself and brought Basia downstairs to stay with her the remainder of the night. Neither Michał nor Zofia would be left behind. Or could be. Anna knew she needed them. Before leaving, Michał took down from the wall the saber that had belonged to Anna's ancestor who had used it when King Jan Sobieski stood against the Turks at Vienna, and for his service had been ennobled. Zofia and Anna each took a pistol. Only Anna had ever fired one–once, a long time ago.

God was with them in that the snow had stopped falling and the moon was as round and bright as a gold ducat. Still, Anna and Zofia had to shield their faces from pelting particles of snow and ice that flew up from the horses' hooves.

Intermittently, Jan Michał called back that he thought he could see marks of the sleigh and horses that had preceded them.

As they came into Sochaczew hours later, however, the wind and fresh, light snow layered the roads, leaving them pure white and smooth as a counterpane on a freshly made bed. No marks at all. They came to the Market Square, and Anna directed Jan Michał to slowly approach the little complex of offices belonging to the *starosta*. But as they drew near, they could see that all was dark within and without. No signs of a sleigh and horses. No signs of life.

Anna's heart dropped. What if she had been wrong? She had guessed they would not stay at an inn because of the prisoner they carried. But what if they had? Or, what if they had continued on, making for Prussia now, traveling straight through? The thought paralyzed her. How could they ever be found?

"Well?" Zofia pressed. "Did you expect someone here? What are we to do now?"

Jan Michał turned about. His expression underscored Zofia's words.

"Take the North Road, Michał." Anna commanded. "It's not more than fifteen minutes. Look for a little drive off to the right. It's planted on either side with tall evergreens."

The sleigh moved on, and the three fell silent.

"There!" Anna cried in a low but sharp tone. "There are the trees and the drive, Michał." The sleigh came to a halt. She stared down the long drive toward the modest manor house of the *starosta*. She had passed this way many times, but had been to the house itself only once–when she had come with her mother, who demanded from Doliński justice for the killing of her husband. Whether it was any fault of his, she had never found out, but subsequently he had somehow allowed the murderer to escape.

At this distance, the house looked tiny, the windows dark. And there were no signs of a sleigh. "We need to go closer," Anna said, "on foot."

Neither companion questioned her. Jan Michał handed Anna and Zofia down from the sleigh.

"Let's go," Anna whispered. "Go slowly and don't talk. Voices will carry on a night like this."

"Wait a minute, then," Zofia said, placing her hand on Anna's arm. "I think your son and I need to know what this is about, Anna. Why would someone here want to take Tadeusz?"

Anna sighed. She knew her cousin was right. They needed to know the circumstances—just what risk there was, and why. In few words she told them now, the silver light from the moon defining their faces as she relayed to them the Brotherhood's plans for Tadeusz—*possible* plans, she underscored. And with few details, she characterized Doliński as a man who would enjoy doing harm to her family.

"Tadeusz—king?" Zofia said, her voice drawing out the second word. She was stunned.

"I would not wager money on it," Anna replied. "I never have."

Jan Michał's eyes had gone wide, but he said nothing. Anna could only imagine how Tadeusz's treatment at the academy now made some sort of sense to him. How could they have helped but treat him differently, knowing there was a chance he would be king of a restored Commonwealth one day? And Jan Michał was a sensitive enough child that he would pick up on the slightest nuance of difference in the ways they were treated.

"I'll lead," Jan Michał was saying. "Mother, you and Aunt Zofia follow in my boot steps."

Child? Anna thought, as they started their single-line procession. *Jan Michał is a man.*

They had gone some fifty paces when Zofia cautioned them to stop.

"What is it?" Anna asked.

"A light! There, to the left of the portico."

Zofia was right. A pale yellow flickered in the windows. Anna's heart caught. She felt she was nearer Tadeusz. But nearer danger, too. "Push on, Michał."

The three moved another two hundred paces without stopping, without speaking, the crunch of snow beneath their boots resonating in the stillness. Jan Michał led them to a cluster of shrubs near the lighted window. "I'll take a look," Anna said.

"No, Mother. I'm taller. I'll get a better view."

He was not taller by much, but Anna deferred. She and Zofia held to each other, watching as he sidled up to the white siding of the house, then slowly maneuvered his way to the window. The crocheted curtains framed the upper width and sides of the window, allowing one to peer inside at its midpoint. Jan Michał remained locked in position for what seemed a long while.

At last, Jan Michał rejoined Anna and Zofia, his face dark with anger. "He's in there, all right. On a couch—tied up and gagged like I was."

"And the other two?" Zofia asked before Anna could.

"Just one is in the room."

"Is it Doliński—the one you called the boss?"

Jan Michał shrugged. "I don't know."

Of course he wouldn't know, Anna realized. He had only heard Doliński's voice. He hadn't seen him. "I'm going to look," Anna said. "Jan Michał, hold your anger in check, do you hear? Now, go around back and see what you can find. Check the stable. Find out where the other one is, if you can. Then come back. For God's sake, don't do anything with that saber. Be careful!"

Jan Michał disappeared. "And me?" Zofia asked.

"Just wait."

"Wait?" —I'm sorry, I didn't bring my knitting with me. Anna, do you have a plan?"

"No, not yet. I wish I had, but we'll put one together once we know where they both are."

"Assuming there are only two."

The thought that there might be more sent a chill through Anna. "Wait for me." Anna moved in behind the shrubs and took short, stealthy steps to the window. Jan Michał's little bit of extra height had given him an edge, for Anna had to stand on her toes while gripping the window ledge. She prayed she would maintain her balance.

Suddenly she caught sight of Doliński's face not two paces beyond the window pane! She froze in place. He had gone near the doorway of the room and turned, as if to survey the human bundle on the couch. Anna closed her eyes, her heart in a vise, fearing he would turn just slightly and see her there in the window. All their lives would be worthless. He would let no one escape.

Upon opening her eyes again, Anna saw that he had left the room. Tadeusz was unguarded, for the time being. The moment hung fire. She half expected the front door to open, allowing Doliński to fly at her.

A full minute passed. Anna let herself down and quickly went to where she had left her cousin. But Zofia was gone. Anna didn't dare call out. She stood there in the numbing cold, wondering what to do next.

Then, out of the dark, she did see someone moving toward her.

"Anna!" Zofia whispered.

"I told you to stay put! Where did you go?"

"To the front door. They're trusting criminals—it's unlocked."

"Praise God, that's good news."

Zofia put the tips of her fingers on Anna's mouth for just a moment. Then she silently pointed to the window of a second-floor room. A light had been made there, and they could see someone's shadow playing against the window.

"Doliński, I think," Anna said breathlessly. "He just left Tadeusz alone."

"Let's go in, then."

"No, let me go in. You go to the window and come in only if I wave you in. We can't risk all of us at once. And you need to be here when Jan Michał comes back around."

Zofia acquiesced, and Anna slipped onto the portico, pushing open the front door and moving slowly into the hall. She stood there for the longest time. The house was silent as an abbey except for the sound of the fire crackling in the room in which Tadeusz lay. Anna turned now, moving for the open door to that room. She stopped on its threshold. It was a little library, dirty and ill-kept. She moved furtively toward the couch. About ten steps away from Tadeusz, the floorboards creaked, and the boy opened his eyes. Anna said a little prayer of thanksgiving to herself. He had his senses about him, and she hoped that once he was untied, he would be able to walk out on his own.

She fell on her knees by the couch. Her son's blue eyes had gone wide with relief. "We'll get you out of here, Tadek. Just be *very* quiet once I get this cravat untied."

Untying the knots in the bad light, however, was no easy thing, and Anna's nervousness worked against her. When she realized it was taking too long, she gave up, and her hands moved to the ropes that had been fastened at his wrists.

She was having more success with these when Tadeusz jerked his head up, his eyes wide in fear—no, in warning! Anna heard a step behind her.

As she turned, some inner sense directed her to move, and she did so—just as Doliński brought down a hearth poker. It clipped her shoulder instead of her head.

Anna rolled to the side and scrambled several paces away.

"We have a visitor, it seems, Tadeusz," Doliński rasped. "Isn't that nice?" He still held the poker. "Good to see you in Sochaczew, Lady Stelnicka."

"I've come for my son," Anna said.

"Have you? That's unfortunate for you." Doliński started for her, his hand with the poker lifting high into the air.

"The misfortune is yours!" The voice belonged to Zofia, who emerged from the shadows near the door.

"Ah, and you brought a friend, I see," Doliński said, turning about. However overweight, he cut an imposing figure and was not going to be easily cowed. But then he fell suddenly silent, for he saw what Anna saw. Zofia had her pistol trained on him.

"You're going to let the boy go," Zofia said. "Anna, untie your son."

"Let's not be hasty," Doliński said. "The boy has a great future. I've taken him into custody for the Brotherhood."

"You're lying!" Zofia cried. "Stay where you are, bastard. I would enjoy killing you."

Doliński took a step toward Zofia. "Have you killed many?" he asked. He took another step.

Zofia raised the pistol.

Doliński wasn't to be deterred. He doubted Zofia's will. Anna did not.

Zofia pulled the trigger.

No explosion followed. Just a timid click of the hammer. Horror flashed like lightning across Zofia's face, and she released the second hammer.

Nothing.

The pistol had not been properly primed. Doliński laughed and started to rush Zofia, the poker held high in the air, ready to strike.

Now came the explosion.

Doliński stopped in midstep, the poker falling to the floor. He had only a few seconds to turn and face Anna, his face screwed into an expression of disbelief and pain.

Anna stood, ready to fire again, but Doliński folded over now and fell to the floor.

A long moment passed as Anna and Zofia stared at him, lifeless on the floor, then at each other. Finally, Zofia said, "Thank God *your* pistol worked, Anna!"

Anna held a finger to her lips, shushing her cousin. The sound of the shot was bound to bring his friend.

At that moment a door at the rear of the room burst open as if by a bomb. Anna swiftly turned, raising the gun, ready to release the second chamber. The order to fire had already gone from her brain to her finger when she sighted the tall figure coming through the door.

"Anna, don't!" Zofia screamed. "Don't! It's Michał!"

Anna was in such a state of fear and panic and shock at taking one life that she moved with no will or mind of her own. It was Zofia's scream that very probably saved Jan Michał's life, Anna would conclude later. The scream paralyzed the finger she had on the trigger. Jan Michał came fully into the room now, his saber drawn, his eyes on Doliński.

"Did you see the other one?" Zofia implored Jan Michał. "Surely he heard the shot."

"He heard it," Jan Michał said in a strange and cryptic tone. His face was a white mask. "He'll not trouble us."

"You killed him?" Tadeusz asked, his face bright with amazement. He had finished the job of loosening his bonds and taken the gag from his mouth, which now formed a perfect *0*.

Anna looked down then at the saber Michał held, its shiny blade dulled with crimson.

25

Mid-March 1807

The long, grueling march to Gdańsk through a cold and muddy terrain was coming to an end. As Jan came upon the outskirts of the city, an important fortified port on the Vistula with access to the Baltic, his lancer squadron was forced to find routes along hills and fields because the roads converging on the city were so saturated with the oncoming French and Polish infantry. His squadron was part of the two divisions led by General Dąbrowski, who had recovered from his wounds and rejoined the legion. Through intelligence briefings—and through the naked eye—Jan took inventory of those marching with them. Supporting the French *Chasseurs à Cheval*, Polish cavalry included the lancers under Dziewanowski, Prince Radziwiłł's Northern Legion, and General Sokolnicki's cavalry—as well as Polish and French infantry numberless as the spring grasses that had yet to appear.

It was an awesome sight. Jan wondered how any Prussian sentinel in the Gdańsk tower could look out at the advancing forces and not tremble. Keeping out of cannon range, the forces made camp in the abutting suburbs. At night a huge fire broke out. The Prussians had set fire to those buildings closest to the city to limit shelter for the advancing masses. Fire burned all night, bright enough for Jan to write a letter to Anna.

The perimeter of Gdańsk was immense, but much of it was neutralized by the River Vistula and floodplains. The city was primarily protected by two forts, the Góra Gradowa and Góra Biskupia, both on the south of the city. These fortifications became the focus of the siege. Once they were taken, the city would not stand.

In the morning, Jan's squadron ran skirmishing operations in the suburbs, all the time advancing closer. Small-arms fire resounded as the enemy stood ground outside the forts. By noon the Prussians had retreated into their fortifications and begun heavy artillery fire. Eight of Jan's men were wounded, two killed. Jan helped in the retrieval of the body of one of the two, young Sylwester Fiszer, who had been disemboweled by a cannonball. Jan blinked back at the horror of the sight. Ironically, the blond boy's face seemed to be merely in repose. Much of the time Jan pushed through the movements of battle like a well-oiled machine, but such moments caught him up, reminding him of the true impact of war and killing. Sylwester was nineteen.

A retreat beyond the cannon fire was called and camp made. The next day work on the trenches for siege-works began. French engineers set an army of sappers to work, digging the trenches at night, like worker ants. Under cover of darkness, the enemy sent out patrols from the forts to locate the sappers, light flares, and pick them off with carbines. Jan and his men worked to good effect in countering them, allowing the siege-works to continue.

A few days later, at some distance from Jan's squadron, enemy cavalry made a daylight sortie from Góra Gradowa with a force large enough to evict the French from the trenches. Some two hundred lance-carrying Cossacks appeared then, like a blur of clouds, and began to take down the fleeing French and Polish infantry. A single French light horse regiment came on the scene, only to soon fall out of line in retreat. Jan supposed it was the first time they had encountered the legendary Cossacks.

Jan had seen them before, fought them before. They were as good as—and sometimes better than—the Polish lancers. Most had been trained in weaponry from their childhood, especially in the lance. They shunned formations, preferring instead hit-and-run operations, running down a confused and routed enemy, as they were doing now.

And their mode of operation concluded just as Jan figured. By the time his squadron descended upon them, the Cossacks turned about and took refuge in the fort, carrying a good number of captives with them. Nonetheless, progress on the siege-works went on, and the installation of heavy French cannon began. Nighttime resistance from the enemy continued, to little effect. They were on the defensive; their raids fewer in number.

Optimism took root in the French camp. Among the officers and enlisted men there pulsed the notion that victory was within sight.

As March fell away, those inside the two forts who watched the French siege-works proceed grew more desperate.

One morning before dawn, Jan's squadron was patrolling the area of the siege-works when they were beset by Prussian skirmishers who had somehow maneuvered to the rear of their position. His squadron stood firm, however, allowing the French sappers to make a hasty retreat. The sky was still dark, but the snow on the ground made for decent visibility. Carbines of both sides, even fired from moving horses, occasionally found their marks.

At this point, full enemy infantry regiments were deployed from Góra Gradowa.

"Stay in skirmish order!" Jan shouted to his lancers. "Hold the line!" The escape of the French sappers took precedence. Then, as dawn began to break, Cossacks streamed out of the fort like wasps from a hive, their impressive lances stingers to avoid. "Form up!" Jan called. "Form up!" He directed the bulk of his squadron to fall back while he and a few others still stood their ground, covering the retreat.

But there wasn't enough time. The Cossacks, breaking into characteristic threes, bore down on them, disrupting their formation. Jan dispatched two with some ease. In the chaos, however, Jan became separated from his men. A party of three Cossacks descended on him now—lances lowered—but sabers raised. They circled around him with dizzying speed.

Around and around. And yet again—as if their interest was only to madden their quarry.

Jan's arms moved with lightning speed, his saber slicing into the arm of one, then glancing off the shoulder of the next. His left hand was reaching for his carbine.

Now—unseen—came the blow to his own neck, and the world of men, weapons, horses, and hooves revolved, swirling about him. He heard his carbine strike the ground.

Something else—something heavier—struck the ground then. It took some moments for him to realize that it was his own body.

He opened his eyes to find himself in the middle of—no, at the bottom of—a whirlwind. Amidst the smoke, swish of swords, and cries of men, the Cossack horses danced around him, their instinct keeping him safe for the moment.

Stunned and immobilized, he waited for a Cossack deathblow. Men and horses spun about him. In the east he could see the first crimson rays. His last dawn. Light went to dark and light again.

And, finally—dark.

3 May 1807

"Listen to me, Anna," Zofia said. "There's nothing for you to worry about. The siege at Gdańsk *still* goes on. That you haven't heard from Jan means nothing. The man probably doesn't have time to put a crust of bread to his mouth, much less a quill to paper."

"I suppose you're right."

"I *am* right! And just how does one get letters out of a war zone, may I ask?"

Anna shrugged and forced a smile.

Zofia changed the subject. "Now, this is really something, Ania, when we stand here ready to go and our girls are still at their toilette! What do you think?"

Anna laughed and called up to Barbara.

"What can they be doing?" Zofia asked. "Choosing bonnets? Ah, if only my Izabel had a sense of style."

In a few minutes, Barbara and Izabel came down the stairs, arm in arm. The foursome moved out into Piwna Street and fell into the flow of people moving toward the Market Square. It was a bright and sunny spring day. Because of the obvious symbolism, the third of May had been chosen for the presentation of the colors to representatives of the three Polish legions. The Third of May Constitution of 1791 had brought democratic reform into the heart of Europe and hope into the hearts of so many Poles. But it had been short-lived. The Commonwealth's neighbors would not tolerate the seeds of democracy being sown so near their feudal lands.

The little group came into the crowded square. "Hold hands, you two," Anna said to the girls, "and don't let go, or lose sight of us."

"Look," Zofia said, "there are the academy cadets!"

Anna craned her neck, straining to see across the square. The many military cadets were given a place of honor near the dais that had been erected. They formed a semicircle about the platform, three or four boys deep. Her eyes searched the clean and alert young faces for her boys.

"There they are!" Zofia cried. "In that little wing off to the right."

Anna and the girls saw them, too, and waved. Anna thought—or imagined—Jan Michał's brown eyes taking notice. Of course, he dared not exhibit any behavior that wasn't military. He stood like a wooden soldier, his little brother at his side.

Jan Michał. Today was his fifteenth name day. He had been born on the first anniversary of the signing of the Constitution. It was a sign, people had told her then. A good sign.

The Archbishop of Warsaw stepped up to the simple altar upon the dais and began the celebratory Mass. A hush descended on the audience almost as if God himself had waved his hand for silence. The mingling of God and patriotism, Anna thought, makes for an iron will. It came to her then that it was that combination that made for the Poles' love of glory.

As the Mass progressed, her mind went back to the events at Sochaczew a few weeks before. She felt blessed and thankful that her two sons were here this day. That they both had lived through that terrible experience.

But she had her worries and guilt, too. For the second time in her life she had killed someone. However deserving Doliński may have been of his fate, she still could not shake the sight of his dying right before her eyes—and those of young Tadek. She could only wonder how soldiers coped with the killing they were forced to do.

They had left the Doliński manor house that night without looking back. Anna had wanted to go to the authorities, but Zofia pulled her aside. It would be too hard a thing to explain and to prove, she told her. There would be questions and hearings and accusations—and no way to avoid bringing in the boys. What would that do to their futures? And what of the secret role of the Brotherhood? Was that to be exposed? At what expense? No witnesses had been present that night, Zofia pointed out. Doliński himself had seen to it that his servants were absent. Only he and the peasant who helped him were there, and they could no longer tell the tale.

After Doliński's death, Anna, Zofia, and the boys had gone to the school commandant, who—no doubt for Tadeusz's sake—suggested, as did Zofia, Anna not go to authorities. He spoke to the boys himself, praising their mother's actions and exacting from them strict silence. They were to tell no one. "Not Father?" Tadeusz asked. "No one," the commandant said. The boys had sworn by the school code, and she knew they would not break their oath.

So none of those present told anyone. In recent days, little articles had run in Warsaw's *Monitor* about the strange death of the *starosta* in Sochaczew. The peasant found dead at the site had yet to be identified.

Suddenly Anna realized it was time for the benediction. At this point, the standards for the three legions—stitched by Polish women—were marched into the square and up to the dais, where ancient custom dictated that the dignitaries there drive a nail into the staffs to show their unswerving loyalty to the cause. The archbishop and others did so first.

Then the general-in-chief, Prince Poniatowski, spoke eloquently of Poland's past, present, and future, conjuring up for his listeners a country large in heart and soul and honor. After moving many to tears with his words, he spoke of the mothers, wives, and sisters who had sent or would send loved ones off to war, many never to return. "These women," he exclaimed in stentorian tones, "Poland recognizes today by asking them to come forward and drive nails themselves into the standards!"

An audible gasp went up from the audience. This was not customary. And then the line formed, folding and winding and looping about many times over, moving slower than the Communion line, but just as sacredly quiet. Basia turned and looked up at Anna as if to say, *Me too?* Anna nodded to both Basia and Iza, directing them to the line. She and Zofia followed.

As the line moved, she watched Prince Poniatowski on the dais. She had always admired him, but now she took him to her heart. He was handsome, brave, forward-looking, and compassionate. And he was the nephew of the former king. Did it not stand to reason he was a fine choice for king, should the throne be restored?

Why, then, did the Brotherhood choose to support a boy candidate? It was true that King Stanisław—under the auspices of Russia's Catherine—had raised Anna from countess to princess. Anna didn't think of it often, and when she did, the thought never failed to come without a little jolt. And it was true that the Groński bloodline could be traced to King Jan Sobieski. But she saw little chance of Tadeusz's being elected king. She wished the Brotherhood had not conceived the notion. It was no boon to her family.

This addition to the ceremony made by Prince Poniatowski added another hour to the presentation of the colors that had already gone more than two. And yet no one seemed to care. The day would stand in everyone's memory. When the few at the tail of the serpentine line had driven their nails, the archbishop offered his final prayer, and the sounds of sniffling and not a few sobs swept the square.

A strong tenor voice sang out:

> "Poland has not perished yet,
> So long as we still live."

Spontaneously, the crowd joined in with the words of the Józef Wybicki song, filling the Market Square with hope that seemed tangible.

Then the throng began dispersing, the academy cadets filing out of the square, two by two. Anna took one long final look at her sons. Sadness coursed through her. The students' activities for the day had been planned by the academy. Jan Michał was not to be released for his name day.

Fifteen. Where were the years going? How few were left before her Michałek would be called to march? Before he would *want* to march? And then, Tadeusz?

Anna wished now that she had birthed only girls.

Zofia steered the little group toward Piwna Street. She felt strangely serene after the ceremony. *Perhaps I should attend Mass more often,* she thought, laughing to herself.

At the corner leading to their street, she caught sight of a soldier who seemed to be staring. No, he *was* staring as they passed. Zofia averted her eyes. Oh, she wasn't above flirting with a young officer, but she wasn't about to encourage an infantryman in the public street. Still, there had been something about his look. She turned back. He was still gazing intently. The corners of his fine mouth moved up to form the faintest smile. A knowing smile. Did he know her?

She turned away again, her nose lifted. She would not give him the satisfaction of another glance.

"What is it?" Anna asked.

"Nothing—nothing at all."

They moved on another ten or twelve paces. The house was coming into view. She fought not to look again. They were nearly home. She thought of Lot's wife who had been told not to turn around. His wife's unhappy fate had no effect on Zofia. Her head turned about as if it had a power of its own.

The handsome soldier still stood at the corner, watching. But he had removed his *czapka*. The late afternoon sun glinted in the white-blond hair. The blue eyes danced.

Dog's blood! Zofia felt her heart start to race. *Is it possible?*

He smiled at her recognition.

Before entering the house, Zofia placed her fan into the sleeve of her little jacket. "Oh, I must go back, Anna. I've left my fan in the square."

"You have a dozen more, Zofia. You'll never find it."

"I know just where I placed it. It was Mother's, and I don't want to lose it."

"Let me go back with you, then."

Zofia was already moving away. "No, you go in with the girls. I'll be back in no time." Anna called something to her, but Zofia couldn't decipher it amidst the noise of the crowd. She pushed against the current of those exiting the square, moving quickly toward the corner. How many years now? she asked herself. How many?

Jerzy, she thought. *Jerzy!*

Paweł arrived in Warsaw two days after the presentation of the colors. Zofia sat at the breakfast table, regaling him with the details of the singular event.

"I'm sad to have missed it," he said. "Had I known, I might have arranged to arrive earlier. Is Anna at home?"

"No—Paweł, where have you been, and how is it you can move about without your squadron?"

"My men are attached at the moment to Napoléon. I'm in Warsaw—on a mission."

"And where is the great Emperor Napoléon?" Zofia asked flippantly. "He's not at the siege of Gdańsk?"

"No, but he's running daily communications there with his General Lefebvre. You can be certain he's in charge from afar."

"But where is he? Or is that a state secret?"

Paweł laughed. "No, he's at Schloss Finkenstein in East Prussia. Has been since the first of April. Where is Anna?"

Zofia ignored the question. "Does he have a young woman with him?"

Paweł nodded. "He brought her in at night in a covered coach. Very few have actually seen her, and we're not supposed to know anything about her."

"Ha!" Zofia scoffed. "All of Poland must know by now! So much for Napoléon's secrecy! It's Maria Walewska, isn't it—his *petite Marie?*"

"Why—yes. Do you know her?"

"I've met her."

"I take it you don't like her?"

"She's a fool!" Zofia cried. "You know she's married and has a young child. It's all a bit much for a girl of eighteen."

"To be consorting with the man who imagines himself the Emperor of Europe?"

"*Does* he? Have you seen *her?*"

Before he could answer, Anna came into the room. Remembering his mission, Paweł stood, pulse racing, and went to kiss her.

"This is quite a surprise, Paweł." Her smile was wide and genuine. "It's good to see you."

"And you, Anna!" he stammered. "I hear I missed an amazing ceremony on Sunday."

"You did! But what brings you here now?"

"He's on a mission," Zofia said.

Paweł felt faint. He attempted a smile—or at least a passive expression—while he searched for the right words. He would prefer the battlefield to this.

"What is it?" Anna asked.

Paweł had not meant to blurt it out in the first few moments of seeing her, but he felt the words coming, tripping up through his throat as if he had no control over them.

"I wanted to be the one to tell you, Anna."

"Tell me?" Anna's face went white and to his right he heard a little gasp from Zofia. "Oh my God!" Anna cried. "It's Jan, isn't it?"

Paweł drew in a breath.

"Say something, Paweł." Zofia ordered. "Tell us!"

"Word reached me," Paweł managed, "that—that Jan is missing."

"Missing?" Anna whispered. Zofia pulled out a chair for her. "Missing?" she repeated. "At Gdańsk?"

"Yes." Paweł assisted Anna in sitting.

"It's a siege, Paweł, isn't it?" Zofia asked, a slight tremble in her voice. "How does one go missing in a siege?"

Paweł kept his gaze on Anna as he spoke. "At night the enemy runs sorties out of the forts there. One night he disappeared."

"Disappeared?" Anna muttered.

"On a particular night, ten or twelve days ago, a large group of Cossacks overcame his squadron."

"Cossacks!" Zofia exclaimed, her hand going to her mouth. "My God!"

Anna cast a confused look at Zofia, then turned to Paweł, her face questioning. "Is it better he died?"

"They do have a reputation, Anna. But they don't usually kill their prisoners. You're not to lose hope."

"Jan," Anna said, the word scarcely a breath. "My Jan, a prisoner." She looked dazed. "Cossacks . . ."

Zofia rose, went to the buffet, poured out a little glass of vodka, and brought it to her cousin. Anna's glazed green eyes looked up at Zofia, then at Paweł. Lifting her hand, Anna took the glass and drank down its contents.

Paweł watched the beautiful Zofia at her vanity, but his mind was still on his missing friend and the news he had had to deliver to Anna.

"So you knew all along about this scheme of the Brotherhood's?" Zofia unclasped her necklace, glancing through the mirror to where Paweł lay on the bed, fully clothed. "And you told no one?"

"I was instructed to tell no one. Not even Jan."

"But why would they choose Tadeusz?" Zofia began to brush her hair, and the flames of the tapers on her vanity danced with her movements.

"They wanted someone they could form from the earliest age. Does it upset you?"

"No—although it's strange to think of a child of Anna's as king."

"You're jealous."

Zofia swung around on her stool. "No, why should I be jealous? Anna is family. Besides, Izabel and I would find our places at a court of a King Tadeusz."

Paweł laughed with mock malevolence. "Already plotting, my dear?"

"No, it's only natural for the mind to wander. Are you going to sleep in your uniform? You're not in the field now, you know." Zofia turned back to the mirror.

As Paweł rose and began to undress, he saw her watching him through the mirror.

"Tell me, Paweł, do you think there's a chance the Brotherhood will prevail?"

"Off the record, I think not. Everything seems to go Napoléon's way, sooner or later. Poland's future will be in his hands, not in the Brotherhood's."

"Nor in Russia's?"

"No."

"So—*you* think he will be Emperor of Europe?"

"If he has anything to say about it, he will. But it remains to be seen. He stumbled a bit at Eylau, and I think that sowed in him a little insecurity, but he may very well put that behind him."

"And we'll be at his mercy, won't we, bowing and scraping at his throne—despite all the Polish blood being shed in the French cause?"

"It's in the Polish cause, too."

"Now, *that's* what remains to be seen! Just watch, we'll find ourselves with a French king. Napoléon, the High and Mighty!"

Paweł said nothing. She had struck upon a strong possibility.

Neither spoke for a while. Paweł climbed into bed. Zofia stood, her back to him. Her mood seemed to have undergone a transformation. "What *are* Jan's chances, Paweł?"

Paweł pulled himself up in bed. He felt his throat closing. "I—I don't count him out, Zofia. The man has strength and determination."

"Cossacks don't murder their prisoners?"

"Sometimes, maybe. But often not—at least in an overt way. Most die as a result of the conditions they're exposed to."

"I shouldn't make Anna too hopeful, then."

"I don't know. She *should* hope. She should pray."

"I don't believe in prayer, Paweł," Zofia said, allowing her chemise to fall to the floor. "I wish I did."

Paweł studied her in the flickering light of the tapers. She had such a beautiful body, he thought. *So beautiful.* Zofia didn't move for the longest time. "Zofia?" He saw now that her back was shaking slightly. At a second urging, she snuffed the tapers and came to him, slipping beneath the counterpane. He took her into the crook of his arm and touched her cheek. "You're crying."

"It's nothing."

"Is it Jan?"

Zofia sighed and remained quiet for a long while.

"Zofia?"

"It is and it's more than that. Paweł, I never loved Jan. Despite the grief I gave him and Anna, I never loved him. You need to know that. If I believed in prayer, I'd ask God to bring him back to Anna. So, yes, these tears are for him—and they're for the loss of my home and estate and my mother and God knows what might be next. And Poland! I've often made light of the fact that we are Europe's plaything and from one day to the next often wake up under new ownership. But I *do* care, Paweł, I do! And I don't know how much more I can take." Zofia started to shake now, and the tears streamed as if she had been storing them up for years. She reached out and clung to Paweł.

Zofia seemed a fragile doll as he held her trembling form. He spoke to her softly, consoling her, wondering where all her strength had gone. If only he could tell her there would be no more losses.

If only he could ask whether she might one day love him.

Paweł opened his eyes to someone nudging him. He stared into the beautiful black eyes of Zofia, and they were laughing at him. She was fully dressed and made up.

"Paweł—you are a slugabed! This is your only full day in Warsaw—are you going to sleep it away? After breakfast you're to take me for a drive." She bent low and kissed him lightly. "Now get up."

Paweł took hold of her, attempting a more passionate kiss.

Zofia pulled back, smiling. "There'll be time for that later—if you behave."

The old Zofia had made a comeback, he realized. And he was glad for it.

26

Anna sat at her secretary writing to Anusia Potocka, declining yet another supper invitation when a knock came at the door. "It's Zofia, Anna. May I come in?"

"Of course."

Zofia entered and took care to close the door behind her. Anna looked up and knew immediately from her cousin's face that something was amiss. "What is it?"

"Anna, you have a visitor." For once, Zofia seemed at a loss as to how to word something. "From Sochaczew—the *starosta.*"

"What foul joke is this?" Anna stood. "He's dead, Zofia. He's dead!"

"The *new* starosta. I'm sorry. I should have said so."

It was no wonder the color had gone from Zofia's face. Anna felt faint, also. Her mouth was suddenly dry. "Is it about—about Doliński?"

"Yes, but that's all he would say to me."

"Sweet Jesus," Anna whispered and fell back into her chair. "They know! They *know!*"

"They *can't* know anything," Zofia said, coming forward. "You must be strong, Anna. You must."

"What are we to do?"

"Nothing. We do nothing. We know nothing—do you understand?"

"We should have told someone at the time. Now it looks as if—"

"Listen to me," Zofia rasped. "It wasn't murder." Her hands reached up to grasp Anna's shoulders. "We both know that. And there isn't another person alive who knows what went on that night. Remember *that.*"

"The boys know!"

"Yes, and if not for your own good, then it's for theirs that you are not to say anything."

"But the *starosta*—he *must* know something. Why else would he come here?"

"We'll find out what he knows when we go down. But we're not to give anything away, do you understand?"

"You'll stay close by?"

"Of course. You're in a fragile condition right now. I've told him that. Play that up as you need to."

Anna paused for a moment outside the downstairs reception room to compose herself anew. She was not playacting. She *was* in a fragile state. Zofia led her in then and introduced her to Lord Bolesław Myszkiewicz.

"Pardon me for this intrusion, Lady Stelnicka." He bowed and kissed Anna's hand.

"Oh, it is no intrusion, Lord Myszkiewicz. I am always glad to see someone from my birthplace."

"Are you?"

"Of course! Please, do sit."

The *starosta* retreated to the couch where he had been sitting when they came in.

Anna sat in the chair across from him. "Will you have tea?"

"I did offer," Zofia said.

Anna saw that she had moved around behind the couch and stood near the window. This would be the vantage point from which she would coach Anna.

"And I declined, Lady Stelnicka."

Anna took in a deep breath. The formalities were over, it seemed. Now came the business.

"Lady Stelnicka, you knew Lord Grzegorz Doliński, my predecessor as *starosta?*"

"Yes. Not well, however."

"And you've heard of his recent death?"

"Yes, I've read of it in the *Monitor.*"

"A tragic thing," Zofia said. "Very tragic."

"Indeed," said the *starosta,* turning his head to acknowledge Zofia. "It was a shock to all of Sochaczew."

"Scavengers, I suppose," Zofia offered.

"Actually, nothing was missing, Lady Grońska."

Before he could bring his head around and gaze back at Anna, Zofia shot her a warning glance. *Be careful, Anna,* it seemed to say. *Go slowly.*

"You say not well, Lady Stelnicka?"

"What?"

"You say you did not know him well."

"Oh. No, I didn't."

"Not in all the years he held that position?"

"No, Lord Myszkiewicz."

"I see."

"I didn't spend all my years there." Anna felt sick at her stomach. The man was fishing.

"Anna lived at my home in Halicz," Zofia offered, "and then in Praga for some time."

Anna nodded. "Before the final Partition, of course."

"You left Sochaczew soon after your parents died, I understand?"

"Yes."

"Your father was killed by a peasant?"

The old darkness descended on Anna. "Yes, and Mother died soon after of depression and a broken heart. She lost an infant son, too, at that time. My brother."

"I'm sorry."

Anna was surprised how suddenly—and with what ferocity—all the pain of those losses rushed back at her.

"Perhaps this is enough for today, Lord Myszkiewicz," Zofia said, coming around to stand to the side of Anna. "As I said, my cousin's health is not stable, and she should go back to her room to rest."

"I'll take only a moment more, Lady Grońska, to fulfill my mission."

Mission? Anna thought. She looked to Zofia, whose face—probably mirroring Anna's—had gone white as chalk.

"Do you recall," the *starosta* continued, his faded blue eyes on Anna, "the name of your father's attacker?"

It was not a question she anticipated. She sat suddenly erect. "I shall never forget it, Lord Myszkiewicz. It was Feliks Paduch."

"I see."

The old bitterness—like tinder dried for a hundred years—was suddenly reignited. "Feliks Paduch killed my father, and Doliński somehow allowed the murderer to escape."

Zofia quickly swung around behind the couch and out of the *starosta*'s view. Her face was full of fear—and caution. Anna realized at once she was stupidly handing the *starosta* a motive for killing Doliński.

"You're still tormented about it," the *starosta* said in what Anna thought an overly solicitous way. "I find that very understandable."

"I—I have found my way to acceptance." It was a lame statement, she knew. A glance at Zofia's expression underscored its impotency. *Just what evidence does he have? Let him say it now!*

"I regret having to bring up all this old hurt, Lady Stelnicka, but I think when you hear what I have to say, you will be glad."

"Glad?" Anna looked from him to Zofia, whose veiled eyelids gave warning. *Glad?*

He nodded and sat forward. "It seems that Feliks Paduch, the peasant from your family's little village, left for a while after somehow managing to escape, but that he came back to the town of Sochaczew and has lived there for some years."

"What?"

"It's true."

Anna thought she would pass out. "Did Doliński know this?"

"Oh yes, he knew. I regret to say that Doliński was corrupt. How corrupt, we are finding out every day. It's shocking."

"He just allowed Paduch to live peaceably in Sochaczew? Knowing what he had done?"

"Yes, we even suspect Doliński aided Paduch in his escape back in '91. He was probably paid for doing so. That was his specialty—bribery."

Anna's mouth fell slack. Any regret she had for killing Doliński evaporated at that moment. If he were in the room now, she thought, she would do it again. She heard Zofia utter some oath.

"What's to be done with Paduch?" Anna asked.

"It's been done. That's what I've come to tell you."

"Been done?"

He nodded. "You no doubt read that a second man was killed the night Doliński died."

Anna instantly knew where this was going, and a numbness came over her. Was that a question? Did he expect a response?

"We read that there was," Zofia interjected.

"Yes, we did," Anna said, trying to camouflage the shock reeling through her, for she knew what he was going to say next.

"The other man on the Doliński premises—run through with a saber, he was—turned out to be Feliks Paduch."

Anna felt the room around her begin to revolve. The *starosta* went on at some length, telling how Doliński had taken in Paduch and given him shelter, all in return for chores about the manor house—and for following through on some of the *starosta*'s dirty work. It seemed that Paduch had not lost his predilection for drink, threats, and violence.

The room spun faster and faster, and the next thing Anna knew, the *starosta* was leaning over her, making his good-bye, saying something about closing a chapter to her life.

"Thank you," Anna said, as if in a dream. "Thank you."

Zofia saw the *starosta* out. When she returned, she sat across from Anna in the place vacated by the *starosta*. The two stared at one another. Anna had no doubt that to some degree they had twin emotions. For Anna, it wasn't so much relief that they had not been found out for the doings of that night. It was sheer amazement and shock to learn that Feliks Paduch, the murderer of her father, ended up being killed by Jan Michał, the grandson of his victim.

Anna thought about the *starosta*'s parting words. She looked at Zofia and spoke at last. "Oh, the *starosta* was right—a chapter has ended, it's true. But he doesn't know how strangely it's ended, Zofia. How strangely."

"And may he never know, Anna," Zofia said. "God's blessing! Luck was with us today!" She threw back her head then and laughed.

Jan vomited into the all-purpose pail. The ship rolled and pitched, and the two hundred Polish and French prisoners belowdeck rolled and pitched with it. Jan had never been at sea, but more than the motion, it was the stench of human vomit and waste that made him ill in those first days.

He was one of six prisoners confined to the tiny compartment. Each morning they received portions of a foul-tasting gruel, and each afternoon they plotted a takeover of the ship. From their limited vantage point, the prisoners thought the crew weak. At night, several of their Russian captors took up places outside their door, speaking in a low Russian dialect, drinking vodka and throwing dice. Jan knew a bit of Russian, and some of the discernible talk was of a coming peace settlement, something that—along with fever, dysentery, and scurvy—tempered the prisoners' thirst for revolt.

When not fighting storms and squalls, the ship of prisoners sloshed and rolled on, endlessly it seemed. Forty-three days passed. Twelve Poles died, their bodies casually carted away and thrown into the sea like slop from the waste buckets.

Jan staved off real sickness until the very end of the sea journey. By the time the ship docked at Riga, he little expected to live. His incarceration and illness aside, Lithuania seemed worlds away from Warsaw. He doubted he would see Poland again.

The medics in the prisoner ward tended to him, bleeding him daily and ignoring his request of quill and paper so that he might write his last thoughts to Anna. After a bleeding, he would fall into a delirium, dreaming of her, wishing that life for her had been different. That he had been the husband she had hoped he would be.

* * *

"You are presumptuous, Major Potecki!"

"General Grouchy," Paweł said, "it is not my intention to be presumptuous. I am merely stating my opinion."

"I don't wish to hear it."

Paweł looked out into the darkening sky. To his right, far as the eye could see, the fields and woods above Friedland and the River Alle shook and rumbled and glittered with guns and artillery. There Napoléon and his other generals were waging a multifront battle that had begun early in the morning. From this vantage point, directly overlooking the village of Heinrichsdorf, Paweł watched as twenty-two Russian cavalry squadrons retreated from Napoléon's main forces, scrambling to the only spot where the River Alle was fordable—and making their escape.

"With all due respect, sir—"

The general's glare and his raised forefinger interrupted Paweł. "General Dąbrowski has allowed you to be attached to me because you know the terrain. When you speak to me, I expect you to speak of the landscape, not tactics." The general lifted his field-telescope and stared out at the vast lands beyond which lay Friedland.

Paweł knew that after the fall of Gdańsk, Prussia was a worry no more, and Napoléon considered Friedland the final victory that would bring Russia to her knees—or at least to the table. And yet the Grouchy cavalry, forty squadrons strong, stood watching the Russians cross the river—effecting their escape—when they might have been surprised and easily beaten.

"Of course," the general said, "another reason for your assignment may be your excellent French and my poor Polish, hey?" He shot Paweł a quick sideways glance. "Oh, I know what you're thinking."

Paweł did not reply. He stared out, gripped by a terrible impotence.

"You think we should be swarming down upon them like locusts. I can tell you, Major Potecki, that I have no orders to attack."

Emmanuel Grouchy was not a bad general. Paweł knew him to be brave and effective. Only that morning he had proved it. And at Eylau, he had led his dragoons pell-mell into Russian cavalry, ripping through it like a whirlwind. When his horse was killed beneath him, he remounted after the charge and led a second attack. But there were other stories about him, too, like his part in a bungled attempt to invade Britain in '96. The French fleet under General Lazare Hoche had reached Britain safely, all but the ship carrying Hoche. Next in command, Grouchy chose to sit on board for three days rather than disembark. A great storm arose and the ships retreated across the channel to France, clinching Napoléon's failure to take Britain.

So it seemed to Paweł that indecision was Grouchy's fatal flaw. He needed explicit orders from above or he was at a loss. At Eylau he had had Murat nearby and under his auspices performed gallantly. *Murat,* Paweł thought now. *If only Murat were here.*

Days later, while waiting for the general in his tent, Paweł's eyes fell on the emperor's written missive to Grouchy concerning action at Friedland. Napoléon had directed the left wing to "maneuver so as to cause as much harm as possible to the enemy when he, pressed by the vigorous attack of our right, shall feel the necessity of retreat." So Grouchy *had* orders. Explicit orders. Did the fact that the Russians were already in retreat negate the orders in the general's mind?

In the end, Friedland was taken, and the Russians, under General Bennigsen, put to flight. Paweł had another mystery to ponder when Napoléon did not take up nighttime pursuit of the tired Russians with the French cavalry that had not seen heavy action. Surely Napoléon had proved in the past the advantages of running down an already beaten foe. What held him back now?

Paweł suspected a treaty was in the offing and that perhaps Napoléon did not want to demonize himself in the eyes of Aleksandr by destroying absolutely Bennigsen's forces, and thus perhaps encouraging Aleksandr to fight on.

This was a lesson about power, Paweł realized. A vast wealth of power used successfully—but unwisely—could lead to failure.

27

July 1807

Barbara knocked and entered the little anteroom to Anna's bedchamber. As she walked over to where Anna sat on a couch by the window, her green eyes narrowed. "You've been crying, Mother."

Anna denied it, braving a smile.

"It's about Father, isn't it?"

"Come sit, Basia. I just miss him, that's all."

Barbara was not about to accept that answer. "I heard Aunt Zofia tell Madame Sic that he's missing. Why didn't you tell me?"

Anna bit her lower lip. "He'll come back to us."

Tears started to form in Barbara's eyes. Her lips trembled. She knew—and loved—her father, if only from his letters and her mother's stories.

Anna put her arm around her, pulling her close. "No tears," she rasped. "I'll not have it. Your father will return."

"Do you think so, Mother? Really?"

Anna took her daughter's face in her hands. "We have to think so, Basia. We *must*." They sat for a long while as dusk settled. Anna thought how she was encouraging her daughter to hold her tears inside—as *she* had always done. Since her childhood, Anna had not cried in front of other people. It wasn't a good thing, such holding back, she had come to learn. And yet she couldn't help herself. She knew she should allow Basia to release her emotions through her tears. But if Basia were to cry, she knew her own tears would start—and there would be no sluice gate strong enough to hold back the flood.

When the news had come that Gdańsk had fallen and that the French and Polish prisoners held within the city had been freed, Anna told herself that Jan would be among them. Then the letter from Paweł arrived, stating that no trace had been found of Jan. Paweł did say that some prisoners had been removed from the city by ship but couched it in such a way that Anna was unable to detect real hope on his part. Anna doubted, too, that good records were kept of prisoners who died in captivity.

The letter had come on the day she visited the boys. She had sat erect and smiling, fending off Jan Michał's and Tadeusz's questions about Jan. "He's fine," she assured them. "Your father's too busy with the business of war to write now. You'll hear from him soon." And then she watched—horrified—as they demonstrated for her with quill and paper how the taking of Gdańsk had played out. It seemed that the siege had already become a tactics lesson in classes at the academy.

She nodded and smiled through the presentation, but all the while she was coming to the realization that her boys were not naïve—and that in accepting her assurance of Jan's safety, they were *humoring* her.

On the ride back to Piwna Street, she had to call for the driver to stop. She alighted from the coach and became ill at the side of the road.

Night had fully fallen when Zofia put her head in the doorway. "You're coming to the Potockis' tonight, are you not?"

"I am."

"Good! I'll give you half an hour," Zofia said, disappearing.

Anna felt relieved that her attending the gathering precluded any questions from Zofia about her frame of mind. Barbara's questions had been enough.

And Anna did truly wish to go. Peace had been made at Tilsit, not long after the Friedland victory, and she was anxious to hear about it. Anusia's father had been there for the negotiations, so she relished the thought of hearing a firsthand report.

Anna and Zofia arrived on time. The Potocki household was brightly lit and resounding with chatter and conversation. Anna could not remember an assembly this ebullient in years.

"What could he do?" Lord Stanisław Potocki asked his hushed audience. He was speaking of Aleksandr. The question brought everyone up, quiet and expectant. "After Friedland he *had* to negotiate. And you can be certain Napoléon was anxious for it because Austria may have been considering breaking their neutrality and going over to the Russians."

Anusia's father-in-law went on to set the scene. On 25 June, the two emperors met on a hastily but well-appointed raft in the middle of the River Niemen. Days of discussions and nights of suppers went by as they hammered out the details of the draft. Queen Louise of Prussia did not arrive until 5 July. She played both the suppliant and the coquette, but Napoléon found it hard to forgive her previous tenaciously militant stance against him. She, more so than her husband Frederick William, had cost the French much. Now, as she saw Prussia shrink back to its boundaries of 1772 at the hands of these two mutually admiring emperors, she wept in humiliation.

Among Lord Potocki's listeners a cheer went up. "Just desserts," someone said.

"The French are to keep a presence in Gdańsk," Lord Potocki went on to say, "but it will remain a free city. I can tell you Napoléon is delighted. The French and Russian control of the Baltic keeps Britain—the little emperor's greatest nemesis—at bay. Britain has been, of course, dependent on the Baltic for much of her navy's supplies, and this will hurt her mightily."

While these were indeed important outcomes, Potocki's listeners were growing impatient while they waited for news closer to home. At a lull in conversation, an elderly aunt of Anusia's took a hearing horn from her ear, and her irritated voice crackled out: "What about Poland, my lord? What about Poland?"

A crest of laughter undulated through the room, followed by a chorus agreeing perfectly with the sentiment. Some had heard rumors of the results of Tilsit, but everyone waited on tenterhooks to hear the true story from one who had been there. Count Potocki smiled, raising his hand to quiet his audience. He had been called to the conference to convene with Napoléon on certain French-inspired amendments to the Commonwealth's Third of May Constitution. "The Constitution is to stand again!" he cried jubilantly.

Anna sensed a ripple of electricity flame up and flow through the entire group. Her own spine stiffened at the news, and her arms turned to goose flesh. How her father and Jan's father—both strong proponents of the Constitution— would have celebrated the news! And then she thought of Jan. *Jan!* Time and again, at Kościuszko's side, he had risked his life for the Constitution. Had he lived to hear the news?

"And Poland?" The cryptic question came from a former deputy to the Great *Seym*, Walenty Sobolewski.

The count compressed his lips, and his shoulders sagged a bit. "We have been granted a good portion of our lands lost to Prussia as long ago as the Partition of 1772. But not all—not nearly all."

"And Lithuania?" a Radziwiłł cousin asked.

"The emperor refused to discuss independence for Lithuania."

The room itself seemed to tense as Poles tried to configure the map in their heads. The news settled in as if in a series of little shocks.

No Commonwealth. A smaller Poland. Slighter expectations.

Anna knew everyone in the room was coming to terms with its immediate personal impact. Zofia's face, one dark eyebrow arching upward, for once could be read like a newly inked page. Her vacant property in Praga was safe, but her very valuable estate in Halicz was not to be recovered. Anna felt relief that Sochaczew would be part of the restored Poland, as would Warsaw, of course. But the Stelnicki holdings in Kraków and Uście Zielone would not.

"Is that even enough to call it *Poland?*" a friend of Potocki asked.

Lord Potocki's face clouded. "It's *not* to be called Poland, Marcin."

"What?" Gasps went round the room unsuppressed.

"It's true," he said. "The word *Poland* seemed to have been deliberately avoided by both Napoléon and Aleksandr."

Lord Sobolewski stiffened in his chair. "Both of whom," he interjected, "you've entertained in this room, Stanisław!"

"I know. I know, Walenty. What we're to have is a duchy."

"A *duchy?*" The word rode the room like a wave.

"It's to be the Duchy of Warsaw," Potocki continued.

"With *whom* as duke?" The question came from Zofia. People turned to gawk at her, but she gazed fixedly at the count.

"Frederick Augustus of Saxony."

With this new little shock came silence. The duke-to-be was a non-Pole.

"We must consider this a start," Potocki said, attempting to put the best face on it. "Our Prussian captors are gone. A number of patriots are to accompany me to Dresden as deputies for the new duchy. On the nineteenth of this month, the emperor is to dictate the finished Constitution and make appointments."

"I daresay," the Radziwłł relation muttered, "that *dictate* is the correct word."

"Why Dresden?" someone asked. "Why not Warsaw?"

"The emperor is eager to get back to Paris, and Dresden is on the way."

"And after spilling our blood, we're given short shrift, Lord Potocki," Lord Mdzewski said, with no little bitterness.

Anna empathized with her friend's father. Lord Potocki had no doubt expected this little mutiny. He had known that his guests' expectations ran high. "Come, come," Potocki said, forcing a smile. "We will do the toasts. It is a beginning!"

Zofia leaned over to Anna. "What will you wager that Poland's darling human dowry, Maria Walewska, will be given short shrift, as well?"

Impulsively, Anna fixed her gaze on her cousin and asked, "Given the chance, would you still trade places with Maria?"

"Anna!" Zofia laughed, drawing her head back. She took only a moment to answer. "In a heartbeat, cousin. In a heartbeat."

August 1807

In sweltering heat, Anna returned from the hospital—where she had recently been volunteering—to find Zofia meeting her at the front door. Her cousin's face was uncharacteristically serious. "What is it, Zofia?"

"Come into the dining hall, dearest."

"There's news of Jan!" Anna stood still as death, feeling only the blood draining from her face.

Zofia silently took her by the arm and led her into the dining hall. Paweł and Emma Szraber were seated at the table. Emma had come for a two-day visit, and both she and Paweł wore the same serious expression as Zofia. Paweł rose and came to kiss her.

Anna immediately thought the worst. "He's dead! He's dead, isn't he?" The room went silent for a long moment. All eyes were on her, and she became very faint.

Paweł grasped her upper arms. "No, Anna," he was saying. "Jan is alive."

"Alive?"

"Yes," Zofia said.

"Where?"

"In your bedchamber," Zofia replied.

"What? Oh, you've been pulling long faces to frighten me!" Anna's spirit soared as she disengaged herself from Paweł and turned to go to the stairs. Zofia's hands immediately grasped her upper arm, forcibly detaining her. Anna's head snapped around. No one's expression had lightened. "We need to prepare you, Ania," Zofia said.

Emma nodded. "Before you see him."

"He's been wounded!" Anna blurted. "Has he—?"

Paweł seemed to read her thoughts. "Oh, he's all of one piece, Anna, and has no wound he hasn't already suffered and survived."

"It's just that he's been ill while in captivity," Zofia said. "The Cossacks bled him. But that seemed to worsen his health. I've never believed in it myself."

"So he's thin?" Anna asked.

Paweł nodded. "And weak. Very, very weak."

Zofia nodded. "He no sooner dismounted his horse than he collapsed."

"My God!" Anna scarcely realized the words as her own. She attempted to withdraw from Zofia's grasp. "Let me go to him!"

Emma stood and came around the table. "Anna, you must be strong. You must try to appear as normal as possible." Emma's tears were coming fast now. "You see, you must be stronger than I."

Anna felt as if an ice-cold hand had reached into her chest in order to squeeze the life out of her.

"You're the one who can give him what he needs, Anna," Zofia said. "And that's hope."

Hope. Is Jan's life at risk?

"I see," Anna said, feeling in that instant some unknown power releasing within her veins, like some quick-acting drug. She remained quiet for a long moment. In this time she put aside her panic, took the facts she had been given, digested them, and stored them away. She gathered up her courage now, just as Jan and Paweł and thousands of brave Poles must have done before every battle, practicing on these three the smile that she would give her husband.

They stood back, sensing her new composure.

And then she made for the stairs.

Standing before her little suite, she collected herself anew. No one had followed her up the stairs. She entered now, passing through the anteroom and moving to the open bedchamber door. Lutisha had heard her coming and left the bedside, approaching Anna, giving her customary little curtsy, her face like thunder. Carrying a razor and basin, she passed out of the room without bringing her eyes up to Anna's.

Anna stood, drawing in a deep breath, allowing her eyes to acclimate to the darkness of the room. At first she thought the person lying on the bed was not Jan but some stranger.

She took short, slow steps. The visage she saw now blended into the whiteness of the pillow. His face, like his form, seemed to have shrunken. His hair—and especially his mustache—seemed more gray than blond. Anna came to the side of the bed.

He heard her at last, and his head rolled on the pillow, as if with a great effort. The eyelids lifted, and the cobalt blue orbs fixed on Anna. They at least had not faded! He smiled, and Anna prayed her smile was as genuine as his.

"Lutisha gave me a shave just in time," Jan said. "You're a . . . sight for sore eyes . . . Ania."

"As are you, my darling," she said, reaching for his hand. The thinness of his arms had startled her, and now the weakness of the pressure his hand exerted horrified her.

"Don't . . . don't pretend," he rasped. "I'm a *sore* sight . . . I know."

Anna feigned a little laugh. If he could think to try a sad little joke, she would not cry. She would not.

His slender fingers twitched in her hand. "Your eyes . . . Anna . . . I thought never . . . to see them again."

"It seems that when peace was signed," Paweł was telling Zofia and Emma, "the prisoners were freed and given a half-pension each. Jan was near collapse, lying like a corpse on the edge of Riga's Market Square, when a Cossack approached him. He recognized Jan from the siege. This man slung him onto his packhorse, and they left the city. He was a Ukrainian Cossack, and the Ukraine was where he was headed. They were days on the road, the Cossack always looking out for Jan. By the time they came upon the Warsaw Road, Jan thought himself revived enough by the air and sunshine and food to strike off on his own. The Cossack gave Jan the horse."

"The Cossack did?" Zofia asked, her almond eyes wide in amazement.

Paweł nodded. "He did. When Jan asked for the name of the man's village so that he might send him fair recompense, the Cossack smiled and smacked Jan's horse on its way."

"Praise God!" Emma cried. "Even in war there are miracles."

"Indeed," Paweł said, "the Cossacks are thought an undisciplined lot, eager to unleash terror and violence, but they can be as fine as our Polish lancers in war—and as we see now, sometimes in peace."

* * *

An hour later, Lutisha entered the bedchamber with a glass of warm milk and a small plate of mashed duck livers. Anna's stomach instantly recoiled, but she remembered that after she had been beaten and raped all those years ago, Lutisha had force-fed her the same meal. And she had taken strength, defied death, and survived.

Placing her faith in the longtime servant, Anna went downstairs to find Zofia, Paweł, and Emma in the reception room. She came to the center of the chamber, remained standing, and spoke in a mechanical sort of way, feeling as if she were delivering the prologue to some Shakespearean play.

"Jan will recover," she said, believing it. Willing it. "We will return to our life at Sochaczew. The boys will come home to live with us. There will be no more soldiering in this family." Anna's eyes moved around the room, as if fixing her gaze on each of her loved ones made truth truer. "We are done with war."

Part Four

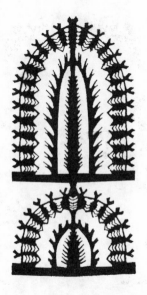

Sweet to the inexperienced is war.

—POLISH PROVERB

28

Paweł sat alone at a little table in a Paris inn. This was the legion's last few days in the capital and a true respite after the years in Spain and the previous month's winter trek over the Pyrenees. He sipped at his drink. He was thinking of the horse, two pack-mules, and a Polish lancer—an acquaintance of his—that had been swept over the side in an avalanche. An inglorious end to an inglorious campaign.

Paweł took stock of his own life. It occurred to him that Jesus Christ died at thirty-three, his life's goal attained, his destiny on earth played out. A strange thought, he realized. He thought also of something Napoléon had been heard saying lately: "Forty *is* forty, after all."

The emperor was nearing forty-three now, one year younger than Paweł himself. And yet both pressed on as if youth were not fading fast with every campaign, every battle, every night and year away from home. Twelve hours on a horse, and Paweł could scarcely walk. Not like in the old days. Was there such a thing as the star Napoléon claimed to be following? *Am I,* he wondered, *following my destiny? To what end?*

A group of rowdy Polish soldiers at the bar broke out into spontaneous song:

> March, march Dąbrowski,
> From Italian soil on to Poland,

Under your leadership
We shall regain our freedom

The large woman tending to the drinks sauntered over. "Another schnapps for you, sir?" When Paweł assented, she poured it out and nodded at the revelers. "How is it they spend everything they have? Poles—not tight-fisted like our Frenchmen."

Paweł laughed. "This is most likely the last they'll see of Paris, madame. They wish it to be memorable. Your Frenchmen will always have Paris."

"Ah, yes," she said, showing her few teeth in an enigmatic grin, "those who aren't laid out all across Europe. *They* have no hope of seeing Paris again, monsieur."

"Touché!" Paweł said, raising the glass.

The woman moved away, pleased with herself.

Paweł was as happy as most of the Polish soldiers going back to Poland—and as war-weary. From the first, subjugation of the Iberian peninsula had been a losing proposition for a host of reasons, not the least of which was France's nemesis, England. It would have taken the whole of the *Grande Armée* to gain success, but now the bulk of the French forces was needed elsewhere. While Aleksandr's treaty with Napoléon forbade trade with England, Russia found it difficult to survive without it. Violations were well known, and as a result, war in the East once again loomed large. Yes, Paweł and his fellow Polish soldiers would see their country again, but Poland would be nothing more than a stopover as the French forces moved toward the great Eastern steppes—toward Russia and war with Aleksandr.

Only the day before, 22 March 1812, at the Place du Carousel, Polish regiments fresh from Spain had marched in review for the mounted emperor. Napoléon's new empress, Maria Louise of Austria, and other pretty noblewomen stood watching from a balcony. He had divorced Joséphine in favor of a political marriage and hopes of a son. Gossip in Paris favored no other subject. His Polish mistress, Maria Walewska, remained in Paris—in seclusion. Paweł heard it whispered that she was none too happy about her current status.

The legions had stood at attention then for a long time. Paweł wondered how many soldiers held it against Napoléon that for the last two years he had left Spain to his subordinates, to desultory effects. He rode up and down now, asking a question here, tossing a compliment there—the sparkle in his gray eyes ultimately eliciting from the men a prideful enthusiasm few other leaders could inspire. "I applaud you all!" the emperor called out. "You are *most* fit to march. I can scarcely believe you have waged such a fine campaign against Spain! Bravo!"

"A fine campaign, indeed," Paweł mumbled to himself. Nonetheless, the emperor went on, at no little length, working his magic on the troops. He was a wizard that way. Somehow—without any *direct* assertion from Napoléon—Polish soldiers had gotten it into their heads that a war with Aleksandr in the East presaged a complete resurrection of the Old Poland. And so, in mighty voices that came from deep within themselves, the regiments called out *"Vive l'Empereur!"* Napoléon seemed quite pleased, but in the end, few decorations were handed out for the risks and sacrifices of nearly four years.

Instead, the men were pronounced fit for travel and the departure date was moved up, cutting short the troops' well-deserved leave in Paris.

Anna opened her eyes. She could hear Jan across the room, probably searching in the dark for his boots. "Jan?"

"Did I wake you? I'm sorry."

"Come here," she said. She didn't tell him that she lay awake most mornings before he went out.

He came over and stood by the bed. "Go back to sleep."

Anna reached up, took his hand, and drew him closer. "Stay with me a few minutes."

He smiled impetuously. "Ah, you're wishing a morning tumble?"

"No, nothing like that!"

"Too bad. There are worse ways to start the day!" He spoke with a mock naughtiness.

"Come," Anna said.

Jan lay down next to her atop the counterpane, bootless but fully clothed. His arm went around her neck, and he drew her to him. "There, is that good?"

"Yes."

"You wish to talk?"

"Yes."

A lull ensued.

"You wish *me* to start?" he asked.

"No, it's just that, well, Jan, I don't always feel a closeness between us."

"I'm holding you, Anna. I'm here. And last night—"

"I know that. It's not just that kind of closeness I mean. It seems like married people should talk about their feelings more. And fears. There should be more sharing. Oh, we have passion, but I long for more." There! She had said it. Would he understand? Jan was quiet for what seemed a long time. Anna waited. She would say nothing that would allow for a lighthearted reply.

"I have my fears," he said at last. "I'm one who acts, though, Anna. You know that. And you must know my feelings."

"I do, Jan, but often I can't read you."

"Read me—what, like a *book?*"

Anna smiled. "A good book—but sometimes—a mystery. Sometimes it is hard to understand you."

"I love you. I tell you so, do I not?"

"You do."

"Perhaps I'm a simpler soul than you think. Perhaps I'm not the type of husband you imagined when you were a girl."

"You are more than I imagined, Jan. *Much more.*"

Jan turned on his side, propping his head up with one arm as he peered down at her. The room was slowly beginning to fill with light now. Anna studied her husband. His face had filled out again after his ordeal with the Cossacks. Despite a limp that was more pronounced in the cold weather, his health and handsomeness had come back to the extent that she could at least *picture* him so many years before, lying in the forest leaves, professing for the first time his love for her. The intervening years were not all happy years, but they were gone, the bad with the good. How very quickly!

"I love you, Ania," he said, as if he had read her mind. As if he, too, had traveled back to that autumnal day in Halicz. "I'm sorry if it seems that I close you out."

"You do."

"You are my heart, Ania, my heart. And our worries are the same, no? Day-to-day life. The boys and Basia—and what kind of a Poland is to be left them."

"They are the future," Anna conceded.

Jan kissed her now, lightly. "Don't be *too* quick to make us the past," he quipped.

"Always a joke," she replied.

As if to refute her gentle accusation, he kissed now with a passion that caught flame in them both, his hand moving over her. Anna had wanted to speak of his lost property, of the new war on the horizon, of their sons' roles in the military. But she felt her body responding to his, felt her mind blurring, becoming a world of colors, not thoughts. After a time, as they made love, his mouth on hers, she opened her eyes. She was startled to find that his cobalt blue eyes were open, too, speaking to her, loving her.

Later, after he had gone out, Anna lay wondering at her chances for another child. She was thirty-eight but not past bearing time. Her courses still came like clockwork. Their children were growing fast, and sometimes she thought she would relish having another little one in the house. Anusia Potocka had just had a little boy, and she envied her. Other times, however, she wondered if she could manage it, for *she* sometimes seemed to be the one in need of nurturing and protection.

Anna often felt at loose ends these days. Her little announcement four years earlier, when Jan came back from Riga, that her family was returning to Sochaczew had come to fruition only in part. The boys had not come with them. The school commandant flatly refused to dismiss Tadeusz. The Brotherhood had invested too much in him. As unlikely as it was that a kingship lay in his future, she was told, they were keeping their options open. They would have allowed Jan Michał to come home, but Anna knew it would break his heart—he had come to love soldiering. And Anna wanted him near Tadeusz.

Jan, who had learned about the Brotherhood's machinations for the first time, took the news calmly, placing no faith in its happening—and after visiting with the boys, voiced no objections to a soldier's life for Tadek and Jan Michał. It was an honorable calling, he told Anna, one on which both boys had already set their minds. Anna realized it was not so strange a reaction, coming as it did from a man with a soldier's heart.

As for Barbara, she had come home to Sochaczew with Jan and Anna, but she was now in Warsaw, pursuing her education at the Convent of Our Lady of the Assumption. It was her fourth year there. On her shorter vacations, she often stayed with Izabel, who was in her third year at the convent school. Anna worried about Zofia's parenting, but all evidence seemed to indicate that her cousin was proving a good influence, and that Izabel—with the help of the nuns—was developing into a true gentlewoman and a good friend to Barbara.

Before Anna and Jan left Warsaw for Sochaczew, they learned just how duplicitous and evil Lord Doliński had been. Paweł remembered him as the Prussian spy within the Brotherhood. And Anna watched as Jan's pallid face became inflamed when she spoke of the threat he had been to her spirit—and person. But it was her turn to be surprised—and angry—when Jan detailed how, in order to hold at bay the Prussians' interest in Anna's estate, he had been blackmailing Jan for years, bleeding his inheritance.

When all Doliński's masks had been removed, Zofia's dark eyes turned on Anna with concern, as if to say, *Are you going to tell?* Talk did turn to Doliński's death then—and to the identity of his accomplice. For a moment, Anna wanted to say that it was she who had killed Doliński and Michał who killed the murderer of his grandfather. But Zofia, perhaps seeing her temptation, spoke out then about the comeuppance the two criminals had gotten. It was enough to give Anna pause—and she kept her silence.

Maybe she should have revealed everything at the time, she thought now, as a way of keeping the boys safe. If they had suffered a bit in the public revelation, they would at least have been removed from the school—no longer cadets, no longer fodder that could fuel still another of Napoléon's campaigns coming this way. She would have confessed, too, had it not been for Zofia and the threats of the school commandant, who wanted no such scandal. Oh, she knew the talk would not have mattered much to the boys. But having to leave school, being forced to give up the thought of soldiering for Poland—that *would* have. They would never have forgiven her.

For years she regretted keeping the secret from Jan.

The thought that war was once again on the horizon made her tremble. Where was her old confidence? Her nerve? Anna remembered the extent she had gone to prior to the last—and final—Partition of Poland. With the capital occupied by Russians, she had hosted numberless meetings of patriots in the Grońska household, putting everyone at risk. She had even the gall to impersonate Zofia in order to warn the king himself of an insurrection within Warsaw. And when Catherine sent her most merciless general to avenge the rebellion, the army descending on Praga, slaying every citizen in its path, Anna had driven a carriage to Warsaw across the burning bridge from Praga.

Anna still wanted a free and independent Poland, as much as ever. But now with talk of yet another war, she felt fear rising up within her, taking a stranglehold. She could think only of her husband and her children. Not a day went by that she didn't imagine the sounds of soldiers on the march, sometimes from the west, sometimes the east, everywhere the tramp of feet.

She recalled Zofia's telling her that countries were merely boundaries that shifted with time, whimsy, and war. Perhaps there was truth in that. She remembered, too, something her Aunt Stella had told her once: "Anna, before there are countries, there are families."

At midmorning, Jan took a rest, sitting down on a fallen tree. He had taken to his old habit of chopping wood on the edge of the estate, where no one would witness the master of Topolostan at such a servile task. It was cold, made more so by a frigid March wind that whipped off the as yet unsown wheat field, but his activity had driven up his body heat so that the chill felt exhilarating. He looked to the east, watching the sun continue its ascendancy.

He knew he had given little satisfaction—other than the physical—to Anna. Instead of opening up more fully to her, he had played the lovemaking card. Why? What would he have told her? That he felt an overwhelming sense of unease in the life he was leading in Sochaczew? He would not say unhappiness. No, he loved Anna as much as ever—more!—but he felt as if he were going through the motions of another man's life.

He had made his choices, after all. He had *asked* to be released from the legion. He would follow Napoléon no longer—no longer looking for promises between the lines of his speeches. Kościuszko had long ago given up on the little Corsican.

Not that Poland had been completely forgotten. With the peace Napoléon had made with Aleksander in 1807 had come the Duchy of Warsaw. The national flag was unfurled once again, and Prince Poniatowski—whom most Poles thought should have been named king—was made Commander of the Army. Napoléon named the king and queen of Saxony duke and duchess of the new duchy. They were benign in their old age, but that they were non-Poles nevertheless stung. It was at least a small blessing that the duchy did not go to French Marshal Joaquim Murat, who had eyeglassed it, or one of the Bonaparte brothers, who were picking up pieces of Europe as if they were chips in a game of cards.

The duchy government consisted of a council of seven ministers and a president. Knowing Jan's past support of Kościuszko and the Constitution, several ministers beseeched him to take a position in the government. Jan declined because it was evident early on that the council operated only with the authority of a kind of proconsul—a Frenchman, of course. And if a truly serious or controversial case arose, its resolution fell into the hands of no one other than Napoléon Bonaparte himself. The Duchy of Warsaw was a puppet government, not the independent nation Jan had dreamed of.

Still, his hopes had been raised less than two years after the duchy was formed. Assuming that Napoléon would be overextended with his troops in Spain and that the French people had lost the taste for perpetual war, Austria had declared a war of revenge on France. Called upon by Napoléon, Poniatowski and his army of sixty thousand did their part magnificently, counterattacking and reclaiming key elements of the old kingdom: the area of Kraków as well as Galicia. For a time it looked as if the Stelnicki town house in Kraków and the Stelnicki and Groński estates in Galicia would be returned—but when Austria sued for peace, Napoléon ceded most of it back.

Time and again, Napoléon broke Poland's heart. And Jan's. Undeterred, Prince Poniatowski continued on under the French aegis. Paweł, too, Jan's greatest friend, fighting there in Spain for years at a time. Why? For what?

Jan's thoughts came back to Anna. She had learned at last of Doliński's bribes to keep her estate from falling into the hands of a Prussian owner. She had paled at the news, cursing the man anew. While she carried no guilt for the death of the man who would have murdered Tadeusz, she seemed little bolstered by his just end. Jan now knew that she could cope with such truths—and yet, he had kept from her an extortion more recent than Doliński's: Once the duchy had been formed, France had demanded an exorbitant amount to keep claim to her own family property. Jan had quietly paid it, using much of the remainder of his family fortune.

So there was this secret and his worries and disappointments that he kept from her. He did it to protect her, to shield her—and his little family. He did it consciously. And he prayed for the day when he could be to her the kind of husband she longed for.

He looked up and saw coming into the clearing the peasant boy who made use of the wood Jan chopped. Hardly a boy any longer. Nearly a man, Jan thought, as he drew closer. Nearly a man, seeing to the needs of his family.

As the boy waved, the noon sun interfered, splashing spangles of light into Jan's eyes. And for a moment Jan imagined him in the blue-and-crimson uniform of an infantryman. Was it a presentiment? Was this the future of every young Pole?

Paweł reached Poznań in early June. It was here that the majority of the troops awaited Napoléon. Paweł experienced the sharpest sense of déjà vu, for all the excitement, triumphal arches, fireworks that had welcomed Napoléon in 1806 welcomed him anew in 1812. The emperor arrived in the evening and could only have been pleased by a lighted crown of laurels displayed on the church clock tower, its inscription reading, *Napoleoni Magno Caesari et Victori!* The citizens and new conscripts, it seemed, placed their faith afresh in the emperor. Of the soldiers, however, there were some of the Old Guard—those veterans that had been there in 1806—who cheered now with less enthusiasm. They were here because they were soldiers and knew no other life. If Jan were here, Paweł knew, he would find his own comfort among this dissembling minority.

As for himself, Paweł had always been an optimist, one who saw the best in people and discounted their flaws. And he would be the first to admit he had worked up no lasting immunity to the emperor's charismatic ways.

Both Jan Michał and Tadeusz were called up to service. As Young Guards in the cavalry, they were assigned to Prince Poniatowski's Warsaw contingent, the Fifth Corps.

In the days prior to their departure, Anna could not bring herself to talk to

Jan about their marching orders. They were to go to Poznań. Now, instead of worrying about her husband away at war, she would have two sons placed in imminent danger. War had become a certainty, and Napoléon's appreciation for the prowess of the Polish soldier was such that he often called on them first. Like other boys of their class, Michał and Tadeusz had been educated to appreciate—no, to *love*—honor, bravery, and the glory of the battlefield. They longed for it. All for the cause of a free and independent Poland.

It was no surprise to her, either, that Jan did not speak on the subject. He remained morosely silent. Anna knew that he—like Kościuszko—placed no trust in Napoléon. But whom else could they trust? Not Russia. Nor Austria. Nor Prussia. And if the good Prince Pepe, as Prince Poniatowski was called, threw in with the Corsican—they told each other—perhaps some good would come of it. The Duchy of Warsaw, flawed as it was in so many ways, was *something*, at least.

And so Anna and Jan stood, shoulder to shoulder and dry-eyed in the Warsaw Market Square, watching the presentation of the colors. This was a more abbreviated ceremony than that she had witnessed in 1806, and this time the attendees were not invited to the dais to hammer symbolic nails into the staffs. Prince Poniatowski and a few dignitaries carried out that tradition. Anna thought it just as well. She hadn't the heart to do it.

Old soldiers spoke in full-throated tones of their valor and deeds well done in past battles won and lost. And it seemed that hovering over the square were the spirits of the many thousands who had died fighting in the Partition years and in the host of wars waged by Napoléon. Now a new generation of Poles had stepped up, mere children really, some with cheeks as soft and smooth as peaches. Children, Anna thought. Children fired with the ardor of war and killing. Her children.

In the midst of the prince's speech, Anna glanced up at the figure atop Zygmunt's column. Suddenly, she was five again, visiting Warsaw for the first time with her father. Craning her neck, she had been awed by the sight. The bronze figure of the long-dead king held a cross in one hand, a sword in the other—like a warrior saint. He had been the one, her father told her, who had moved the capital from Kraków to Warsaw. Even then she had precociously wondered at the strange juxtaposition of the symbolic cross and sword. But some years later, while Jan risked his life in the army and she worked behind the scenes for Kościuszko and the Patriotic Party, she would often quote the proverb, "Sometimes it takes a sword to bring the peace."

Anna looked back to the dais. The ceremony was ending. Jan took her hand to lead her away, applying just the slightest pressure as his fingers encircled hers. Either he knew not to speak or could not. For once she was thankful for his silence. This was no place for tears.

* * *

Anna and Jan arrived back in Sochaczew late into the night. Jan had held her for much of the trip. When they did speak, it was of mundane goings-on at the estate.

Marta received them at the front door, her face tearstained, her blue eyes lifeless.

"What is it, Marta?" Anna asked.

The servant's lower lip trembled as she tried to maintain her composure. "It's Mother, madame. She's—she's dead." Marta's grief betrayed her now, and she shook as she tried to hold back sobs.

Anna took the middle-aged woman into her arms and held her. Unexpected heartache was heavy, indeed.

"Where is she, Marta?" Jan asked. "You sent for the doctor?"

"We took the liberty, my lord. But by the time he got here she was gone. She's in our quarters. Apoplexy, he called it."

"Apoplexy?" Jan said. "Heart seizures can be quick, to be certain."

Marta withdrew from Anna's embrace, embarrassed but thankful.

"No one had a bigger heart," Anna said. "No one."

Servant or not, Lutisha was waked in the Stelnicki reception room for the prescribed three days and nights. Her family and friends maintained visitation around the clock. Anna chose the latest shift, sitting—often alone—near the open pine coffin from midnight until dawn.

Lutisha had been more than a valued servant. She had been also a maternal figure and a friend to Anna.

Years before, many thought Anna would not survive the violent attack at the pond. But Lutisha had stood by her, giving her hope and encouragement, single-handedly nursing her back from the dead. She had insisted that she eat, force-feeding her when necessary. She stayed by Anna's bedside, keeping her well covered against what she called the vapors of the night.

And so now it was Anna's turn to sit with her through the night. A childhood prayer came back to her:

> Angel of God, guardian of mine,
> Stand by my side all of the time,
> Morning, evening, day and night,
> Be with me always to keep me right!

She continued to think about the past. When Anna had gone to the Groński estate at Halicz after the deaths of her parents, Lutisha had welcomed her with her large smile and her sincere concern. Anna remembered, too, how the King's Guard had come into the Praga town house, searching for incriminating writings of Zofia–and how it was Lutisha who managed to find Zofia's wicked writings and secrete them in her skirts. She saved Zofia and perhaps the whole household that day.

Lutisha had served as midwife to Anna for all three of her deliveries. Anna had not given up thoughts of having another child–but what would she do without her Lutisha to bring it into the world? Anna smiled to herself now: Who would tie the red string around the little one's wrist as a protection against the evil eye?

Was it God who granted nobility to a few, leaving the life of the peasantry to so many more? Or was it mere chance? Anna didn't know, but she did know that Lutisha lived her life within its confines to the fullest, demonstrating more love, dignity, and loyalty than most titled people Anna knew.

Anna was thankful that during much of those three long, long nights, she was able to shake free of her sadness and morbid thoughts about sending her sons to war. Even in death, Lutisha continued to serve. But there were times, too, when she thought how Lutisha, nearing eighty, had lived a full life, a life that–like the seasons–was a circle that had come to its completion.

Death was something Anna had feared since her parents and infant brother died years before, one so close upon the other. As the years went on, however, she came to realize that the darkness of death that shadowed her served a purpose, for it was such a perfect foil to the brilliance and joy of life and living. It was a reminder to live and to put aside fear.

Her thoughts, however, eventually came back to her sons, and to the sons of so many others, all soldiers now and in the sweet bloom of youth. So many of them would not live to see the circle of life move to a natural end.

29

y God!" Paweł exclaimed. "Tadeusz, you are the mirror image of your father!" The words were no sooner out of his mouth than he recognized the gravity of his blunder. If he thought for a moment that his insensitivity would somehow slip by unnoticed, one look at Jan Michał—with his Groński features and darker hair and complexion—told him otherwise. Michał's face was reddening with a painful embarrassment. The brown eyes were at once hurt and indignant. Tadeusz seemed oblivious of his stepbrother's reaction. "That's what everyone says, isn't it, Michał?"

"Yes," his brother said, trying to put a good face on it. "And it's no compliment for Papa."

"And Michał, you have Jan's ability to make quick quips," Paweł said, hoping to assuage the hurt. He was eager to change the topic. "Ordinarily you would be meeting with your billeting officer, but in your case, I'll be showing you to your quarters and then around Poznań."

"Excellent!" Michał said. "Say, you were expecting us?"

"Yes, your father wrote, telling me to keep a lookout."

"And the emperor?" Tadeusz pressed. "You'll introduce us?"

Paweł laughed. "He's not here yet."

"But when he does arrive?" Michał asked. "We can meet him?"

"No promises, gentlemen. Is everyone in the Young Guard so enamored with Napoléon?"

Both boys nodded. "He's a strategist like none before him," Michał said.

"The others would kill to meet him," Tadeusz added.

"And no doubt they'll probably have to do so," Paweł said. "Now let's get your gear to our quarters."

"*Our* quarters?" Tadeusz asked. "Are you nearby?"

"Closer than you think. I'm one of the Old Guard assigned to mentor a company of Young Guard."

"*Our* company?" Tadeusz asked.

Paweł nodded.

"We weren't expecting a babysitter," Tadeusz muttered.

Michał's brow lifted in mock petulance. "I suspect our father had something to do with this." He seemed less offended than did his brother.

"He merely wrote to say you were coming, as I mentioned," Paweł said. "The rest was my idea, I admit. Don't worry. In the company of others, you will address me as Major Potecki—and I'll stay out of your way as much as possible. Now, just deny that you're hungry!"

The boys could not, and as they made their way to their quarters, they fell to complaining about the day's long ride. Over supper, Paweł regaled them with his tale of forty-eight hours in the saddle during the Spanish campaign. When he was gotten down off his horse, he couldn't walk, and his feet were so swollen, his boots had to be cut off. A fever kept him on the sidelines for two weeks. Paweł thought that the boys—or rather, young men—might as well know from the start what they were in for.

In turn, they told him of their dream of becoming lancers.

"Don't rush it," he told them. "You'll need decent cavalry service first."

Napoléon arrived the next day to much fanfare. Jan Michał and Tadeusz received no special audience but did get a close-up look when the emperor reviewed the Polish troops, complimenting Prince Poniatowski for all to hear.

For many, the condescending attitude of the emperor contrasted poorly with the natural gentility of the Polish prince. Nonetheless, the Stelnicki brothers were duly impressed.

A few days later, Paweł called his company of Young Guard to horse, and they set off for Wilno as part of a much larger host, with Toruń as a stopover. The ground was level, so the horses were not overly taxed. They were walked the first hour, then given a drink and short rest, whereupon they were made to keep to a lively canter for two hours, and as this process was repeated, the horses managed to maintain strength and endurance.

Paweł got to know the two special charges in his assigned company. While both boys were passionately patriotic, Jan Michał was the more thoughtful and practical. He was a bit insecure and consequently appreciative of his superiors' approval. Tadeusz was surer of himself, perhaps because he had always the protective wing of an older brother. He was the better spoken and smarter of the two, but he was intensely emotional and possessed an impulsiveness about him that kept Paweł on guard.

Their school had pumped a love of war into their veins, it seemed, but before they tasted their first skirmish with an enemy, they were to be subjected to the hardships of a forced march. These hardships were multiplied exponentially by the size of Napoléon's Grande Armée. Whereas the little emperor had been adroit at managing forces of 100,000, a force of 650,000 challenged him in ways he could not have counted on. The roads were clogged with Württemburgers, Badeners, Bavarians, Italians, Poles, and French—all under his aegis. When the June heat became unbearable and rations dwindled, many of these soldiers took it upon themselves to go foraging—and plundering. Napoléon and his generals turned blind eyes to inappropriate behavior. As the days went by, morale dropped and desertions became common. Typhus, dyptheria, and dysentery claimed thousands.

The Young Guard marched to the front of Paweł, and as the long days passed, stragglers fell to the side here and there, their bodies interspersed among those of dead horses. It was all Paweł could do to keep track of his own company.

On 21 June, as confrontation grew near, Napoléon addressed the forty thousand Polish troops: "Soldiers, the Second Polish War has begun. The first one ended at Friedland. At Tilsit, Russia swore eternal alliance to France and war on England. Today she breaks her oath. Destiny must run its course. We are still the soldiers of Austerlitz. What a triumph that was! Let us march beyond the River Niemen and carry the war into her territory. This Second Polish War will be as glorious for our French armies as was the first one. Our victory this time will guarantee peace for at least fifty years!"

While Paweł could not help but notice he had made no mention of independence for Poland, Jan Michał, Tadeusz, and the entire Young Guard burned like human flames for the cause of the little Corsican. *"Vive l'Empereur!"* they cried, until their voices were worn threadbare.

On the next day, the Grande Armeé, the marching babel of tongues, came upon the River Nieman, and everyone's heart beat faster, for to cross it meant invading Russian territory. They made camp. The emperor drew up to the front on his gray horse and with his field-telescope surveyed the high and fast-flowing river. He—and the cheering men—seemed to have forgotten that in the early morning a rabbit had run between the hooves of that very horse, causing it to throw the Emperor of France. Paweł could not help but wonder if it was a bad omen. To his mind, an invasion of Russia should have been initiated much earlier in the year. The seasons turned like a well-oiled wheel—quickly—and Russian winters were deadly. Best not to be there when the snows came to the steppes.

Napoléon, normally superstitious and watchful of omens, seemed not to take the episode of the hare seriously. He immediately put General Elbe's engineers to work creating three pontoon bridges on the Niemen, for the wooden bridges had been burnt by the Russians. But impatience must have consumed him, just as it did his men, because he sent an urgent request to the Poles to find a place to ford the Wilia, a tributary of the Niemen. Paweł's company was one of several to immediately mount and begin the search. No sooner had some of the Young Guard reached the river's edge than they let out a great whooping sound, so overcome were they with the thought of being the first forces on Russian ground. Later some claimed to have seen on the other side Cossacks who taunted them, causing them to toss caution aside.

While the river's surface appeared calm, the current was treacherous. Paweł noticed a nearly submerged tree branch shooting down the river as if it had been shot from a cannon. Then, to his horror, he sighted a number of the cavalry direct their horses head-on into the deceivingly swift waters. He immediately rode to the front of his company, waving and ordering them to halt. "Not safe!" he called. "It's not safe!" His men, deflated at being held back as others forged ahead, drew up around him, disappointment stinging their faces. Paweł saw Jan Michał now. "Tadeusz—where is he, Michał?"

Jan Michał pointed. Tadeusz was maneuvering his horse among a group who were testing the water. A few were actually taking the plunge, crying out excitedly, *"Vive l'Empereur!"* Tadeusz seemed only moments away from doing the same. Already Paweł could see that many who had gone into the river were in serious trouble. The bottom dropped away from under them, and the rapidly moving water was tearing them from their horses.

Paweł had to make a split-second decision: he must either go for Tadek himself or send Michał. He knew that if he went himself, some of his Young Guard would allow the emotion of the moment to overrule discipline, and they, too, would attempt the river.

He turned to Jan Michał. "Go get him, Michał! Bring him back at once! Tell him he's under orders! He's to come back or be sent home in disgrace!"

Paweł watched helplessly as the scene before him became more and more horrific. Both men and horses were unable to withstand the force of the river. A number were swept away. And still he could hear among the boys' calls and screams the foolish cries of *"Vive l'Empereur!"*

His heart pounding, Paweł watched now as the pantomime played out between the Stelnicki brothers at the water's edge. Tadeusz was resisting Michał's command, the command of an older brother. He pulled his horse away and started into the water.

Michał's horse followed—and for a moment Paweł feared he would have to tell Jan and Anna of the senseless loss of both their sons.

"Tadeusz!" he called out, his voice lost in the pandemonium. He fought back the urge to go after him himself. He could not afford losing others of his company.

And so he watched as the brothers' horses moved into deeper water. Jan Michał attempted to grab the reins of Tadeusz's horse, but his brother pulled away. He screamed at Tadeusz, spittle flying from his mouth, and pointed out to the middle of the river where a horse and rider were being swiftly swept away. This seemed to give Tadeusz pause, and in a moment both he and his brother turned their horses, just managing to get to shore amidst the confusion.

Ten of the overly zealous cadets and nearly twenty horses were lost that day.

Paweł turned to survey the hillock from which Napoléon had issued his request. He was nowhere to be seen. *"Vive l'Empereur,"* he muttered.

Late the next day, with the pontoon bridges in place, everyone made the crossing without incident. Napoléon gave over the horse he had been riding–named Friedland in honor of his magnificent victory there over Russia–in favor of a fresh mount named Moscow. The symbolism was not lost on the men. The march continued.

Despite a fortnight on the road in deplorable conditions, when the troops at last assembled on the heights above Wilno, the generals called them to arms. A palpable thrill ran through the Young Guard. Jan Michał and Tadeusz sat alert in their saddles, their faces all anticipation. They were to see action! But a light rain soon gave way to a deluge. Up from the rear–on a white horse this day–rode Napoléon. His riding coat was gray, as were the angry eyes under his trademark bicorne, the brim of which ran off rain like twin waterspouts. He cursed the weather as he tried to make out the city below through the gray screen of rain.

In a little while, word came through the ranks that the city was unprotected, and the troops moved down into the center of Lithuanian culture, coming across cooking fires and items hastily abandoned in the Russians' haste to evacuate. There would be no battle this day.

Jan Michał and Tadeusz found that the houses to which the company was billeted were filthy and strewn with human waste.

Worse, Paweł sensed that the Russians were–like a spider–luring them across the great Eastern steppes and into the center of their web, a winter web of cold and ice and snow.

July 1812

Zofia was sitting lost in thought in Princess Charlotte Sic's reception room when the maid came in, a befuddled look on her round face.

"Madame, the princess has another visitor."

"Charlotte is too ill to see anyone today. Who is it?"

"I didn't think to ask, madame. She seemed upset. Cryin' she was."

"Show her in here, then. I'll speak with her."

In a few minutes, a young blond woman appeared wearing a beautiful slate blue day dress and a handsome bonnet of dark navy. Zofia stood, startled by the apparition. She immediately recognized that the ensemble was from Paris, and recently so. Under the bonnet, the young woman's face possessed a perfect ivory-and-rose complexion, marred, however, by the tracks of tears. "I am so sorry to barge in like this." Several steps into the room, the woman fixed her gaze on Zofia, and she abruptly halted. "Oh!" she said, her eyes then traveling about the room.

Only now, when the surprised and helpless expression of a schoolgirl flashed across the woman's face, did Zofia recognize her. It had been several years. Zofia wondered whether the woman recognized her.

The woman blushed deeply. "I . . . I came to see Princess Sic."

"I am afraid that Charlotte is ill and unable to receive today."

A long awkward moment ensued. The woman looked like a sparrow about to take flight. Choosing to stay for the moment, she forced a little smile and gave a curtsy. "I am Lady Maria Walewska."

Zofia nodded. "I am Lady Zofia Grońska."

"I . . . I know."

"You remember, then? I'm afraid I behaved rather badly at our last meeting. Your memory of me cannot be flattering."

Lady Walewska afforded a wider smile, evidently taking Zofia's comment as a kind of apology. "It was a long time ago," she said. "Charlotte saw that you were reunited with your beautiful shawl, yes?"

"Yes." Zofia's back involuntarily stiffened, and she felt a flush of discomfort come into her face. There was no trace of malice or sarcasm in Lady Walewska's voice. She seemed completely ingenuous, and it was that innocence about her that made Zofia feel embarrassed and petty about the incident so long ago. She would have preferred sarcasm from the woman. She could deal better with that. "You've just come from Paris?"

"Recently, yes."

A little shadow passed over the woman's face, catching Zofia's interest. "Will you be seated, Lady Walewska?"

"No, I should be going."

"Do let me ring for some tea." Zofia approached Lady Walewska and led her to the sofa. She had paled a bit since coming in. "Are you well?"

"Yes, thank you."

Zofia made short work of requesting the tea, then seated herself across from Lady Walewska. "Are you comfortable?"

"Yes. This is very kind."

"Paris! Is it like they say? The seat of culture?"

"It's lovely, Lady Grońska, but I should not trade my Poland for twenty of all of France."

"Really?"

Lady Walewska nodded. "Truly."

Zofia was becoming more and more eager to find out what was going on behind her weakening facade. She suspected the woman was a tinderbox of emotion. "I would imagine that a woman of your . . . *standing* in Paris can only find life there fascinating. You must be afforded every convenience, every pleasure."

A slight lift of an eyebrow indicated that Lady Walewska understood Zofia perfectly—that as mistress to the emperor, she had the city at her feet. And yet she seemed not to take offense. "Appearances are not always what is real, Lady Grońska."

"Still, I'm sure Warsaw is very provincial by comparison. What is it that has brought you back?" Zofia was certain she knew the answer. Napoléon's *petite Marie* had followed the emperor, who was coming east again to wage war. What could be more obvious?

Lady Walewska's huge blue eyes brimmed suddenly with her unhappiness, and she looked away. As her eyelids closed, tears rolled down her cheeks.

The maid entered now with the tea tray. As soon as she set it down, Zofia dismissed her. "I'm so sorry," Zofia said. "I spoke out of turn. It is none of my business." She poured tea for them both, her curiosity at fever pitch.

Lady Walewska accepted her cup, took a sip, and looked up at Zofia.

Zofia put on her most compassionate expression. "You will forgive me?"

The woman's rounded chin trembled a little, the tears started up again, and her facial veneer shattered completely. Her shoulders sagged forward, and the cup and saucer rattled.

Zofia was at her side in an instant, relieving her of her tea and comforting her, one arm around her shoulder. "There, there, Lady Walewska, cry if you wish. Cry—do let it out."

It was all the encouragement the woman needed. Lady Walewska broke into sobs as if on command. Several minutes went by before she was able to collect herself. She lifted her head to Zofia. "Thank you so much. I don't know what came over me. You must call me Maria."

"And you will call me by my Christian name, as well."

Maria sniffled and attempted a smile. "Zofia, I came by to cry on Charlotte's shoulder, and I end up crying on yours. You're very good to allow me."

"Not so very."

"During Charlotte's stay in Paris last winter, she helped me through a number of crises, big and small. She gave me advice–good advice–as a mother would give."

"Did she? Well, I'm hardly of an age to be your mother, but anything you say to me will be kept in confidence."

"I'm certain of it. I can't talk to my own mother or to my brothers. They are all against me." Zofia waited, hoping she wouldn't have to prompt her. "You see," Maria continued, "I've come back to Warsaw to obtain a divorce." Tears threatened again.

This news did surprise Zofia. Divorce *was* easier to come by in these days of the Napoléonic Code. Zofia knew half a dozen middle-aged women who had shed their husbands to take on lovers, to marry again, or simply to become independent. But by all accounts, Lord Walewski was a content enough cuckold who had done everything to smooth Maria's path to Napoléon, except drive the carriage to the assignations.

"And your family is set against it."

"Oh no!" Maria cried, blinking back the tears. "They *want* me to divorce Anastazy. They do! . . . But it's against God and the church, Zofia. It's against my beliefs . . . my conscience."

"Then–why should you consider it?"

"Because *he* wishes it!"

"Napoléon? But he has divorced Joséphine and married Maria Louise. Does he intend then to–?"

"Oh no, he'll never divorce her to marry me. He's made that clear. Oh, for a moment I thought I had my chance at happiness when he divorced Joséphine. But he quickly snuffed that thought like a candle in a strong wind, do you know? Oh no, France comes first with Napoléon; only a dynastic marriage would suit him. He was shopping for a womb–a royal womb, he said. Can you imagine?"

"Then why is he urging you to divorce your husband?"

"My son. It has to do with his inheritance."

Zofia took a deep breath. "Your second son is *his*, isn't he? Napoléon's?"

"Yes, oh, I suppose it's no secret. Here or in France. Anyway, the emperor will be very generous with Aleksandr–"

"Wait a minute," Zofia rasped. "You've named your child–*Napoléon's* child!–Aleksandr?"

Maria nodded. "It's a Walewski family name."

And it's also the name of Napoléon's Russian nemesis–Tsar Aleksandr, Zofia wanted to blurt out, but held her tongue. What had possessed the woman? Maria continued talking at some length about the concern Napoléon had for lands and monies that he meant to leave to Aleksandr. It seemed that Maria's octogenarian husband was weakening in mind, but he remained as proud and prodigal as ever, spending his fortune away at an alarming rate. Anything left to little Aleksandr by his true father–the emperor–would not necessarily be secure–unless Maria obtained a divorce. Zofia placed her hand on Maria's. "So you have little choice, then?"

"I suppose. But I just dread it. I really do. In order to get the divorce, I have to go through both civil and ecclesiastical proceedings. And I have to be nice to Abbé Pradt." Maria grasped Zofia's hand. "Oh, Zofia, he may be an archbishop, but he's a lecherous one that makes my flesh crawl when he's merely in the same room as I!"

"I've only seen him from a distance. He's certainly a short and ugly little man, pompous as Nero, they say. But has he behaved inappropriately?"

"Just his *gaze* is inappropriate. I try to dress like a nun when I'm in his presence. Napoléon told him to watch out for me, and he has taken that to mean much more."

"But you need his help?"

Maria nodded. "Because of his connection to the emperor, his influence will be a telling factor in not only the church court, but in the civil court, as well."

"What are the grounds?"

"My family will testify that they coerced me into marriage with a man fifty years my senior."

"And Lord Walewski will not contest?"

"He has signed a declaration to that effect." Maria gave a little shrug. "Truth is, Zofia, he's a bit senile now."

"I see. Now, if I were Charlotte, what advice would I give you?" Zofia made a show of thinking.

"Your listening has already helped, Zofia."

Zofia ignored Maria's comment. "First, I will say that you should reconcile yourself to the divorce. If your church doesn't understand, your God will. You must think of your son's inheritance. It is no small thing that you have given Napoléon his first son–and that he is recognizing him in this way. And you, too! Fortune may have kept the crown from you, but in your Aleksandr you have something Joséphine did not have. You have *power,* Maria."

"Do you think so?"

"Absolutely!"

Maria seemed to brighten. "Thank you, Zofia."

"And as for our ugly archbishop, once the divorce is granted, you need not see him again."

"That's not quite true."

"Why is that?"

"It is the emperor's wish that he and I *together* shore up Polish support for this war in the east."

"Ah, I see. You with your patriotism and he with his Catholicism."

"Something like that."

"Has he written to you?"

"A few letters and invitations. Mostly harmless."

"I see. Let me give some thought to the nasty little man, Maria." Zofia said. "I'll see what I can do."

"Really? Oh! you must be careful not to antagonize him."

"I know. But I'm not without some influence."

Maria rose to leave. "Charlotte said you are clever."

"Did she?"

"She sets great store by you. Oh my, she thinks of you as a daughter."

"Really—she said that?"

"Yes."

This bit of news caught Zofia by surprise. It came home to her how often she had taken Charlotte for granted, how often she had used her, how often she overlooked her huge heart. "Well," Zofia said, trying to catch herself up to the conversation, "the divorce is the correct path to take for you, Maria." She stood now. "And who knows, you may wish to marry again."

"Oh no!" Maria let out a little gasp. "Maria-Louise or no, I am bound to Napoléon Bonaparte—by my son and by my Poland. I must see to the protection of both."

Zofia was taken aback by the fervor of the countess, but she said nothing to deflate her hope. Zofia was convinced, however, that Maria Walewska, her son, and Poland were all pawns in the chess game Napoléon was playing—with all Europe as a board.

After Maria left, Zofia sat with her tea for some time. She had started her tête-à-tête with Lady Maria Walewska with a falsely solicitous attitude, determined to acquire as much information as possible about her success with the French emperor. Zofia's plan was to supply bad advice to the little snippet who had eclipsed her own intentions for the emperor. It would amuse her to do so.

But something had happened as Maria poured out her heart to Zofia, as if to a true friend or sister. She could not recall the exact moment, but as she heard the plaintive cries of the guileless and naïve woman, her own heart had been somehow touched—so much so that by the time she sent Maria on her way—with sincere advice—Zofia had become determined to be of help.

Maria reminded her of a young Anna, Zofia realized now, wincing at the bad marriage advice she had given her cousin years before. She had lived to regret it. If there is a God, she wondered, had he sent her Maria as a test? She chuckled to herself at the notion. Standing and ringing for the maid to collect the tray and bring a cordial, she considered the possible dividends of be-friending the mistress of the Emperor of Europe.

Later, into the evening, Zofia went into Charlotte's room. Each time she saw her, she was surprised by her thinness. She was wasting away.

"I don't think there's to be a comeback for me, Zofia."

"Nonsense! You'll survive this, and we'll be going to the French Theatre in no time, gossiping in the balcony, laughing at the people below."

Charlotte smiled. "I remember your saying that one goes to the theater mainly for the intermissions. We did have our times, didn't we?"

"We did!" Zofia cried in a loud whisper. "We laughed at the old men in their silly powdered perukes and spindly legs and the women who think rouge and jewels can cover a multitude of sins."

"But the time comes, Zofia, when we are *all* laughable. When it is God's turn to laugh."

"No! God's turn be damned! You're going to survive this, do you hear?"

"I think not. Now, do sit and tell me what Maria had to say."

Zofia described the interview in considerable detail. The predicament of Maria Walewska had its effect. "I should like to give Monsieur de Pradt a good piece of my mind," Charlotte said afterward, a new strength in her voice, "preying on the innocent like that. He was an odd choice for minister to Poland. I said so at the time."

"I suspect Napoléon thought an archbishop would make the church in Poland heed the French calling. He knows how Catholic Poland is."

"Then he should have chosen someone truly religious." Charlotte gave a little laugh. "But Napoléon wouldn't recognize someone like that even if he bit him in the arse."

Zofia laughed at full volume. "Nor would we, Charlotte. There! You can't be dying if you can trade quips with me."

"Zofia, bring a quill and paper. I want to dictate a letter to Pradt."

"No, you're not to worry about him. I'm making Pradt *my* business."

"Zofia, you're not going to complicate things for Maria?"

"No, nothing like that. I don't hold her conquest of the little Corsican against her."

"Ah, good. That's good of you."

"Dog's blood! I'm not doing it to be *good*. Don't go and spoil my reputation by putting *that* about. I'm doing it because it'll be fun."

"Maria deserves a good turn."

"She needs *someone* to take her by the hand, it seems."

"Why do you say so?"

"She's so terribly naïve. To have faith in a man who shuttles her back and forth across Europe in a carriage as fits his needs, while he is concocting a divorce and marriage to *another* for political reasons. I think I would have smothered the dwarf in his sleep."

"Ah, you seem to have missed something in your chat with Maria—you see, she's in *love* with Napoléon."

"She could not possibly—"

"Oh, she is. Hopelessly, as they say." Charlotte lifted herself a bit higher on her pillow. "Zofia, love has eluded you thus far. Perhaps you cannot recognize it."

The surprise that Maria could still love Napoléon fell away, dispelled by the sting of her friend's words. *Why* did they hurt as they did?

Charlotte's hand reached for Zofia's. "That's another thing we laughed at from the balcony, isn't it?"

"Love?"

"Yes, dear, love. There you have it."

Zofia made no reply.

30

Alone, Jan sat on the steps of the portico, staring down at the tributary of the Vistula that flowed by Anna's family home. Anna had gone to Warsaw to help make room at the hospitals and prepare for the expected flow of the wounded that would be sent back from the east. She would be staying with Zofia for some time. Jan regretted seeing her go and deeply missed her. She was the single star in what had become a dark constellation. A word from him would have kept her home, but he knew she wanted to help with the war effort. Doing so gave her purpose, making her feel she was somehow aiding her sons. He could not help but wonder what had become of *his* purpose.

"Excuse me, milord." The deep voice was all politeness.

Jan looked up to see Walek's son. "Tomasz!" Jan stood. Tomasz was tall and lanky, a man of few words, and he seemed tongue-tied now. A bit older than the Stelnicki boys, he had often watched out for them before their days at the academy. "What is it?"

"It is," he began, drawing in a long breath before starting again. "It is this, milord. I want to join the little emperor."

"How old are you, Tomasz?"

"Twenty-eight, milord."

"You're married, yes? With two children?"

"Three, milord."

"Why do you want to go?"

"Papa fought with Kościuszko, milord, as you know. He did his duty. You, too, milord. And your sons. Now—well, it's come to me."

"That's a brave and decent thought, Tomasz. You're a good man and a good worker. We can't easily spare you on the estate. So many others have gone. Why have you waited till now to ask?"

"My woman was against it—and big with child she was."

"And now?"

"I have to be a man, milord. I have to be a Pole."

"You are both, Tomasz. You know that you may not come back?"

"I know, milord."

"Who's to look after your wife then—if you don't come back?"

Tomasz stood silent, and a shadow crossed his face, as if he had not considered this.

"Tomasz, Napoléon has six hundred fifty thousand men. Do you know how many that is? I'll tell you—it is more men than the blades of grass in that meadow yonder. More!"

The peasant's eyes widened.

"The little emperor has enough men. Everything depends now on how he uses them. Do you understand? How smart he is."

He nodded.

"You have a duty here, Tomasz. Poland is going to need you to raise wheat here, and she is going to need you to raise your fine family to carry on our traditions. We pray that every Pole will come back from Russia, but we know there will be losses, terrible losses."

Tomasz's long face looked especially so at Jan's words.

"I must ask you to stay, Tomek. I must say no."

He nodded, his face reddening to the roots of his blond hair. "Thank you, milord." He walked slowly away, shoulders sagging.

Jan sat staring at the river long after Tomasz had returned to his little cottage in the village. Dusk was falling, and the frogs in the marsh began to stir and croak. He looked down now, a little surprised to see that he still had in his hand a copy of Warsaw's *Monitor*. Once again—despite the failing light—he read Napoléon's address. The emperor called the war against Russia the "Second Polish War."

What did that mean? Jan knew what it was *meant* to imply—that Poles were fighting for the resurrection of their country. But there was no use of the word *independence*. Nor would there be, he feared.

And yet his countrymen, his best friend, and his sons had gone off to fight and be killed for the French emperor. And here he sat. Was he right to let them go while he stayed at home? Or to deny Tomasz's request?

I should be there with Paweł and with my sons, he thought. *I should! I can still handle the rigors of the march—and war.* The old bloodlust he had held at bay for so long broke through, rising up from his gut as he schemed how he could leave the very next day, be in uniform and in camp within the week. How Paweł and the Old Guard would welcome him! His sons, too! Damn Napoléon! Damn the upstart Corsican! *I'll go. I will!* After a while, Jan stood, dusted himself off, and walked with a good pace down by the river, body and heart enlivened by the decision.

It was nearly dark before he returned to the house. As he neared the lighted dining room windows, he saw Marta within, scurrying about with the supper preparations. For a moment he imagined Anna sitting at table waiting for him—annoyed at his tardiness—but smiling nonetheless. He halted abruptly.

He had for a few intoxicating minutes forgotten Anna. The excitement coursing through him like liquid fire slowed, stopped, cooled. He couldn't leave her, not again. He looked up at the darkening sky. His boys were under that wide canopy somewhere this night, perhaps in danger, perhaps not. *God be with them,* he prayed. *I cannot.*

Zofia's carriage clattered onto the cobblestones of the courtyard of the Brühl Palace, a rococo design and the most impressive residence in Warsaw. It took little more than the possession of a title to gain entrance to one of Archbishop Pradt's receptions, but through her friendship with Anusia Potocka, Zofia had managed a seat at the archbishop's table.

It seemed that Pradt was heavily in the debt of the Potockis. When he had arrived in Warsaw to take up his ambassadorship, he found the interior of the palace wholly unacceptable and set about having it completely refurbished. The undertaking took some weeks, and not wishing to stay at a hotel or rent an apartment—thereby depleting his significant salary of two hundred thousand francs—he prevailed upon the Polish hospitality of the Potockis to take him in for the interim.

More than a hundred people were assembled in the main reception hall, talking in clusters and sipping French wine. Anusia appeared out of the crush, moving forward to Zofia. "Oh! I'm so glad you've come, Zofia," she said, kissing her on either cheek. "I do hope you don't find the event as dull as the host."

"That bad?"

"Oh, I just thank God he's gone from *our* house. What an annoyance, as you're likely to see."

"Is Maria Walewska here?"

"Not yet." Anusia moved her fan to her face. "Oh, dear, here he comes. Do be gracious, Zofia."

"Why, Anusia, I am *always* gracious!"

Ignoring Anusia's giggling, Zofia watched him approach. He *was* quite short. If she didn't see his feet kicking out from under the dark ecclesiastical robes, she would have thought the man was walking on his knees.

Anusia introduced the abbé to Zofia. "I am most charmed to meet you, Lady Grońska. Each day I am surprised anew by the beauty of the Polish women."

Zofia had worn a high-waisted low-cut gown of violet, and the archbishop's eyes were trained for the moment on her décolletage.

"Thank you, Your Eminence," Zofia said, dropping to her knees, the violet tulle skirt spreading out around her like the petals of a peony.

Pradt held out his ring for her to kiss. Rising, Zofia said, "Our Polish men have long kept us a secret, but now with them off to fight for the French, we must assume the stage."

"It is not the French you Poles fight for, Lady Grońska. It is for your own country to be recalled to life."

"That, Your Eminence, remains to be seen, doesn't it?"

The abbé bristled, and the small beads that were his eyes widened slightly. "Do not doubt my word, Lady Grońska. It is true. One day you Poles will be grateful to the emperor."

"A smug little man," Zofia whispered as the abbé sauntered off to visit with a nearby group of people.

"Indeed," Anusia said. "He entertains very grandly, though he's thrifty as a squirrel. Do you know what he gave my father-in-law as a gift for our housing him?"

"I'd venture to say it was not money."

"It was a painting. He was impressed by Lord Potocki's collection of excellent art, so he sent to the archbishop's palace in Malines for what he called a 'masterpiece.' Knowing the man's taste, my father-in-law had a presentiment that the gift would ruin his gallery."

"A gift that no doubt cost Pradt nothing."

"Exactly. And its arrival vindicated my father-in-law's fear." Anusia let out a little gasp. "Zofia, it is the most pedestrian rendering of a scoundrel once famous in that area."

"An unlikely subject for a bishop's home. He was ridding himself of it. And did Lord Potocki place it in his gallery?"

"He would sooner swim the Baltic." Anusia chuckled. "No, he gave it its own little gallery—in the *garret* of the Wilanów residence."

Zofia smiled slyly. It would be sheer fun, she decided, to put this haughty man in his place.

Maria Walewska arrived just in time for supper. Zofia suspected her tardiness had been calculated so she would miss the abbé's tour of the reception hall and his incessant small talk. Not that his jabbering stopped at table. He chattered on throughout the meal, commenting on every course, boasting of the chef he left behind in Malines, lamenting the absence of certain French dishes. He berated his servers loudly for the slightest infraction—something *not done* in Polish households.

He had Maria Walewska sitting at his right hand, as if she were his queen. Pradt would finish every commentary with a look in her direction, that look facilitated by the use of a lorgnette that swept over her shapely form like a searchlight. Maria had dressed most modestly, however, allowing the abbé little to ogle. Sometimes in his private discourse to Maria, his hand would cover hers as if to make a point, and it would linger there.

The sight caused Zofia to involuntarily stiffen in her chair. And it took only a few glances about to realize that no one was ignorant of his infatuation with Maria. The young women smiled with ironic amusement, their mothers' tongues clucked with disdain, and the older men glowered behind spectacles, as if at insult. The ambassador was no diplomat; that was certain.

"The bean soup reminds me of a story about Madame de Pompadour," Pradt announced suddenly. "Everyone knows she favored the use of multiple beauty spots on her lovely face, yes? Well, one little rebellious spot chose suppertime to take a little dip in her soup bowl!"

He paused, waiting for some reaction. He had the attention of everyone within hearing, but the prelude to the story elicited little response. "You'll never guess what Madame de Pompadour did!" he exclaimed. "Rather than admit to her embarrassment, she spooned up the beauty mark. Looking down to where it floated in clear broth, she declared: 'Look! What good luck—a raisin!' And before anyone could manage a good look, she ate it down!"

Pradt's audience did afford a little surprise and laughter now, but not so loud and cloying as Pradt's own hiccuplike laugh. Amidst the polite response, Anusia leaned over to Zofia. "*I* could have guessed it," she said. "He told the same story a dozen times at Wilanów. It won't be the last of the Pompadour anecdotes, you can be certain."

It wasn't. "Did you know," Pradt asked, retaking the stage, "that Madame de Pompadour believed a beautiful woman is more frightened by the end of her youth than by death? And she certainly proved it! On her deathbed, about to breathe her last, she gathered up all the strength left to her and called out to her Creator, 'Wait a moment!' With arms she could barely lift, she took her rouge, drew crimson circles on her pallid, lifeless cheeks—and promptly died!"

"Isn't it odd," Anusia wondered aloud, "that an archbishop is so consumed with a courtesan out of the past?"

"Perhaps not," Zofia said. "Look at the way he leers at poor Maria. And the stories he chooses are not particularly flattering to women."

As the courses continued, Pradt told two more Pompadour stories.

"Your Eminence," Zofia said at the next lull, "isn't it so, that much of the time Madame de Pompadour was the power behind Louis the Fifteenth's throne?"

Pradt flashed a wide insincere smile. "Her influence was overrated, Lady Grońska."

"Really?" Zofia persisted, her dark eyes fixed on her target. "Here in Poland, we heard she was called the last uncrowned queen of France. Is that a falsehood?"

Pradt's lower lip trembled very slightly. "Hearing such a thing does not attest to its veracity, my lady."

Zofia was not about to acquiesce. She proclaimed in a lilting voice: "Wasn't it Cato who said, 'The Romans govern the world while women govern the Romans'?"

A little cheer and rattling of silver went up from the women in the room. Anusia elbowed Zofia in the ribs. "You've gone too far, Zofia."

The abbé's olive complexion smoldered red. His lips thinned and tightened.

"*Au contraire,*" Zofia murmured. "He needs to know I will not melt away in the heat of his hot air."

"But why anger him?" Anusia whispered.

Ignoring her friend's question, Zofia raised a spoonful of her dessert to her lips. "I must say, Your Eminence," she announced in her stage voice, "that the raspberry mousse is divine!"

A small orchestra played after supper. According to Anusia, at his first reception, the abbé had said he wished to provide dancing for the young people. He failed to realize that all the young men had gone to war. No one danced this evening, either.

"Lady Grońska." The strange little voice came from behind.

Recognizing it immediately, Zofia turned around. "Your Eminence," she said, nodding slightly.

"Would you care to see some of my paintings?"

"Yes, please." Zofia had been calculating how she might privately talk to the abbé, and now her problem was solved. He led the way, chattering on like a parrot about his interest in art. They came to tall white doors gilded with gold, and he pushed them open, standing to the side as Zofia passed. She felt his hand on her waist as she entered. The contact lasted but moments, and yet the skin at the back of her neck prickled at his touch. He closed the door behind them.

"You have but *one* painting in here," Zofia said, nodding toward the fireplace.

"And it is worth looking at, my dear. Come." He took her hand.

Zofia allowed herself to be led. She had an idea now just how his attention made Maria feel.

"It's a Dutch seascape. Do you like it, Zofia? May I call you that?"

"If you wish."

When they stood before the painting, Zofia withdrew her hand.

"Well?" he asked.

"Yes," she lied, "it's lovely."

"You may speak your mind, Zofia."

"What do you mean?"

"I saw your expression the moment you took it in. You may say what you think."

"Very well—it's dreadful. Perfectly dreadful."

The abbé laughed. "Exactly! A poor imitation of a Dutch master."

"You were testing me? I thought so!"

"You have shown me tonight that you are quite independent."

"Have I?" Zofia asked, her tone all flirtation. "Anusia Potocka thought I overstepped myself."

"Not at all." Pradt pivoted now and stood looking up at Zofia.

Drawing in a deep breath, Zofia turned to face him. A light gleamed in the little man's eyes. A lurid light, Zofia thought, even as she smiled. His face reflected an impetuosity she had encountered before–but never from an archbishop. "I am glad to have this private audience, Your Eminence."

"Are you?" he asked, smiling up at her. "You may call me Dominique. We should not be so formal."

"I wish to confide in you."

"By all means, my dear."

"I am certain that in your lifelong position in the church you cannot be used to gossip. Even if the gossip is swirling like a tide all around you."

"Gossip?"

"Terrible, vacuous talk, Your Eminence. With you at the center."

The abbé paled slightly. "About *what?*"

"I do hate to be the bringer of bad news."

"You must tell me, Lady–er, Zofia."

"It's about Maria Walewska."

"Maria?"

Zofia nodded. "And you."

The small eyes widened. "Nonsense! There is no cause for gossip. I am duty-bound to the emperor to watch out for her. He *personally* directed me to look after her. He calls her his *petite Marie*."

"I know and you're right–I'm certain there's nothing to the talk. I'm convinced of your innocence."

"Thank you."

"Still–the gossip persists. It's rather ugly."

"I hadn't realized."

"If word should reach the emperor's ear–"

"There is no foundation for such stories!"

"Well, there are the letters, you see."

"Letters?"

"Yes, the ones you wrote to Maria. I read them quite by mistake, you understand, and Maria lectured me for doing so. But I must tell you that should the emperor see the one or two of them–well, as innocent as they are, they might be viewed in a different light by some people."

Pradt's eyes narrowed, his face white as his collar. "Ah, I see what you're up to. You are even more independent than I gave you credit for."

Zofia smiled. "Some would say dangerous."

"And you know the emperor?"

"Oh, yes."

"How well?"

"Very well, Your Eminence."

"I imagine that you do." He gave a wicked smile. When Zofia returned it in kind, Pradt turned his attention back to the painting, his face pinched.

A long silent minute passed.

"You know, Lady Grońska," he said in a dark drawl, "that I could have you excommunicated."

"And *you* should know," Zofia said, "that–like you–I'm not a very good Catholic." She heard him draw in a deep breath. Unable to help herself, she followed up on that thread of thought. "And isn't it so that the pope himself has excommunicated the Emperor of France? It doesn't seem to have slowed him a jot."

"Maria has kept the letters?" He turned back to Zofia, all business now. "Look at me, Lady Grońska."

Zofia slowly turned, smiling. "You were to call me Zofia."

"Never mind that. Has Maria kept the letters?"

"Yes."

"And to get them back?"

The business mode became infectious. "You are to leave Maria alone. She is an innocent and should not be placed in a compromising position. You know her attachment to the emperor–and his to her." Zofia paused, then said with soft authority: "No more letters, flirtations, lingering touches, or sitting at your right hand."

"I see." The abbé turned and stared blankly at the seascape. He muttered the old proverb, "Where the devil can't manage, he'll send a woman." After a while he spoke in a stronger voice: "We understand each other, Lady Grońska."

Zofia smiled at the painting, certain he often used it as a way of deciphering friend from sycophant. Well, she was neither. "You know, you've done wonders with this palace. I hope you'll stay in Warsaw a long time."

Pradt turned back to Zofia. "*Ma chère!* It seems you can shape-shift from silky ingenue to the meanest shrew and back again in the blink of an eye."

Zofia chuckled. "Do you know the Pompadour maxim about the hedgehog?"

"No, I'm afraid not."

"Madame de Pompadour said that the hedgehog gives up its quills only when the wolf loses his teeth."

31

Having finished their various duties for the day, Anna, Anusia Potocka, and Maria Walewska were preparing to leave the hospital.

"You won't disappoint me now, Anna," Maria said. "You *are* coming tonight? Pradt's reception will be much more fun with the two of you there."

"Only a funeral for the grotesque little man would be more fun!" Anusia said, laughing. "We'll be there, Maria, guarding you on either side. And Anna *dares not* miss. She had a special invitation from Pradt. What did it say, Anna?"

Anna shrugged. "The archbishop had the temerity to command my presence."

"Maybe he's lost interest in Maria," Anusia said.

"Good God, I hope so!" Maria cried.

"Seriously," Anna said after they had a little laugh, "it's a little mystery. But I look forward to any news coming back from the march east."

"This reception for King Jérôme should be more interesting than the others," Anusia said, a sparkle coming into her eyes. "There are so many stories that preceded his arrival in Warsaw!"

Prior to beginning her toilette for the royal reception, Anna went to visit the ailing Princess Charlotte Sic. She was about to start up the stairs when she came upon Izabel making her descent. Her eyes were red from crying.

"Iza! How good to see you!"

The girl came to the bottom of the stairs and tried to smile.

"She's very ill, your mother says," Anna whispered.

Iza nodded, allowing Anna to enfold her in her arms. The girl shook, and her tears started afresh. "Oh, I didn't cry in front of her, Aunt Anna. I didn't. I waited until I closed the door behind me."

"Good for you," Anna said.

After a while, Anna held her at arm's length. Iza was fifteen now and developing into a young woman. She lacked Zofia's dark Tatar looks. The startling difference in Iza's appearance had prompted Zofia to occasionally refer to her daughter as a cuckoo or changeling, and Anna had reprimanded her for doing so in the girl's presence. The child had Zofia's dark hair but her features, light complexion, and eyes could only reflect her father's traits. Anna had often wondered over the years who the father was, but this was one issue the chatty Zofia would not talk about. It was clear now, though, that for Iza the awkwardness of childhood was falling away and nature was transforming her into a real beauty. It had happened in a matter of months, it seemed, this caterpillar-to-butterfly miracle.

Iza wiped at her tears. "I'm sorry," she said. "I'm being silly and stupid."

"You are not, Iza. You have a tender heart. That's nothing to apologize for."

"Thank you, Aunt Anna," she said, sniffling. "I should be going."

"When you get home, will you remind Basia that she's promised to help at the hospital tomorrow?"

"I will. Oh, may I help, as well?"

"It's nothing of great interest. Procuring bedding and making bandages— that sort of thing."

"I should like to help."

"Then be ready at six sharp."

Anna took a deep breath before entering the French princess' room. She had not seen the princess for at least a year, and although Zofia had told her that Charlotte hadn't long to live, her appearance still shocked Anna. Once quite round and robust, she was now drawn and emaciated.

"Hello, Anna!" Genuine delight shone on her face as she pushed herself up a bit against the pillows piled behind her.

Anna masked her shock, quickly advancing and kissing Charlotte on either cheek.

"You just missed Iza!"

"No, I did see her downstairs."

"Oh?—I hope she was all right. You know, she's taking all this very hard. Sit down, dear."

"I'm so sorry you're not well, Charlotte," Anna said, sitting in the bedside chair.

"Thank you, dear. Have you heard anything of your sons?"

"Nothing recently."

Charlotte reached over and took Anna's hand. "It must be a great worry."

"I try to keep busy. Now, how are *you?*"

"A little better now that I won't let the doctor bleed me anymore. I've got water on my heart—now what good is bleeding going to do? They need to drain the water, not my blood, for pity's sake."

Anna stayed and chatted for a space of time, but when she saw that Charlotte was tiring, she stood and prepared to leave.

Charlotte spoke now, as if to detain her. "Iza's becoming quite the young woman, isn't she? She's going to give her mother a run for her money."

Anna laughed. "Surely Zofia doesn't see her as competition."

"Perhaps not," Charlotte conceded. "Anna, please sit for just a few more minutes."

"Yes, surely." Anna obeyed.

"Iza calls me her *grand-mère*." Charlotte sighed, and seemed to think for a long while. "Have you ever heard Zofia call Iza anything other than Izabel?"

"No," Anna had to admit.

"There's something in that, you know. Oh, I've tried to lavish the girl with affection, as if I could make it up to her. And so now I worry."

"Zofia *does* love her, Charlotte. Deep down—I'm sure she does."

"In her way, perhaps."

"Don't worry about Iza. I'll be staying in the capital more as—God help us—the hospitals start to fill up with our wounded. I'll keep an eye on her."

"Good! Oh, please do, Anna. You know, Zofia has plans for Iza. Marriage plans."

Anna drew in a deep breath. "*Marriage* plans?"

Charlotte nodded. "To a magnate."

"Oh, I don't think so, Charlotte. Zofia herself rebelled at the prospect of her own arranged marriage to Antoni Grawliński. I don't think—"

"Oh, parents are often quick to forget what it was to be a child. A child who has had a birch rod used on him will, years later, use it on *his* child."

Anna sat in silence a long minute. At last she asked, "What magnate?"

"Adam Czartoryski."

"Charlotte, you can't be serious."

"Why? Because she herself has romanced him—to no avail? Him, that Prince Podolski and a dozen other magnates over the years! Zofia's not thinking about Iza's welfare, Anna. She's intent on marrying into a magnate family, if only by proxy. For herself, time is running out. Between the two of us, I think it already has. The emperor himself said something to the effect that forty is forty, after all—didn't he?"

"Has Zofia launched this—this campaign?"

"Yes, to what extent, I don't know. I do know that the prince is now at the age where he cannot avoid marriage—and that Iza is proving to be a nice little morsel for a middle-aged man."

"That doesn't mean she couldn't love him."

"No, it doesn't. But when you fell in love with Stelnicki, you were, what, eighteen?"

"Seventeen."

"Very well, seventeen. Could you imagine yourself then falling in love with someone your *father's* age?"

It was a paralyzing thought. Anna was forced to admit that she could not.

"You see," Charlotte said. "You must use your influence with your cousin, Anna. Do what you can to see to Iza's happiness—and I will do what I can."

"I will," Anna said, kissing Charlotte. Suddenly, she felt tears brimming in her eyes and took her leave before they could spill. "Good-bye, Charlotte. You've been a good friend to Zofia—a good friend."

As Anna walked toward Piwna Street, an odd mixture of sadness and new respect for Charlotte gave way to the subject of an arranged marriage for Iza.

Charlotte's last words came back to her: *And I will do what I can.* Only now did Anna wonder what the dying woman could have meant.

Flanked by Maria Walewska and Anusia Potocka, Anna sat at the far right of Abbé Pradt's long table. Anusia leaned forward, directing a quiet question to Maria. "How is it you're not sitting at the archbishop's right hand?"

Maria shrugged. Holding her fan to her face, she said, "I told Abbé Pradt that I should like to sit with my two friends—and to my surprise, he deferred. I think I have a good fairy who has reduced his fire of desire to a simmer."

"Really?" Anusia asked. "The man gives me a *chill.*"

Servants poured into the room with the first of many courses. The supper commenced. Anna stole now and then a glance at the King of Westphalia, who sat at the archbishop's left. King Jérôme's entrance had been ostentatious. As a marshal of Napoléon, he had been free to design his own uniform, and had created an imaginatively flashy one of red and green. Its peacockery matched the wearer's rule. As the twenty-eight-year-old brother of Napoléon, he had been granted a kingdom comprising Hesse-Kassel, Brunswick, Prussia's former western provinces, parts of Hanover, and other tiny fragments. He had a reputation for the extravagance and hubris that touched all Napoléon's siblings. While he was capable of great bravery, he thought himself a young genius and demonstrated great foolishness.

Catherine of Würtemburg, his wife through a marriage engineered by Napoléon, was not present, so that his notorious roving eye luxuriated in the presence of a multitude of unchaperoned Polish ladies. His marriage, it seemed, had not dulled his appetite for pretty women—women he was often heard referring to as "sweet peaches" or "supple strawberries."

"How long has he been here?" Anna asked her friends. "A week? He seems in no hurry to go east and catch up to the Grand Armée."

"A week of operas, suppers, and parties, I might add," Maria said.

"Well, it ends tomorrow," Anusia announced. "I had it straight from my father-in-law that today a courier brought a message from the emperor demanding he bring up his reserve corps at once. An *angry* message! He leaves at dawn."

Unspoken conjecture among Anna's friends and among many in the room had it that should Napoléon resurrect the Polish nation, the throne would likely go to Jérôme. The player-king. It was a thought that tempered the ambrosial celebration.

"Lady Stelnicka, is it not?"

Taken by surprise, Anna turned to face the lord of the hour himself. Her introduction to the king before supper had been formal and full of ceremony, but now she could see he was trying to inject warmth into his manner. "Yes," she said, managing a smile.

He smiled, too, as his eyes moved over her shoulders and breasts. "You have two sons in service, I understand?"

"Yes, in the Young Guard, Your Highness."

"I trust they have fared well."

"I hope so. Fortunately, a family friend in the Old Guard has taken them under his wing. And Jan Michał—my older son—looks out for his little brother."

"How old *is* Tadeusz?"

Anna blinked back her surprise. How had he known his name? "Seventeen," she heard herself say as a strange numbness set in.

"A delightful age!" the king declared. "At that age, one feels as if he is discovering the world for the first time. And soldiering brings you to so many new places."

King Jérôme went on to speak of the coming war effort with Russia and the great destiny of the Bonaparte family. Anna pretended to listen and nodded occasionally in response, but her mind was in a ferment. He had known Tadek's name! How? Who had told him? Perhaps it was innocent, merely a casual mention by the same person who had told him she had sons in the service?

But some sense told her that it was not innocent, that he had asked with some purpose in mind. Despite his leering glances that continued as he spoke, she ruled out his attention to her as physical attraction. He was a decade younger than she—and there were many beautiful young women in the room.

"How has young Tadeusz adapted to Poniatowski's Corps?" he asked now.

His coming back to the subject of her younger son confirmed what she already felt at her core: that the King of Westphalia held some special interest for Tadeusz.

"He's become quite the soldier. He hopes to become a lancer one day." Anna spoke with no enthusiasm, as if she were listening to someone else deliver a stage line. She felt the room tilt, begin to spin about her. Fear ran through her like an icy wind off the steppes.

"I don't know what my brother would do without the Polish lancers, Lady Stelnicka. They have been invaluable to him—but I'm certain you know that."

Anna nodded mechanically and then the king was wishing her well, bowing stiffly at the waist. With a start, Anna noticed on his belt the raised images of the compass and the square, the same images King Stanisław had worn—symbols of the Masonic Brotherhood.

As he moved off, the red-and-green uniform colors blurring among the other costumes, thoughts flew at Anna like bullets. Was King Jérôme attached to the Prussian Masons? To the same arm of the Brotherhood that had paid Doliński to kidnap Tadeusz and to deliver him to almost certain execution? Did he think that Tadeusz was somehow a threat to his own chances of claiming the Polish throne? Did he hope Tadeusz would not survive the war in the east? Would Tadeusz be in danger if he did survive?

Was Tadeusz in danger *now?*

17 August 1812

At dusk, Paweł stood on a hill above Smolensk, a city at the eastern border of the old Poland. It was situated on the left bank of the River Dnieper and so an important crossing point as the French moved into Russia. A large Russian force had repaired behind the strong city walls. Smaller units occupied the outer buildings that clustered nearby. After two days of a frontal assault and gritty house-to-house engagements, the French moved in, taking to the suburbs. Three major fires, most likely set by the enemy, still burned ferociously, however, feeding on wooden buildings and old towers.

Paweł turned to see Napoléon riding forward at a trot to survey the situation. He was accompanied by just two officers, and they moved perilously close to the old town, its fifteen-foot-thick walls still patrolled by Russians. But Paweł had learned by now that the emperor often took such unnecessary risks.

The Russians had suffered and would not hold out much longer, Paweł thought, but it had been at the cost of ten thousand French casualties. His own company of Young Guards had lost two youths. Later Paweł would take up the sad task of writing home to their families.

On the march prior to this point, the company had seen action half a dozen times without losses, but the Grande Armée as a whole was losing five thousand men a day to disease and desertion. Nonetheless, the lofty enthusiasm for the emperor on the part of young Poles had neither waned nor wavered.

By morning it was clear that the Russians had vacated Smolensk, and the French forces entered the city. The Young Guards were not the only ones to be sickened by the sight and acrid stink of dead bodies, soldiers and citizens alike, many piled like a fishmonger's wares. Paweł and others of the Old Guard had to hold themselves back from vomiting. As for Napoléon, famous for his delicate olfactory sensitivity, he seemed quite unaffected. It was put about that he commandeered the saying of one of the Roman emperors: "The corpse of an enemy always smells good."

Into the afternoon, Tadeusz approached Paweł, requesting that he accompany him to a little stone residence that had been shattered by artillery. Inside, Jan Michał was standing over the supine form of a Russian soldier.

"He's still alive," Jan Michał said.

Moving closer, Paweł saw that the soldier amidst the rubble on the dirt floor was no more than a boy, younger even than Tadek. Not even a bit of fuzz on his chin. "Is he conscious?" Paweł asked.

"Now and then," Jan Michał said.

"What is your name?" Paweł asked in Russian.

The eyes—pain-filled but fearless—opened. "Chapaev," he said.

"What are we to do with him?" Tadeusz asked in a pleading sort of way.

Paweł took in the expressions of the Stelnicki brothers now. Jan Michał and Tadeusz had come through several battles and a half dozen skirmishes, each time acquitting themselves with the zeal and bravery of the young. But now he saw dark wonder and fear in their eyes—for when they looked into the eyes of the dying Russian youth, it was as if they were looking into a mirror.

"We're going to take him to our surgeons, Tadek. This is war, too. We will be judged not just by how well we fight—but by how well we treat the fallen enemy."

The boys looked from Paweł to the boy. They remained mute.

Paweł knelt at the boy's side. "We're going to move you now," he said. "We're taking you to the doctor."

"It is too late," the boy spat. "Too late for me." He looked up at his captors, some unseen strength taking hold. "What devil your tsar must be to try to conquer Holy Mother Russia! What devils you all must be! You cannot win on holy soil. You will be driven out with tails between your legs, like wounded wolves."

"Michał," Paweł ordered, "take him from under his arms. Tadek, grab his feet. Let's get moving."

As he followed them out, Paweł admired the fire that still burned within the mortally wounded young Russian. But it came with a warning—if the millions of Russian peasants across the steppes and into the cities harbored the same zeal, what a great mistake the emperor was making. Russia would not fall that easily.

The brothers came to Paweł in the evening, their faces drawn. The boy had died on the table.

"What were you doing in that hovel?" Paweł asked now. "Plundering, yes?"

The boys looked down, shamefaced.

"Leave that to others, do you hear? You need worry only about carrying yourself into Russia and out again. I've seen what happens to those who try to carry out the riches of a country. Time and again they don't make it with their lives. Do you understand? Polish warriors fight for independence. Not paper rubles or silver goblets. Make your mother and father *proud*, do you hear? Look at me!"

The boys—still silent and rooted like sticks to the ground—fixed their eyes on Paweł. "On the other hand," Paweł said, "should you run across fur hats, gloves, or coats that will protect us from frostbite on this God-forsaken steppe, you are not to forget Paweł, old friend of the family, yes?"

This little speech coaxed at last smiles from the two, and Paweł pulled them together in a bear hug.

It was Polish infantry who, with the help of two artillery pieces, had gained entry into Smolensk—but when the *Bulletin de la Grande Armée* was sent back to Paris via Warsaw, Napoléon gave credit to French soldiers. The lie incensed Paweł, and in his letters to the two dead soldiers' families—traveling by the same courier—he made certain to underscore the truth.

The forces remained in Smolensk a full week. Paweł suspected that

Napoléon was allowing time for Aleksandr to consider suing for terms. Because they had yet to bring the Russians to a decisive battle, Paweł doubted Aleksandr would weaken—and therefore the week was time lost. On the other hand, the conservative move might be no move. Nearly all Napoléon's marshals thought that they should winter in Smolensk, for the hardships of the Russian winter were not far away.

Again, perhaps afraid to remain away from Paris for too long—where plots against him sprang up like weeds—Napoléon followed his own star and chose to move on. On 25 August, the Grand Armée left Smolensk, its sights set on Moscow.

32

September 1812

"Have you ever been in love, Zofia?"

"What?" The bedchamber was dark, and Zofia had thought Charlotte asleep. The raspy, labored voice had surprised her, as had the question itself.

"In love?" Charlotte said. "Truly in love?"

"I don't know. Sometimes I think so. Have you?"

"Oh, yes! A great love—before I met you. Before I left France."

"You never told me."

"A lady should have some secrets. The pain remained too close to the surface."

"After all these years? Who was he?"

"A duke. Aubrey was his name."

"An unusual name."

"It means 'blond ruler.' "

"And did he love you?" How strange, Zofia thought. That this conversation was taking place in darkness. And that she had never spoken of it before.

"He did."

"What happened, Charlotte?"

"He married another. At the wishes of his family. I was untitled at the time, and they could not see beyond that."

"I see. It was your only love?"

"It was."

"What happened to him?"

"He died on the scaffold. Like so many. And you, Zofia? Was it Jan Stelnicki?"

Zofia thought for a long moment. "No, I think not."

"Who, then?"

"Someone you never met."

"Iza's father?"

"You're very talkative, Charlotte. You should be resting."

"It was, wasn't it?"

"He was just a boy."

"But it was—different?"

"Yes, it was different. He was so innocent. He taught me how to carve some silly little figures out of linden wood. I even imagined myself staying in that tiny, pathetic village—living the life of a peasant." Zofia forced a laugh. "He was a peasant boy. Isn't that silly?"

"Perhaps. Perhaps not. What was his name?"

"Jerzy."

"And you never saw him again?"

"I did see him. Once. Years ago at the presentation of the colors ceremony. He had joined Poniatowski's infantry."

"Was he different than you remembered? Still innocent?"

"Still innocent, yes. But a man. He had become a man."

"And?"

Zofia sighed. "I gave him the send-off a man deserves." Charlotte seemed to be waiting to hear more. "I never saw him after that."

"He knew about Iza?"

"Yes. And he wanted to come back to Warsaw after the campaign. He wanted to meet her. He wanted to—Oh, it was impossible, and I told him so."

"And?"

"He probably died in the campaign. The infantry often gets the worst of it, you know."

"What do you tell Iza?"

"That he was a great lord and that he died fighting for Kościuszko."

"I see."

"You know, Charlotte, I've had many conquests." She gave a little laugh. "Perhaps even more than you!"

"Indeed."

"I've bedded King Stanisław and the little French emperor himself, for God's sake! But there's nary a night I don't think about that blond peasant boy. Isn't that strange?" Zofia sensed Charlotte shifting in the bed, then felt her take hold of her hand.

"Not so very," Charlotte said. "Not so very." And she lifted Zofia's hand to her lips and kissed it.

Charlotte was weeping now, Zofia realized.

On 15 September, the main arm of the Grande Armée, a hundred thousand strong, reached Moscow. The sight of the oriental-flavored city, with its many hundred golden spires and colored onion domes rising above glittering palaces and numberless rooftops of wooden buildings caught Paweł's imagination as much as it did the members of the Young Guard. Paweł stared long moments at the cathedral with its nine copper-covered bell towers, the tallest of which supported the thirty-foot-high silver cross of Ivan the Great. Days later, orders came down that the magnificent cross—and the great eagles on the Kremlin towers—were to be detached and trucked as trophies to Paris. In removing the oversize treasures, however, the carpenters and workmen nearly lost their lives as the icons crashed to the ground. The booty would prove too heavy to cart away.

It seemed inconceivable that they were here. The march from Smolensk had been the most demanding Paweł had experienced. The temperature in the course of a single day swung like a pendulum, arcing from sweltering afternoon heat to temperatures below zero at night. And the strong winds of the steppes whipped up dust that pelted the soldiers, forcing them to invent face coverings of odd rags. Water was bad or nonexistent, and food became extremely scarce, with horseflesh and corn providing the most common ration.

Natural elements aside, skirmishes had been plentiful and brutal. Besides huge casualties, the number of stragglers—those wounded or victims of hunger and disease—mounted into thousands upon thousands. But the battle that had turned aside the Russian army, permitting entry into Moscow, occurred at the village of Borodino. The victory had not come easily, for the Russians fought and fell in continuous forward movement as if they were mechanical soldiers that according to the emperor "only cannonballs can demolish." The Russians suffered an estimated forty-five thousand men, dead and wounded; the French, thirty-five thousand.

Before abandoning Moscow, its governor, Count Rostopchin, removed fire-fighting equipment and put hundreds of arsonists to work. The resulting fires lasted five days, devastating palaces, churches, homes, and businesses—so many made completely of wood. The Jewish quarter was reduced to ash and cinders. Fortunately, the Kremlin complex was spared. Paweł could not imagine the Poles burning Warsaw or the French burning Paris merely to slow an enemy. It was barbarous. Word filtered down that an enraged Napoléon had written to Tsar Aleksandr that Moscow no longer existed and that Count Rostopchin's four hundred arsonists had been summarily shot.

Poniatowski's Fifth Corps, along with General Murat's cavalry, made camp in Voronov, a small abandoned village a bit southwest of Moscow. Paweł saw his Young Guard billeted in small wooden houses with thatched roofs. He admonished his men against destroying property or taking anything other than food, blankets, and warm clothes. While his men seemed to obey, much of the French army was bivouacked within Moscow, and with the fires providing diversion, plundering there went unchecked for several days. Men looted anything of value, heedless that they would have to carry it on their backs the long, long way they had come. Their consciences were cleansed, it seemed, when it was confirmed that the fires had been set by the Russians themselves.

The entire army should have been billeted outside the city, Paweł thought, but the temptations of real roofs, stoves, and beds had been too much for certain army authorities who must have prevailed upon Napoléon.

On the first morning in Voronov, Paweł knocked and entered the little dwelling that had been assigned to Jan Michał and Tadeusz. "Hello, soldiers! Hello!" he called.

Both boys had been sleeping. They jumped to their feet.

"Still abed, are we?" Paweł said, with a laugh. "One would think you've been on a forced march!"

The boys smiled, wiping at their eyes.

"Get dressed now, while I put some wood in the stove."

A little while later, the three sat at a tiny table, sharing a meal of preserved deer meat that Paweł had fried up.

"What now, Major?" Jan Michał asked.

Paweł shrugged. "That depends on Napoléon."

"And the tsar," Tadeusz said.

"You're right there, Tadek."

"Will he sue for peace?" Jan Michał asked.

Paweł snickered. "Who knows the will of the gods, hey?" He drank down some warm mead. "Personally I don't think we've done our job convincingly enough on their army, but we'll see."

A blue fire ignited in Tadeusz's eyes. "At Borodino we should have followed Kutusov—allowing him to steal away into the night like that! A final frontal assault is what we needed."

"We had been pushed to the limit, if you hadn't noticed, Tadek," Jan Michał corrected. "And full frontal assaults can be ruinous. Isn't that right, Major?"

Paweł nodded. "Sometimes, Michał, yes." He took another drink. "As for Napoléon, I expect he'll wait and see what comes."

"You think we'll winter here?" Tadeusz asked.

"Any extended waiting and we'll have to," Jan Michał said. "Yes, Major?"

Paweł nodded. "Your tactics classes taught you well. Winter on the steppes is deadly. How's the meat?"

When the boys complimented Paweł, he laughed, calling them liars. "It's tough and salty—but compared with what we've had, who's to complain?"

"What's that?" Tadeusz asked, his ears pricking up and his eyes shifting left to right.

"What?" Jan Michał asked.

"I heard nothing," Paweł said.

"There, again!" Tadeusz cried.

"I think I did hear something, Major," Jan Michał said.

"I'm afraid the artillery has taken much of my hearing," Paweł said with a little laugh.

"A goat?" Jan Michał suggested, half to himself. "Or a cat?"

Tadeusz stood and made for the door. He pushed his head out, surveying the front of the hut. After a long minute, he closed the door and returned to the table.

"Nothing?" Jan Michał asked.

"Nothing."

And then came the noise again.

"I heard *that!*" Paweł declared. "A baby!"

They listened in wide-eyed silence. It came yet again, more sustained. The three stood as if on command, their eyes moving to the ceiling. "Is there an attic?" Paweł asked.

"More of a loft," Jan Michał said. "You know, for the animals when it gets cold enough."

"Which is often in this God-forsaken tundra," Paweł said. "Where's the access? Outside?"

"No," Tadeusz said. "There's a ramp behind the kitchen area."

Paweł drew his pistol. "And you didn't check it out?"

"I stuck my head up there," Tadeusz said. "A lot of hay. Too dark to see much of anything."

The three moved to the ramp without further words—and listened. Silence.

"Come down!" Paweł called, his voice authoritative and demanding. He drew his pistol. "Come down from there at once, or you will be shot!"

They could hear a little shuffling going on. Then the sound of someone moving on the boards. A red booted foot appeared on the ramp.

"Come ahead," Paweł ordered. "If you have a weapon, drop it now, or you will be shot."

"No weapon." The tremulous voice was scarcely audible. The second boot and the hem of a brown muslin garment appeared. It was a woman, and with great hesitancy, she moved down the ramp, carrying a bundle of blankets that held the little crier that had given away the hiding place. She was scarcely more than a girl, a terrified girl, younger than Jan Michał and no more than a year older than Tadeusz.

"What are you doing here?" Paweł asked in Russian.

"I live here."

Her response was in Polish, but Paweł took care not to register surprise. "Who else is up there?"

"No one."

"Have a look around, Jan Michał."

"I'll go, Major!" Tadeusz cried.

"I said Jan Michał!" Paweł's snappish delivery underscored that it was an order, and Tadeusz blushed at the censure.

Jan Michał started for the ramp.

"Damn it, Michał!" Paweł shouted, stopping him in midstep. "Get your pistol!"

It was Jan Michał's turn to be shamefaced now. He went for his pistol and in no time was ascending the ramp. They could hear him moving around overhead. How had they not heard the woman and baby before this?

"Nothing!" Jan Michał shouted.

"All right, come down!" Paweł ordered.

The woman looked as if she was about to faint. The baby started to cry now.

"Go sit down," Paweł told her.

The woman sat, and the three drew around her. The crying grew louder.

"Your baby is hungry?" Paweł asked. "If you're able to feed it, do so."

The woman went red as a ripe apple, adjusted the blankets in a camouflaging manner, and obeyed.

"You're Polish," Paweł said.

She nodded.

"What are you doing living here?"

"My husband is Russian."

"In the tsar's army?"

"Yes."

"Why didn't you take to the forest with the rest of the villagers?"

She flinched, and her eyes brimmed with tears. "I'm afraid of them. They are all Russian. They do not accept me. They would kill me. I know they would kill me."

Paweł believed her.

"What are we to do with her?" Jan Michał asked.

"I can stay?" she asked.

Paweł looked down on her, this pathetic but pretty peasant madonna and her child. "It is your house. These soldiers are in your house."

"I can cook for them," she said. "My name is Metody."

"The deal is struck!" Paweł cried, turning to the wide-eyed brothers. "They'll watch out for you, and you'll cook for them."

"But, Major—," Tadeusz started.

"I expect," Paweł interrupted, "she'll do a damned sight better than I or either of you at the stove."

Tadeusz knew not to question any further.

Paweł's eyes narrowed on his two charges. "Jan Michał, when you get up from the table, take your pistol, danger or no, and next time, my friends, *thoroughly* examine your quarters. Be aware of every bedbug! The enemy could have slit your young throats in your sleep. Understood?"

"Yes, sir," the brothers replied in tandem.

33

October 1812

Anna sat with Anusia Potocka and Maria Walewska in the reception room of Charlotte Sic's rented town house. They had come an hour earlier from their volunteer duties at the hospital to visit the French princess and to support Zofia, who would not leave her bedside. After a short visit to the princess' chamber, they took up vigil in the reception room below. A servant went about the room, lighting tapers against the increasing darkness. The painted porcelain Gdańsk clock on the mantel ticked loudly.

The three friends, acutely affected by the sight of Charlotte and her labor to draw breath, sat in silence for what seemed a long while. Anna noticed that hers were not the only eyes to move toward the ceiling, as if the drama being played out in the upstairs bedchamber might be visible.

"Maria," Anusia asked, "was there by chance a letter for you in the packet containing the emperor's latest Paris bulletin?"

Contrary to the present mood in the room, Napoléon's fall *Bulletins de la Grande Armée*–passing into Warsaw and the temporary care of Abbé Pradt, then on to Paris–had been filled with the telling of splendid results. The Grande Armée pursued the Russians, stalking the enemy who retreated, evaded, fought only when cornered, and retreated yet again. Smolensk had been a marvelous victory, the emperor boasted. And now Moscow itself had been won. Warsaw received the magnificent bulletins of the emperor with great fanfare. Anna, however, was one of the few to question–if only to herself–a cake with so much icing.

Maria took good time in answering. "I did have a letter," she finally said with a sigh. "He avoided the subject of my going to Moscow."

"Ah," Anna said. "He must have a reason, Maria. Perhaps he doesn't expect to be there long."

"Perhaps," Maria said.

"Although," Anusia said, "my father-in-law believes the emperor has no choice–that with winter all but upon them, they'll have to stay." As if suddenly realizing her observation did not lighten Maria's mood, she added, "I'm certain that by the next bulletin we'll have an indication of what he's going to do. If he's to stay, I know he'll send for you."

Maria braved a smile and Anna agreed, knowing that Maria longed for a repeat of the happy winter she had spent with Napoléon at Schloss Finkenstein. How difficult it must be for a mistress who truly loves a married man, she thought. There was no question that Maria Walewska loved Napoléon Bonaparte.–But did *he* love *her?*

For Anna and Jan, the latest mail packet from Moscow had been more reassuring. As usual, Paweł had been able to include in it a letter, this one detailing Anna and Jan's sons' safe installation in a little village outside Moscow. To hear Paweł tell it, they thrived in the Grande Armée. And her fears regarding the possible danger to Tadeusz from King Jérôme were allayed a bit when she read that Jérôme finally joined the French forces, Napoléon took away command of the right wing of the French army, placing him instead under the command of General Davout. So incensed was the young self-proclaimed genius-king that he resigned in protest and returned to Westphalia.

Anna read and reread Paweł's letter, wondering if he–like Napoléon–

painted a picture of the march with a brush dipped in colors that did not reflect reality. She found herself accepting his brief reports much like Warsaw
accepted the bulletins of the emperor—with great celebration. And a greater
wish that the news was true.

A noise on the stairs was heard now, then soft voices in the hall and the
front door closing on the doctor. Zofia came into the reception room. "Thank
you so much for staying," she said to the three, her face a white mask. No one
needed to be told what had just occurred. The French princess who had
cheated the guillotine years ago had died.

"It was peaceful?" Anna asked.

Zofia nodded, walking to a window and staring out into the twilight. "I
asked Char if she was afraid, and she said the oddest thing, Anna. She said
that when you think of yesterday without regret and tomorrow without fear,
you are near contentment."

When Zofia turned back to face Anna and Anusia, Anna realized there
were transparent pearls in her cousin's eyes—a rare thing.

The days in Moscow ticked by slowly, like a clock winding down. It seemed
clear to everyone that Aleksandr was passing on his turn in the game: He was
not about to sue for peace terms. Speculation as to what Napoléon would do
ran rampant among his officers and soldiers. Some envisioned him taking action soon by seeking out Kutusov for a decisive win, then marching to Kiev
and the Ukraine, where the weather was better. Others thought he should retreat to Smolensk, but that meant a fifty-day journey with an army woefully
underclothed for the sub-zero winter blasts of the steppes. The surviving
horses lacked frost nails for their hooves. Staying in Moscow had its proponents because there was adequate shelter and a good six months' supply of
food. But that decision ran a serious risk: Would the Russians not gather up
confidence and amass an army for a winter engagement? And the French
could not hope for reinforcements now until spring.

Paweł could understand why the emperor vacillated. While he wished
Napoléon would pause in his novel reading—for this is what seemed to occupy
most of his days—Paweł was glad it was not his decision to make. Even now,
in these dark and portentous days, he felt Poland could be the key to success
for Napoléon. If only he would declare Poland free and independent, then
send the Poniatowski Fifth Corps southeast to Minsk in support of the two
Polish forces there that were supporting the Austrians in the southern French
flank. Combined, Poniatowski, Dąbrowski, and Bronikowski would muster a
real Austrian offense against Russia's Third Army of the West and the Russ-

ian Army of the Danube. And the thousands of Poles back home, who had doubted Napoléon, would engender a new wave of recruits. *If only* . . .

But Paweł guessed that Napoléon judged such a declaration of independence for Poland too great an incitement to Russia. Aleksandr did not like the idea of a free people living under a democratic constitution on his western border any better than Catherine had. And Napoléon seemed to hold out hope that he could still make his peace with the tsar. It was a delusion, Paweł thought.

Lines of communication with the French detachment in Smolensk began to break down as Russian partisans there rose up in great numbers, committing such atrocities that demoralized French soldiers came to fear capture far more than death in battle. The interception of Napoléon's dispatches containing his *Bulletins de la Grande Armée* became routine. In light of political problems in Paris, Napoléon at last made up his mind on 17 October: The order came down that French forces were to evacuate Moscow in two days, retreating to the River Niemen.

The next day, as Paweł directed his Young Guard in the collecting of supplies and packing in Voronov, word came that General Murat was under full attack at the nearby village of Winkovo. Poniatowski mobilized the Fifth Corps and came to his rescue, but not without twenty-five hundred casualties. It was an unhappy omen for the retreat.

At three in the morning, Paweł knocked and entered the quarters of Jan Michał and Tadeusz, afraid what he might find. He had seen Jan Michał in the midst of the battle, holding his own—but nowhere had he seen Tadeusz. The room was dimly lighted by two candles, and it took some moments for his eyes to adjust. Cooking oil permeated the little hut. Two forms stood over the third, which lay on one of the cots.

"Major!"

Paweł sighed in relief to see it was Tadeusz saluting him. His eyes then moved to the young woman, who was cleansing a shoulder wound Jan Michał had incurred.

The patient tried to rise from the cot. Metody pushed him down, uttering a sharp word, so he settled for saluting from the supine position, apologizing profusely.

"That's all right," Paweł said, moving closer. "How bad is it?"

"A flesh wound," Jan Michał said. "Nothing at all."

"It's to the bone," Metody contradicted.

"That's because I'm *all* bone. Mama always said so—no flesh. It's nothing, I tell you."

"Lie still," Metody said.

Tadeusz laughed. "Isn't she something, Major?"

Paweł nodded, then addressed Metody. "You've cauterized wounds before, I can see."

Metody gave a little shrug as if it were nothing.

Paweł addressed Michał: "The convoy of wounded has left already, but perhaps we can catch you up to them."

"No, Major—please! I'll be able to ride. I will!"

"We'll see about that."

"But, Major—"

"Ah, no arguments tonight, Michał. We'll see how you are tomorrow. I do have some news."

"We trounced them!" Tadeusz cried. "What could be better news? Ran off their main guard like they were a handful of drunken Cossacks!"

"Not without taking our lumps, as Jan Michał here demonstrates. Remember that, Tadeusz. In war, everyone loses. And don't *ever* underestimate Cossacks!"

"Yes, Major."

"The news is that the Young Guard is to stay behind with Marshal Mortier long enough to explode the Kremlin and its arsenal. There are sixty thousand Russian muskets there that we're not going to leave behind to be used against us later."

"Good lord!" Tadeusz punctuated his cry with a whistle. "The Kremlin—what fun that will be!"

"It's a duty, Tadek."

"Yes, sir. Duty *and* pleasure."

"Once that's done, the Young Guard will catch up and ride rear guard."

Picking up the washbasin, Metody moved toward the little kitchen area to tend to her baby, her face dark. Paweł could see that she had been crying recently, and he became immediately suspicious. "Michał," Paweł asked, "you have not—become involved?" He cast a sidelong glance at Metody.

"No," Jan Michał said. "Nothing like that!"

Paweł turned a questioning look to Tadeusz. "And you, Tadek?"

"No," he said, tossing off a laugh. "Too old for me, and married besides!"

"What are the tears for, then?"

"She's afraid," Tadeusz said.

"Terrified is more like it, Major," Jan Michał said. "She feels safe with us, and she's convinced that she and her baby will be killed once we leave, if not by the Cossacks or the Russian soldiers, then by the returning villagers who thought her an outsider before—before all this."

Paweł wished that he could deny the likely fate—but he could not. Metody was in a precarious and dangerous situation. He watched her now as she lifted her baby from his crudely made crib.

"She wants to go with us," Tadeusz chimed.

"To Poland?"

Jan Michał nodded.

"What about her husband?"

"She doubts he's even alive. She's thinking about her baby, Major."

Paweł thought. "Perhaps we can place her in one of the camp followers' vehicles. Her nursing or cooking skills should come in handy." Both boys brightened at the suggestion. "Now," Paweł asked with a wink, "are you going to offer me a vodka, or not?" It was only after a second drink that Paweł revealed his other news. "I won't be leading the Young Guard with you tomorrow," he said.

The boys looked stunned.

"I've been assigned to the advance guard as Napoléon makes his getaway." Paweł could tell the news had a profound effect on the boys, but they both quickly donned masks of acceptance. This was the way of the army. "You'll be riding under Major Mortier."

Jan Michał stoically nodded as Tadeusz said, "Yes, sir."

The subject was dropped, and the facade of nonchalance continued, and after a third drink, Paweł left the hut. Walking back to his quarters, he worried that he had failed Jan and Anna. He had tried to hold on to his present duty, but Poniatowski told him Napoléon himself had made some positive comment when he saw Paweł's name on the proposed list, recalling the days in Poznań when Paweł and Jan had taken him on day trips into the country. The man's memory was remarkable.

Both Michał and Tadek had grown into fine, self-sufficient soldiers, he told himself. He had taught and they had learned fast. He had tried to capitalize on Michał's tactical prowess—to great success—and to curb Tadek's impulsiveness—to considerable improvement. But he could not play guardian angel to them throughout their military careers. In fighting for a chance at independence for the Commonwealth, they were following through on Jan and Anna's dreams started twenty years before. They would prove worthy of the challenge. The day had come to let fly the unhooded falcons—and it had come at the behest of the emperor himself.

God grant them both glory in battle and long life!

"No news is good news," Abbé Pradt kept repeating as his arriving guests asked if he had reports from the front. "We are here to dance—to enjoy!"

"Again, the man has nothing to say," Anusia Potocka murmured to Anna as they waited their turn in the reception line.

"And he says it," Anna replied. "You have to give him that."

"Why do we show up at his doings?"

"In the hope that some news will have come through."

"I know, I know. Oh, Anna, you and Jan must be beside yourselves with worry."

The archbishop's splendid receptions had continued without interruption despite the fact that no dispatch had come through Warsaw for weeks. Was Napoléon now sending his bulletins on directly to Paris? Or were the dispatches not making it through the lines? Most believed the latter true. Rumors of tortured and murdered messengers abounded.

Anna and Anusia moved forward. "What is this?" the abbé asked in mock horror. "Lady Potocka, you have worn black to my soirée! Is this a wake, I ask you? A funeral?"

Anusia smiled tightly. "It is my favorite dress."

"Ah," he said, "at least your diamonds redeem you." He turned his attention to Anna. "The green of your gown is dark, too, Anna. Although it shimmers beautifully."

Anna curtsied. She had grown to thoroughly dislike the little archbishop.

"Is Maria with you?" the abbé asked.

"No," Anna said. "She's a bit under the weather."

"Spending too many hours at the hospital, I'll wager. As both of you do, I hear."

"Don't rely on hearsay, Your Eminence," Anna said, emboldened by the man's insouciance. "Come see for yourself." Anna and Anusia broke free of the abbé, whose smile soured slightly, and he went on to the next in line.

"Good for you, Anna!" Anusia whispered. "It wouldn't hurt him to bring a little of his false enthusiasm to the men in the hospitals. Let's sit here. Do you think anyone will dance tonight?"

"I doubt it—unless they transport some of the hospital's ambulatory patients. Besides, no one is in the mood to dance." A darkness had come to Warsaw, blanketing it like a pall of black crepe. The hospitals had filled with men who had been wounded at Wilno, at Smolensk, at Borodino. They were the bravest of the brave during the day but cried out in their sleep, sobbing for the many more wounded and stragglers left behind. To hear them tell it, more men died of disease than in battle. And groups of marauding Russian peasants had risen up, not Cossacks but common people incensed with the disruption of armies—and no doubt nourished by the generations of abuse on the part of their own government. Victims were murdered in gruesome ways.

Eyes were gouged out. Men were dropped into vats of boiling water or repeatedly propelled to the ground with such force that no part of their spines were unbroken.

When the famous Napoléon bulletins ceased, all of Warsaw and all of Poland held a great collective breath. And as fear for fathers, brothers, and sons—as well as for a free Poland—set in, rumors and speculation became rife. The Polish imagination knew no bounds. No news was *not* good news, Anna thought, listening to the strains of a polonaise. In his last letter to Maria, Napoléon told her that he would not have her there at Moscow. Anna thought this only gave credence to the widely held belief that the French were in retreat. That some terrible defeat loomed.

Zofia approached them now. She wore a lovely berry-red satin gown, cut low at the bosom. "Hello, Anna. Anusia, it's good to see you. I haven't been to one of Pradt's receptions in the longest time." After an exchange of greetings, Zofia sat and the three watched as a young woman was escorted to the floor by an octogenarian. They were the only couple to attempt the mazurka.

"Pradt pushed them out there at gunpoint, no doubt," Anusia said.

"Pradt!" Zofia huffed. "The man has a piss-pot on his shoulders!"

Anusia laughed, nodding at the odd couple on the dance floor. "I'll wager the old goat doesn't manage to stay vertical the length of the dance."

"Shush!" Anna rasped. "That's Maria's husband."

"*Former* husband," Zofia corrected.

"Indeed, by God, you're right, Anna!" Anusia cried, her hand going to her mouth. "Just look at him—and those spindly legs."

It was not long before Zofia grew restless. She made her good-byes to everyone—with the omission of Abbé Pradt—and left.

"This is the first I've seen Zofia since the funeral, Anna," Anusia said. "She's taking Charlotte's death very hard. Not a real laugh or even a genuine smile tonight."

"It's more than that, Anusia." The words were scarcely out of Anna's mouth before she regretted them. She had learned over the years to consider content before speaking. But she still failed at it occasionally.

"What?" Anusia was already pressing. "What is it? Do tell!"

"You must swear secrecy. If Zofia wants you to know, she'll tell you." When Anusia duly swore, Anna said, "She went to the reading of Charlotte's will today."

Anusia gasped. "Oh! She didn't get the diamonds?"

Anna shook her head. "Nor the château in Brittany."

"What did she get?"

"Nothing."

Anusia was dumbstruck. "Nothing? Precious lord, I thought Charlotte had no one in the world but Zofia."

Anna would bait her friend no longer. "She had a granddaughter of sorts."

Anusia caught on immediately and drew in a great breath. "Izabel!"

Anna nodded. "Iza received—everything."

"*Everything?*" Anusia's mouth formed a perfect circle. Catching her breath, she said, "Well, at least it's in the family. But Zofia must feel as if she's been stabbed."

"For now, she does. And you might say the knife was double-edged."

"What do you mean?" Anusia asked.

"The answer to that lies in the why of Charlotte's bequest."

"I'm listening."

"Zofia has had every intention of marrying Iza off to Prince Adam Czartoryski."

"But he's old enough to be her father—and didn't she try to get him to the altar herself?"

"She did, years ago," Anna answered, "and although the prince has been an inveterate bachelor, he, like most men of some stature, wish to bring children into the world. That, coupled with Iza's beauty—the dark hair and light coloring and eyes—would most likely have turned his head."

"All right, assuming that's so, what was Charlotte's intention?"

"Can't you guess? She didn't want Zofia deciding Iza's future. Now, with her own fortune from Charlotte, Iza need not be bullied into an arranged marriage."

"Ah, I see!" Anusia let out a great sigh. "A sleight of hand by Charlotte—and orchestrated from her grave, no less. Everyone always thought Zofia the clever one. She must be angry as a hornet."

"It'll pass—I hope," Anna said. "She should know the dangers of arranged marriages."

Anusia shrugged. "Mine was an arranged marriage, and it didn't turn out badly."

"Well, my first one was, too, and it turned out *very* badly! Now, you're not to allude to your knowledge of this, Anusia."

"I know. I have a secret I'm bound to tell you now, too. Once, when Zofia was well into her cups, she told me how she had never quite gotten over King Stanisław's elevating you to princess. After all, she had had a little fling with his Royal Highness, as you must know. I suspect her machinations with Czartoryski were partly due to her jealousy of you. Had he married her, she would have been a princess, too! There, now we are even. One secret for another. Don't you think it's time to leave?"

"I do." Anna stood, choosing not to tell her friend that her disclosure about Zofia was no secret.

34

November 1812

Inside the hut, Jan Michał was watching Metody tend to her baby when he heard the commotion outside. He recognized one of the two raised voices as belonging to Tadeusz and hurried to investigate.

"You will! You will!" Tadeusz was screaming in Russian, his face inflamed.

The bearded Russian civilian was lashing a canvas covering to the contents of his wagon. He was perhaps fifty. "Never," he said, physically brushing Tadeusz aside as if he were a pesky mosquito.

"You must!" Tadeusz insisted. "It's been *ordered*."

Jan Michał saw Tadeusz's hand move toward his saber. Striding toward the two, Jan Michał placed a restraining hand on his brother's arm. "What seems to be the matter here?" he asked, his narrowing eyes cautioning Tadeusz.

"No matter," the Russian said. He walked to where the brothers stood. "No one rides in my wagon." He stood a head taller than Jan Michał. Much heavier, too. An imposing figure.

"He refuses to take Metody and the baby," Tadeusz said.

"Tadek, there are wagons and carriages lined up the length of the street."

"And they all have passengers!"

"I see," Jan Michał said, assessing the situation. "Tadek, Metody could use some help inside."

"No, damn it! I'm not about to—"

"Tadek," Jan Michał said, lowering his voice and switching to Polish, "let me take care of this."

When Tadeusz put up further argument, Jan Michał tossed him a severe look of warning that immediately silenced him. Tadeusz looked at the peasant, fighting back his instinct to win him over—one way or another. He looked back to his brother, sighed, and moved off toward the hut.

Jan Michał smiled tightly at the civilian. "My brother sometimes flies before he walks." His Russian was not as polished as his brother's, but it was serviceable.

The man shrugged, continuing his cold glare while Jan Michał affected a conversational tone. "Both horses look strong enough." The man grunted, mumbling something Jan Michał could not make out. "You have passengers, then?"

"Yes."

"How many?"

"One."

"And that one is yourself?"

"It is."

"I see. We have a young mother and a baby here. They'll not take up much room, and they weigh little."

"They'll take up no room on *my* wagon."

"What's your name?"

"Oleg."

"Oleg, I am Jan. Did my brother Tadek explain the emperor's orders?"

"Your emperor is not *my* emperor." The man sneered. "I don't take his orders."

"Ah, I see. Just what is it you're transporting here, Oleg?"

"That's my business."

But Jan Michał was already walking around the wagon, lifting the canvas here and there, peeking beneath. He saw a gilded French desk and other furniture, as well as paintings, furs, and brocaded material. "All from *your* house, Oleg?"

The man had followed him. "Perhaps."

"You must be very rich."

"That's my business."

"What is this number 142 painted on the side?"

"All the vehicles have been given one."

"Then you are going under the auspices of the French?"

"Auspices?"

"Protection."

The man stood, expressionless.

"My brother was trying to tell you, Oleg, that Napoléon has ordered that no vehicle is to have fewer than two of the wounded or civilians."

When the man persisted in his indifference, Paweł said, "Perhaps he didn't tell you also that any vehicle not conforming to this order would be *burnt* on the spot. All up and down the line here, you'll find that every wagon has its passengers. If you wish to keep your nice things, you will take the woman and baby tomorrow."

The man started to bite at his lower lip. He had been boxed into a corner and knew it. A long moment passed before he gave the slightest of nods.

"Good! We are in agreement, then."

Another grudging nod.

"And you are to take good care of the two. If we should find, my friend, that they've come to harm because of you, my brother and I will search you out and make you familiar with a Polish lance." Jan Michał grinned widely now. "And you, Oleg, will find yourself opened up like a sow being made ready for sausages."

The man's eyes widened. "Yes, soldier."

Jan Michał smiled to himself as he moved toward the hut. Evidently the threat had suffered little in the translation to Russian.

The next day, 19 October, the main forces quit Moscow. Paweł knew that the word *retreat* was taboo. The plan was to join the large French force left at Smolensk. Conditions and supplies there were thought to be good, and Napoléon would be able to fashion one of his *Bulletins de la Grande Armée* that would transform the pig's foot they had come away with into a plump roast. Oddly enough, Napoléon had not ordered his men to travel light, and they started out carrying as much in spoils as they could, resembling more the Israelites fleeing Egypt than soldiers.

Their route to Smolensk had been kept secret. Upon setting out, Paweł guessed that they would take a southern route so as to avoid the inward path that had already been stripped clean of supplies. The southern route was the smarter route.

The Grande Armée moved like a great tortoise and by the twenty-third, the hare, General Kutusov, had moved in behind it at the town of Malo-yaroslavets. The next day a deadly battle commenced, and control of the town switched sides seven times. Paweł would remember it as one of the bloodiest conflicts of the campaign. This time it was the Italian corps that finally drove the Russians out, and while the French licked their wounds, Napoléon met with his generals. The resulting decision—to take the northern and supply-poor route to Smolensk—incensed Paweł. It seemed unfathomable. It had long been wrung dry of food sources. And the army was already in short supply of rations. While the men had up until now shared their foodstuff and put in shares of flour for the common soup, they started hoarding any flour, rice, biscuit, or potato in their possession. The common soup became one flavored by horseflesh, the only commodity at the ready.

The ammunition warehouses and the Russian army barracks went up in a magnificent explosion. Jan Michał and Tadeusz had helped in the laying of the fuses, and they were both awestruck by the results. Ammunition and thousands upon thousands of muskets were destroyed, muskets that the Russian nobles had not dared pass out among the populace for fear—a justified one—they would turn them on the nobility that had held them down for generations.

"What now?" Tadeusz asked.

"We're going to do what we were told to do—search out supplies."

The brothers were on one of the streets untouched by the fires. Hundreds of the Young Guard swarmed the streets on the same mission.

"But what about the Kremlin *buildings?*" Tadeusz whined. "You know as well as I that they were to come down!"

"I thought so, too. Plans must have changed."

"No, you heard Paweł just before he left. The Young Guard was commissioned to bring down the Kremlin. By the emperor."

"And you're disappointed?" Jan asked.

"Damn it all—yes! I was looking forward to the flame and ash. And a fire that would outshine the sun. I don't think Napoléon relented."

"You think it was General Mortier?"

"Yes!"

"Deliberately disobeying the emperor? Now why would he do that? You do grant we'll need the supplies for the long trek back to Smolensk, or wherever it is we'll winter."

"Yes, I give you that. But we can collect supplies and still blow the place sky high. Listen, I say we go now and set some explosives. Let's do it, Michał! This is our chance."

"Wait a minute!" Jan Michał could see that he was serious. "Tadek, who's going to suffer if it's destroyed?"

"What do you mean? The *Russians* will suffer!"

"Not the leaders. Not the army. Think, Tadek! The *people* will! In taxes and in broken backs."

"Who cares?" Tadek started down the street that led to the Kremlin compound.

Jan Michał had to double his step to catch up. "You'll be disobeying orders yourself, Tadek!"

"Not the emperor's orders. Those are the ones that count. Don't you realize we must be the only ones who know about them? It's up to us to finish off the Kremlin. If it weren't for Paweł letting us in on it–"

"Stop!" Jan Michał cried, his hand clamping on to his brother's arm. "Listen to me. Mother told us about the massacre and destruction at Praga in '94, yes?"

"Exactly, all the more reason!"

"No, it's not. Warsaw itself went untouched. The Royal Castle still stands, as does Zygmunt's Column! The Russians could have destroyed the city. And when the Prussians left much more recently, they could have done likewise. War may seem to be without limits, Tadek, but it isn't. It isn't!"

Tadek thought for a long moment, his blue eyes fixed unflinchingly on Jan Michał's brown.

Jan Michał now delivered the coup de grâce. "What would mother do, Tadek?"

Tadeusz was caught off guard. He blinked, and his face became pinched. "Damn it, Michał, don't bring her into this!"

"Why not? Is it something you'll proudly tell her? Is it? Would blowing up those incredible buildings make her proud?"

Tadeusz pulled away. "She'd light the fuses herself."

"You know that's not true!"

Tadeusz laughed. "You're right, but bringing Mother into it was such a low blow, I had to counter somehow. All right, Michał, you win. Let's get the damn supplies."

Jan Michał grinned. "There's a building there that looks as if it hasn't been searched. Let's try it."

"Fine. But I have to say Mother would not approve of the three Cossacks you dispatched the other day."

"Oh, now that's where you're wrong. If she had been born a man, she'd be riding in the vanguard."

Tadeusz laughed again and threw his arm around his brother's shoulder. "Say, didn't our own King Zygmunt's army take Moscow?"

"It did, in 1610, and he held it for two years."

"A better showing than Napoléon's."

Jan Michał nodded. "But in the end, Russia's a hard nut to crack."

The Young Guard withdrew from Moscow on the twenty-third, leaving the Kremlin intact. Carrying with them important supplies, they followed the path blazed by the Grande Armée. It was an easy thing to do, for the roads and fields were littered with broken wagons and abandoned booty that included paintings, books, and silver too heavy to carry. Mortier put out an order that any soldier caught salvaging goods would be summarily shot. Jan Michał told Tadeusz to keep his eye peeled for wagon 142 among the abandoned vehicles, but it was nowhere to be seen. He prayed that boded well for Metody and her baby.

The Young Guard joined the main forces at Maloyaroslavets two days after the battle there. The soldiers moved in, stunned to find seven thousand of their own—and nearly as many Russians—lying in the environs of the town like macabre fallen statues, crimson on uniforms, on lifeless faces, on the earth.

The Young Guard cursed General Mortier and themselves for their tardiness. As for the emperor, Napoléon was glad to see them. Whether Mortier told Napoléon about the sparing of the Kremlin, Jan Michał never learned, one way or the other.

Late that night Jan Michał quietly returned to the camp of the Young Guard.

"Did you find Metody?" Tadeusz asked.

"Yes, thank God. The wagon is still in decent shape. Oleg had lightened it considerably, but he appears to have taken my threat seriously. She's good, it seems. I left them what food I had with me, biscuits mostly." Jan Michał sighed. "She was depressed, though, to find lice on herself and on the baby."

"Good God, I can imagine. She kept that little hut clean as the gold buttons on a general's coat."

"Probably caught the creatures from the Russian—he's dirtier than a pig."

A silence ensued as Jan Michał wrapped himself in his bedding. Long after he thought Tadeusz must have fallen asleep, his brother spoke up. "You like her, Michał? Yes?"

Jan Michał looked up at the clear night sky, taking in a thousand stars. "Yes."

"Much?"

"Yes, Tadek."

Neither spoke after that, and soon Tadeusz's regular breathing indicated sleep had overcome him. It took a good while longer for Jan Michał to sleep. He feared that when the Grande Armée moved out in the morning the forty thousand camp followers—Metody among them—would fall far behind. He wondered if he would ever see her again.

The Grand Armée moved with greater speed, covering the fifty miles to Mojaisk in only two days. A day later the march brought them through Borodino.

While Paweł was disappointed that they were taking the already plundered route, he was struck dumb that no one had thought to avoid the Borodino battlefield. The horrors war had imposed as they moved toward Moscow a matter of weeks before now seared the eyes as the exodus from Russia continued. No one could look away. Spirits plummeted at the sight and stench of thirty thousand corpses torn to pieces by wolves and carrion crows. And yet, Paweł thought it perhaps a good thing that the Young Guard realize war meant more than courage and glory. The starving, ragtag army pushed on, passing through Gjatsk and arriving in Viazma at the end of October. A muster revealed that sixty-five thousand troops remained of the ninety-six thousand accounted for in Maloyaroslavets.

Cossacks and peasant bandits were unrelenting in their guerrilla attacks upon the stragglers who more and more were falling to the wayside, but the Russian army allowed the Grande Armée to stumble forward. In the meantime, another force was moving toward them. On 5 November, before Smolensk could be reached, it began to snow. "General Winter"—in the words of Napoléon—made himself known. By the seventh, heavy snow was falling, and the roads were iced over.

Without winter shoes, horses by the thousands slipped and fell on the ice, thousands more just dropping to the ground out of starvation, exhaustion, and cold. For many miles before reaching Smolensk, soldiers and stragglers survived by eating horseflesh and blood soup.

Several hours after the entry into Smolensk on the ninth, Paweł went in search of Jan Michał and Tadeusz. He found the Young Guard billeted in an overcrowded barn. Tadeusz's thin and unhealthy appearance came as a shock. "Have you eaten yet, Tadek?"

"We ate, shortly after arriving."

"What?"

Tadeusz gave a little smirk. "We dined on horse liver with snow for drink."

Paweł suppressed a grimace. "It'll keep you going, at least, yes? Where's Michał?"

"He's gone to look for Metody. Major, are we to winter here?"

"It was a possibility, but it seems unlikely now. The city is already depleted of supplies, and we have word that the Russians are not about to leave us on our own for the winter. Their numbers have increased, while ours—well, you've seen the results of the march. Fewer and fewer men and almost no discipline."

"How long do you think we'll stay?"

"Not long. We have intelligence that the enemy plans to thwart our crossing the Rivers Dneiper and Beresina. Two days—three at the most."

* * *

Some of the camp followers had managed to keep pace. Jan Michał found Metody not far from the city gates, sitting, her back against the battered and crumbling wall. "Metody?" Had it not been for her holding the baby, he would not have given her a second look. Her appearance had changed so. She was deathly ill. "Metody?" he repeated.

She lifted her head and stared, seeming not to recognize him. Her once charming face was skeletal now.

Jan Michał knelt down in front of her. "We must get you to the hospital, Metody. Do you hear?" It was as if she weren't aware of his presence. She drew her legs up into herself, clutching the baby tighter. The covered bundle had made nary a noise or movement. "Is Nelek all right?" Jan Michał asked, making a move to pull back the corner of the blanket that covered the child's face. Metody pulled away, but Jan Michał spoke to her in reassuring terms, gently insisting that he see the baby.

It was as he had feared. The child was dead. But the sight was unimaginable. His skin, splotchy with raised sores, was as dark as black raspberries. The little body was completely frozen, one tiny fist raised as if to rail against its fate. Metody clung to a baby that must have been dead for days.

Jan Michał didn't attempt to pry the baby from her grasp. He did, however, try to get Metody to her feet. As she struggled against him, a piece of fur covering one of her feet came free, and he could see that she was badly frostbitten.

"We need to get you to the hospital, Metody."

The young woman refused, fighting him off with surprising energy. He stood then and looked down at her. Metody returned his look, and he knew for certain that she recognized him. And that she understood. But she fell on her side now, drawing herself up into a fetal position, the baby still in her grasp. She was giving herself over to her fate.

It was an easy thing to die of the cold, they said. One just went to sleep. It seemed almost pleasant. Jan Michał turned now and ran for help. It took good time to find what accounted for a hospital and convince an orderly to help him. By the time the two came upon Metody, she was fully asleep and could not be roused. Someone had stolen her feet coverings.

"It's too late," the orderly said.

"It's not!" Jan Michał screamed. "Let's get her to the hospital!"

Hesitant, the orderly nonetheless helped Jan Michał envelop her in a blanket that they had brought.

The hospital was a vortex of confusion. Jan Michał fought for a place for

her and was assigned a narrow space on the floor against the wall. The orderly had been right, of course. Metody was but one of many that he had seen
in the same condition. Jan Michał stayed nearby, intermittently attempting to
rouse her, but by early morning, she was dead.

"There's a trench in front of the city walls," he was told by a doctor. "Take
the bodies there. The French army dug it before going on to Moscow. Little
did they know how it would be used."

Jan Michał found the trench, hundreds of paces long, half-filled with bodies frozen in the most surreal poses. He stumbled into the trench, laid down
his burden, and arranged it as best he could, placing the hospital blanket he
had stolen over Metody—and the baby that he had returned to her arms. He
said a quick prayer and climbed out of the burial site. A city worker there assured him the most recent bodies would be covered before nightfall with lime
and dirt. "Are you certain?" Jan Michał pressed, afraid that the bodies of
Metody and her little son would be cannibalized.

"I am, soldier."

Jan Michał gave a grudging nod and dropped a few coins into the
worker's hands. "Cover them now, if you please."

35

When the Grande Armée left Smolensk on the twelfth, after a stay of
three days, they numbered no more than forty-one thousand. Be-
sieged by blizzards and icy roads at first, Jan Michał knew that he
could not continue to fasten onto thoughts of Metody, for the dead and dying
were all around him and it would take every iota of concentration, cleverness,
and determination to bring himself and his brother out of this catastrophe alive.

The Young Guard marched in the van now. Jan Michał and Tadeusz often
walked their overworked and underfed horses. In this way, the cavalry managed to keep their animals alive longer while most of the horses that had
pulled wagons and caissons had succumbed or been killed for food.

On the seventeenth, the Russians—ninety thousand strong—staged an attack on the road to Krasnoi, severing the Grande Armée in two, putting at risk
the Beauharnais Corps. Napoléon sent the Young Guard back to fend off the
attackers. Jan Michał and Tadeusz stayed close to each other as they descended
into the swarm of men and weapons. In all the young men, reserves of energy

and mettle seemed to come from places that had seemed hollow only minutes before. Like Jan Michał and Tadeusz, they longed to see Poland again, hungered to embrace mothers and sisters again. They longed to live their lives.

The Young Guard pushed into an open area littered with Russians laid out on the snow, apparently wounded or dead. At a given signal the Russians jumped to their feet and started firing into the Young Guard, who turned their horses aside in order to make a half-loop around their attackers. They had heard about this favorite stratagem of the Russians. Experiencing it served only to motivate them further. And so they killed, ultimately routing the Russians in this contingent—but at the cost of a good many Young Guard, friends of Jan Michał and Tadeusz. No sooner had they claimed victory than they turned to see the Old Guard, the sixteen thousand "immortals," riding to protect Davout's corps at yet another point of attack. Jan Michał said a quick prayer for Paweł.

The Old Guard lived up to their legend, repelling the Russians, just as the Young Guard had met expectations, and the army trudged on—through Dubrovno, then farther west, happily discovering that the bridges over the River Dnieper had not been destroyed. They crossed safely, coming to Orsha.

One third of their forces had been left behind, dead and dying.

Paweł found Jan Michał and Tadeusz in a large stable with many of the Young Guard, all in spirits revived by the Russian rout, a decided thaw in the temperature, and decent food rations that included a little brandy and vodka.

"We're going into a peaceable Latvian area," Paweł said, raising a toast to a group of ten or twelve youths. "We're done with Russian citizens from here on out. No more angry partisans wishing to hack off our heads in lieu of those of their own nobles."

A little cheer went up. All of them had passed fallen French stragglers on the road who begged to be finished off before they were found by human wolves. Only occasionally had they been obliged.

"And the Cossacks, Major?" someone asked.

"Ah, we'll have their lances tickling our sides for a good while longer."

"Well, in these temperatures," Tadeusz said, "at least we can sleep at night without fear of not waking up!" Several soldiers spoke up in affirmation.

"The thaw is not all good news, gentlemen," Paweł said. "You see, the Orsha citizens tell us that the River Beresina, which is usually well frozen over at this time of year, has thawed with the milder weather. A week earlier and we could have safely crossed on the ice."

"What about the bridges at Borisov, Major?" Jan Michał asked.

"Our own spies tell us the Russians will get to them before us."

"And destroy them, of course," Jan Michał muttered, his face dark. Paweł did not deny it. He was sorry to have been the lever by which the Young Guards' optimism escaped. He didn't go so far as to tell them that three massive Russian armies held them virtually surrounded against a raging river. They would learn that soon enough.

The long, cold, and arduous march to Borisov—by way of Tołoczyn and Bobr—commenced, nonetheless. The Grande Armée navigated much of the way through massive forests of unusually tall birches on a road made of pine timbers elevated enough for the way to be seen in the snow. It seemed that they were moving slowly toward self-destruction. Napoléon, who traveled ahead by a few miles, ordered all official documents, as well as the tricolors, burned to cinders. Word got about that he now believed his guiding star had deserted him. It seemed so, thought Paweł, but more than that, the emperor's military genius had evaporated into the thin, cold air of a Russian winter. General Winter.

Jan Michał and Tadeusz, still gently urging their horses, intermittently walking them, passed thousands of French soldiers, mostly infantry, who stumbled along dumbly, their eyes, like their bodies—iced over. More and more, the road became blocked with stalled carts and dying horses. Traffic slowed even as the temperature dropped and the North wind increased its frigid fury. They fell more than a day's march behind Paweł's legion. "Maybe we should take a rest," Tadeusz called, nodding to groups of men who were making bivouacs under the birches, feeding their fires with wood from the broken carts for the roasting of horseflesh.

"No!" Jan Michał spat, scarcely able to put down the temptation himself. He knew that many of these good men, warmed and fed, would lie down in the snow and sleep, never to rise again. Tadeusz looked longingly at the fires, then nodded in submission to his brother. He understood.

Upon reaching Borisov, Paweł learned that French troops under General Dąbrowski had been forced to abandon the defense of the bridgehead. This came at the hands of Russian General Cziczaków, a Pole. Napoléon ordered General Oudinot's corps to recapture the bridge, and although they were successful in routing the enemy, the bridges had been put to the torch.

But Lady Fortuna had saved a small smile for the little emperor. It was the revelation in the form of a note that arrived on 23 November. In coming to Napoléon's aid from Wilno, west of the River Beresina, French General Corbineau had bribed a peasant to point out a secret ford in the river near the village of Studienka. The bit of luck revived Napoléon's genius. He ordered General Elbé's four hundred-man engineering team to erect two bridges on the eighty-five-yard-wide site, to be completed on the twenty-sixth. Then he himself knitted the wool that went over the Russians' eyes by ordering a series of feints that misled and confused.

When one bridge was completed on the twenty-sixth, the Eighth Regiment of Polish lancers crossed first, putting to flight Cziczaków's Cossacks. General Oudinot's and General Ney's corps crossed next, forming up as potential protection against the Russian army on the left bank under General Cziczaków. Finished that afternoon, the second bridge was larger and allowed for the transport of the artillery. Crossings continued all day and all night.

In the early afternoon of the twenty-seventh, Paweł crossed with Poniatowski and the Old Guard, and from the heights on the left bank he watched as the Imperial Guard passed with Napoléon's battered carriage, followed by the Young Guard. He let out a little sigh when he caught sight of Jan Michał and Tadeusz, unsteady on their feet as they walked their horses, but a sight for sore eyes just the same.

Discovering what the French were about, Cziczaków initiated the last battle of the campaign on the morning of the twenty-eighth, coming down hard on the left bank, wave after wave, upon the French forces. Fighting raged on the right bank, as well, with General Victor's rear guard repelling the enemy for a second day so that the crossings could continue. The battle drew out—with advantages passing from one side to the other and back again—until dusk, at which time Cziczaków withdrew his forces. Napoléon claimed victory although French losses numbered in the thousands.

Paweł, never one to count his kills as some did, still felt his pulse running fast at the thought of winning. He gave thanks that he had come through it unhurt and wondering at the dark irony that all the surviving Poles coalesced to face an enemy that was led by a Pole. Giving credit where it was due, he would well remember the French—especially the cuirassiers led by General Ney, who were responsible for two thousand casualties—but without the Poles that fought and died that day, the retreat would have ended in defeat. Generals Dąbrowski, Kniaziewicz, and Zajączek all sustained wounds; Zajączek, amputation of a leg. Prince Poniatowski, too, suffered a leg injury and had to relinquish his command to Marshal Ney.

After dark, Paweł searched out the Young Guard. Knowing they had suffered significant losses, he prepared himself for bad news.

At last he found a few faces he remembered from that night in the stable at Orsha. None of them had any post-battle knowledge of the Stelnicki brothers. His ebbing hopes seemed justified.

Paweł went then to the rise above the river where the wounded were laid out on the hill, like a supine audience in an ampitheatre. A handful of surgeons and orderlies worked among a thousand men. He walked the width of the rise, moved down a few rows, then walked back, peering into faces either full of pain or numbed by it.

"Major Potecki!" someone called. Paweł recognized Jan Michał's voice at once. A little thrill ran through him. Michał was alive! Paweł saw the waving figure in the dark now, and moved fifteen parallel paces, then down two rows of men.

"Michał!" Paweł's first impulse was to embrace Jan Michał, and having done so, he immediately held the young man at arm's length, fearing he had done further injury.

"I'm fine," Jan Michał said, reading Paweł's expression. "A bit bruised from a fall off my horse."

"Thank God!" Paweł cried. "And Tadek?"

"Right here," Jan Michał said, his eyes directing Paweł's down.

Tadeusz stared up from his position on the ground. In the dark, his face seemed as white as the snow. "I was hoping you'd say hello to me, too, Major." He attempted a laugh.

"Tadek!" Paweł dropped to his knees. "What is it?"

"My leg," Tadeusz said. "It's nothing."

"Nothing?" Jan Michał said. "Nothing is relative. He took a ball in the lower calf."

"I tell you it's nothing."

"Has the surgeon seen it?"

"An orderly has," said Jan Michał. "He's fourth or fifth in line for the surgeon to come by."

"And when the ball's gone, I'll be as good as new." The pain went out of his eyes for a moment. "We beat him back–Cziczaków, yes?

"That we did!"

"I was this close to him," Tadeusz said, stretching out his arms. "This close–and then I took the ball in my leg. I could have killed the turncoat!"

Paweł chuckled. "Damned inconvenient, Tadek. Forget about him."

"He's a traitor to his country. He's–he's immoral."

"There is *no* morality in war, Tadek. There is only kill or be killed."

"And I should have liked to have killed him!"

"In any case, we'll be away tomorrow. Even now the rear guard is crossing the bridges. Enough talk for now." Paweł stood. "Michał, don't let the surgeon start until I get back."

"Yes, sir." Jan Michał's quizzical expression spoke his question for him.

"I'm going for a bottle of brandy I have squirreled away. Good stuff!"

"Major?" Tadeusz asked, pain in his voice. "I'll ride tomorrow. I'll be fine. I won't go in the wounded wagons."

Paweł smiled. "We'll see how you do, my friend."

Walking away, Paweł prayed that Tadek would be up to riding in the morning. He knew that there were no wounded wagons, that only caissons and Napoléon's carriage had been allowed to cross the rickety bridges. All other vehicles were being abandoned and burned. He cringed to think what would happen to the thousands of stragglers and wounded left behind. No plans had been made for them. They would be left to the Cossacks. It was as he had told Tadek: there was no morality in war.

The next morning Jan Michał pushed Tadeusz up onto his horse. "All right, Tadek?"

"Yes, I can do it—how far to Wilno?"

"About a hundred sixty miles." Jan Michał saw Tadek wince but say nothing. "The major came by while you were sleeping. I told him we'd be fine."

"He's left already? When did the order come?"

"Last night. There's been a steady stream ever since."

"And the Young Guard?"

"Gone. That is, those that survived the battle."

"And you just let me sleep?"

"You needed it, Tadek."

"Dog's blood! So we'll be *last* now?"

"Not if we get a move on." Jan Michał and Tadeusz entered into the battered remnants of the Grande Armée now as it proceeded away from the Beresina, utilizing a wooden causeway raised above a extensive area of marshland. Here and there a temporary bridge had to be thrown down, but everyone counted it a small miracle that the Russians had not destroyed the causeway. Had they done so, Jan Michał mused, their escape might never have been possible.

Tadeusz remained quiet for a long time. Jan Michał knew he felt the effects of the surgery and the brandy. After the operation, the doctor had taken Jan Michał aside, telling him that he had not gotten all the shrapnel and cautioned them to get to a good surgeon soon. In time, Jan Michał would have to pass that news on to his brother.

Jan Michał had not slept at all the previous night. There was more cause for alarm than his brother's operation. He had sat at his brother's side watching Victor's rear guard cross the bridge in the early morning hours. Napoléon's genius had won the day, but the losses had been staggering.

During the night, the wind was such that he could hear General Elbe on the far side of the river urging the stragglers and wounded who could walk to cross the bridges immediately because they were going to be blown to bits. The Grand Armée wasn't about to allow the Russians access for pursuit.

By morning, however, most of the stragglers, apathetic or dazed, had kept to their campfires, ignoring Elbe's advice. It was only at 9 a.m., when the explosions began, that they came to their senses and a crush of ten thousand rushed the bridges. Many were burned to death, and many more drowned as the bridges collapsed into the water with a great hissing sound, like blazing blacksmith tools being immersed in water—one, then the other.

The thirty thousand remaining stragglers awaited their fate at the hands—and lances—of the Cossacks. There was nothing to be done for them. Pushing down an impulse of nausea that licked at the back of his throat, Jan Michał turned away from the sight.

Travel through the heavy snow became tediously slow, more so now because of a few empty amunitions wagons that were carrying the seriously wounded. Jan Michał heard some of them begging to be finished off, so great was their pain, so dark their prospects. The thaw had retreated, and General Winter returned victorious. Temperatures, night or day, did not rise above zero. The crimson sun offered no heat. The sides of the road were strewn with frozen corpses, and near Zembin, Jan Michał and Tadeusz stopped to stoke the dying embers of a fire that had been built by eight soldiers who had since fallen asleep—and frozen to death. Already some of them had had their boots and coats stolen. Jan Michał had to push several bodies aside to gain access to the fire for himself, his brother, and the horses.

Getting Tadeusz off the horse and on again with a minimum of pain proved such an ordeal that Jan Michał mentally noted he would not attempt it unnecessarily. The horses were weak with cold and hunger, too, so they stayed only long enough for Jan Michał to melt some snow in a stew pot he found, adding to it a crumbled biscuit and a sliver of dried horsemeat. Nothing was to be found at the site for the horses.

Setting off now, the brothers were a pair among small bands of soldiers and a few camp followers who had not lost their nerve at the Beresina crossing.

Some thirty hours after leaving the Beresina, they came to Pleszenice—a distance of a mere twenty-five miles. Neither brother spoke of the pace they had been reduced to. Here, at least, at a peasant's hut they found—for a price—shelter and food for themselves and their horses.

Jan Michał went out after the meal and returned an hour later with a pair of crutches.

"Who the hell are *those* for?" Tadeusz asked, indignant.

"Well, they're not for me."

"I don't need them. Carrying crutches will set me apart as a straggler!"

"We aren't far off from that."

"Oh? And you blame me? Why don't you just go on, then?"

"Listen, Tadek. With my help, you can hop fairly well, but you're still in pain. You may need these."

"The pain will go away."

"The surgeon said he didn't think he got it all. You may as well know, Tadek, that you're going to need another operation."

The color drained out of Tadeusz's face. "You took good time to tell me."

Jan Michał shrugged. "If you weren't so stubborn, I wouldn't have told you until we got to Wilno. Now, you're going to practice on these before we leave."

"Damn!" Tadeusz said through clenched teeth. He pushed himself up from his chair and took the crutches. Jan Michał pulled the chair to the corner of the room, making room for his brother's first clumsy attempts with the crutches. He found himself absently feeling for the gold ring his mother had given him for his first Holy Communion, the ring he had used to buy them.

During the night, Jan Michał kept jerking awake from the recurring dream in which he and Tadek were sleeping in the snow—and would go on sleeping forever.

Their journey continued in the morning as they joined the ranks of others that had stayed the night in the village. Once on the road, however, the numbers of those who had fallen to the wayside seemed to have increased. General Winter had conquered most of those they passed, but some had been slain by marauding Cossacks, too.

The next day at dusk, they were not far from Ilia and had just sighted the steeple of the parish church when Jan Michał's horse gave way beneath him, collapsing and dying on the spot. It came as no real surprise, and Jan Michał did now what he had to do. He worked mechanically, hacking away at the poor animal's emaciated haunches, carving steaks that could feed him and Tadeusz, as well as be used as barter in the village ahead. He caught what blood he could in his regulation saucepan and once the cutting was done, helped Tadeusz down into a ravine, where a fire others had left behind would warm their blood-and-horseflesh soup.

By the time they climbed back onto the road, much of the dead horse's remaining blood had seeped into the snow, freezing immediately. From the crimson-colored ice Jan Michał and Tadeusz chiseled out neat little cakes that they placed in their saddlebags. Later they would suck on them for sustenance.

Jan Michał could not think about the horse he had come to love and protect, just as he could not think about those stragglers who called weakly now from the side of the road, begging for assistance. He walked, leading Tadeusz's horse, both brothers keeping their eyes trained forward as they went, as if they could not see those calling out, as if the cries of the dying could not pierce fur-covered ears.

At Ilia, Jan Michał insisted Tadeusz practice more with his crutches. He reluctantly obeyed. In the morning, Tadeusz suggested that they both ride his horse. Jan Michał demurred. He would walk. How long the surviving horse could hold out was already in question.

Two days later, with only brief stops to relieve themselves, they came to Molodeczno. Tadeusz was so stiff with cold and pain that when Jan Michał helped him down from the horse, he could scarcely stand. Jan Michał's feet were numb, and he worried about frostbite. "Halfway to Wilno?" Tadeusz asked.

Jan Michał shrugged. "Give or take," he said, immediately depressed by the thought. *Only halfway!*

They were given a room in the cottage of an old couple on the outskirts of the town. A wounded French soldier being housed there overnight told how the Cossacks had staged a heavy attack on the rear guard as the Grande Armée remnants trudged through.

"What day was this?" Jan Michał asked.

"Two days ago," the soldier replied in French.

Jan Michał and Tadeusz looked at one another. There was no need for words. Each was thinking how far they had fallen behind the main force. They knew that the danger of Cossacks only increased for stragglers. Just the same, they had bargained to stay the night, and they would do so. They needed the rest.

In the morning, they came to regret their decision. Jan Michał and Tadeusz sat at the tiny table waiting while the old woman stood at the stove stirring gruel and grilling some corn. Suddenly, her husband burst into the cottage, the cold wind rushing in behind. He could hardly speak. "A thousand pardons!" he cried. "Dear God in Heaven, a thousand pardons!"

"What is it?" Jan Michał asked—even though he thought he knew what had happened.

"Your horse, milords! Your horse!"

"It's dead?" Tadeusz asked.

"No," the old man said, his eyes round as coins. "The horse is gone. Vanished!"

"Stolen?" Tadeusz asked, his face paling.

Jan Michał grew dizzy. His appetite went the way of the horse. He blamed himself. He had been weak in will—he should have stayed in the pathetic little barn with the horse. It had been a foolish gamble. But the old man had locked the barn, assuring him the horse was safe, that the penalty for horse theft was death. There was no law in war, he thought now. It was a hard lesson. What was the penalty of death these days to anyone? Nothing. For many, death was merely a quicker way out of misery.

Tadeusz attempted to stand. "We should find the horse thief out, Michał. Shoot him!"

Jan Michał pulled his brother back into his chair. "We don't have the energy to spare, Tadek. What use would it be? The horse is long gone and if not on the road, its haunches are probably in someone's fry pan at this very moment."

Tadek's shoulders slumped forward. "May the bastard die."

"Very likely. But we won't, Tadek. We won't!"

Tadek nodded. Jan Michał turned to the old man. "Are there any horses for sale here in Molodeczna?"

The man shook his head. "Not one." A grim expression on her lined face, his wife came up to the table and slopped the gruel into the brothers' bowls. She returned to the stove then for the corn. Jan Michał forced himself to eat.

"It's a good thing you robbed some poor cripple of his damn crutches," Tadeusz said, picking up his spoon. "I'll give you that."

After their meal, they readied their things. The old man provided Jan Michał with a sturdy piece of leather with which to bind Tadeusz's bad leg. They set off at midmorning with a band of seven other stragglers, mostly camp followers of one occupation or another. They passed a tiny element of the rear guard that had stayed behind for some reason. As they were mounting up, one of them was heard to say, "Look at them, will you! Stragglers! Let's get the devil out of here before we join them!"

So now we *are the stragglers,* Jan Michał thought. We *are the pitiful ones not to be looked at, not to be heard, as the army moves forward!*

Once they were out on the road, Tadeusz turned to Jan Michał as he maneuvered his crutches in the snow. "Do you think the old man was lying, Michał?"

Of course, he had considered it, too. The peasant could have sold the horse. God knows what the market price might be—despite its condition. Or he might have hidden it in the forest. "I don't think so, Tadek. His humiliation seemed quite real."

Tadeusz gave out with a little harumph. "I thought so, too."

Jan Michał's thoughts were on the road now. If they were about halfway to Wilno, that meant they had eighty miles to go. On foot.

He would not think about Wilno . . . Smorgoni would come first. . . .

Neither brother spoke for hours on end. By nightfall, they realized that two of the group had slipped behind. Everyone paused in their tracks for a minute, looking back. The two were but dark dots in the snow a mile distant. The remaining seven looked, said nothing, turned again to the northeast, and moved on. Stragglers could not wait for other stragglers. Doing so would mean their lives, too. By morning—against a crimson sky—they realized another two had fallen off from the band.

At noon the remaining members stopped to relieve themselves. Tadeusz was sitting on a stump when Jan Michał emerged from the trees at the side of the road. "I don't think I can go on," he said.

"What do you mean, Tadek? You're doing fine."

"My leg—the pain's too great."

"It's a lucky thing you can feel it and that it hasn't gone numb! Let me take a look." Jan Michał unwound the leather covering, then the dressings that had not been changed for two days. It was an ugly sight. The open wound was obviously infected, the flesh around it darkening.

"You see?" Tadeusz said, pulling back the woolen material protecting his face and ears. Jan Michał took note that he was flushed and feverish. "They're moving on, Michał," Tadeusz said, nodding toward the other three farther up the road.

"So?" Jan Michał said, all the while trying to think, trying not to let his mind go as blank as the snow stretching out in every direction. Here and there he could see mounds that he was sure were bodies, men who had sat down without the ability or will to go on.

"You need to push on, Michał. I won't have you stay for me."

"Push on for what? To tell Mama that I left you on the road to Wilno. Left you to freeze to death?"

Tadeusz went into one of his old rages even as tears formed in his eyes. "Don't play some goddamn hero. There's nothing here for you, Michał. You still have a chance! Take it, goddamn you!"

"I won't leave you here!" Jan Michał screamed.

"I've got plenty of company," Tadeusz said, nodding at a mound in the gully at the side of the road. "You must save yourself!"

Jan Michał jerked Tadeusz to his feet and held him there while he reached for the crutches and roughly set them under his brother's arms. Now he tied

the wool about Tadeusz's face, leaving room for him to see, and securely replaced the fur hat.

Tadeusz relented, pushing forward. They got no more than fifty paces before Tadeusz fell over, too faint to go on. "I'll carry you, damn it," Jan Michał
said, lightly slapping his brother's covered face. "Do you hear me, Tadek?
Stay awake!"

Jan Michał used his belt to fasten the crutches to himself, then pulling
Tadeusz to his feet, he pulled him onto his own back. Tadeusz was too weak
to hold on, so Jan Michał grasped his arms, one on each shoulder. And he began to move forward, one step at a time. Unsteady at first, he moved patheti-
cally slowly, but as he got the weight on his back positioned just right, he
advanced a little faster and with more assurance. "Stay awake, Tadek. Don't
go to sleep, hear? We'll sing, all right? All right?"

Tadeusz mumbled.

Jan Michał started in on the only song he could think of at the time:

> Darling war, darling war,
> What a lady you must be
> For all the most handsome boys
> To follow you like this.

Every so often, Jan Michał had to shake his brother to coax a semblance of
the lyrics out of him. Several hours passed in this way. Of course, the other
three stragglers were long out of sight.

A rise came in the road ahead, and when Jan Michał saw it, both his body
and spirit faltered for a moment. His singing stopped. He didn't know if he
could last . . . if he could make it. *Dear God in heaven,* he cursed, *how far to Smorgoni? How far?* He prayed for it to be just over that hill. That his feet had not
stopped came as a surprise to him. They moved like spokes of a machine.
"Come on, Tadek," he cried. "Sing with me!"

Tadek obeyed, his voice a mere rasp.

> Darling war, darling war,
> What a lady you must be
> For all the most handsome boys
> To follow you like this.

They came at last to the crest. The road stretched ahead, as far as Jan
Michał could see. Reason told him Smorgoni was still miles and miles away.

"We'll rest here, Tadek." Jan Michał gently set his brother down near a fallen tree that jutted out onto the road.

Tadek was nearly delirious. But not quite. Every so often he mumbled, "Go, Michał. Go on."

Jan Michał knew how his brother thought, and so he relieved himself very close by out of fear that Tadek would try to take his own life so as not to be a burden.

He came back and sat on the fallen tree, near Tadek, forcing him to mindlessly sing again. Neither of them had eaten for twelve hours. And yet food did not matter.

What seemed an hour passed. The air grew colder, and the wind picked up.

Jan Michał was losing faith. They were to die as stragglers—it was their fate. His mind had gone blank when his brother touched his arm. He looked up to see fear bring alive Tadek's blue eyes. Then he turned to see what had caught his attention.

In the far distance—ahead—he could see two or three dark spots on the snow-bleached road. Three moving figures. Moving toward them.

"Cossacks!" Tadeusz hissed without moving his jaw. "Cossacks!"

Fear ran through Jan Michał, too. He stood. "Let's get you into the gulley—now!"

"They'll see us moving, Michał."

"And they won't see us sitting in the road? Get up, damn it!"

Jan Michał pulled his brother down into the ravine, positioning him behind the mound where snow covered a corpse. He pushed snow atop him. "Don't move, hear?"

Suddenly, Jan Michał remembered the crutches. They lay where he had cast them in his panic—in the middle of the road. There was no time now to retrieve them. From his crouched position in the gully, he could not see the riders, but he could hear the hooves against the hard winter earth. He folded himself into a fetal position, hoping that he, too, would be taken for dead.

Time stretched out in the most surreal way as the horses came closer. He kept his hand on his saber. He would manage a fight. If death had come for him and his brother this day, it would be an honorable death. A soldier's death. Preferable to dying from the cold.

The thud of the horses' hooves slowed. The Cossacks had seen the crutches and been put on guard. And yet he heard no voices.

The horses had stopped—just above him now. There was no escaping. He heard the crunch of boots in the snow coming nearer, nearer. His grip on his saber so tight it hurt, he held his breath, waiting for the Cossack cry, waiting for them to leap into the gulley, lances in hand. Well, he would take at least one with him into the next world.

A long, long minute passed. He could hear the hard breathing and occasional snort of two horses.

Slowly he turned his head and looked up at the road. The sight formed a kind of queer human *wycinanka,* a papercutting formed by the silhouette of a tall, dark figure against the failing daylight. Behind him was what seemed the side planking of a sledge.

The man's head was tilted down, his vision directed to the gulley, to him.

Jan Michał stood up, fully prepared to die.

Now came the man's deep, sonorous voice, wonderful and miraculous. "Jan Michał?"

Jan Michał stared up, a shiver running through him. "Major Paweł?"

The sledge sailed slowly northwest through the pitch of night. Tadeusz lay nestled in furs in the coffinlike bed of the vehicle. For the first few miles, Jan Michał rode up front, next to Paweł who still marveled that he had come upon Michał and Tadek when he did. Were it not for crutches left in the road, the boys would not have survived. Was it mere happenstance? He had always thought that there was some scheme of things in the universe—and this seemed to bear that out. Was it God? Fate? The powerful prayers of their parents?

"How is it," Jan Michał asked, "you were able to leave your duty and come back for us?"

"While the Cossacks are still biting at us like flies, the campaign has been suspended."

"For the winter? Or for good?"

"That depends on Napoléon's luck in Paris. He left Smorgoni yesterday in a closed sleigh."

Jan Michał's well-covered head tilted up at Paweł. "Left? He just left his Grande Armée? Hightailing it back to Paris?"

Paweł pointed to a clearing to what had been a little campsite. Whereas most of the fallen up to this point had been the wounded and camp followers, the men here—frozen like ice sculptures—were ordinary soldiers of the French infantry. "Not so grand anymore," he said.

"Will he come back?"

"There was a little matter of an attempted coup at home, but I have no doubt he'll put it down and come back with a new army."

"You have faith in him."

"I do. What choice is there? You know, your brother needs medical help as soon as possible."

"Wilno?"

"Too far. Too many days."

"Smorgoni? Is there a surgeon there?"

"Its little hospital is jammed. Filthy, too, and full of typhus. I wouldn't take him there. I do know of someone, though."

"Who, Major?"

"A man that put a few of us up the last two nights."

"A doctor?"

"A bear tamer."

Jan Michał gasped and laughed simultaneously. "A bear tamer!"

"There are many of them in these parts."

"Bears or bear tamers?"

"Both. The man's good with wounds. Believe it or not, he uses bear fat to draw out shrapnel. I assisted him in an operation. I nearly fainted dead away, but he was good at it, Michał. I have faith in him."

"Like you do in Napoléon?"

"*Touché!* But, yes, I guess faith is faith. Still, the decision is for you and Tadeusz to make. You're men now."

"My brother's in no condition to make a decision. And I don't see there's much choice. The bear tamer, it is."

"It'll at least make a good story one day," Paweł said.

Jan Michał laughed. "You should introduce your bear tamer to Napoléon before he goes after the Russian bear a third time."

Paweł laughed, too.

A small movement on Jan Michał's right caught his eye. They were passing the three fellow stragglers who had gone on ahead. In a snowy clearing they sat in a cluster around a pitifully tiny fire.

One of them looked up to the road as the sledge passed, watching it passively, too weak or too hopeless to call out.

36

"You're awake awfully late, Marek," Anna whispered. "It's midnight. Are you a little better today?"

"A bit, milady." Even in the dimness of the ward, it was evident his cheeks were reddening.

Anna smiled. The twenty-four-year-old infantryman stared up at Anna as if she were the madonna. She suspected that no titled woman had ever even spoken to him before. "You should be going home soon."

He nodded and his eyes became distant. It was as if Anna could read his mind. She was certain he was wondering what his homecoming would be like when he returned to his little village near Poznań. He was anticipating–fearing–how his wife and two boys would react to the loss of his arm. She touched him lightly on the forehead before moving on.

Marek had come to the hospital in a convoy, one of many that had brought countless wounded from the early battles at Wilno and Smolensk. As the patients arrived, the veracity of Napoléon's early optimistic *Bulletins de la Grande Armée* was put in serious question–by the sheer numbers of wounded and by the sobering accounts the soldiers themselves provided.

Anna went back to the little wooden table that served as her desk in the fifty-bed ward. The truth was that she had volunteered for the nighttime shift because of her insomnia. If she were at Zofia's, she knew sleep would not come. She worried constantly about Jan Michał and Tadeusz. No letter had arrived in months. And with the interruption of bulletins from the east, no word had come from Paweł, either. Were they even alive?

Anna had not been home to Sochaczew in months, had not seen Jan in that space of time and missed him terribly. She knew instinctively that he was going through his own hellish nightmare. As a soldier for so many years, it had been difficult for him to send his sons off to war, a war he questioned. That his best friend Paweł was trying to watch out for them no doubt complicated his feelings. Jan would be doing that for himself–had not his faith in Napoléon been tapped dry.

Restless, Anna stood and walked the length of the ward, coming across now a bed that death had made vacant the night before. A new face lay upon the pillow, eyes open. He was staring at her. Anna drew near. "Do you need something, soldier?" He shook his head. Anna studied the young man with blond hair. He seemed to be regarding her strangely. "What is your wound?" she asked.

"A lance wound in my backside," he said ironically.

"I won't insist on looking, then," she said, her tone light.

Anna's comment provoked a smile. Oddly, it was a smile of familiarity that made her think he knew her. She set her taper on the little bedside table, watching him closely all the while in the better light. His eyes were very blue. Did she know *him?* "Are you unable to sleep?" She looked up at the paper pasted on the wall. "Jerzy?"

He paused, then shook his head.

"Tell me, Jerzy, do you know who I am?"

He stared at her, his eyes narrowing and his handsome face serious, and for the moment she thought he did indeed recognize her and that he would clear up the matter in short order. The smile came back then, wider and capricious. "Queen Maria-Louise, the emperor's latest flame?"

"Very funny!" Anna went back to her little station and sat, searching her brain. She sensed that she knew this man and was quite certain he had recognized her, too. Half an hour passed and she put the matter to rest.

At one in the morning she heard voices at the far end of the ward. Four men had entered and were looking about. When they saw her at the table, its single taper a tiny beacon in the darkened room, they started to move toward her, their heavy boots reverberating throughout the ward. Anna could tell by their bearing that three of them—dressed in dirtied white caped greatcoats—were French military officers. The fourth was dressed in a fur-lined green velvet coat with fancy gold fasteners. Atop his head was a sable cap that shaded his face.

One of the officers quickly introduced the others, all French names. The foppish fellow, she was told, was the speaker's secretary. Formalities done with, the speaker said, "Lady Stelnicka, we were informed by a servant at the Walewska town house that Lady Maria Walewska could be found here."

Anna tried not to show her surprise. "She was here earlier tonight," Anna said, "but you missed her by two hours."

"Then where is she?" The snappish question came from the one in velvet.

Suddenly it dawned on Anna that this man was no secretary and that the other three deferred to him. Anna's pulse quickened. Her eyes went immediately to the shaded gray eyes under the hat. And she knew his identity at once.

Anna curtsied.

"Well? Now you know!" Napoléon Bonaparte said, realizing he had been unmasked. He removed his cap and gave a little bow. "We played at whist once upon a time, Lady Stelnicka, did we not?"

"We did, Your Highness. And we danced once, too."

"I was no doubt as bad a dancer as I was a loser at cards. I trust you don't hold it against me. Now, my dear—where might I find Maria?"

"I'm afraid she's gone back to her country house."

"Damn!" Napoléon's anger flared like a new torch. "At Bronie? Not to her town house? Perhaps we just missed her."

"No—she received word earlier this evening from Bronie that her son had become ill."

"Aleksandr?" The emperor's anger was transformed into genuine concern. "Is it serious?"

"No, Your Highness, just a cold. Nothing more."

Her assurance seemed to satisfy. He *should* be concerned, Anna thought. Aleksandr was his firstborn son.

The four spoke among themselves then in rapid French as if she were not present. Anna managed to glean that they were headed to Paris via Dresden, and Napoléon now wanted to take a side trip to Maria's manor house. The other three argued vigorously against such a venture. Anna recognized one of them now as General Caulaincourt, one of the emperor's inner circle. It was he who stressed bluntly that they didn't want to lose the time and that the appearance of calling on Maria at such a serious time for Poland would make no friends.

"I have friends enough," Napoléon thundered. "It's an army that I lack!" But a sour wince on the emperor's face made it clear that the majority had won out.

Napoléon turned and kissed Anna's hand. "Lady Stelnicka, please do give the Lady Walewska my best. Tell her I will write—soon!"

Anna curtsied. "Yes, Your Highness." The words came with little feeling.

He gave a thin little smile. "Except for Maria, you will keep my appearance here in confidence?"

Anna nodded. Good-byes were abbreviated, and the four moved noisily to the far entrance. Anna stood there a long time, the emperor's words ringing in her ears: "It's an army that I lack!"

Only now did she allow her anger to stream up from her center, sending a high heat into her face. He had shown real emotion for his son. She wanted to scream after him now: *Where are my sons—my sons that you have taken to war, my sons that you have now abandoned—where? Trudging the frigid Eastern steppes? Or worse?*

She stood, stunned for some moments, until she heard two words being rhythmically recited by someone in the ward. "Jesus Christ!" one man was saying, over and over.

Anna stirred herself, picked up her taper, and moved toward the voice. She was glad for the diversion. "That was Napoléon," came the stunned voice.

"Yes, Jerzy, it was."

"Jesus Christ!"

Anna moved closer. Suddenly she remembered—a day long past came back to her, a serious face at the front door of Paweł's town house. "Jerzy, you know Lady Zofia, do you not?"

"Who? No, I don't," he said, a bit too quickly. He seemed to forget Napoléon.

"Lady Zofia Grońska, my cousin. You came to her house on Piwna Street a long time ago—asking for her."

"No, milady. You're mistaken."

"It was *years* ago, of course." He shook his head. "You don't recall?"

"It must have been someone else."

"You're certain?"

"Yes, milady."

"I see." Anna turned and walked back to her table, convinced he was lying.

The early morning Mass-goers were spilling out of Saint Martin's into Piwna Street when Anna arrived back at the town house. After a little breakfast, she dashed off a note to Anusia Potocka, inviting herself to the Potocki home in Wilanów that evening. Anna knew she was always welcome there. If there was significant news in Warsaw, it was often spoken there first, often by the makers of the news. And with Napoléon's appearance—incognito—in Warsaw, there *had* to be news.

"I was delighted to get your note, Anna," Anusia said, ushering her into the house. "You should come by more often. Never wait for an invitation."

Anna smiled. "Thank you. That's very kind." She walked in, expecting groups of people, chatter, uplifted brows.

Nothing. The house was quiet as a convent. No one stirred. "Any word from your husband in Wilno?" Anna asked.

"Nothing recent," Anusia replied. "Supper won't be much—it's only us. My mother-in-law is in bed with a cold, and my father-in-law has gone out. What with so little news about the war effort—and none of it good—he's been very depressed of late. He was called to the ambassador's palace."

"So Pradt is still here in Warsaw? I've heard he's had his bags packed for months, just waiting for the bad news."

"Oh, he's ready to hightail it to France, but he'd never do anything without hearing from Napoléon. And you know as well as I there hasn't been a bulletin coming through Warsaw in weeks."

Anna took in a gulp of air. How could she not tell her good friend what she knew? That the man himself was in town running about in a green velvet coat and fur hat like the ostentatious Osric in *Hamlet*.

"How did the night go at the hospital?" Anusia asked. "You do look tired, Anna."

"I suppose that I do. I tried to sleep this morning but couldn't."

"Well, I'll send you home early."

Anusia did try to send her home, two hours after supper, but Anna held out, certain that her friend's father-in-law would come back with substantial news.

Count Stanisław Potocki finally arrived at 10 p.m. That he seemed to be in good spirits amazed Anna. "Come sit down, the two of you," Potocki said. "You will not guess in a million years who was at the ambassador's."

"I think I could," Anna said, forgetting herself.

"Oh, you do?" Potocki said, taken aback. "Then tell me, Anna."

"Napoléon Bonaparte, Emperor of France," Anna said, smiling smugly.

The count's mouth fell slack for a moment, but then he laughed. "You little witch! I know you are merely joking, Anna, but your joke couldn't ring with more truth. It was indeed Napoléon."

Anusia gasped. "He's here? The army's come home?"

Anna knew the answer to that, too, but she waited now on the count's answer. What details would he provide?

"There is not much of an army left." Lord Potocki's eyes lost their sparkle. "The emperor was very blunt about that. He claims a hundred twenty thousand, but we have other sources that put the figure lower. Much lower."

Anusia's eyes widened in horror. "But he took *half a million* men into Russia!"

"Indeed," Potocki said. "And he's returned to Warsaw with three officers. Those who have survived the trek from Moscow are straggling back to Wilno."

This news also alarmed Anusia, whose husband Aleksandr held a post in that city. "But the last Aleks wrote," she said, "the city was already in turmoil, dealing with those wounded on the way to Moscow. Not to mention the countless French deserters."

Potocki offered up an unconvincing smile. "I pray things have improved." He turned to Anna. "I also pray for your sons, Anna. How it must worry you. May they both be safe in Wilno."

"Thank you, Lord Potocki."

The count went on to detail Napoléon's report to the Duchy Council. The report seemed unbiased. The emperor, he said, had detailed the setbacks, the losses, the deaths of hundreds of thousands and he had done so without romanticism, without masking the scope of the disaster. And the Russian campaign had been just that—a disaster. " 'From the sublime to the ridiculous there is but one step' were his words. His exact words."

Anna held Lord Potocki's eyes when he had finished. "He takes responsibility?"

He shrugged. "He does own up to mistakes. He says his famous star deserted him, and in its absence the winter—General Winter, he calls it—brought him low."

"His *star?*" Anna gasped. "*General Winter!* You call that owning up?"

Lord Potocki's eyes widened.

"And *now?*" Anna pressed.

"Well, that's the amazing thing, Anna. The man is not broken! Not the least, so it seems. He presented to the Council a very accurate contemporary picture of European politics and demonstrated clear vision of a plan. And in that plan there is to be an independent Poland. He went so far as to say he should have seen to it before now, and that that might have helped the cause. He's off to Paris now to raise a new army."

"A new army," Anna echoed dumbly.

"Just how did the Council receive this?" Anusia asked.

"Most of the members fell under his spell, I must say. He kept saying that he who hazards nothing gains nothing."

Anna inwardly seethed, thinking that the count himself was included among those whom the emperor had transfixed. She could only think now that Poles were either the most hopeful of all nations—or the most gullible.

Later, after the count had retired, she voiced this last thought to Anusia. "Aha! The emperor is as clever as a cat. Dangle independence in front of a Pole, and see what happens—he'll follow you over a cliff! Like geese in a row, one after the other."

"Were you and I there in the wizard's presence, Anna," Anusia said, "we would likely have been won over ourselves."

"Ah, there's the difference, Anusia. We weren't there," Anna said. "Nor was any woman, you can be sure."

37

Jan stood shaking the snow from himself in the front hall of Paweł's town house on Piwna Street, watching his daughter descend the stairs, taller and more beautiful than he remembered. It was early evening, and outside the winter darkness had fallen like a curtain.

"Father! You've come!" Any ladylike graces instilled by the nuns at convent school went the way of the wind as she rushed into his arms. "I'm so glad," she confided in his ear. "Mother's been distraught. She puts on a good face, but I can tell. You should take her back to Sochaczew for a while."

Jan held his daughter at arm's length, his face registering his question.

"News hasn't been good," Barbara offered.

Jan's grip instinctively tightened. "What do you mean, Basia? Has your mother heard something—about the boys?" The moment seemed to hang fire for the longest time as he waited for his daughter to speak.

"No, no, I didn't mean that!" Barbara cried. "I just meant news in general—from the front, you know."

"Oh," Jan said. For the moment, he had thought the worst. His equilibrium returned and he released Barbara. "I do know. News comes to Sochaczew, too."

"I know, but her hospital work—it gets to be too much for her, I think. And they say four of every five Polish soldiers perished, Father." Tears glistened in her eyes. "Some eighty thousand young men."

It was a bitter thing to hear from one's daughter. "Our boys will come home. We will not think otherwise, Basia. Do you hear?"

"Yes," she said, sniffling a little.

"Where is your mother?"

"Lying down. She goes to the hospital at midnight."

"Oh. And you? Is this a holiday from school?"

"No, I asked to come home for a day—but it won't be long till *wigilia* and Sylwester celebrations. Not that anyone seems to care about such things these days."

"We'll celebrate Christmas and New Year's as always," Jan said. "Come what may, you may be sure of that." He kissed his daughter on the forehead. "Now, I'm going upstairs."

"Yes, Papa," she said, seeming to understand that he meant to go alone.

* * *

Having taken off his boots in the antechamber, Jan entered the bedchamber, carrying a taper that threw a halo of light in the darkened and silent room. Closing the door behind him, he paused, listening. Only a few embers glowed in the grate, occasionally spitting, but the chamber retained its warmth. A long minute passed before he could distinguish the soft and regular breaths of his wife. Like a high wave rushing at him, it suddenly came to him how he had missed her, how he loved her.

He longed to wake her. And yet he knew that he shouldn't, that she needed her sleep. She had taken too much upon herself, pushed herself too far. Only God knew what horrors she witnessed daily at the hospital. She should sleep.

Still, he could not bring himself to leave the room. He moved noiselessly to the bed. He realized that she lay on the left side of the bed, her usual side, as if she expected her husband at any time. Did she leave his usual place in bed undisturbed as a way of having him there in spirit? At home in Sochaczew, he had done exactly the same thing, but it was only now that he realized he had done so.

He drew down the covers. He stripped himself of his shirt and breeches and carefully slipped into the bed. The feathered mattress beneath was softer than the one at home, the enveloping quilt somehow more welcoming. He lay on his side, facing Anna, whose back was to him.

She stirred only slightly, but in such a way that brought her backside closer to him. He felt the warmth of her body radiating against his and was immediately aroused.

Half of an hour passed. It was more than his arousal for Anna that kept him awake. It was the whole history of his knowing her. His meeting and secret courting of her. Their marriage, their children, and little pieces of happiness stolen from a tapestry of turmoil, war, and separation. Too much separation. Life had dealt her such terrible blows—the premature deaths of her parents; the rape and subsequent pregnancy; the arranged marriage to a man who sought only her money, her land, and her death. And yet she had always gone forward somehow. How had she managed? Any man would be thankful to have her strength.

Jan silently cursed himself. When they had married, he hoped to protect her, to be always at her side. And yet he had left her—time and again—for the life of a soldier. For years at a time. Those years of waiting, the wondering whether he would ever return—this must have been harder than any march he had ever endured, any battle he had ever braved.

Anna turned in bed now, rolling onto her back, her side flush against Jan. Her eyes opened at the sensation, stared at the ceiling for a moment as if distrusting, then turned to him full of fear. He imagined he could make out the green of her eyes as she pulled back and turned onto her side, propping her head up with one arm. "Jan!" she rasped, fear replaced by wonder.

"I'm sorry, Anna," he said. "I didn't intend to startle you."

"How—how long have you been here?"

"Half an hour or so." He gave out with a little laugh. "I gave you a fright—I'm sorry."

She smiled. "I—I haven't been so happily startled—ever!"

"Indeed," he said, pushing his arm under her and pulling her to him.

Anna's head came down on his chest. "Oh, Jan, I'm so glad you've come."

He caressed her hair, then leaned forward to kiss the top of her head.

"I should have come home, Jan. I'm sorry."

"No, Anna, I should have come here before this. Your work here is more important than anything I was doing."

Anna picked her head up and stared at Jan. "But, Jan, I could—"

Jan put his finger on her lips, silencing her. "In an arguing mood, are you?" He kissed her lightly. "Save it for later."

He kissed her again, a kiss that held—and held.

It was a night of lovemaking he would savor for a very long time.

Several days later, on a Saturday evening, Jan and Anna arrived at the Potocki home in Wilanów for a small supper in honor of Anusia's uncle, Prince Poniatowski, who had returned to Warsaw from the Russian campaign a few days earlier. The general had badly twisted his leg in battle and was still experiencing pain. The Potocki family had welcomed him into their home while he convalesced.

Jan's disillusionment in Napoléon and in his sincerity regarding Poland's possible independence was always close to the surface, and so it was with deeply mixed feelings that he bowed before the reclining Poniatowski, who had taken so many of Poland's youth into Moscow. Jan's own feelings about Napoléon were not likely to change—but nonetheless, in the presence of this Commonwealth patriot, he felt somehow that he himself had failed the Polish cause. That he had failed his own sons, who had heard the call.

The prince was most gracious. "Jan and Anna, it is good to see you both once again, to see that life here somehow continues." Jan saw a pain in the general's eyes that was much more than the physical pain that plagued him. He read in Poniatowski's face the cold harshness of the Russian terrain, the faces of the Fifth Corps he had led taken there, and the battles that had taken such a toll in death.

The general seemed to immediately decipher the concern in Anna's eyes. He wasted no time in addressing himself to the issue. "Ah, my good friends," he said, drawing in a long breath, "I only wish I have brought some news of your sons."

"You're aware of nothing bad—or good?" Anna asked.

"I'm afraid not, Anna. I *can* say that their names were not on any of the lists of the—lost—at the time we left Moscow."

"They left in good health?" Anna asked.

The general squinted and gave a little forward sag of his shoulders.

Jan squeezed Anna's hand, hoping she wouldn't press him for more. "Thank you for that much, General Poniatowski," he said. "It's hope enough for us to have for now."

A little later—but before supper—a few of the other guests managed to get the prince to speak of the ill-fated campaign. He spoke honestly, most likely forgetting that toward the rear of the music room where he held this spontaneous and sober court were Jan and Anna.

"So many died," he said. "So many. French, and Italians, and Saxons, and Poles. The French emperor faltered this time and faltered badly. His gut decisions no longer amazed us. He deliberated, vacillated, and I can tell you he often made the worst possible choices. The army was cut to pieces in battle after battle. And all along the trail, the blood-thirsting Cossacks and outraged peasant partisans snapped and bit at us like unrelenting wolves. Many of the brave men surviving such attacks died of hunger or typhus or cold—brave men! To them, the greatest disappointment was not to die in battle." The prince paused, as if the words tore like a saber through his heart. A moment later, he drew a deep breath. "I am not to stay long in Warsaw. It may seem inconceivable to you—but the Polish army is to be reconstituted, and I will again lead them."

A few gasps in the audience preceded complete silence.

"Do you know," the general resumed, "that even amidst the chaos and lack of discipline in Moscow when whole units fell to searching for loot to take back, not one—not one!—of my men deserted his station?"

As fate would have it, it was at that moment that Lord Potocki stepped forward to announce to the prince that a number of his soldiers had just arrived in Warsaw and were petitioning to see him in the reception room.

Prince Poniatowski stood at once, wincing in pain. With the aid of his crutches, he maneuvered through the double doors into the capacious room adjacent. A single motion from Lord Potocki indicated that the other guests should follow.

Jan and Anna fell into the flow, too. Jan's heart beat fast. Was there a chance—just a chance—that Jan Michał and Tadeusz were among them? Anna's face had a stricken look about it. She, of course, was thinking the same thing. His arm around her waist tightened. He could sense her whole body trembling.

Jan, a seasoned warrior himself, was shocked nonetheless by the sight of these thin, bedraggled soldiers, not more than an hour off the road from Wilno. Few of them had any remnants of the proud, colorful uniforms in which Warsaw had sent them off. They were but skeletal figures in filthy clothes and snatches of furs. Jan looked to Anna, wishing he could shield her from this pathetic scene. But she seemed not shocked at all. And then he realized that for weeks she had been seeing men like this limping or being carried into the hospital. The sight was familiar to her. She had no doubt seen worse. Her eyes, like his, hopefully raked the faces in the room, once, then twice. Their sons were not to be found in this group. Neither dared voice the razoredged disappointment that set in.

Several of the dozen soldiers stepped forward and placed at the general's feet the eagles of their regiments. Although in the worst moments of the retreat, Napoléon had ordered staffs, flags, and eagles destroyed rather than suffer the indignity of losing them to the enemy, these good men had hidden away the eagles. Prince Poniatowski stared down at them, his eyes immediately tearing. "Only one," he said, "only one is missing." And he saluted his men even as tears rolled unabashedly down his cheek.

"No, it's here, General," one soldier said. "Kazimierz has it. He's ashamed because it's no longer intact." A young soldier was pushed forward. The gaunt and frightened youth—no more than a boy—placed the final eagle before his commander.

Jan leaned over the general's shoulder to see that the eagle's head was missing.

The blushing soldier looked up at the general. "A bullet took its head, sir."

General Poniatowski was at first speechless. "God bless you," he said at last. Then, louder, "God bless you all!"

The ragged band of brothers stood at attention, crying out, "Long live Poland! Long live Poland!"

Jan would remember this always—this exchange between a general and his men, one that spoke so well of Poland and its spirit.

"Lord Potocki," the general called out, "can we feed these young patriots?"

"Indeed, General!" Potocki tossed back without a thought. "Indeed!"

After supper, Prince Poniatowski approached Anna and Jan. "My men brought with them a packet of mail—and in it is this letter for you both from your friend Paweł." The prince handed the envelope to Jan and bowed slightly. "I trust it contains good news." He moved away then, allowing Jan and Anna their privacy.

Jan turned the letter over to Anna. Anna's amber-flecked green eyes fixed on Jan's for a long moment. In them was the greatest hope . . . and the greatest fear.

"Open it, Anna," Jan whispered.

Breaking the seal, Anna opened the letter and her eyes quickly scanned the few lines. "Oh, Jan, Tadek was wounded in the leg!" Anna clutched the letter to her heart for a moment.

She read on then, her face darkening.

"Anna?"

"They operated—three times. The third time was in Wilno."

"They're back in the Commonwealth, then!"

Anna came to a sudden stop, and all life left her face.

"And?" Jan pressed.

"Gangrene," Anna said, her face bleeding to white.

Jan could barely make out the word. He saw that the emerald eyes were tilted up at him. He had never seen them so vacant. "Anna?"

"He's gone, Jan." It was scarcely more than a murmur. "He's gone." Anna teetered for a moment, and Jan was certain that he would have to catch her to keep her from falling. But she stood firmly planted and fell silent. She gave in to no tears.

Jan's first thoughts were for his wife—rather than for his dead son. He put his arms around her, almost forcing her to grieve in his arms. They stood for the longest time as the news settled in. Finally, he asked, "And Michał? When is he coming home?" He held Anna at arm's length so that he could see her face.

Anna shook her head. "He's not, Jan. His unit's leaving for Toruń, then Poznań."

Zofia had waited for Anna to leave for the hospital before knocking on the second-floor anteroom.

"Come in," came Jan's voice.

Zofia entered. "I hope I am not disturbing you, Jan." The room was well-lighted with a dozen tapers.

Jan stood. "It is your house, Zofia."

Zofia took a chair across from his. She read into his face and tone that caustically ironic attitude that he had never discarded toward her. He had never forgiven her for her sins against him and Anna all those years before. She could not blame him.

"It's not my house, Jan. It's Paweł's house. And as his good friend, you are always welcome here."

Jan sat down. "And as your cousin's husband?"

"Just as welcome."

Jan nodded in a slightly exaggerated way.

"Will you always hold me in such contempt, Jan?"

He seemed momentarily taken aback. "We're relatives," he said, striving for humor, "we need not be friends."

"I hope one day we might. I sincerely apologize for my past . . . behavior."

"An apology is like a cleaned spot, Zofia—some of it still remains. I have no wish to continue this thread of conversation. Why have you come?"

"Jan, I wanted to tell you how sorry I am about Tadek."

"Thank you."

Zofia cleared her throat. "I've come to speak to you on behalf of Anna."

"What? Why would she—?"

"Oh, she has no knowledge of this, you can be certain."

"Then, what is it?"

"I'm here to ask that you do not go to Kraków with Poniatowski, Jan. Your place is with Anna."

"What? Where do you get your information Zofia?"

"You plan to take up arms for Napoléon again. You plan to join Paweł and Jan Michał."

"I've said nothing of the kind to Anna!"

"And I have not talked to her of it, either. But I know—and if I know, you can be certain your wife knows."

"Have you become a seer now? . . . Or am I so predictable?"

"Only in that you are a good man, Jan Stelnicki, and a good Pole to the marrow of your bones. Be a good husband to Anna. Don't go, Jan."

"You're something for the birds, Zofia. You're still trying to manage people's lives. When will you learn to stop trying to play people like pawns on a chessboard? When?"

"I plead guilty. But my wish in this matter is not one born out of a wish to direct other people. Enough Poles, young and old, have died. And for what— the vanity of a little Frenchman?"

"I wouldn't be doing it for *him*. There's Jan Michał."

"Ah, Anna's son."

"He is *my* son, too."

"I don't want to see Anna lose you, Jan. The French cause is doomed. I think Poniatowski knows that. I think you know that. Napoléon himself has a sense of doom about him, following him like his shadow."

Jan shrugged. "All warriors face defeat at one time or another."

"I know the proverb: 'Through bravery you may win a war; through bravery you may lose.' You've shown your courage already, Jan. Think about your wife. Would it not be braver for you to stay at home?"

"Thank you for your advice, Zofia." Jan stood, as if to see her out.

Zofia took the hint and rose from her chair. When the door closed behind her, she wondered if perhaps Jan hadn't softened just a bit in his stance toward her. For the moment, at least the irony was absent from his tone.

Zofia walked downstairs and sat in the darkened reception room. He was right, of course, she thought. She *was* trying to manage people's lives. Charlotte had told her as much, too. And Charlotte had worked to ensure Izabel's independence by leaving her such a great inheritance. Zofia laughed to think how angry it had made her. It wasn't because she herself had lost out on the wealth and lands in favor of her daughter—it was because the power of exerting her will on her daughter had been corrupted. In time, however, the anger had passed.

Zofia thought of Izabel's father. It had been so long since she had seen him. She had had little hope that Jerzy survived. The toll on the infantry was staggering. What a waste of life, she thought. He had been so young, so full of promise. Handsome, too. Many times, in thinking of his innocence and his attachment to her, she thought that she could have loved him—were it not for their difference in provenance. She often dreamt of him.

And not many days before, when Anna told her of the young infantryman in her ward that she thought to be the same Jerzy who had once come looking for Zofia—despite his denial—Zofia had rushed to the hospital. But a day had elapsed, and in that time the soldier had been released. *Had* it been Jerzy? That she cared—and cared deeply—surprised her. The thought of him evoked strong emotions and vivid memories of her stay in that simple peasant's hut so many years ago. She could remember momentarily wishing that she were but a peasant girl engaged to the handsome young Jerzy. She realized now that the wish—ridiculous as it was—had not died.

38

Anna entered the second floor bedchamber that had been her own as a child. "I sat in that window seat often," she told Barbara. "With my legs pulled up, just as yours are."

Anna stared out the window, down the long, curving, poplar-lined drive.

When the Russians had occupied Warsaw in February of 1813, establishing the Duchy as a Tsarist protectorate, she had taken her daughter back to their home at Sochaczew. There was nothing in the capital but a quiet, like that preceding an execution. On 13 March, Prussia declared war on France. The omens looked bad for Napoléon, but things could go worse, for the question remained whether Austria—with Napoléon's father-in-law on the throne—would join the allies against the French.

"What are you thinking?" Barbara asked.

"Thinking?"

"Your eyes, Mama, they became so distant for a moment."

"Oh? I was looking down the drive and thinking how I was sitting where you are now when they returned my father's body in the back of a wagon. It was a terrible day. The first of many terrible days."

"You said once you would tell me things when I was old enough. Am I old enough now? Will you tell me, Mama?"

Anna sighed. "Yes, Basia, I will tell you now." Anna sat down opposite her daughter in the window seat and took the better part of an hour telling her about the deaths of her parents, her rape, the arranged marriage to a man who tried to kill her—and through it all, her enduring loved for Jan Stelnicki.

"And so you always loved Papa?"

"Always."

"It's a lovely story, Mama."

"Lovely? Yes, I suppose so. But not always happy. Basia, he's at war—again."

"But he'll come back—you said so! Don't you believe it?"

"Yes, of course, I do, dearest."

"He will—and so will Michał!" Barbara scooted down and pressed up to her mother, her arm moving around her shoulders, her lips brushing her forehead. For the moment, daughter took on the role of mother. Then Barbara's other hand gently caressed Anna's slightly rounded belly. "You're happy about *this,* aren't you?"

Anna stood. "Yes, Basia, I am."

"Do you wish a boy or a girl?"

"A girl," Anna answered, tweaking her daughter's cheek. "One just like you."

They heard a rustling on the roof, and Anna laughed.

"Is that—?" Barbara asked.

"It is!" Anna laughed. "The storks have come home!"

Late that night, a fire in the reception room grate cut the nighttime chill. Anna sat staring at the family weapons placed upon the wall above the hearth. She marveled at the paradox: These instruments of violence and the books making up a little library were symbolic components in homes of the *szlachta* everywhere.

Anna *would* prefer a girl. She had already given one boy over to the ceaseless machine of war. She vowed to go to hell herself before surrendering another.

She thought about her Tadek, the beautiful little baby that so resembled Jan. She thought about the wonder in his blue, blue eyes as he grew. It was still there the day he and Jan Michał marched out of Warsaw, their souls afire for the French emperor and the implied independence of the old Commonwealth.

They were children—what did they know? What did anyone know? And whatever hopes the Brotherhood had had for Tadeusz—that was all gone now, washed away like wishes written in the sand. Somehow she had never thought their schemes of placing Tadek on the throne would amount to much, so it was only her little boy that she mourned. Only Tadek.

As unhappy as Poles had been with the little Duchy of Warsaw, thoughts of it now gave way to melancholy longing. With the advance of the Russians, Prince Poniatowski had taken his men to Kraków. Lord Potocki told how the tsar made an overture to Poniatowski that if he would change sides, he would have the throne in a Russian-ruled Poland. It was more than thirty pieces of silver, but less than what it would take for him to go against his sense of honor and military discipline. Only Napoléon had taken on Poland's longtime enemies, and—win or lose—Poniatowski was part of Napoléon's Grande Armée. He and his unit would remain so. It was the Polish way.

Anna had not discouraged Jan from going. She knew she could not hold him. On the day Jan left, he had showed Anna documents relating to the disposition of her estate. Anna insisted on perusing them at once, and it took lit-tle time for her to discover the huge amount of money Jan had paid the French treasury to hold on to Topolostan.

"Your family money, Jan!" she rasped. "It's all gone?"

"Not all," he said. "And it is *our* family money, Anna."

She nodded. "Just as Topolostan is ours, Jan. You never said a word!"

"I'm sorry, Ania. There shouldn't be secrets between man and wife."

Anna thought her heart would break—for the secret that he had kept—and the one she still held.

"You're crying, Anna," Jan said. "I'm sorry to have kept this from you."

Anna gave a shake of her head. "No, it's not that. Jan, I've been living with a secret, too."

"What—what is it?"

"It was I, Jan—I who killed Doliński. I did it!"

Jan took her face into his hands, and what seemed a smile formed on his lips. "I know," he said.

"You *know?*"

He nodded. "And Jan Michał killed Feliks Paduch, the man responsible for your father's death."

"But—*how* could you know?"

"Jan Michał told me."

"Michał? He confided in you?"

"He did—and why not? I'm his father, yes?"

"Yes," Anna said, dizzy, her heart too full to say more. It was at that mo-ment that her old worry—that Jan had not truly accepted Jan Michał as his own son—vanished.

"Don't worry, Anna," he said, his arm encircling her at her waist and his mouth going to her ear. "I'll bring Michałek back home."

"Bring him back if you can, Jan," Anna said, kissing him. "But come back to me. Come back to me, do you hear?"

She sent him off dry-eyed and with a smile on her face, a real smile.

April 1813

"My God, Jan," Paweł said, "to see you in uniform again—well, I can scarcely believe it!"

Jan laughed. He saw the amazement on Paweł's face, felt it in the powerful bear hug. "Now don't go thinking I've changed my mind about the little Corsican."

"Oh, I don't expect that. I know you're here for Jan Michał."

"Yes. And for Tadek, too, you know. I need to unhorse a few in his memory."

"Still a soldier, you are. Welcome to Nuremberg, my friend."

Jan shrugged. "Once a soldier, always a soldier, isn't that what they say?"

"There's truth in it, too. You came with Poniatowski from Kraków? Any engagements?"

"None. Not a skirmish. Has Napoléon come back from France?"

"He's due any day now."

"How's Michał?"

"Good! He'll be so glad to see you." Paweł's face darkened. "You can't imagine what he and Tadek went through in the retreat to Wilno. He stood by his brother every step of the way in weather that seldom rose above zero. And Tadek almost made it, too, Jan. Near the end, in Wilno when he knew he wasn't going to—my God, how he cursed the fact that he was dying in a hospital and not on the battlefield."

"I imagine it crushed his spirit."

"It did. I had to remind him his wound occurred on the field. Thousands like him died just from the cold or typhus. I made certain he was given the cross of the Legion of Honor for his bravery. He insisted on sitting up in bed for the little ceremony even though the end was just a few hours away. Jan, your boy died peacefully."

"He died a man," Jan said, wiping at his eye.

"He did, indeed."

"Now, where is Jan Michał?"

Minutes later, Jan was walking toward the campsite of the Young Guard. It did feel good to be in uniform again. His blood seemed to travel through his body at an accelerated rate. Poniatowski had welcomed him back into the fold with a genuine warmth and enthusiasm. Jan had brought to the effort 102 horses he had raised at Sochaczew. These Polish-raised animals, smaller than the Grande Armée's horses, were easy to maneuver—and very welcome, for the shortage of horses had been more difficult for Napoléon to remedy than the shortage of men.

Poniatowski was to take the remnants of the Fifth Corps and piece them together with the remainders of several other legions, incorporating them into the Eighth Corps. Here was a man who had served as an Austrian general, received Prussian decorations, and acted as Poland's Minister of War under Russia's overview. If he saw that Poland's future was with France, turning down Aleksandr's bribe of a crown in the process, Jan would do no differently.

Jan sighted Michał standing in a small, lively cluster of the Young Guard. "Michał!" Jan called, waving. Jan Michał, in the midst of some story or joke, looked up with a jerk. His eyes narrowed, and his mouth dropped a little. He abruptly left his friends and ran the thirty paces to his stepfather.

For a long moment they stood *vis à vis*, silent as stones. The look of shock on Jan Michał's face seemed to shift into one of awkwardness. Finally, as if at a loss for what to do, he saluted his father. Jan did not return the salute. He laughed instead, and pulled his son into his arms.

After a while, he could feel Michał trembling against him. "I tried to watch out for Tadek, Papa," Michał said. "I did try."

Jan could feel on his neck the wetness of Michał's tears. He thought his own heart would break. He struggled—unsuccessfully—to hold back his own flood of tears. "I know you did your best, Michał. I know."

On the last day of April, Napoléon rejoined the Grande Armée. His strategy, Paweł learned, was to move on Dresden by way of Leipzig, retake Gdańsk and push the enemy behind the River Vistula. He wasted no time, staging a victory at Weissenfeld on 1 May. There the emperor lost an old comrade, Marshal Bessières, and Napoléon took it badly.

The next day fighting accelerated at Lutzen as the emperor set his green recruits upon the Russian veterans. By midafternoon, the tide had so turned against the French that Napoléon boldly rode to the front, barking out orders, adjusting plans, shoring up spirits. A series of maneuvers then brought a reversal of fortune, and both the Young Guard and Old were moved to the front. The allies' line cracked and broke.

Only the French shortage of horses prevented the fullest victory. Nonetheless, it was a victory, and Napoléon seemed to everyone a prodigy once again.

The French wasted no time in pursuing the retreating enemy cavalry and artillery. During the march to Dresden, Paweł witnessed constant skirmishes between their advance guard and the rear guard of the enemy. They entered Dresden on 8 May and on the eighteenth left for Bautzen, reaching it the same day. It was there that news filtered down through the ranks that the King of Saxony had stopped dithering and joined the French side, providing fresh troops. On the twentieth, Napoléon drew up his forces against the Prussian and Russians at Bautzen, and by nightfall they had control of the town.

The following day, however, the French found that the allies fought with what Napoléon called a fanaticism. The daylong battle was protracted and brutal. It was only by sending in his last-ditch Guard at the end of the day that the allies withdrew. The French lost twenty thousand and estimated the allies' losses as just as many.

The French followed the allies the next day and a confrontation at Reichenbach took another of Napoléon's best loved and trusted men. General Christophe Duroc, Napoléon's greatest friend, was struck in the middle by a ricocheting cannonball. He died with doctors standing helplessly by, the victim himself apologizing to the emperor—who had maintained an all-night vigil—that his service had come to an end. "Napoléon has lost most of his best generals," Paweł told Jan. "And yet three of his worst—Macdonald, Soult, and Ney—go on, often misunderstanding or outright disobeying orders."

Napoléon called off the pursuit and accepted an offer from Austria to negotiate terms with Russia. A truce ensued. Because his Austrian wife, Maria-Louise, was French regent, the emperor trusted in the neutrality of the mediator. Surely her father would not move against his daughter, who ruled France in her husband's stead.

Still, well out of earshot of the emperor, officers argued the subject. Many, like Jan and Paweł, found the current struggle between the French-led forces and the Russian-led allies an even one. Should Austria discard her neutrality and throw her support behind one or the other, however, it would make all the difference.

Just days after the truce was established, Jan learned that an old friend and longtime lancer, Dezydery Chłapowski, had asked to be discharged. Jan found him in his tent making preparations to leave. "What is it? This isn't like you."

The man sat on his cot. He didn't look up from some papers he was organizing and gave no answer. He seemed thoroughly depressed.

"Your family in Poznań?" Jan pressed. "Is that it?"

Dezydery shrugged. "No."

"Then what is it? Why can't you say?"

"Jan, my reason needs to remain confidential."

"Then you may swear me to it. I swear, Chłapowski. I swear by the Black Madonna."

"Very well. I escorted General Caulaincourt for the negotiations of this truce. While he was in consultation with the enemy's representatives, the emperor's secretary, Baron Fain, showed me terms that Napoléon had dictated."

"Why would he do that?"

"Oh, Fain has seen me for so many years as part of the Guard that he has come to think of me as French rather than Polish."

"I see. And the terms?"

Dezydery looked up at Jan, eye-to-eye for the first time. His face had become empurpled, his tone deliberately restrained. "There, Jan, at the very beginning of concessions he would make to Aleksandr—at the very beginning!—was the Duchy of Warsaw!"

"Good God, man! You're certain?"

"I saw it myself, Jan! We're to be the *first* sold down the goddamn river!"

Stunned, Jan watched his friend pull the paperwork and letters together and place them in a satchel.

"I've served that man since I was scarcely more than a boy, Jan," Dezydery said, his voice low and cracking. "It's been my life. My *life!* And to find it worth nothing at all. *Nothing!*"

"What will you do, my friend? Poznań is occupied."

Dezydery stood. "I'll go to Paris—and then maybe England. I just know I'd rather dig ditches than see that man again. You know, they say he had a grand strategy for Europe. He had no *strategy!* He's good at tactics, that's all."

Jan walked over and hugged his old friend. "Godspeed, Dezydery. May we meet again one day."

Dezydery held Jan at arm's length. "And what about you, Jan, now that you know?"

"Me?" Jan asked, giving a tortured little smile. "For me it's different, my friend. I haven't believed in the little Corsican for some years. I don't know that I ever did."

Jan left the tent, his head down. He would keep the news to himself, as he had sworn. He would not even tell Paweł, who served north of Leipzig, in Dąbrowski's division. To what end? Jan thought. Paweł had regarded the emperor as a demigod for too long.

Not long afterward, word came that treaty negotiations had failed. Worse, Austria now declared war on France. The die was cast.

*   *   *

In later years, the events leading up to the Battle of Leipzig would become a blur in the memory of its survivors. While Napoléon longed for one decisive battle that would tell the tale, his allied enemies played tag and run, teasing and taunting him, causing him to move his armies from one place to another, wearing his soldiers down, bit by bit. Skirmish warfare became a day-to-day thing. His army soon became exhausted and hungry. Their uniforms were tattered, and some soldiers even went bootless.

News coming into camp worsened. Bavaria defected from the French, and her army went to strengthen the allies. In Spain, Napoléon's forces were beaten back by the English under Wellington. It seemed all of Europe was aligning itself against the little emperor. Nonetheless, Napoléon held fast to the idea that his was the new order of things, one favoring the rights of man, as opposed to the old order and the privileges of a few. To hear him tell it, one great battle was all that was needed to turn the tide.

Prince Murat deployed Poniatowski's Eighth Corps, as well as the forces of Generals Victor and Lauriston, to guard the south and southeast perimeters of Leipzig. On 14 October, Russian forces under General Wittgenstein came against the French in six powerful waves, each one beaten back by courageous cavalry charges. Despite the years, Jan fought much as he had as a young man, staying as close to his son as possible without being too conspicuous. While Tadek had been a perfect reflection of Jan's light eyes and complexion, Michał's appearance was very different since he carried in his Groński blood certain darker Tatar traits. Just the same, Jan saw his younger self in Michał—in his vigor and horsemanship and prowess with the saber.

After that battle and all battles in which they partook, neither father nor son spoke to the other of lives they had taken. There was no counting, no boasting. The killing was something they stored away in their memories, not to be visited willingly. Jan was just glad that they both lived to see another day.

The battle for Leipzig was in no way finished, but the Eighth Corps so impressed Napoléon with that day's fighting—despite significant Polish losses—that in a makeshift ceremony on the putrid and body-littered battlefield, he presented Prince Józef Poniatowski with a marshal's baton. He was the only non-French officer ever so honored. Among the able-bodied and wounded Poles alike, chests were swollen and eyes moist with pride. Even Jan—who had had his fill of war and killing and Napoléon—found himself wiping at his eyes.

* * *

In the early morning hours of 16 October, Napoléon's one decisive battle came to him. The enemy allies attacked, their plan—it was clear—to outflank the French right that was defended by Prince Murat and Generals Victor, Lauriston, and Poniatowski. Two hundred enemy cannon—followed by massive columns of soldiers—descended six times in all, each time beaten back by Murat, each time suffering ten times more casualties than the French. By night Jan learned that elsewhere on the Leipzig battlefield the French had held—but at the cost of twenty-five thousand men.

The seventeenth passed without fighting. A small Saxon force and General Bernadotte's command of seventy thousand bolstered the French, but reinforcements were being welcomed into the Russian camp, too, starting with General Bennigsen and his estimated forty thousand troops. On the eighteenth, it was the enemy again that initiated the attack on the right flank. Employing French artillery to the fullest, Murat's generals held off the allies, triumphing by the end of the day. Late into the night, however, word filtered down that 220,000 rounds of artillery had been sacrificed to the little victory. There remained a scant sixteen thousand rounds, or enough for a two-hour battle. Napoléon ordered an immediate and full retreat westward to the nearest ammunition depot at Erfurt.

To reach the first town along the way, Lindenau, some six bridges had to be crossed, necessitating troops to march in narrow files. Nevertheless, by the early morning hours of the nineteenth, two-thirds of the Grande Armée had evacuated Leipzig. Generals Macdonald, Lauriston, and Poniatowski served as rear guard during the operation.

The morning light, however, made Napoléon's intentions clear to the allies, and they came down in force upon the rear guard. Jan kept one eye on Michał as cavalry battled cavalry. The Poniatowski forces purposely yielded ground as the tail of the Grande Armée moved toward the main bridge between Leipzig and Lindenau. Jan knew that the bridge had been laid with mines the night before, and that once the last of the rear guard passed over it, Napoléon's engineers would send it sky high, effectively leaving the enemy on the wrong side of the River Elster.

But long before the crossing could be completed, an explosion rang so loudly in Jan's ears that he faltered for a moment and beat back the thrust of a Russian's saber only at the last moment. After he had dispatched the foe, he turned to look toward the bridge. Of course, he knew what he would see.

With at least ten thousand soldiers and hundreds of wagons yet to cross, the bridge had been destroyed. Why had it been blown to pieces so prematurely? Those unhappy souls who had been unable to cross would likely be slashed to ribbons.

Chaos ensued as the French forces tallied the situation and made for the river's bank. The allies gave no respite and began to close in, killing as they went.

Jan found Michał at the river. They both quickly sized up the situation. The bank was steep and slippery, a pitfall for the horses. While the river was not particularly wide, they could see that the current's power was deadly. The roiling water pulled at the broken timbers of the bridge, making short work of ripping them free and sending them on their way. Jan looked about for Poniatowski. In the confusion he found no sign of the general. The choices were clear to both father and son. If they stayed and fought, they would die. If they stayed and laid down their arms, they might be spared, in which case they would spend the rest of the war as prisoners. If they attempted to cross the river, the risks were high.

Already, hundreds of their comrades had made their decisions, choosing the river over capture. Horses and men slipped down the bank and into the water. In the moments that Jan and Michał watched, it seemed that for every soldier that held his own in the water—mounted or not—another was carried away by the river. One faltering horse could take with it several other horses and soldiers.

To the rear, Jan could see the enemy descending in a swarm, shooting and slicing as they went. He knew that every moment he and his son hesitated could be their last. Michał nodded to his father. Their thoughts were the same, it seemed, words unnecessary. The two directed their horses down the bank and into the icy cold water.

In no time water was washing over the horses' manes. "Hold tight to your mount, Michał!" Jan called. "And keep your head down and your sights forward. Only forward!"

It was at that moment that Jan felt a stinging sensation. His hand went to his neck and came away bloody. He had been hit by carbine fire. While he had suffered his share of lance and saber wounds, he had never been hit by gunfire. Dumb Russian luck, he thought, for the aim of guns fired from horseback was notoriously bad.

"Papa!"

Jan looked up ahead at Michał, whose horror-stricken face registered the sight of the wound.

"Papa!" Michał called, reaching out to Jan. "Give me the reins!"

"No!" Jan called. "I'm fine! Forward, Michał. Go forward. I'll make it before you!"

As a race, however, progress was painfully slow, hampered not only by the strong current but also by the bodies of horses and soldiers being washed away. What seemed half an hour passed. For once, Jan wished for a larger horse.

One man tried to save himself by fastening on to Jan's horse's neck. By this time Jan could offer the man no aid. He knew by his own failing strength that he had lost a great deal of blood. He had no choice but to force the man to release his grip. The man fell back into the river and disappeared.

They were at the middle—and deepest—part of the river now. He put his head to the side of the horse's neck, hugging her mane much as he had done as a child, whispering for it to go on.

He felt another sting at his right shoulder. For a moment his eyes focused on the water rushing past him, crimson with blood. He had no doubt that the allies had dismounted by now and were picking off their targets like fat fish in a pool.

His horse had been hit, too. He felt it falter beneath him, falter and lose its footing. He knew enough to get his boots out of the stirrups so he would not be swept under and away. In what seemed like moments, the horse was gone and he found himself attempting to stay afloat, attempting to avoid objects and bodies that relentlessly came at him.

In time, his diminishing strength fell away altogether. He prayed now, not for his own life, for he was accepting of his death, but he prayed for his son Jan Michał. That *he* would live and make it back to his mother at Sochaczew.

Anna, he thought, *my beautiful Anna Maria! Forgive me.*

On the previous day, the eighteenth, Paweł had stood with Dąbrowski to the north of Leipzig. Their orders were to hold the suburb of Halle. It was every bit as important as the bridge over the River Elster, for it provided a narrow passage through which the Grande Armée had to pass in its retreat from Leipzig. Despite Dąbrowski's reputation, the task was a risky one because his division had been reduced to a handful of cavalry, a mere sixteen hundred infantry and six cannon.

At 9 a.m., Prussians attacked, and an hour later the Russians joined in the effort. Paweł was speaking to Dąbrowski about maneuvers when Gourgaud, one of Napoléon's aides, rode up to inquire about the defense of the gate. Dąbrowski brusquely told him that each Pole would sacrifice his life before giving over the Halle Gate—and cantered off.

Gourgard shot Paweł a questioning glance. Paweł grinned. "I think that Dąbrowski got his back up over your inquiry. Polish pride, you see."

"Ah—what *are* the chances then, Paweł?"

"We have the little French company manning the gate," Paweł said, "but without further reinforcements—it's two to one, and I doubt we can hold it."

Gourgard's lips thinned and, thanking Paweł, the aide rode away.

Within an hour, two divisions were sent in, and with their considerable support, the Polish forces held until night fell and the battle ended.

It wasn't until late into the evening of the nineteenth that Paweł learned of the tragic events that took place at the bridge over the River Elster. Napoléon's engineers had rigged the bridge to explode once the rear guard had passed over it. He placed responsibility for the premature ignition order to a colonel who, in turn, passed on the task to a corporal. As the fighting between the allies and the French rear guard moved nearer and nearer the bridge, the chaos caused the corporal to panic—and he ordered the fuses lighted.

Along with important wagons full of supplies and the wounded, some twelve thousand men had not made it across. Resisting capture, many of those men drowned—or were shot.

With tears in his eyes, Dąbrowski told Paweł the worst—that Prince Józef Poniatowski was among the dead. A strange weakness came over Paweł at the news.

"He was attempting to cross the Elster," Dąbrowski said. "The enemy fire on those attempting to evade capture was unrelenting. One of his men said that before entering the water, he refused to surrender and called out something about duty and honor and that he had already stared Death in the eye." Dąbrowski paused, drawing in his breath. "And then, midstream, he was hit by a hail of bullets. He slipped from his horse, and the strong Elster current took him."

"May God take his soul," Paweł said.

"They say a Hungarian gypsy once told him that he was to beware of magpies."

A little chill ran along Paweł's spine. *Elster* was the German word for "magpie." He had no time to dwell on Poniatowski's bad fortune. Something else pulled mightily at his heart. Paweł felt certain that Jan and Michał would have attempted the crossing. He hurried now to search among the survivors for the two, praying as he went.

39

Zofia sat motionless—but for her darting eyes—at the window of the covered carriage. She had spent the better part of the morning driving along the rough road that ran parallel to the eastern bank of the River Vistula. Her driver had obediently responded each time she called for him to slow or stop in order to take a better look at a little peasant hamlet or particular hut. In the three hours of tedious travel, she had seen nothing familiar. The overcast sky opened now and began to spit down little showers of rain.

"Stop!" Zofia called, her body going tense, her eyes narrowing.

The carriage ground to a halt. There, one hundred paces away, sat the dwelling she had been searching for. What set it apart from a thousand other peasant huts? The single poplar that stood to the side like a sentry? She wasn't quite sure, but she could not be more certain that this was the hut in which she had convalesced after having been snatched from the Vistula.

Time lengthened as she stared, thinking back nineteen years to those months she had spent there. Images of the old man and his daughter came to her with surprising vividness. And the face of Jerzy, too, but that had always stayed vivid in her mind. Somehow he had always been with her. Was it because Izabel resembled him so? Yes, there was that. Their daughter had become a link to that past. But there was an invisible link, too, one of strong and convoluted emotions.

Zofia saw that some children had taken notice of the stalled vehicle. Here the carriage of a noble was not an everyday sight. They whispered among themselves, their eyes wide with wonder. They moved a few paces closer.

What had drawn her to this place after so many years? Jerzy had. Zofia recalled how young and innocent he was. It had been so easy to seduce him. He had given her his heart without a thought. And she had taken it, wishing for the moment she were a peasant girl who could make a life with him—but knowing that was impossible.

So many men had passed through her life. Why was it she had not forgotten this one? This Jerzy? He had no title, no money, no power. She remembered how he had come to see her, years later in Warsaw, after he had joined the infantry, and they spent a torrid afternoon together. He had become a handsome man, but he was still the innocent boy beneath. Their difference in age meant nothing by then. But other differences remained.

She smiled to herself, thinking how he was the only person she had ever allowed to call her by the diminutive Zosia. The afternoon had been only that, an afternoon, and she saw him off to war, avoiding the slightest suggestion that they would ever meet again, giving him no encouragement. But–ever since Anna had told her she thought she had tended him in the hospital, Zofia could not shake her head clear of him. She had to know if he was that soldier laid up in the hospital. If he had returned home to pick up his life. If . . .

The children were calling out to her driver now, asking him what he was about and who was inside the carriage. "Scat!" he shouted at them. "Move off, urchins!"

At that moment, the door to the hut opened, and a woman appeared. It was not the woman Zofia remembered. This one was younger, about thirty, but pretty, and even in colorless sacklike broadcloth, Zofia could see she was shapely. She looked at the carriage with some interest. At once Zofia drew back from the window, but she continued to watch.

The woman cupped her hand to her mouth and called "Zosia!"

The strangest thrill ran through Zofia like a little bolt of lightning. How was it this woman could be calling her by her diminutive? She grew dizzy at the notion.

"Zosia!" the woman called again, more demanding this time.

And then a tiny voice squeaked out an answer: "Coming, Mama!"

Zofia saw now the little mystery unraveled. A little girl had detached herself from her friends and ran toward the woman. The daughter's name was Zosia.

The exchange between the driver and the children had gone silent during this little episode, but it now resumed. Zofia could see the mother questioning her daughter, the woman's eyes moving to the carriage now and again. The drizzle turned to a light rain.

Zofia couldn't think what to do. Should she order the driver to move on? Dare she get out of the carriage and approach the woman?

A man emerged from the other side of the house now and moved toward the mother and child. Zofia's heart caught.

The little girl called out something to the man and went running into his arms. He lifted her high into the air as if she weighed no more than a shaft of wheat. The hat he had been wearing in the fields fell off his head.

Jerzy.

Zofia had known it was he the moment she had seen his long and confident stride. The woman said something to him now, and the girl pointed to the vehicle. Jerzy shaded his eyes against the rain and looked to the carriage.

Zofia fell back against the seat, her heart racing. When she dared look again, she saw that in one motion he was setting down the child and retrieving his hat. The rain was steadily increasing now, and a clap of thunder sent the children back to their homes.

Jerzy said something to the woman, evidently telling her to take the child inside. As the woman took charge of the little girl, Jerzy looked again at the strange sight of the carriage—and then he started moving toward it, his face glistening in the rain.

Some nameless emotion erupted within Zofia. She shifted to the other side of the carriage, lifted the shade, and called to the driver. "Move on! Do you hear me? Move on *now!*"

The horses were immediately set in motion, and the carriage began to bounce along the pitted road. Zofia did not look back and prayed he did not suspect the identity of the occupant of the coach. But she could imagine his beautiful face there in the road, blue eyes staring after the mysterious vehicle—much like the rain-spattered face of an icon in one of the roadside shrines.

After a little while, Zofia gave orders for the the carriage to swing around and make the return trip to Warsaw. When they once again passed the little hut, Zofia dared lift the shade to look. Nothing stirred. Pools were forming all about. The heavy rain had driven animal and man alike to shelter. Set against the thunder and lightning, the dwelling appeared a pitiful thing, but the smoke from its chimney somehow tempered the effect. No doubt, inside the three sat about the little hearth. In a little while they would have a modest meal.

Jerzy had found his life, Zofia thought. *Dog's blood!* There was nothing for her here.

Zofia lay awake that night for many hours, her mind turning like a mill wheel in a storm-swept stream. The trip to the country had been silly and impulsive. She wondered why she had done it, but she had no regrets. Regrets were foreign to her.

She was forty now. What was it Napoléon had said about being forty? It was something cryptic, she knew. And then she remembered. He had said, "Forty is forty, after all." Where *had* the years gone? They had gone as quickly as the bubbles in French champagne. She felt no older than she had at sixteen back in Halicz—but she knew differently. She was not immune to age.

Her dream of marrying a magnate had not materialized. The Radziwiłłs,

Czartoryskis, Poniatowskis, and a half dozen others had given her notice—but no nuptials. Even her plan for Izabel had been scuttled. She let the thoughts pass. She could live another forty years. How was she to live them? Would she live them alone?

There were few constants in her life. There were Izabel and Anna. Izabel would soon find her own path. And Anna had her family—and a new baby on the way.

There was Paweł. Dear Paweł. How had he put up with her as long as he had? Zofia laughed to herself. How had he become so smitten with her? The man was a saint.

Perhaps it was his years away soldiering, always soldiering, that kept her endeared to him—and he to her. Absence had made his heart grow fonder.

He would come back. She never doubted that he would. Napoléon would lose his grand dream one day soon in a grand catastrophe. Paweł would then come back, and they would settle into a life together. She was surprised by the pleasure the thought conjured up.

Paweł would come back. She would make him happy. He had long ago stopped asking her to marry him. She tried to imagine his face when *she* would ask *him*.

She would live as Charlotte suggested—without regrets, without fears. She imagined herself finding happiness.

40

Anna ran her hands over her belly, round as a pumpkin. Within a month, the baby would be here. She had that at least to look forward to.

It was the second of November, All Souls' Day. She could not help but remember the holy day in 1794. Her aunt had died that day, just before the Russians descended on Praga. Even now—so many years later—a chill pulsed within her veins when she recalled the thousands of innocents who had died in the massacre. And when it was over, the last partition had been put in place, and Poland ceased to exist. Later, the Duchy of Warsaw appeased a few, but greater hopes were placed on the shoulders of Emperor Napoléon Bonaparte.

After the retreat from Russia, however, hopes thinned. And now, with news of the death of Prince Poniatowski, the Polish spirit seemed altogether crushed. Like so many of her fellow Poles, Anna had come to love the prince, who valued his word and honor over power and position. Had he switched sides, Aleksandr might have made him King of Poland. So many others had switched—and prospered. Prince Józef Poniatowski might have saved his uncle from the epithet, the last King of Poland. But in the end, his sense of honor won out.

It was the Polish way.

Anna's thoughts returned now to concern for her husband and son. What of them? Had *they* tried to make the crossing of the River Elster? Had they survived it? Or had they stayed behind to become captives of the allies? Anna knew at her core that they had attempted the crossing rather than allow the Russians to take them.

Did they make it across? Why had no word come?

Anna had lost one member of her family. Her dearest Tadek. She prayed no more would be taken. *"No more. Let my husband and Michał live,"* she whispered.

An hour later, Barbara called to her from her bedchamber. "Mama, come here! Come quickly." She sounded as if she was in distress.

It took some doing for Anna to get up out of the chair, much less move quickly, but in very little time she was in her old bedchamber.

Barbara sat in the window seat, her back stiff, her eyes wide with—what? Fright?

"What is it?" Anna demanded. "What is it, Basia?"

Barbara's mouth fell slack. "A wagon in the distance—turning into our drive!"

Anna moved to the window. For another minute the two silently watched it wend its way down the poplar-lined lane. Anna's temple pulsed as she re-lived the day her father's body had been brought home in the same fashion.

"It's a single driver, Mama."

"I see." Anna felt her heart start to hammer in her chest. "Is it a soldier? Can you make him out? Your eyes are better than mine."

"I can't tell. It looks like he's wearing *rags,*" Barbara said. "What kind of a wagon is that?"

"It's a caisson, Basia."

"What is that?"

"It's a military wagon. It's used for transporting weapons—or the dead."

They stared without speaking for another minute—until they both were able to recognize the driver. And then—as the caisson drew near the drive in front of the manor house, they both saw the body of a soldier in the wagon.

Anna drew herself up and took her daughter's hand. Barbara's face was white with pain and fear. "Let's go down, Basia. You will help me on the stairs."

They moved out to the staircase, and as they descended it was Anna who seemed to be lending assistance to the trembling Barbara.

The wagon was drawing near just as the two went out onto the portico.

"Mama!" Jan Michał called, pulling the caisson to a halt. He jumped from the driver's perch, his eyes immediately flushing with tears.

He was in Anna's arms then, and Barbara's arms encircled the two of them.

The moment lengthened. It seemed as if all of them had lost the power of speech. Anna pulled away then and moved to the wagon.

"He'll be fine, Mama."

Anna turned back, facing her son, uncomprehending.

"He went into a deep sleep half an hour ago," Jan Michał explained. "He tried so hard to stay awake."

Disbelieving, Anna peered into the wagon.

Jan lay, still and white as a corpse. She reached in to place her hand on his. It was warm.

"Jan," she said. "Jan!"

Jan Stelnicki's eyes opened wide at the sound. His head rolled toward her, his eyes taking in her hand, then her face. While his body had been bloodied and bruised, his eyes were as blue as the sky had been the summer day they had met in the meadow.

"Anna," he said, "is it you? Am I dreaming?"

"It is, Jan. It is no dream."

"Good God, Michał!" Jan cried out suddenly, rearing up. "You let me sleep for my homecoming."

"The doctor said you should sleep!"

"If you hadn't pulled me from the river, I'd give you a good thrashing! Now help me get out of this coffin. It's not my time yet, by God!"

Michał and Anna both assisted him in getting out as Barbara ran forward to kiss him.

"You can hug me, too, Basia," Jan said, his arms going around her. "I won't break. Three Russian bullet holes, but the doctors swear I'll survive."

As he released his daughter, his eyes came back to Anna. His hand reached out to tenderly touch the roundness of her belly. "You have me back, Anna," he said. "You have me back."

Ignoring the tears that wet her cheeks, Anna reached up to Jan, drew his face to hers, and kissed him. It was a kiss that transported her to an autumn meadow long ago in Halicz, a kiss that would carry her forward all of her days.

Epilogue

She who is satisfied with little
is not so poor as she who
never has enough.

–POLISH PROVERB

3 May 1814
My Dear Zofia,

I pray you and Iza are well. My love comes to you both.

Pass on my warmest congratulations to Jan and Anna on the birth of their son Józef. The prince would have been proud to have been his namesake.

No doubt, you have heard of our defeats at the hands of our enemies. Even France itself is lost. The emperor has abdicated and the Bourbon rule is being reestablished. The old order has won out.

So the days of the Duchy of Warsaw are numbered? Everything is relative, is it not? Just as we mourned each partition of the old Poland and grumbled about the duchy, I suspect that whatever plan the allies construct for us, we will come to feel sentimental for the dear old duchy.

Zofia, you have written to me of your love, and I have taken your words into battle with me. In my lowest moments, they lift me up. Know that I love you, that I always have loved you. I don't wish to hurt you.

However, today we arrived on the little island of Elba, the miniature kingdom the allies have deigned to grant Napoléon. He seems to have already won over the 12,000 residents who, aside from fishing, exist on the lead, granite, and iron industries.

This pitiful little place is a far cry from the emperor's dream of uniting the mainland of Europe. Quite a comeuppance!

And yet I cannot help but feel the allies have been too lenient. Elba will quickly bore an emperor used to so much more. He brought with him his chefs, musicians, and two of his favorite singers, but he will never be content here.

Yet, here we are. And so, I must tell you that I will not be coming home— at least any time soon.

You will ask me why I have followed him into his exile. You will upbraid me, as you did Prince Poniatowski when he followed Napoléon, passing up Aleksandr's offer of a crown. You will call it a suicidal bravery—or a lethal sort of honor, so typical of the Poles. And I can understand that.

But you see, the emperor was allowed some sixty guards to accompany him into exile. Napoléon chose the Polish lancers, Zofia. There were those who refused and who are on their way home even now. But I could not refuse—even though I hear you scoffing at me across the continent.

I could not refuse.

I hope that you understand, my love.

Paweł

Author's Note

*P*ush *Not the River* was based on the actual diary of Countess Anna Maria Berezowska, translated by her descendant, John A. Stelnicki. The countess began keeping a diary when her life, like the Polish nation itself, fell into a downward spiral. With strength and spirit, both she and her country encountered, endured, and survived unimaginable trying times.

Push Not the River took her story to the end of the diary. When asked by St. Martin's to write a sequel, I considered the surviving characters and imagined how their lives might have played out during the fascinating Napoléonic period. Knowing my characters so well, after living with them for years, made the task of writing *Against a Crimson Sky* less daunting than I had thought it would be at the outset. After studying the history of Poland during that era, I wanted to first outline the story in full and then fill in the details. But my characters would not cooperate. They had minds of their own and they had to take me through their story in their own good time. I consider myself blessed that they did.